KEEPING WILLOW

The Prototype Book 3

JACINTA HOWARD

KEEPING WILLOW PLAYLIST

Keeping Willow Playlist

Elevators (Me & You)- OutKast
Get Bigger/Do U Luv- NxWorries
Keep You In Mind- Guordon Banks
The Ballad of Dorothy Parker- Prince
Hello It's Me- Isley Brothers
Backseat- Ari Lennox
Rockets- LION BABE
All in My Head- SIR
Think of You- Terrace Martin
Come Live With Me Angel- Marvin Gaye
Hey- KING
Hypnotized- JMSN
Best One- NxWorries
Good Luv'n- BJ The Chicago Kid
Summer Breeze- Isley Brothers
Cranes in the Sky- Solange
I'm So Famous- Joi
PRIDE- Kendrick Lamar
Same Ol' Mistakes- Rihanna
Terrified- Childish Gambino
To Live & Die- Jhene Aiko feat. Cocaine 80s
Hereditary- J.I.D.
Weary- Solange
Missing You- The Internet
Gemini- Alabama Shakes
Always Will- Tweet

Voyage to Atlantis- Isley Brothers
Never Catch Me- Flying Lotus feat. KDot
Do What U Wanna Do- Devin The Dude
Liberation- OutKast
Aquemini- OutKast
Partners in Crime- The Internet
Prototype- OutKast

WILLOW

WE WERE GOING to get arrested. We were going to get arrested, I would go to jail, and my parents would kill me. No, they'd disown me. And *then* kill me.

I sucked in a breath, willing my heart to slow down, because in spite of that reality, which was hovering over me like the thick Texas air that was clinging to my skin like syrup, I felt *alive* for the first time in months. Two months, to be exact.

"Stay close, Willow."

Devin's bass filled voice was low in my ear when he grabbed my hand, pulling me into his hard body as he led us through the dense crowd, and my heart raced even more quickly. It felt like forever since I'd heard his baritone in my ear, but the familiarity of his voice also made it feel like yesterday. I blinked and sucked in a short breath, the conflicting emotions I always felt with Devin threatening to surface and take over everything, again. I pushed them down as I exhaled.

I gripped his rough fingers, burying my nose in his shoulder, because I couldn't help it, as we maneuvered through the swarm of bodies, careful to keep my head down. Sweat threatened to drip into my eyes but I didn't dare release Devin's hand.

For one, we'd be separated and the crowd was way too large to find him again quickly, and two, he was using his bossy voice on me. That bass filled one that pricked at my nerves but at the same time felt like a shot of tequila because it warmed my blood and made me feel like I was floating. Two months ago, I told myself I was immune to this. Yet here I was again, entangled. Ensnared... It was too much and not enough.

That was Devin though—always able to bring out the extreme side of my emotions. Emotions I knew existed but had never really experienced before him. With Devin I didn't just get mad, I got *pissed*, so angry that it felt as though a ball of fire was burning in my belly and heart. With him I didn't just get excited. He aroused my senses so that it felt as if everything in my body was floating and tingling, aching and yearning to be connected to him in every possible way. Devin was my highest high and my lowest low. It'd been that way since the very first time I saw him three years ago, coming out of the campus library with my roommate and his best friend, Jersey. He was like a magnet. Just being near him did things to my insides because when Devin touched me it was like every feeling, every sensation gathered and pulled, toward *him*.

"Keep up," he said now, impatiently, pulling me along with him.

He glanced down at me, as if daring me to deny him. I didn't say anything though. I just willed my feet to go faster, trying to match his long strides. He was moving quickly, keeping his head down with his fitted low so that he wouldn't easily be recognized. We were running late, and even though he was easily the coolest person I'd ever known, Devin hated being late. You'd think it'd be the opposite—that the party wouldn't start until he got there, which it didn't. But Devin detested people taking advantage of his time, and so he made it a point not to waste theirs either. He sidestepped a guy holding a huge sign that simply read *"I Am Human,"* and I mumbled an apology that I knew the guy couldn't have possibly heard.

All around us there were chants—cries, really—voices rising in cadence, filled with anguish, rage, even helplessness despite the power of the gathering. The rally on the campus was for Jamal Waters, the 15-year-old who'd been killed by campus police at Colorado Tech just before summer, sparking another wave of outrage in a nation that was already tense and on edge. I remembered hearing the news like yesterday—the feeling of helplessness and rage and *fear.* I glanced up at Devin, wondering if he remembered too.

It'd just been announced that the cop who murdered him wouldn't even be indicted. The atmosphere was charged, the energy coiled tight like the rattle snakes that sometimes hid themselves in the tall grass at my grandma's country Galveston home, ready to strike if the mood swung just an inch in any direction.

People were so *angry.* I looked up, directly into the eyes of a girl whose face was contorted into hard lines as she shouted, tears gathered in her eyes that didn't fall, maybe because her rage held them at bay.

I felt the knot in my stomach tighten as my feet sank into the dewy grass as I followed behind Devin. I wasn't sure what I felt. It was like I was balancing on my tippy-toes looking over the edge of a cliff, and at any given moment I might topple over into something unknown, or worse, like my constant confusion about everything going on the world was changing me *into* something unknown.

Actually, there'd been a knot that slid from my chest to my stomach at random times for the past couple of months, ever since I watched the video of Jamal Waters being shot to death by campus police who didn't look much different than the cops that patrolled my campus at South Texas. Jamal though—he looked *so much* like Devin. His walk. His smile in the pictures they showed of him on TV following his death. His nose ring. His full lips that were so well-shaped they could only be described in feminine terms like "pretty." He was even a drummer for the high school's marching band.

Subconsciously, against my will, I rubbed my thumb along Devin's wrist, burying my nose deeper into his shoulder as we walked briskly toward the stage, which was hovering just 50 feet in front of us, blocked off by flimsy metal gates. I could smell Devin's after shave, his spicy deodorant, his sweat, which calmed me down a little bit, confusing and irritating me.

The energetic crowd switched to another chant, *"No Justice, No Peace,"* and seemed to grow even louder. I was surprised there were even this many people here. School wouldn't start until Monday. But then, this crowd was a mix of students, locals and kids from other schools who'd driven down for the Progressive Union/Common Collective rally—that and to see The Prototype.

The Prototype ran South Texas University. There was no other way to put it. They were regional celebrities who were on the brink of stardom, recognizable to everyone in the area, whether they liked their brand of alternative-soul music or not. Plus, all the members—Devin, Jersey, Zay, Travis, Kennedy and Bam— went to the university. *Or used to.*

I frowned, pushing the unpleasant bit of reality out of my mind. Ever since Devin told me he was dropping out, everything was different. Different in a way that I was still coming to terms with. I told myself what Devin did wasn't my issue any more though. Dropping out was about his music. And Lord Jesus knows nothing ever came before Devin's music and The Prototype.

Devin's grip on my hand tightened as we continue to press through the crowd, the evidence of The Prototype's popularity evident on the t-shirted bodies of the students and locals who'd gathered for the rally and my belly tingled in response. Maybe because it'd been so long since I'd seen him. Since he'd touched me...

I distracted myself by studying the faces in the crowd. I didn't recognize many folks, although a lot of them were wearing the newer Prototype t-shirts I'd rode to Dallas to pick up three months earlier. It seemed like a life time ago.

The stage was now directly in my line of vision when I lifted my head from the back of Devin's muscled shoulder, and he kept us moving briskly, pushing past shouting people, where there was finally a bit of clearing, as bodies began to separate and large swaths of green grass became visible. Security had escorted the rest of the band to cleared area, the only space in front of Merner Hall and the ancient library that wasn't overflowing with bodies.

We finally reached the rest of the band—Jersey, Zay, Bam, Travis and Kennedy— who were standing off to the right of the stage in a small clearing. I was winded from how quickly we'd been forced to walk. I wiped my brow, releasing Devin's hand, and then pulled at the material of my thin cotton sundress. I'd worn it because it was lightweight, but sweat still trickled between my breasts, and I knew my cheeks were flushed under the oppressive late afternoon Texas heat. I felt Devin's eyes on me, but I diverted my attention across the patch of grass. His gaze was hot and consuming and I didn't need the drama. When I did look up at him, he was studying me beneath the brim of his fitted, his brown eyes full of unsaid things that echoed loudly in my heart anyway.

"Hey, you guys," Kennedy greeted us, giving me cause to break Devin's disruptive gaze. Her eyes were wary. Her mass of hair was tamed down into two French braids than hung over her small shoulders. For such an itty-bitty thing, she had a strong voice on her.

"This crowd is restless," Kennedy said to no one in particular, the light from the beaming sun bouncing off the tiny gold hoop in her nose. Her voice was like cotton, full but with a tendency to float away, and you sometimes had to lean in to hear her. She looked up at Travis before her gaze landed on Devin.

"Something's gonna go down. I can feel it."

Devin said nothing, only exhaled as he met Travis' gaze, even though his was covered by shades. Travis dipped his head, moving to stand behind Kennedy and spoke low in her ear, as he drew her to his chest with one arm. They'd been together pretty much since Kennedy moved to Tyler, Texas about a year ago. Their relationship was so... *intense*.

Kennedy nodded and inhaled deeply, closing her eyes as if she was meditating. I automatically glanced at Jersey, before I remembered that I was still mad at her. Unsurprisingly, she only smirked at my glare, her gaze flitting to Devin then back to me. It was her fault I was left to ride with Devin.

The five-minute ride was awkward and silent, with Devin typing on his phone every time we came to a stop sign. He'd said all of three words to me the entire time. I felt stupid for coming back early. Stupid for thinking that Devin and I could... I closed my eyes briefly, breathing deeply. I didn't know what I thought. All I did know was that the eight weeks apart had only made him better looking. His reddish, dark caramel skin that was almost walnut because of his time spent in the sun, the smattering of freckles that dotted his straight pierced nose, the stubble on his strong jaw, his thick eyebrows that showcased cola-colored eyes enhanced by eyelashes so long they tangled at the tips, and his lips. *God,* his *lips...* They were perfectly shaped for everything—biting, licking, kissing, and whispering things in my ear no one else ever had. Dreams and promises that made me feel connected to life in a way nothing else ever had.

I opened my eyes and glared at Jersey again. She'd begged me to come back to Tyler a few days early so that I could make their show at the rally, and I did. Jersey was my best friend and I always wanted to see The Prototype. They were hands down, my favorite band, *ever*. Every single member just dripped with talent, and I knew that at any given time, they could each realistically entertain solo careers if they wanted. They were also my extended family. I was even staying with Kennedy and her Grandma Pepper for a few days until I moved into my dorm room. But since Devin and I broke up, it'd been different, strained, for me at least.

I was glad to head back home to Houston after the end of last semester. I needed to breathe, to get my head on straight, and to think without Devin Walker clouding my thoughts, invading my heart. And now, within just a few hours of being back in town, I was under his spell again. I rolled my eyes at Jersey but she only frowned, her attention diverted by a group whose voices suddenly swelled with their "No Justice, No Peace" chants.

"Something's gonna go down," Kennedy said again, her gaze darting around the anxious crowd.

"They need to tear some shit up," Jersey spoke up, her face scrunched. "How tired of this racist shit are we supposed to get?"

She too, had on large shades that drew attention to her pouty lips, which were painted deep burgundy. Like Kennedy, she was gorgeous, but Jersey's sexy-pretty was downright sultry, even when she was being mean. She drew men like a fly to honey, though ever since she'd met Zay, she'd paid them no mind. Jersey's release from life was her music but her salve was Isaiah Broussard.

Devin shook his head, releasing another breath when she stared at him as though she expected him to answer her.

"*What?*" she snapped, glaring at Devin.

"Cool out, Jersey," Devin responded gruffly. "Direct that energy where it needs to go."

Jersey shook her head, shifting her weight like she was ready to throw blows with someone, as Zay and I exchanged a glance. We were used to the two of them bickering like siblings. Devin looked at me again, but once more, I redirected my attention. Being around him again was too much, too fast, because one thought kept invading my mind: I wanted him.

"All I know is, if I get hit with one of those water bottles they were throwing earlier I'm hopping off the stage, swinging."

It was Bam who spoke up, the band's keyboardist, who looked like he should be playing linebacker instead of the keys. A broad smile was on his handsome face, as usual. I could count the number of times Bam was in a bad mood.

"You know people are even more on edge because it's hot as the devil's cage out here too? Got me out here Samuel-L-Jackson-*Black Snake Moan*-greasy-sweatin'..."

I laughed, exchanging a smile with Jersey, who playfully pushed at Bam's shoulder. He grabbed her putting her in a headlock, and ruffled her hair, as she squealed and slapped at his huge arms.

"Bam, are you crazy! My hair! *Stop*!"

Devin shook his head and looked around, frowning at the frumpy security guard who was standing nervously at the gate, his hand on his pepper spray. He looked like he really wanted to use it on the girl who was shouting in his face, waving her sign really close to his head.

"Kennedy is right. Some shit is about to pop off," Zay, the other lead singer and guitarist, glanced at Jersey, then Travis and Kennedy, before his gaze landed on Devin. "I don't know why these fake-ass cops are out here antagonizing people." He eyed the girl who was now full-on arguing with the guard.

I could feel the tension radiating from Devin, as he lifted his cap from his brow, his eyes assessing the crowd, contemplating the right move for the band. That was his thing. Reading the crowd was as natural as breathing for him, and he could play into their needs or desires before they probably even realized what it was they were searching for. He used to be that way with me too.

The noise in the crowd swelled again, along with my heart rate. What was going on right now... seemed a little unwise, dangerous even. Who knew what people were capable of when they were enraged and in a mob?

"Devin, maybe you guys *should* think about this..."

The words were out of my mouth before I had a chance to stop them. He looked down at me. My heart flip-flopped, and again, I willed it still. "I mean, if something happens..." I looked toward the girl, who was now being approached by another cop. "You could get *arrested*. Right?"

The chanting was getting louder and people were beginning to shake the flimsy metal gates that separated the stage area from the rest of the crowd. Devin followed my fearful gaze then looked at me, his eyes wary and alert but still shaded with slight amusement. It was the first expression that I'd gotten from him other than disinterest since I'd been back in Tyler.

"Ain't nobody getting arrested." His deep voice was confident. He looked down at me, his chest expanding with the breath he took. He leaned closer, speaking directly into my ear, causing goosebumps to rise on my skin despite the staggering heat. "You know I'm not gonna let anything happen you."

"I'm talking about *you,*" I returned just as quietly, my nose nearly brushing his cheek because he was still so close.

His eyes flickered again and he cocked his head. "So, you worried about me now?"

His voice was heavy with double meaning, though barely audible, and I sucked in a breath. For the first time, he was visibly angry. I turned away, stomach churning, glancing at Kennedy then Jersey, who still looked as though she was ready to fight.

Out of my peripheral I saw the organizer of the rally and head of Progressive Union, Danica, approaching us quickly.

"Thank you-*thank you,*" she breathed once she reached us, winded from her power walk. "Thank you guys so much for actually showing up, Devin."

Devin frowned slightly, probably at the idea that if they'd made an arrangement to appear, they wouldn't honor it.

Danica was smiling now. Her coiled hair had come undone and she swiftly pinned it back out of her eyes as she turned her attention to Devin. She was pretty, with a small waist and a huge butt that was amply noticeable in her short jean shorts. Her eyelashes were long, accented by charcoal eyeliner and her eyes were wide and expressive. She looked like Devin's type, physically, at least.

"What's up, girl," Devin greeted her, accepting her hug. Another girl, probably an underclassman, sidled up behind Danica with water bottles, which she promptly passed out to the band members. Of course, there wasn't one for me.

"You mind grabbing another water?" Devin asked the smiling girl.

He handed me his, without a second thought, and I took the bottle gratefully, wiping the ice-cold plastic over my forehead before twisting off the cap and taking a long, soothing sip.

"You guys have no idea how much I appreciate you agreeing to play today," Danica said, watching as I handed the bottle of water back to Devin. He promptly took a long swallow, his eyes on me. I shifted my weight, tugging at a lock of my hair again. Danica tore her eyes from Devin's mouth, and her eyes darted to the crowd. She shifted uncomfortably, shaking her head. "I'm afraid something is about to go down."

"So are we," Zay, spoke up, his gray eyes appeared almost icy blue under the unrelenting sunlight.

"I think once you guys get on stage— you can calm everyone down," Danica suggested. "I thought maybe you could do some of your more laid-back songs, change the air a little. There's a lot of... non-students here."

Devin handed the bottle back to me, so I could have the final bit of cool liquid. I hesitated for a second before pressing the bottle to my lips.

"This isn't what we were expecting when we put this rally together," Danica admitted. "I didn't expect for all of these... other people to show up."

I glanced at Travis, who'd narrowed his eyes. Out of all of us, he was the one with the most ties to Tyler, Texas. His grandma, Pearl, left her house to him when she passed, and most of the band lived there now. Kennedy's grandma, Pepper, lived right down the street, which is partly how she'd joined the band so quickly when she moved here last year, and how her and Travis got together. Travis loved Tyler, and Danica's snide remark wasn't lost on him. He was chewing on his toothpick double time now, though his handsome face remained void of expression.

"So, what's up? You're sayin' you want us to pacify these 'other people'?" Travis asked, in his raspy voice. His tone was calm but cool, and Danica shifted uncomfortably.

"I wouldn't say 'pacify,'" Danica said, eyeing the crowd again, who'd began chanting loudly.

"Then what would you say?"

It was Jersey who spoke up; of course, her water bottle pressed against her lips. She cocked her head to the side a little, her gaze assessing and I bit the corner of my lip, bracing myself for some drama. Jersey rarely held her tongue. And neither did Danica—I knew that much from seeing her around on campus. She was in my Civics class last year and liked to wield her opinion around like a sword, slicing up anyone who dared to disagree with her.

"I'm gonna be honest with you guys," Danica said meeting Jersey's gaze head on. "The crowd is getting out of control, and Progressive Union can't have that. We can't have the organization's name tied up in any campus riots."

"A riot is the language of the unheard," Travis said, exchanging a glance with his cousin Zay, who was standing behind Jersey, pulling absently at the belt loops on her short shorts as she subconsciously leaned against his chest. After two years of rooming with her, I knew Jersey and Zay's relationship dynamics, and I knew that was Zay's subtle way of keeping her cool before she spazzed.

"Maybe it's time to get a little rowdy to wake people up," Zay added.

"Everyone here is 'woke.' It's not about that," she said, turning toward Zay.

"Then what's it about?" Jersey prodded.

Danica released a breath and shook her head, casting a pleading look in Devin's direction. She was bothered but trying to flirt simultaneously, which just made her look desperate. I lifted my long Senegalese twists from my shoulders, immediately relishing the heavy hair being off my damp back. Devin's hot gaze skirted over me, before he returned his attention to the discussion at hand.

"We're just trying to understand what you're saying, Danica. What's your objective here?" Bam finally spoke up, his deep voice uncharacteristically serious.

"This is the first co-event we've done with Common Collective."

Danica's worried gaze skated over to a group of two white girls and three white dudes who were wearing t-shirts bearing the organization's name. I recognized one of the sandy brown-haired guys from class too. I think he was dating one of the girls from my dance team.

"Progressive Union is the only black organization on campus and if anything goes down, *we're* gonna get the blame. Not them."

She lowered her voice though it wasn't necessary because no one besides could hear her given the crowd noise. "The difference between the way that white protestors and black protestors are treated... I don't have to break that down to you, do I?"

Danica's eyes were still pleading and she glanced at Devin again, silently asking for help, as she pinched the material of her yellow halter between her fingers, and pulled it, accentuating her chest. I shifted my weight, my wedged sandals denting the dewy grass.

"I thought maybe you all could start with 'Space' since it's everyone's favorite and..."

"We make our own set list," Jersey said, her irritation evident.

"Look, I love The Prototype. That's why I paid almost half of my yearly entertainment budget for the set-up to—"

"We're doing this show for *free,*" Travis reminded her. "Because we're about this movement."

Danica shook her head, pushing out a breath. "We need people *calm*. It's not time to be irresponsible."

"The cop who killed Jamal was 'irresponsible,'" Jersey countered. "How dare we be expected to downplay our anger for the sake of looking 'respectable' to these white folks?"

"Do you understand what's going on here?" Danica erupted.

"Do *you?*" Jersey countered loudly, just as Devin moved to step between her and Jersey. Zay grabbed Jersey's arm, his gaze on Danica.

"Maybe we need to just pull the plug on the whole thing," Danica goaded, looking directly at Jersey.

"No one is pulling the plug on anything," Devin interrupted, using his commanding voice on her now. "We cleared our schedule to be here and we're doing this show."

Danica's mouth was a tight line and was still glaring at Jersey.

"Danica." Devin waited until she looked at him. "We got it under control, a'ight? You said it yourself. You wanted us here for a reason. You go do what you need to do and we'll do what we need to do up there."

Devin jerked his head toward the stage, and waited until Danica nodded in acceptance, softening under the hum of Devin's voice. She hesitated for another second, staring at Devin before folding.

"Alright. I'll go introduce you."

She walked away, throwing a glance at Jersey over her shoulder. I looked up at Devin, who expelled a breath. There was always so much present in his eyes, passion, intelligence, determination, and an intensity that seemed new. It was a focus that dimmed everything else. He stared into my eyes for a minute, melting everything inside of me that might have wanted to fade away from him.

"Go Bruce Banner," I whispered, staring into his eyes. Something shifted in his and he inhaled and held the breath before letting it out slowly.

"Stand right there by the steps."

His voice was gruff and he bobbed his head toward the stairs that lead to the stage, and I nodded again, accustomed to the routine, even though I'd been out of practice. If it was large enough, sometimes I could be on stage with them but in this case, it wasn't feasible.

He turned away from me and I followed everyone toward the stage, stopping near the steps as we all huddled together for Travis to deliver his customary prayer before they went on, grabbing Jersey and Kennedy's hands so that I could avoid Devin's. I didn't miss the look he flashed me though.

When we broke apart and they headed up to the stage steps I could see Devin silently signaling to everyone else.

I could only see their backs on stage now, but the crowd's attention was instantly drawn to them, the chanting growing louder, mixed with shouts of "Prototype" now as well. Danica climbed down the stage steps and stood next to me, casting me a wary glance. I wondered briefly what she knew about my status with Devin, but worked on keeping my attention fixed on the stage. The band never did any talking before they got into the music, ever. It was their thing. And today was no different.

Devin started tapping in the rhythm and the rest of the band began playing along, the sound stretching into the thick air and popping back toward the stage like elastic. And when they uttered the first words to the song, I didn't know whether to laugh, or cry. Out of the corner of my eye I saw Danica's face drop and she closed her eyes as on cue and completely in sync, The Prototype shouted out the menacing words of N.W.A.'s song, chanting along aggressively with the crowd, *"Fuck the police."*

2

DEVIN

I COULD STILL the hear the crowd, still feel the beat of the drums in my body when I stepped onto the front porch of the house, swatting at the moths that were drawn by the soft light that Kennedy or Jersey probably left on for us.

Our show was *lit.* It's always like that after I gig—the music doesn't leave me. I can still feel the beat in my blood—it's dormant until I get on the sticks, but once they're in my hands, it's like something inside of me wakes up, and starts clawing to get out. "Bruce Banner" is who Low started calling me after I explained it to her. But tonight, it was intensified and more meaningful because we were playing for a reason that extended even beyond the music. It felt like we were playing for our existence, for our right to breathe as people.

I was so in the zone, I fucked around and broke one of my sticks tonight. We were closing out one of our older tracks, "Come Undone" and the drum pattern breaks down completely. I was Bruce Banner alright. It worked out though. I just played with one hand for a minute. The crowd went crazy when Zay drew their attention to it—almost like it was part of the show. I had to signal Low to grab me a new one from Bam's van. All I had to do was look back at her, where she was standing off behind the stage, and she nodded, already knowing.

That was an indescribable feeling—knowing that I could rely on Willow to come through in the clutch but also realizing that she was more disconnected from me than she'd ever been before. Seeing her again today, after two months, and after she decided that we needed "space" and bounced to Houston for the whole summer, made it hard to concentrate. And that wasn't acceptable.

I knew she was coming to town because Jersey couldn't hold water, plus the last semester of her senior year was starting in a couple of days, but nothing prepared me for being able to breathe her again.

Low always smelled like honey and sunshine. Light, sweet, inviting, like life itself when it was good. She gave substance to every space she entered because her energy was so pure and genuine. Like her being present made everything more real, more accessible. Seeing the way she smiled, hearing her voice, the way she said my name, the way she still looked at me, even when she didn't want to, wasn't lost on me. Willow felt me, the same way I did her. We were best friends and she was my heartbeat, even when it felt like it didn't make sense for us to be as connected as we were. Me and Low were in a constant state of turmoil but that never meant that she wasn't my pulse—steady as my breathing. She was the one thing besides music that I knew in my soul.

I loved Willow Elizabeth Harden.

She was supposed to come on tour with us over the summer. When she up and left after another argument that went too far, but not far enough for her to just dip on me without a word, I just did what I always do—turned to music. We were headed out tour with another soul group out of Atlanta called Black Bottom at the time anyway, 36 cities, and I barely had time to think about the fact that she'd up and bounced on me at 6 in the morning, like we were in one of them goofy-ass romance movies she was always watching. I didn't let myself. I couldn't. But when I did focus on it, when thoughts of us inevitably infiltrated my mind, I couldn't breathe. Couldn't think. Couldn't function. And that wasn't an option.

My phone buzzed in my hand and I answered it quickly.

"What's good?"

"Sent," Nikitta said promptly. "To you and Travis."

"Good lookin' out."

"Let me know what you think, Devin, for real. Don't sugar coat it. I need your opinion."

"Do I ever not keep it 100?"

"No," she paused, as if thinking. "So maybe do sugar coat it a little, actually," she laughed. "Tell me the truth but be gentle about it."

"Imma check 'em now," I said chuckling. "But I'll holler at you in a minute, okay?" Nikitta liked to ramble if I let her. I didn't have the time for that tonight.

"Okay, don't forget to let me know."

I hung up, already tapping out a new rhythm that popped into my head, beating my thumb against my thigh as I pulled open the heavy wooden front door to the house. When I was nine my dad bought my first drum set, a gift of guilt for missing the birthday party mom scraped up her pennies to have for me at this go-cart racing place, Tire Tracks.

I love my dad, but that dude is unreliable, and the quicker I realized it, the better our relationship got. I lowered my expectations for what a father should be and it made him easier to deal with.

For my ninth birthday, he didn't help out with any loot for the party—he didn't even show up. I wonder now if it was because that was right after he and my moms divorced and he just couldn't deal with seeing her. Either way, it was messed up. But it turned out that his sometimey-bullshit resulted in the best gift I ever got.

Funny how life works out like that.

Before I picked up the sticks, I could never sit still. Like, ever. I was constantly moving, like there was an internal battery in my organs and I could never rest. It drove my mom and all my teachers crazy.

"He can't pay attention and he's disruptive," Mrs. Herman told my mom when I was in the third grade before suggesting she take me to the doctor to get drugged. She already had me sitting off in a corner by myself away from the rest of the class, like I was a nine-year-old derelict or some shit. Moms had a fit about it when she found out though—called Mrs. Herman racist, but in a real polite way. Moms had politely calling people on their bullshit down to a science.

Still, moms ended up putting me on Adderall for about a month, until she saw the side effects, how it made me shaky and withdrawn, so she took me off it. Three months later, I had the drums. She was as surprised as my dad that his bullshit make-up gift ended up being my "cure." I just needed somewhere to put my energy, to let it out so that it could turn into something. From the moment I touched the drums, I knew that was it. Even at nine years-old I knew what my purpose was. This music.

"Nikitta came through with these pictures," Travis was saying as we headed into the small house his grandma Pearl left him after she passed a few years back. He finally decided he was tired of it looking like 1952 inside, and had it renovated. Travis was serious about keeping the wood floor though. I didn't blame him. It was cool; had character.

The house smelled like garlic and pasta, and my stomach rumbled in response, as I glanced toward the small kitchen entrance.

"I didn't even know she was into photography," Trav said, closing the front door behind him.

"I haven't even checked what she sent yet. You put 'em on social already?" I asked, nodding at Kennedy as she came through the living room entrance from the kitchen. That meant Low was here somewhere too, since she was staying with Kennedy at her grandma's a few houses down the street.

"Doin' it now." Travis perched himself on the edge of the large sectional couch, his attention on his phone. Still, without looking, he grabbed Kennedy's hand, and pulled her to stand between his legs.

Kennedy left right after the show because she was weird about crowds, and people in general. I couldn't blame her. Baby girl had been through some mean shit, an experience that would've had a lesser person staring at four walls in psyche ward. I was concerned when she joined the band about a year ago, at first anyway. Kennedy's voice was magic but she couldn't mess up the vibe being scary, no matter how dope she was. But when Kennedy was on stage, she lit up like a Christmas tree, like she had another being lying dormant inside of her. We connected on that level. Always though, after we hopped off stage, she was antsy and ready to kick rocks.

Willow and Bam left with her after the performance tonight— Low because she said it was too hot to function and she probably wanted to get away from me. I hadn't heard her voice in *two months*. I texted and called her, more times than I could count, all of which went unanswered. If it wasn't her, I would've just taken the L and moved the hell on. I wasn't in the habit of chasing women, especially women who didn't know what they wanted from me or themselves.

But it was Low. And we had so much history. I could admit that a lot of my identity was tangled up in what we'd built over the past couple of years. How we went from being up under each other every day for two years to practically not talking for a straight two months had me reevaluating damn near everything. Shit that didn't even have to do anything with my up and down with Low. Being out of control with emotions wasn't my lane. Not anymore. I couldn't let anything, even my heart, mess that up for me. There was too much at stake. We were too close.

"That was soul-stirring today," Kennedy said, looking at Travis then me for affirmation. "I don't think I've ever felt like that on stage before."

"That energy was on some other. Even more than the rally we did at Cassie's school," Travis agreed, referencing Kennedy's older sister. We'd performed in Colorado earlier in the summer, not too long after the shooting, but the vibe was different, looser maybe. The crowd today was wound so tight, I thought they would burst at any minute on some Ferguson-type shit.

"I felt..." Kennedy hesitated, glancing up at Travis then to me. "I don't know... too in control of their energy. I don't know if I like it."

"Nah, get off that." I shook my head, eyeing her. "That feeling you're talking about? It's power, Kennedy. *That's* what we do. The only thing we gotta worry about is giving credit where it's due," I said, pointing upward, "and not abusing it. But that control? It's our gift."

Travis smirked and Kennedy nodded her eyes solemn.

"I could feel him. Jamal's presence," she said quietly, glancing at Travis again.

"Me too," I admitted.

"Not just his either," Travis added. Kennedy blew out a breath and Travis kissed her temple.

"I hope this is the last rally we have to do," Kennedy said softly, though she sounded like knew better.

I glanced toward the kitchen, focusing on the garlic scent lingering in the small house instead of the black people being shot in the streets by police like dogs. Actually, dogs were worth more than black lives, so even that analogy was bullshit. I blew out a silent breath.

"Pepper cooked?" I asked Kennedy. Kennedy's grandma was the best cook ever.

"Yeah, chicken fettuccini. It's warming in the oven. Willow made sure I brought it over."

"Right on." I tugged her braid as I passed by her, making my way into the mid-sized kitchen to fix myself a plate, ignoring her obvious comment about Low.

"Aye, don't forget—"

"I already know," Travis called from the living room, cutting me off.

We needed to call our manager, Jay Little so we could solidify our schedule for the next month.

The constant buzz, that almost-high you get when you know you're right on the brink of changing your life, it was thrumming in my chest with more intensity. I pulled the food from the oven and grabbed a plate from the dishwasher.

The kitchen got the bulk of the summer's renovation, and I perched myself against the new stainless steel stove as I ate quickly, trying not to think about Willow, who was probably right outside on the back patio, or downstairs. It was doubly hot in the kitchen with the oven going on top of the 85 degree night time temperature, so I pulled my shirt off, stuffing it into the back of my pocket, before focusing on my food again.

"Slow down, greedy."

I frowned around a forkful of pasta as Jersey strolled into the kitchen from the basement. I balanced the bowl in one hand and flipped her off. She rolled her eyes as she walked further into the kitchen. I heard her messing around downstairs when me and Trav walked in, the bass pumping in a steady rhythm that I was sure we'd revisit. She grabbed a fork from the dishrack, stood directly in front of me, and attempted to stab her fork into my bowl. I pulled it out of her reach and stared at her.

"You're trippin— get your own. There's a whole pot right there."

I bobbed my head toward the pan sitting on top of the stove, still chewing.

"I only want a bite, Devin. I need to lose five pounds," she whined. I rolled my eyes, and extended the bowl toward her. She helped herself to some noodles, satisfied now that she'd gotten what she wanted.

"You must have the munchies," she observed, as she chewed. "You and Trav never let me know when you smoke."

"You didn't put in on this," I teased her, grinning with my mouth full.

She rolled her eyes again and pushed off the counter, crossing the small room and plopping down into the worn, canary yellow dining room chair, one of the few things Trav kept during his renovations. She pulled her wild hair up, securing it sloppily with a rubber band.

"You still going home tomorrow?"

I nodded. I didn't feel like making the 12-hour drive to Atlanta, but it'd be worth it. I'd head there, take care of business and turn around and get right back on the road.

"How is your mom?" she asked, a little tentatively.

"Better. Once she gets everything situated, she'll be all good."

"Maybe we should canc—"

"I'll be back Tuesday." It would be a stretch because we were leaving out again Tuesday night but I wasn't going to start rearranging our schedule for my personal life. Jersey gave me a sympathetic look, which I ignored.

"My pops asked me to come home next month. He's having a grand opening for his new shop and asked me to be there."

I eyed her. Jersey's pops was recently remarried. He was also a straight-up dead beat.

"Zay ain't feeling that." It wasn't a question.

"He said it was bullshit because he texted me the invite instead of calling."

"It is."

"You're probably both right. But it's like sometimes when he calls... I just. I dunno."

"Want him to be your dad."

She looked at the floor, releasing a deep breath.

"Guess who hit me up? Tanya," I told her, deliberately changing the subject because I knew she needed me to.

Tanya was an old friend back from high school that used to hang with us back in the day. Jersey looked up, clearly appreciative of the topic shift.

"She called me too, wanting to know when we're moving to Atlanta."

"She asked you for tickets to the New York show?" We had a show coming up in NYC in a few days and Tanya said she'd be out there, interviewing for a job.

Jersey nodded. "I don't know why she asked us both."

"Probably because you don't ever remember nothin'," I teased. "You woulda left her ass hangin'."

She flipped me off, smirking.

"What are you doing?" she said after a long second, licking the back of her fork.

"What're you talking about?" I asked, swallowing.

"Willow is outside on the back patio with Bam and Zay." I stabbed another forkful of pasta, spinning it around my fork before stuffing it into my mouth.

"She's gonna think you're ignoring her," Jersey prompted when I said nothing.

I shook my head, forking up the last of the pasta. Shit was delicious. Pepper deserved a cooking Emmy or Grammy. Something.

"Low don't care what I do any more. She made that shit real clear when she dipped this summer."

"Oh my *gosh*. You are so in your feelings. You can't seriously be serious," Jersey retorted, giving me one of her "duh" faces that reminded me of when I first met her, when we were 14. She lived down the block from me and was the first person I was able to actual jam with. We sounded like shit at first, but our musical chemistry was instant.

Jersey kept staring at me, waiting for a response. Her brow was arched and she was smirking, like she knew something I didn't.

"Why you always tryin' to start some shit?"

Her eyes grew wide. "I'm *not*. I'm just trying to help you wake up and get her back."

"She shouldn'ta ever left."

"Your ego is so *massive* sometimes, man. She was freaking overwhelmed, Devin. We went on tour, and now we're about to leave *again* to perform and record but she'll be here still, stuck in Tyler. And with all those thirsty birds always squawking around you guys and after the parking lot incident..."

"Man, whatever," I interrupted. "That's a bullshit excuse. You know it and I know it. And you know who else knows it? Willow."

Jersey rolled her eyes. "You just need to be like, *aware* of how she feels."

I sat my bowl down in the kitchen sink, which was stacked with a few dishes, and ran a little bit of water in it. Jersey's words were nagging at me a little bit, but it was still some bullshit. Low knew she had me, anyway, anytime she wanted. I was hers and she fuckin' left anyway. Talking about she needed to "explore," whatever the hell that meant. Actually, I knew exactly what it meant, which is why I didn't want to hear shit Jersey was yelping about. Low made her choice. She didn't even tell me that shit to my face. She sent it in a damn text message *after* she was already back in Houston.

"She came back early for *you*, not just for our show. You know that," Jersey was saying. "And—"

"You worry about you," I cut her off, irritated. "I got me and Low."

I pushed off the counter, and grabbed a beer out of the refrigerator, enjoying the momentary cool that greeted me before I closed it again.

"Don't say I didn't try to help you, Stubborn," she called out as I headed out of the kitchen, throwing goodnight deuces toward Trav and Kennedy, who were still perched on the back of the couch, looking at Trav's phone.

I headed down the narrow hallway, passing old football and soccer pictures of Travis and his little brother Cam hanging on the walls, ignoring the urge to go outside and be near her. One good thing that came from Low leaving this summer was it freed up the head space I gave her. The void she left was filled with music now. Almost.

I ran a hand over the back of my neck, blinking back memories of when I'd push my bedroom door open after a gig and find her lying on my bed in one of my shirts, typing on her phone, or doing her homework. The old wooden door creaked when I swung it open and flicked on the bedroom light, urging the ceiling fan to start spinning in a pitiful attempt to circulate air.

It smelled stale in the room, unused, because we'd just gotten off the road two days ago and it still hadn't readjusted to having life in it. I flicked on my stereo, and The Isley Brothers started singing about hearing "footsteps in the dark." I sat down on the edge of the bed, which was just a small box spring and mattress stacked on top of each other, taking a swallow of beer, before, tapping the cool bottle against my knee. I was wired and I knew why. Yeah, life was changing a lightning speed. But the real reason was right outside the patio door, chilling with my people, like she wasn't even concerned about what was going on with us.

A few minutes later, there was a light tap at the door and I looked up, not really surprised when Low gently pushed the door open.

"Hi," she said, hesitating in the doorway.

"What's up."

She'd changed into cotton shorts and a tank top since I'd last seen her, her lounging clothes. Her eyes were low but bright, probably from the beer she was holding.

"I'm about to leave with Kennedy but I just wanted to say 'hi'." She shook her head. "Or bye. Or whatever."

She shrugged, offering an adorable half-grin. She shifted her weight uncomfortably and I bit the corner of my lip. The tension was thick, stretching between us like smog, making it hard to think about anything other than what I needed to get off my chest.

"Which one?" My voice was probably gruffer than necessary but I didn't care.

She blinked, tugging at a lock of her hair.

"Huh?"

"Hi, bye or whatever? Which one you gonna go with?"

She stared at me through her thick eyelashes, and then looked at the floor, heaving a soft breath that hit me right in my groin, as she stared down at her toenails.

"Come in and shut the door if you're comin'."

She looked up at me then. After a second, she did as I asked, stepping inside of my small, hot bedroom, and shutting the door softly behind her. Immediately the staleness that previously lingered in the air succumbed to Low's sweet honey scent.

"You were in here decompressing?" she asked, seating herself on the crate near my record player, which was on the opposite end of the bed. There was at least six feet of distance between us, I could feel her body heat, smell her, causing the pit of my stomach to tighten even more. It wasn't just that I hadn't seen her in way too long. It was her. My body instinctually reacting to her presence.

"Somethin' like that."

She glanced up at me, a tiny smirk on her lips. I knew her skin was as smooth to my touch as it looked, her dark butterscotch complexion playing against the thin cotton material of her shorts that barely covered her ass and thighs now that she was sitting. She was a dancer but not the skinny, ballerina type. Nah, Willow had an *ass*, and thick, firm thighs, even though she was fairly petite. She'd gotten a little thicker over the summer, and it looked good on her. Too good.

"I can't believe you guys did that." My gaze slid slowly up from her thighs to her face. She was blushing, trying to act like she didn't see me looking.

"Did what?"

I stood then, moving toward the dresser, mostly as a distraction. She licked her lips, fanning absently at her neck as she lifted her hair off her shoulders with her other hand. Travis' old house didn't have any central air, so a tan box fan was propped up in the window, pushing out thick, hot air, but it was better than nothing. At least something was circulating besides the creaky wooden fan that hung from the ceiling.

"Opened the show with 'Fuck the Police'."

Her brown eyes were wide and I couldn't help but grin. Just uttering the phrase aloud probably made her feel rebellious. I pulled my wallet and keys out of my pockets, emptying them onto the cluttered dresser.

"It's not funny. You guys totally could've started a riot."

"Nah. We 'totally' had control of the crowd the entire time," I mimicked, messing with her on purpose, as I pulled some loose change from my pockets.

"You weren't there in the crowd to see how people were reacting, the *rage* on people's faces."

I turned toward where she was seated on the crate.

"I *felt* the crowd. I ain't need to see their faces. And that rage is valid." I pulled my phone from my pocket, sliding my thumb over the screen. Our Instagram was lit up with comments and likes. *Hell yeah.*

"Of course it's valid. But..."

"Those people weren't stupid, Low." I looked up at her. "If we woulda started off with some Kumbaya, 'we are the world' shit, they really would've been ready to tear some shit up. We needed to help them channel their energy, let them know we understood what they were feeling, and then, once we had them, once they were connected with us, let them release it, all of that emotion, through us... Feel me?"

She bit her lip and smiled, and my gaze automatically trailed to her mouth. Her lips weren't exactly pink but dark salmon, almost like she smoked weed, which I knew she didn't. She'd gotten high with me once and was so paranoid; she'd fucked up my high too. After that, she was turned off completely, which I wasn't mad at. I actually liked that about her. She hadn't seen much outside of the bubble her parents kept her in, but she was curious and down to try whatever, at least once. Being the one who got to show her things— the one who put her on to new experiences was its own high.

I pushed out a breath, leaning against the dresser, which was situated directly across from her crate, and stuffed my hands in my pockets. There was so much unspoken between us but I wasn't ready to go there, not tonight. All I really wanted to do was to slide inside of her, feel the familiarity of her tightness and heat, let out some adrenaline and some of this unidentifiable energy that had me feeling heavy. Willow blinked, as if trying to outrun the weight of the moment, running her thumb distractedly over her beer, before wiping her brow with the bottle, running it down her neck.

"It's *so* hot," she murmured absently, closing her eyes.

I pressed my beer to my lips, relishing the cool of the liquid, my arousal increasing as I watched her. There were times when what I felt for Low was so all over me, so everywhere, the only thing I could think was the simplest: *mine*. She was *mine*, in every sense of the word, and not just because I was the only one that she'd ever given herself to sexually. Or I thought I was. I didn't know what the fuck she'd been doing in Houston for the past two months. Willow was mine... but not. I didn't live my life in limbo, yet here I was.

"Bam forgot to buy water," she explained to me, eyes still closed, as if I didn't already know that, seeing as how I lived here.

Willow blinked her eyes open and took another long swallow, tilting her head so that her long twists fell over one shoulder. It was a new style for her. She put me in mind of ol' girl from that boxing movie, *Creed,* with the style. Her nipples were hard beneath her tank top and my gaze landed there for a second before I was able to focus on her mouth, which was apparently moving again.

She was talking about the dance team now, what plans she had for the upcoming semester and how she'd just brought in a new transfer student. For a second, I just let her talk, even though I felt myself becoming heated, my resentment building the longer her lips moved. She was acting like everything was all good. If it was, she wouldn't be all the way across the room, sitting on a damn crate after two months of us not seeing or talking each other. I shook my head. *This was some bullshit.*

She stopped rambling and was watching me now, her almond eyes full of emotion I was too tired and agitated to decipher. Willow never had a problem telling me what was on her mind but now she was quiet, taking her cues from me. I wasn't giving her much. Instead I just stared her down. She knew what was up. Her chest expanded and she heaved a breath.

"Kennedy's probably waiting for me..." she finally managed. Her voice was soft. "I should probably..."

She trailed off and stood abruptly, pulling at the hem of her shorts, her beer nearly sloshing out of the bottle.

"A'ight."

That was all I could manage. I wanted to push her against the wall and pull those little shorts to the side and remind her of us. I wanted to shake her silly. I wanted to make her tell me why she decided to dip the way she did and explain every picture she'd posted when she wasn't with me. I wanted to ask her why, after two years, she chose now, the most pivotal time in my life to flip the script. But I didn't say shit. Instead, I crossed the room and sat with my elbows on my knees, watching her fumble with the door knob to the bedroom that we used to practically share.

"Good night, Devin."

She didn't look at me when she murmured the words, just slid out of the room and left...again.

BACK THEN: TWO YEARS AGO

WILLOW

"WILLOW! We're about to have a *Gilmore Girls* marathon!"

I barely paused as I waved a hand at Ana, who was seated in the spacious lounge inside of Doyle Hall. There was a huge flat screen hanging from the egg shell wall and vending machines that sold only organic snacks like granola bars and all-natural juices. Rory Gilmore's face was frozen on the screen, and Ana was beckoning for me to join her and the small group of girls who had gathered on the beige sectional couch with their organic popcorn to watch the old television show about a quirky mom and daughter and their love and life escapades.

"We saved some popcorn for you," Katy, Ana's bestie spoke up, her cornflower blue eyes wide.

"I can't," I said, frowning.

I loved *Gilmore Girls* almost as much as *A Different World*. Well, that was an exaggeration because no one could touch Dewayne Wayne and Whitely Gilbert, but still, I got a kick out of Rory and Lorelai's antics and non-stop fast-talking. "I have dance practice." I glanced at my phone. "Which I'm about to be late for."

Ana frowned at me, as if my busy schedule was somehow imposing on her. "I'll catch up with you guys later," I called, as I made my way past the lounge, toward the front doors, where the R.A.'s desk was situated. I waved at Brittany, our R.A. who was seated behind the desk, typing on her phone, as I made my way outside into the damp air. It'd just rained, turning the 80-plus degree heat into a sticky mess. Being from Houston, I was used to the humidity but today it was nearly unbearable, even though it was late in the evening and the sun was taking its last breath, before night fell. I walked swiftly toward the asphalt parking lot on the side of the large brick building, my flip flops slapping on the pavement. I was already in my practice clothes—gray spandex and a peach spaghetti tank.

I spotted my car, the one I begged my parents to get me before I left to college the year before, and hustled over to it, my duffle bag nearly falling off my shoulder as I clutched my keys, and hit the unlock button. I slid into the hot interior, immediately pushing the key into the ignition so that I could circulate some air and breathe in the stuffy car. Nothing. *Um...* I tried to crank it again and was met with a clicking noise.

"Ugh!" I clutched the steering wheel, heaving a breath as I stared out over the nearly empty lot.

My dad forced me to learn enough about cars to know that the battery was probably dead. I tried to start it again anyway, only to be met with the same annoying ticking noise. I sighed and pushed open the door, allowing the hot outside air to rush into the car, while I contemplated my options. I glanced at my phone. I had less than fifteen minutes to make it. If I was late, then I couldn't perform. It was a student-ran dance troupe but we made our own rules and abided them. Ironically, I was the one who introduced the tardy rule. I considered my options. I tried Gia, my friend who was also on the team. She didn't pick up, probably because she'd already turned off her phone. Maybe Jaden, the guy I'd been sorta-kinda dating since last semester, would come get me. No, he was at work. *Shoot.*

"Who you about to shoot, Low Low?" I didn't even realize I'd said the word out loud. But I did recognize the bass filled voice. Immediately my heart started pounding and blood shot to my cheeks.

I looked up to see Devin Walker practically hovering over me. He was so good-looking it literally made my insides ache sometimes. Full lips, long eye lashes that practically curled at the ends, square jaw, sleepy bedroom eyes that knew entirely too much, encased by thick eyebrows. I never thought of eyebrows as sexy, until Devin. He had dimples in both cheeks and hair on his face that rested between a full beard and five o'clock shadow most days. Today, he was rocking the 5 o'clock shadow.

He rested a hand on top of the opened car door and arched a brow, his stance casual, with a small smirk playing on his full lips. Not many people called me "Low Low" except my family and close friends, but Devin used the nickname freely from the first time we met, just about a year ago, when Jersey and I became roommates freshman year.

I had .2 seconds to get it together before it would start looking like I was ignoring him, or was socially-impaired. Sometimes, I thought Devin kind of figured I was anyway. It was the looks he gave me, with his lips slightly quirked up and his eyes narrowed in amusement. It was like he was always a half-second away from doubling over in laughter at me.

"No one," I finally said, licking my dry lips.

His smile increased, showing his dimples, as he stared down at me curiously. The smattering of brown freckles on his nose was visible, even in the fading sunlight, and his Braves ball cap was backwards on his head.

"What's up with you? Why you sittin' in this hot car lookin' like somebody shot your puppy?"

My mouth dropped open in horror at the imagery and he chuckled at my stricken expression. I'd only talked to Devin a handful of times over the past year, even though he was best friends with my roommate, I don't think he'd ever seen me without my cheeks being bright red. My crush on him was turning from ridiculous to just plain crazy. Which was pitiful and sad because Jersey told me on more than one occasion that Devin had "attention problems" when it came to women.

"It won't start," I finally answered, which made him smile again for some reason. "I think my battery is probably dead."

He twisted his lips, his eyes narrowing.

"Mind if I try?" he asked before leaning over me, smothering me with his intoxicating vanilla, cedar wood scent. I held my breath, my heart thudding because of his nearness. He smelled so good, I wanted to sniff him. I let out a slow silent breath and then subtly inhaled. Unaware that he was sending me into cardiac arrest with his closeness, he turned the key, listening to the clicking noise. Finally, he pulled back, allowing me to breathe normally again.

"I think you're right. Pop the hood and I'll give you a jump."

He nodded toward his beat up blue Ford pick-up truck, and I briefly wondered if it would completely fall apart if he connected jumper cables to it. I pushed the thought out of my mind, wondering how I hadn't even heard him drive up. His truck was *loud*.

"Thank you," I said, sliding out of the car, after popping the hood. "I don't want to keep you if you had things to do."

I shrugged, shifting my weight on the gravel, which was poking through my cheap sandals I'd picked up from Old Navy.

"It's all good," he said, without even looking at me.

He was busy popping his own hood and then digging cables from his truck which he expertly attached to my car in just a few seconds. His phone was in his hand the entire time though, and he was texting, his handsome face fixed into a half-grin. The phone rang in his hand and he answered.

"Quit trippin," he answered in greeting, though his deep voice was almost playful. It had to be some girl. I looked away, staring down at my own phone before dropping it into my oversized bag.

"I said I'll get at you. Don't worry about that." He laughed. "A'ight, peace."

A second later he was off the phone, though his fingers quickly swiped over the screen for a few seconds before he slid it into the back pocket of his shorts. Devin dressed so... *cool.* A black beaded bracelet and one with green, yellow and red, were on his wrist and his hair was grown out a little, his kinky curls sticking out of the back of his cap. He was wearing a black tank top with the army green shorts and a pair of Vans. He looked like a rock star. I'd even noticed more guys around campus wearing Vans since last year, and I knew it was only because of Devin.

"You were visiting Jersey?" I asked, feeing the need to make small talk, as I tried not to stare at his tattoos, as he wiggled the wires under my car hood.

"Nah, she left her macro book at the crib and was whining for me to drop it off to her. Guess she has a test."

"She does. She's really stressed about it. She said she needs an 'A'."

I felt an inexplicable pang of jealousy, which was dumb. Even if Jersey weren't my roommate and good friend, I was *so* not Devin's type. Devin liked... worldly women. The cool, sultry girls like Jersey who were all like, smart but whose beauty was interesting. I was not cool or sexy. People told me I was pretty a lot but I knew it was all-American cute and I wondered how much of it had to do with the fairness of my skin and my long, so-called "good" hair. I wondered how many of those people who said I was pretty actually saw *me*.

My phone was buzzing in my oversized bag, and I had to search before I could find it. It was Tre, the team captain, wondering where I was. I quickly texted him back telling him I had car trouble. When I looked up from my phone, Devin was studying me, his back leaning comfortably against the front of his truck. Again, my heart started beating faster and heat spread to my face. Gosh, I hated being so transparent, especially to Devin. Every girl on campus tripped over themselves trying to get his attention and I was no better. He was looking at me almost curiously, as if he was really seeing me for the first time. I tucked a strand that escaped my top knot behind my ear, shifting my weight uncomfortably.

"Why do women do that?" He cocked his head to the side, his smirk back on his lips.

"Do what?" I managed.

"Carry big-ass bags like that?" He nodded toward the black bag that hung from my shoulder.

"We have a lot of stuff?"

"But you can't ever find anything in them. Doesn't that defeat the purpose?"

I shrugged. "Not really." I met his eyes. "Seems like you've spent a lot of time thinking about women's purses though."

He chuckled, a low and throaty sound that sent my heart racing again, and nodded his head toward me.

"Try it now."

I released an inaudible breath, and slid back into the hot car, trying not to make a big deal out of the fact that this is the longest I'd ever even talked to him one-on-one. I turned the ignition and once again got nothing. I looked up at Devin and shook my head. I sighed and stared at the group of girls who passed by us, waving at Devin. Two of them lived on my floor and one even asked to borrow a tampon the other day, but didn't even bother to greet me. I never understood girls like that—who deemed other women invisible if a cute guy was around.

Devin wasn't paying them any mind though. He frowned and jumped into his truck, pumping the gas a few times before yelling for me to try it again. When it still didn't start, I got out and he met me in front of my car.

"Might be your alternator or your starter," he said apologetically. "This is a new car though- so it's probably under warranty if you can find a dealership."

I rolled my eyes up to the steadily darkening sky, studying it with my hands on my hips. If I didn't make practice I wouldn't get to perform Saturday.

"Where were you headed?"

"Dance practice."

"I'll take you."

I stopped staring at the sky and looked at him. But he wasn't paying me any attention as he unhooked the cables.

"Are you sure? It's not on campus. It's across town at the Beverly Theater and..."

"I wouldn't've asked if I wasn't sure, Low," he said, turning toward me. "I don't mind if you don't mind riding in the truck. I know it's not the cleanest."

"No, no," I said, hastily shaking my head and locking my car door. "I like your truck," I lied.

He grinned again, that same smile that made me feel five years-old.

"Yeah, okay."

"I do!" He chuckled and walked around to the passenger side, yanking the rickety door open for me, his biceps flexing with his exertion. He held out his hand and I took it, biting my lip, feeling a jolt rip through me as soon as our fingers touched. I didn't dare look up at him though, as I climbed awkwardly into the truck, which wasn't dirty at all but did smell like air-freshener and oil. Within just a few seconds we were pulling right up to the front of my dorm building, where students trickled in and out.

"I know you gotta get to practice, but I'mma run this up to Jersey right fast and then we can roll, cool?"

I nodded. I was already late at this point and I know Jersey really did need her book. I watched him jog to the entrance of the building, smiling at four girls as they exited through the doors. One of them said something, and he turned, walking backward quickly and said something in return, a sexy grin on his face. I shook my head, feeling even stupider for having a crush on him. It was so cliché.

Absently, I rifled through the CDs that were scattered on the worn gray seat, next to an old black boombox. I frowned, and turned the knob on the radio since he'd left the truck running, and figured out why he carried around a portable radio. I jumped when he suddenly opened the door, sliding into the truck and pulling off from the curb in one smooth motion.

"You weren't in here going through my shit were you?" He tossed me a teasing grin, the soft light from the road dancing across his features since it was now nearly dark.

"I was admiring your radio," I said, glad he couldn't see how red I was in the dim light of the truck's cab. I patted the boombox between us.

"My dad bought this truck for me when I graduated. The radio never worked. I never got around to putting one in."

"Well, I like it. It's authentic."

He glanced at me and chuckled.

"I actually prefer the sound of cassettes."

I smiled. "Must be a musician thing, right?" Jersey always said the same thing.

He only glanced over at me, grinning again.

The ride over only took about 10 minutes and we didn't talk much because Devin wasn't a very safe driver and was texting on his phone the entire time, intermittently singing along to the Bloodstone record that was filling the cab.

"I *love* this song."

Devin looked over at me, clearly surprised.

"You know about that?"

"My dad loves them. I grew up on this. They make music for the soul. Soul. Music."

He chuckled and nodded appreciatively, returning his attention to the road.

"I really appreciate the ride," I said when he parked in a space near the front of the box-shaped building once we arrived. For an arts center, the building's design was bland and generic, though there was a huge mural of children playing in a water fountain that was vibrant and colorful, and helped liven it up some.

I paused with my hand on the door knob, surprised when he opened his door, and started to slide out.

"You're coming in?"

He stopped and looked over his shoulder at me. *Gosh, he was so fine.*

"Is that cool? You'll need a ride home right?"

He hopped out of the truck and was on my side before I could formulate a response. He yanked the crotchety door open and held out his hand again to help me out.

"I know you have other things to do. I could've asked someone to take me home," I said, my voice barely above a whisper because it's all I could manage, with my hand in his larger, rougher one. I jumped out of the cab, the movement putting me directly in line with his chest, just inches away from his body. He smirked and looked down at me.

"I don't offer things I can't give." His voice was low and my entire body heated.

"Okay then." I tucked a strand of my hair behind my ear again and he finally backed up enough for me to move around him, leading the way into the air-conditioned building. It's a wonder I was even able to walk, my legs felt so shaky. I closed my eyes for a second, internally cursing myself for being so obvious... again.

"Your people are gonna be cool with me hanging out, right?" Devin asked from behind me, though his inquiry was late because we were already entering the small theater.

"Rehearsals are usually closed but every now and then people come to watch."

"Cool," Devin said, as he followed me from the small lobby area into the ancient one-story auditorium.

He slid into a one of the burgundy cloth-covered seats all the way in the back and grinned at me. I waved like a dork and I heard him chuckle as I headed quickly down the carpeted aisle toward the group who was already warming up. It smelled like wet wood and the air was cool but I didn't worry about it because I knew I'd be sweating once practice was over.

I felt Devin's presence while I sped through my warm up and the entire time I ran through the routine on the worn wooden stage. But instead of feeling like a ball of nerves knowing he was there, it surprisingly had the opposite effect, I felt, relaxed. Emboldened even, knowing Devin's eyes were on me. I'd looked up a couple of times to catch him watching us. I couldn't really read his expression, since he was all the way in the back but he wasn't staring at his phone so we must've held his attention, at least a little. I half-expected for him to announce his presence, his personality was so big, and he was so used to the attention. But he was low-key.

I didn't hang around to chit-chat the way I usually did when we were done rehearsing. Before nosy Tre could start asking questions, I gathered my stuff and rushed straight back to Devin and told him I was ready to go.

"I can't believe you," Devin said, once we were settled inside of his truck again. I was starting to like the oily smell, the way it mingled with Devin's scent. He stared at me, shaking his head after he'd stuck his key in the ignition. "That wasn't college-level dancing, Low. That was like *Ciara-level* dope, or better actually."

"No way."

"Yeah, Low, real talk. I don't know anything about choreography or none of that but..." he shook his head, eyes wide, "I'm surprised you ain't on TV. You definitely got the look too." His gaze dipped from my chest to my thighs, and immediately the air constricted a little in my chest. I tried really hard not to fidget. I know he meant his off-handed remark as a compliment but I was suddenly really concerned with making sure Devin saw me beyond the box everyone always put me in.

"I actually choreographed this one," I offered.

Devin tilted his head, his eyes growing wide. "Damn, Low-Low. For real?"

I smiled, my belly tingling, at his praise as we finally pulled out of the lot, onto the street, which was lined with small businesses, mostly local spots like a drycleaner and a small liquor store.

"I thought it would be different if we incorporated more contemporary West African dance. So, it's that, but it also has a little West Indies influence. I was trying to give it some pop."

I popped in the seat a little to emphasize my words.

"You succeeded," he said, his eyes low as he grinned at me.

He suddenly honked his horn at a dirty blue Camaro passing by on the opposite side of the narrow street, throwing deuces out the window.

"Trav's cousin, Zay just moved here," he explained.

"Yeah, I think Jersey might..." I stopped, realizing I was about spill of Jersey's beans, which she may not have appreciated.

"Might what?"

"Nothin." I looked out the window, avoiding his gaze. "She's just mentioned him a couple of times."

He glanced at me with the same thoughtful looked he given me earlier.

"When's your performance?" he asked, thankfully dropping it.

"Friday. Same day as your gig at Jimmy's." I smiled proudly. "I said 'gig' in an actual sentence." Devin chuckled loudly.

"What time?" he asked, still grinning amusedly.

"What?"

"Your performance, what time is it?"

"Six."

He nodded, his lips twisting. His eyes were on the road as we maneuvered through the surface streets back toward campus.

"I wanna come check you out. But we have sound check at 6."

I was still staring at him, in a semi-state of shock. He'd turned on the Isley Brothers, and they were singing about summer rain. The music was what I needed after listening to the Rihanna dancehall track we'd been rehearsing to over and over. I was familiar with The Prototype's soulful sound from the handful of shows that I'd been too, but it was interesting finding out that Devin rode around listening to old school soul music.

"We were actually kind of off tonight," I admitted, suddenly nervous. "I keep trying to tell them the formation isn't exactly right."

"I thought you choreographed it?"

"I did but I have to run everything by the captain and some adjustments ended being made. Could you tell?"

He looked at me for a second, as if debating on what version of the truth to tell me.

"You need to be in the front, in that middle spot instead of buddy with the blue hair."

I blinked. I didn't expect him to go into so much detail.

"Well, 'buddy with the blue hair' is Tre and he's the team captain so..." I shrugged.

"So, he's a hater?" Devin supplied. I shrugged again. He flicked another glance at me, driving with one hand on the wheel. His phone buzzed next to him on the seat, illuminating the small space but he ignored it.

"He shouldn't be captain if won't do what's best for the team."

I looked out of the window at the passing scenery. "Tre is definitely about doing what's best for him."

"Then you need to be in charge."

I laughed. "Now that's hilarious. It's not that easy. Usually only seniors are elected to that position."

"Then change it," Devin said, almost off-handedly, finally grabbing his phone.

I studied him while he studied his screen. The line of his jaw, which was covered with stubble, the outline of his full lips, his strong nose, those eyelashes that encased bedroom eyes, and had my body flushing with heat.

"Yeah, right." I finally managed.

"Don't talk yourself out of common sense, Low Low." He tossed the phone onto the seat next to him again and glanced over at me. "Buddy ain't lettin' you get your shine the way you need to, so common sense says you need to be in his position instead."

I couldn't help but laugh a little at his assuredness. He only smirked, his gaze sliding over my face, and my skin heated as if he'd physically touched it. Once again, his gaze was assessing like he was really looking at me for the first time. His phone buzzed again and he cursed under his breath, glancing at the road, then back to the seat, as if contemplating rather or not to answer. I shifted in the seat, pulling my leg under me when he finally grabbed the phone, sliding his thumb over the screen.

"What's good," he said, his tone was cool even though he was clearly irritated. "Right now? We can't do it tomo—" He pushed out a short breath shaking his head as we came to a stoplight. "A'ight. Hold up."

He covered the phone with his hand and looked at me, his expression apologetic.

"I need to make a run right quick. You mind riding or do you need to get back right now?"

My heart sped up with excitement at the thought of spending more time with him. It was pathetic, but I managed to play it cool, lifting my shoulders and nodding.

"It's cool."

"You sure?" he asked, arching a brow.

I nodded again.

"A'ight, I'll be there in ten," he said to whoever was on the phone.

Devin slowed down and made U-Turn at the next intersection we hit, taking us to the opposite side of town. "I gotta pick up the t-shirts for the show."

"The ones Jersey designed?"

He nodded, the headlights from a passing car briefly illuminating his handsome features.

"Can I have one? I mean, I'll buy it."

Devin chuckled. "Nah." My face fell. "Come on with that. You know I got you."

The way he looked at me, the way his voice lowered when he said,

'I got you,' had my body on fire. But that's the way Devin talked to every woman. He flirted. It meant nothing. I shifted in my seat, blowing out a silent breath, distracting myself by thumbing through the CDs scattered on the seat between us. I picked up one, grinning, and ejected the Isley Brothers from the boombox.

Devin tilted his head and looked at me, giving the "oh really?" face that was probably supposed to be stern but was only tempting because I wanted to close the space between us and like, *lick him*—his arm, his lips, his neck. My face was hot as the thought slid through my brain. I'd turned into a perv.

"You just gonna be bold with your hands all over my radio?" Devin was saying when I snapped myself back to reality. His baritone was deep, laced with amusement.

I smiled innocently, pretending to be unaffected, and popped in the CD. Devin's eyes widened when the music poured through the speakers.

"*Hell nah*, what you know about Devin the Dude?" he asked, smiling with his eyes round as he glanced over at me. The Dude was crooning "Do What You Want to Do" and I sang along, going silent only on the curse words.

"I am from Houston, remember?" I turned in the seat to face him, pulling up the strap on my spaghetti tank. "*Everyone* loves The Dude."

Devin chuckled again, shaking his head, still looking at me incredulously. "Hell nah, Low-Low," he mumbled again under his breath. "I can't lie, I'm impressed."

I raised a brow. "Oh, I impressed *the* Devin Walker!" I put a hand over my mouth and widened my eyes. "Did I earn a cookie? Or a gold star?"

He looked over at me grinning. "Nope, you gotta do a little more than that." I rolled my eyes, smiling.

"So, you're actually from Atlanta?" I asked after a few long seconds of listening to the music.

"Born and raised."

"My grandmother on my dad's side is from Atlanta. We always used to stop through there on the way to Florida during the summers. She lived in Decatur."

"Yeah?" he asked, his gaze genuinely interested.

I tended to ramble a little when I was nervous or excited, and so Devin was forced to spend the next few minutes listening to me go on about the summer vacations I took as a kid. Real interesting stuff. But Devin actually did seem genuinely into my long-winded chatter, peppering me with questions here and there. By the time we pulled up to the apartment of the t-shirt printer guy, I'd gone through the basics of most of my high school years.

"What you got up for the rest of the night?" Devin said glancing at his phone after we'd pulled off with the box of t-shirts securely sitting in the back bed of his truck.

"Nothing really," I said shrugging, feeling a little lame.

It was 10:30. Normally, I'd been in my room, studying or talking with Jersey when she was around, or I'd be in the lounge downstairs, watching silly re-runs with group of girls that lived on my floor. Sometimes, Jaden would come by and we'd watch a movie in my room or we'd go out and hang on the quad, just watching people walk by.

My stomach rumbled loudly and I rubbed a hand over it, embarrassed.

"Hungry?" Devin teased, chuckling.

"I am little. I might go steal one of Jersey's hot pockets. Or try to bribe this girl named Ana that lives down the hall from me into giving me some ice cream."

Devin grinned. "You wanna go grab something to eat?"

"Do you mind?" I asked, turning in the seat unable to keep the excitement out of my voice. He offered me a half-grin, glancing at me before refocusing on the road.

"I know spot where you can get some ice cream too so you ain't gotta bribe anybody."

I expected him to take us somewhere quick, like McDonalds but he informed me he doesn't do fast food very often, when we passed by one.

"Gotta keep my energy level up," he explained. "Can't do that with junk clogging your veins. You get sleepy after eating that bullshit for a reason."

Instead, we drove to a little spot called the Pancake Shack not far from t-shirt guy's apartments that sold ice cream, burgers and pancakes, and smelled of syrup and grease, but not unpleasantly so. We sat inside the little diner, that was maybe supposed to be 50s -retro at some point in its existence, but just looked old now, with its faded red booth, dingy eggshell tables and dull white and black checkered floor, and... talked. About nothing. About everything. He told me about starting The Prototype, how he had class with Travis and Bam and they got cool and that's how the band expanded beyond just him and Jersey last year. He told me about goals for the band, how music was the only thing that made sense to him. He was so passionate when he spoke, his brown eyes glinting with so much determination it was infectious, and his dreams quickly became visions in my own mind. I could visualize them on stage, in front of sold out crowds in Amsterdam or Japan. I could see them selling out venues across the country, hear their fans chanting their names.

And when our bubbly waitress brought the ice cream out— vanilla with chocolate sauce and coconut sprinkles— I made him try it, and quickly recruited him, in spite of his claims that my ice cream looked like "glittery boo-boo."

"What's that on your finger?"

Devin furrowed his brow, turning his hand back and forth, studying it.

"On your *finger*," I emphasized, smiling as I leaned forward in the worn both and reached across the small table top for his hand. He let me grab it leaning back against his seat, watching me. I held my breath, struggling to keep the heat from rising to my cheeks so that he wouldn't know I was blushing.... Again. *Why'd I have to go and touch him?* I shifted in my seat, dropping my gaze to the tattoo that'd drawn my attention. It was the numeral two in the space where his thumb and index finger met.

"That ain't my finger," he corrected.

I kept my eyes on his hand, because I couldn't touch him and look at him without dissolving, and ran my thumb over it. I released his hand, leaning back in the booth again, forcing myself to breathe normally as I tucked my hand under my thighs to hide how they were practically shaking. Just from touching him. *So pathetic.* He was smiling when I finally inhaled enough air to meet his eyes without passing out.

"Whatchu think?" he questioned, his bedroom eyes low.

"The number two? Were you born at two a.m.? Do you have two siblings? Oh!"

My eyes widened and I pulled my legs under me, so that I was sitting cross-legged in the booth, and leaned forward, resting my arms on the laminate white table, which was edged in dull silver. "It's because you're a drummer and you play with *two* sticks!"

He laughed, shaking his head as he leaned forward, tapping his thumb against the laminate table in a steady rhythm. He picked up my spoon and scooped up more of the melting ice cream.

"I'm a Gemini." His answer was slightly muffled because he'd stuffed the spoon into his mouth. My eyes dropped to his full lips and I bit the inside of mine. *Good grief—his lips*. I tugged at a lock of my hair that had escaped my bun, trying to hold in my smile. It was so mundane, but also so intimate, sharing a spoon.

"I don't think you meant to—that one was mine," I managed, pointing toward where his spoon was still lying on his plate next to a few uneaten fries, and then back to mine, which was in his mouth.

He frowned for a second as if confused. His eyes were low when he looked at me, that same half-smile on his face, and pulled the spoon from his lips. "You seem clean."

"I *seem clean?*"

He raised a brow, still smirking adorably.

"I *am* clean, thank you very much."

His lips twitched. "We're good then." He put the spoon back down in the steadily melting ice cream in the bowl, just as his phone buzzed. He grinned and returned the text quickly, and I glanced outside at the darkened parking lot, my eyes barely able to make out the frame of Devin's worn blue truck. Somehow, it oddly matched him. It was vintage, maybe a little rough around the edges but you couldn't help noticing it. Devin finished his text, tossing the phone back on the table next to his nearly empty plate.

"Then that's your version of a Gemini symbol? For the twins?" I asked, refocusing on Devin. My gaze fell to his small tat again.

He nodded, stretching his arm along the back of the booth. Now his thumb was thumping against the top of the seat. "Yep. You into astrology?"

"No, I love Jesus."

At that his head fell back and he laughed so loudly that the group of local guys who were sitting at the bar near the cash register looked over at us. I giggled along with him. He was still chuckling as he looked at me, sending tingles dancing in my belly.

"That means you basically have two people living inside of you," I offered.

Without thinking I grabbed the spoon, scooping up the last bit of melted ice cream. It wasn't until it was in my mouth that I realized what I did.

"I'm clean too," he said, smirking when I looked up at him. I raised my brows.

"Your reputation precedes you, Mr. Walker."

"Word? So you think I'm dirty, Willow Elizabeth?" He cocked his head to the side, his lips curled up in a half-smile.

"No, I think you're... busy. With women. A lot. And how do you know my middle name?"

"How many times have I been in y'alls room? It's written on that blue puppy that you keep on your bed."

His eyes were dancing with amusement when warmth spread through me again and I reached for my water, taking a long sip. *How embarrassing.*

"What is a reputation anyway?" Devin questioned ignoring my mortification. His baritone was calm and low, though his thumb continued tapping out a rhythm on the back of the booth. He met my eyes unwaveringly, a hint of *something* in his. "Other people's thoughts about you? Other people's perceptions based on what they feel, or what they're projecting about themselves onto you? Or is a reputation what actually is?"

I chewed on my lip, considering because his eyes were so serious. My gaze dropped to my napkin before I looked up at him. "Both, I guess. Perception and actuality combined, but probably mostly perception."

He grinned a little, his eyes skirting over me. I deliberately stuck the spoon into my mouth, eating the rest of the ice cream, and then placed it into the empty bowl. He met my eyes, chewing on the corner of his lip thoughtfully, as he grinned.

"The best musicians are Gemini's," he said.

"Is that right?"

"Andre 3000, Prince, Tupac, Biggie, Miles Davis, Kendrick Lamar, Curtis Mayfield, Lauryn Hill, Ice Cube, Kanye West, your boy Devin the Dude, your boy *Devin Walker*..."

He grinned when he mentioned himself and I rolled my eyes. He was cocky but so *cute*.

"You mean the *weirdest* musicians are all Geminis. Almost everyone you just named has multiple personalities."

Devin laughed. "Take away any of the musicians I just named and think about what music would sound like. No Prince? No Miles? No Pac?"

He arched a brow and I thought about it, begrudgingly admitting he was right. A world with no Prince was just crazy.

"I think it's because we're so communicative. Creative expression, you know? Most of those artists I just mentioned don't just make good music, they were game changers. Genre-defining. Genre-*defying*. The didn't follow paths, they *paved* them."

"Sheesh, you are like, super serious about this Gemini thing. It's not weird or anything."

He laughed, and once more it was boisterous, as if he wasn't expecting it.

"That's just what I'm about too. How many bands can you name that play the way we do?" He'd leaned forward slightly; his brown eyes glinting with seriousness that made my heart beat a little faster.

"I don't really know any other contemporary black bands, except maybe The Roots and The Internet."

Again, he looked impressed. But I knew a little about music—not as much as Devin or Jersey—but I loved *sound*, the way it got into your skin and *made* you move.

"Black musicianship is the foundation of every single genre—blues, jazz, gospel, rock, hip-hop, soul. I'm about preserving that, and taking it to the next level at the same time."

I smiled because it was impossible not to. "So, you think being a Gemini gave you your creative spark?"

He grinned. "Nah. I give the Creator the glory. But I ain't gonna lie —when I'm on stage sometimes it does feel like something is trying to get out of me. Like another version of me is waking up."

His elbows were resting on the table, his thumb steadily tapping silently against the surface.

"Bruce Banner," I supplied, matter-of-factly. "That's why you practically rip your shirt off like the Incredible Hulk every time you guys perform."

His laughter was open, genuine. "I never really thought about it like that." He was still grinning when he met my eyes.

"So, guess what I am. What's my sign?"

He cocked his head to the side, studying me again.

"*It's him and I...*" I prodded, offering the famous OutKast line. "... *Aquemini*."

Devin leaned forward slightly, his smirk broadening into a smile. A super, super sexy smile that had my stomach tingling.

"Bullshit," he said, his voice low, his eyes glinting with interest. "You're an Aquarius, Low Low?"

"Born and raised."

He laughed again. It was significant because Devin's favorite group of all-time was obviously OutKast, seeing as how he'd named his band after one of their songs, and OutKast's most revered album is *Aquemini*- a combination the group members—Andre 3000 and Big Boi's—zodiac signs.

"That means we match," he said, meeting my eyes, leaning back comfortably in the booth.

He reached out, brushing a finger over the tip of my nose, grinning. My face flushed again. Was he flirting? Or was it wishful, desperate thinking on my part? I mean, only my cousins tapped my nose, my older cousins who were well over 50 at that. I was confused and aroused and confused some more, so I did the only thing I could—I put my straw in my mouth and drank some more water.

We didn't get back to the dorms until after 12, when campus was dark and quiet.

"Let me know if you need some help with your car," Devin said, as he walked me to the front entrance. Campus was pretty empty but lamps were shining protectively overhead. It smelled of nighttime dew and the end of summer, sweet and savory.

"I'll just call my dad in the morning," I said, knowing he'd take care of it, even remotely. "Thank you for the ride and for waiting for me. And for the food. And for the glittery boo-boo ice cream. And for the t-shirt which fits very nicely into my big, functional bag." I patted it, looking at him pointedly.

He laughed, pressing his shoulder against the brick wall next to the heavy metal doors, his stance casual and relaxed as he looked down at me.

"You're good peoples," he grinned. "I like you."

I shifted my weight, moving my bag from my left shoulder to my right, warmth spreading hard and fast from the tip of my fingers to my toes at his words.

"So are you." I bit my lip, looking down at my flip-flops. "I like you too."

Although when I said it, I meant it, in a completely different way than he did. "You saved me from a night of hot pockets," I hastily tacked on in an effort to hide the truth behind my words.

When I glanced up at him again, he was grinning, one of those sexy smiles that showed both of his dimples and made women all over campus drool and run into light poles. No, really. Some girl literally ran into a light pole staring at him earlier this year. Jersey was there and had laughed about it for a solid week. I felt kind of sorry for the girl because I understood how it could happen. Devin was still staring at me. He looked relaxed but like he'd discovered something for the first time and was deciphering whether it was true or not. My stomach was tingling, the air so tight in my lungs I was surprised I was still breathing, or standing upright.

"You're kind of a sleeper." His voice was deep and quiet.

I tucked a strand of hair behind my ear and looked up at him confusedly. "A sleeper?"

"You're an obvious kind of pretty... but you have a lot more going on."

He cocked his head to the side, still considering me. But his look wasn't lustful; it was more... observatory. As if he was an artist and was considering how to paint me. Either way, my knees felt like jelly and I bit hard on the side of my bottom lip, staring down at the freshly paved sidewalk as I tucked a strand of hair that didn't need to be tucked behind my ear again.

"Well, thank you," I finally managed, still looking at the concrete. I wanted to get away from him before I melted. I wanted to stay with him all night long and just absorb his energy.

Devin's phone buzzed loudly, breaking the moment and he grinned as the screen illuminated his features, and then quickly tapped out a message. He pushed off the wall, stuffing his phone back into his front pocket.

"I'll let you get inside," he said, his baritone sleepy and husky. Arousing.

"Okay." I ignored the flash of disappointment that settled in my chest.

"Later, Low-Low," he said. Then he tweaked my nose, like I was his kid sister.

He flashed me another half-grin when I pulled the door open, then turned and headed back down the sidewalk to his truck, probably off to be with whatever chick had made him smile like that. And I went upstairs and went to bed, convinced I was crazy for being half in love with Devin Walker.

DEVIN

"I WANT you to hear my cousin play. I'm thinking we need to bring him in."

I put Travis on speaker then grabbed the joint I'd rolled out of the ashtray that was sitting on the concrete floor, lighting it and taking a long drag, staring at the swirls on the large black and turquoise rug we'd put down a few months ago. It was a throw-away from Trav's gig at the moving company but worked out cool for our rehearsal space. I was downstairs now, messing around on the keys, trying to flesh out a beat I'd had in my head for the past week and a half, ever since I dropped Willow off outside of her dorm room.

"...with this band back home and..." Travis was still talking about Zay but my brain was on Willow, where it didn't need to be. I had other shit to focus on. Andre 3000 and Big Boi were looking down at me from their spot on the wall, judging how unproductive I was being.

I'd had that poster since I was 16, and started really getting into to OutKast because I was finally able to understand what they were talking about—the spirituality and mortality and how that mixed with experiences being two regular dudes from south Atlanta. I figured out why they thought of themselves as outcasts. Moms always had them playing around the house but the summer I turned 16, that was the year. It was all Dungeon Family everything—OutKast, Goodie Mob, Killer Mike, and any Organized Noize beat I could get my hands on. That was the summer that music became real to me, not just some hobby, but something I knew I could pave a path with. That was the summer I developed a vision. I didn't have the exact plan for how I was gonna make it happen yet, but I had the vision, and that was the most important thing.

I refocused on the conversation with Trav. I hoped he hadn't asked any questions because I sure as hell hadn't heard shit he'd said for the past three minutes. He sure was going hard for his cousin though. I already knew Zay would probably join Prototype. I watched his videos online last week, after he popped in on our rehearsal, flirting with Jersey and shit. He sounded a little like Marvin and played a little like Prince and that was an ill combination. And he had a look that fit our vibe. I wasn't on no gay shit but buddy had gray eyes and curly hair and I knew enough to know women liked to look at pretty boys— liked wearing their t-shirts and using them as screensavers. The music and the brand would benefit from him joining. I'd check him out at the show at Jimmy's though. He was gonna open with a band out of New Orleans, so I'd be able to see how he handled himself on stage before we made any real decisions.

I thought of Willow, who'd be at the show too. I smiled, remembering the way she was looking up at me just outside of her dorm the other night.

Just *open*. Straight *Bambi*.

I was so tempted to kiss her, so tempted to suck on that plump lower lip she kept pulling between her teeth, just to see if it'd taste like the ice cream we'd shared. I had to get the hell on. Fooling around with Jersey's roommate was not the move, especially Jersey's roommate who was a virgin and acted like one. All innocent and brand new. Like a little kitten just learning how to walk, getting into shit it knew nothing about. Willow didn't even know what she was workin' with yet, hadn't really figured out her best features, or how to use them to her advantage. She wore dresses a lot, so I always got a glimpse of her thick thighs, but the dresses were more for style than for sex appeal, I could tell.

Bottom line was I couldn't play around with her. I knew that before we ended up spending time together the other day, which is partly why I had always kept my distance before. I knew she was digging me a little, was probably curious about me, but I couldn't entertain any of those cute little nervous glances she'd given me over the past year. She was too adorable, too innocent for her own damn good, and it could get messy quick. Willow just wasn't that type. Whatever went down between us would be serious, for her at least. And I wasn't gonna be the dude to mess with her head like that, just because I was curious to see what she was about too.

I hung up with Travis after firming up some details for the gig and stared at my phone. I wasn't interested in getting caught up with any chick at all. I gave them time when I had it and they all were on board with that, or pretended to be, which was the same thing as far as I was concerned. I wasn't about doggin' women out or no shit like that, but I didn't have the time for anything but my music. There weren't any "music or me" ultimatums going down in my world. The band was just getting to a place where I felt comfortable about what we were doing. And if we added Zay, it'd really take us to another level.

I inhaled another hit of the weed, and bobbed my head to the beat I was sketching out. It actually sounded like Willow—something she'd dance to maybe, with its jazzy, downbeat vibe. I picked at my hair, shaking my head, pushing out a laugh. Low had me intrigued, for sure. I hadn't realized that underneath all that sweetness she was sexy as hell. Nah, she was *sensual* with those lips and eyelashes that went on for days, hovering over soft brown eyes that were more aware than I expected. She was graceful—she had the legs of a dancer. Ever since I'd seen her at rehearsal, every movement she made was amplified in my mind. She was *dope*. I wasn't bullshitting when I told her that. She'd surprised the hell out of me, the way she moved. The way she was watching *me* watch *her* move.

And her voice. That was almost as surprising as her dancing. It was like warm sand on the beach, fluid like water, even when she was talking a lot, which I found out was pretty often. I don't know how I hadn't noticed it before. But then, we hadn't exactly had any heart to hearts. Her voice was airy and mellow...just happy. Carefree. I didn't even care what she was talking about half the time when she was rambling. I wanted to hear more of her. I wanted more of her off-kilter humor. I wanted more of her cute little laugh. And I'd had more, every night for the past week and half. We stayed on the phone talking about anything she wanted to—my music, her classes, even the corny dude that was after her, Jaden. She said she'd been "sorta-dating" him since the end of last semester, which is how I knew buddy was a punk. If he wanted her, he should've locked her down a long time ago. She was *that* type.

I put the joint out, debating. I swiveled in the chair Bam usually occupied when he was on the keys and scrolled to her number.

"*You awake yet?*" I knew she was. It was 1 in the afternoon.

"*Who is this?*" She typed a few seconds later. I laughed aloud. That was another thing that caught me off guard, her sense of humor.

"*Got jokes, I see.*" I replied.

"*Ha. Well, yes, I'm up and feeling great. Yay!*" She put a smiley face after it and I chuckled. So damn cute.

"*How's the music doing today?*" I grinned at her question. She asked me that every day, like my music was its own entity. I liked that shit.

"*Grindin. Workin on a beat now that I think we may end up using.*"

"*Super cool, Bruce Banner.*" She put a smiley face next to it and I grinned.

"*What you on today?*" I typed.

"*Um?*"

I twisted my lips, holding in another laugh.

"*What are you doing today, Willow Elizabeth?*" I tried again.

"*Oh. Hee. Headed to English class. YUCK. I wish you could come rescue me again and take me away to the Pancake Shack.*"

I was thinking of what to say that wouldn't sound like I was pressed because I still wasn't sure what the hell I was doing texting and calling her so much in the first place, when my screen lit up again.

"*I took your advice, btw.*"

"About?"

"I'll tell you later," she wrote back, with a winky face emoji. *"Gotta run, Bruce Banner. James Baldwin awaits."*

"Baldwin is a master truth-teller. Have fun."

The next emoji was one with its tongue out. I wasn't exactly sure what that was supposed to mean but she followed it up with another smiley face. I sat my phone down on the keyboard, then thought better of it because Bam was always complaining about us sitting shit on top of it, and put in my pocket, leaning back in the chair. I was buzzing off that little text exchange, like I was every single time I'd talked to her this week.

The other day, I'd fallen asleep on the couch at 11:30 after playing NBA 2K. I was trying to clear my head, get some down time in the middle of the stuff that was always on my plate. When my phone buzzed, I answered it automatically, half-asleep, my business philosophy book falling off my chest to the hardwood floor.

"Devin, I can't believe you're asleep!" It was her. The "her" that was making the other "hers" that circled around my space look dimmer and dimmer.

"I can't believe it either. What time is it?"

"11:30. But you have to go downstairs right now and make a beat."

I smiled sitting up on the couch, swinging my legs to the floor.

"Why is that Low-Low?" I asked through a yawn, running my hand over my head.

"There's a full moon."

I blinked, scratching under my chin before grabbing the remote and flicking off the TV.

"You've lost me, love." She inhaled sharply when I said that and I grinned a little. So damn Bambi.

"I just... the moon is full so it means the energy cycles are different," she explained after a short pause. "So it's a good time to create. I know you're into astrology and whatnot, right? Shouldn't you know this?"

I chuckled again, shaking my head as Bam came through the door, plopping down on the opposite end of the sectional, giving me dap.

"I ain't all that into it to be watching the moon and shit."

"Well, I was talking to Travis' neighbor lady when I dropped Jersey off today—"

"You were over here today?" My heart started beating faster and I shook my head myself. I was on one.

"Only for a second to drop off Jersey. You weren't home. So anyway, Mrs. Pepper was talking about the garden back home and how plants grow by the cycles of the moon and it made me think about you. How you said your music is like a living, breathing thing? Therefore, your music should 'grow' too. You should go downstairs right this second and see what you come up with."

I laughed again. "Wow."

"That was too much, huh? I was doing too much?"

"Nah, not at all... I like that you care." I paused, debating again on far to go with this girl.

"Okay, well then go," she said before I had a chance to say anything else and get myself caught up.

"A'ight."

"Seriously!"

"Okay, I am, right now." I grinned again because no other women checked in on the music, aside from Jersey and my moms.

I was still smiling when I got off the phone.

She ended up being right too. I made three beats before I went to bed. That's the thing. Low kinda threw me because she was so down to earth. I knew from the pictures in her and Jersey's dorm room that her parents were way older, so I thought she might be a little entitled and spoiled. I could tell the spoiled part might still be right but she was cool as shit. First, knowing something about music, obscure hip-hop at that, and then later, at the diner that first night I'd given her a ride.

I was lightweight testing her when I took her to the Pancake Shack but she hadn't even batted an eye. She just slid into the worn, fake leather booth and launched into another one of her stories that had me laughing because she was so *cute*.

I was actually dead ass broke... had less than $14 and some change in my pocket. My stomach was rumbling but I couldn't pay for her meal and mine, so I just ordered a small fry to play it off, planning to wait until I got back to the crib to eat. But instead, Low asked the waiter for another plate, and while she was still talking, cut her burger in half, scooped up more fries and pushed it across the booth toward me without losing a beat in her story. That's when I knew shit was real.

I hadn't come to any conclusions but I did know I wanted to see her again, without Jersey around cock-blocking, acting like Mother Hen to Willow's baby chick. And I wanted to see her soon. I pulled the chair back up the keyboard and focused on getting the beat in my head out in the meantime, feeling newly inspired.

5

WILLOW

I CAN'T BELIEVE Devin came. I'd just gotten off stage, sweaty but full of adrenaline from performing in front of a packed house, when I spotted him, coming in through the side door that led to the crowded backstage area. It was a compact, boxed shaped room with ugly maroon carpet and a lingering smell of moth balls. There were people milling all around— the theater staff members, and a couple of staff from the community organization who was putting on the program, along with the group of poets who were going on after us.

I blinked to make sure Devin's appearance wasn't some sort of illusion, especially since I hadn't stopped thinking about him for the past week and a half, but he was real, and he was smiling when he sauntered over to me, his gait confident and relaxed.

I inhaled, buzzing at the sight of him before reality seeped in. *Jaden.* He'd showed up and was across the room, getting a bottle of water for me, and I was holding the half-dozen red roses he'd bought for me. I was pining after Devin and Jaden had actually showed up, with flowers.

But I couldn't help it. Devin stood out without trying. He was wearing gray sweats and a plain white t-shirt with the sleeves cut off but still managed to look fashionable somehow. He just looked *cool*, like whatever he was wearing would soon be the next trend, even if it was just sweats and t-shirt. His Braves fitted on turned backward on his head, so I could see his eyes. I couldn't move, though I did manage to close my mouth when Gia nudged me in the ribs. I wasn't comfortable talking about my feelings for Devin with Jersey. It was weird. So I did all of my venting and swooning with Gia. Tre stood next to me in the hot room, giving Devin the once over. I almost rolled my eyes.

"What up, Sweet N' Low," he said when he reached me, brushing his finger against my nose once he was close enough.

My face was on fire and I opened my mouth to try to get something out, but he just grinned. "You killed it. You stole the show, for real."

"You came." I couldn't think of anything else to say. "But you have sound check right now."

He stuffed his hand in his sweat pockets a small smile on his lips.

"I moved it back an hour. I'm headed there now."

I blinked again, staring up at him. Devin never changed rehearsal times or sound check; Jersey was always complaining about it.

"I told you I wanted to check you out. I meant that."

I opened my mouth to say what, I don't know, but Gia nudged me subtly from the back again, just as Jaden walked up and stood next to me. I turned accepted the bottle of water from him, with a smile, murmuring a "thank you." I shifted my weight, biting the inside of my lip.

"You got it," Jaden replied, with a smile, though his attention was directed at Devin.

Devin glanced at me, before greeting Jaden. "What's up. Devin," he introduced himself.

"I'm so rude, sorry," I quickly apologized, as Jaden responded. I introduced Devin to Tre and Gia as well, who began fidgeting and flipping her hair. I did roll my eyes at her when she asked if he was staying for the rest of the show. Our dance troupe worked with the kids from the elementary school near South Texas, and we'd choreographed a routine for them to perform as well.

"Wish I could but I actually gotta roll," Devin answered, as I took a sip of water. His voice low when he directed his attention back to me.

"I just wanted to come holler at you before I bounced." I glanced at Jaden, who looked at me and then back to Devin, his handsome face impassive.

"So how do you two know each other?" Jaden looked at me then at Devin.

"Devin is friends with Jersey. They play in a band together, The Prototype."

"Oh, so you're friends with Jersey," Jaden clarified, emphasizing the word "friends." I looked up at him but he was staring at Devin.

"Me and Low Low been cool for a minute," Devin responded, grinning over at me before returning his attention to Jaden. "Heard y'all been friends for a while too." Devin also emphasized the word "friends," though his smile was still on his face.

I looked at Devin but he only continued to smile, his brown eyes amused.

"Walk me out." He nodded his head toward the door.

"Okay." I turned to Jaden. "I'll be right back, okay?"

Jaden rolled his tongue in his mouth but nodded. "Cool. I'll be here."

I tossed Gia a look who raised her brows at me, and turned, grabbing Tre's arm as she whispered something in his ear. Jaden walked off in the opposite direction. I exhaled, feeling a mix of emotions as I weaved my way through the small crowd of parents and performers with Devin on my heels, toward the doors that led straight to the parking lot.

My heart was racing, my brain working overtime as the natural sunlight and humidity hit my skin. The air was fresh and clean compared to the staleness of the back room. *He came to see me.* No. Devin rearranged his schedule to see me. And what was that whole thing with Jaden about? My thoughts were going 100 miles per minute as I made my way toward his old truck, which was parked in the space nearest to the side door of the building.

"I see what you mean about taking my advice," Devin spoke up, pulling me out of my thoughts. "Your boy needed to be in the back. The audience had to see you. I'm glad you decided to value yourself," he teased with an adorable grin.

We paused in front of his truck and he leaned is back against it, stuffing his hands in his pockets again.

"I asserted common sense," I smiled, kicking at a pebble next to his tire. He laughed at that, biting on the corner of his bottom lip, causing the pit of my stomach to tighten.

"You didn't seem too tired up there."

He gave me a knowing look and I grinned, staring down at the ground. Last night, Devin and I talked for over three hours, until 1 in the morning, even though I had an 8 o'clock the next day and he said he needed to be working on a beat that he said was stuck in his head.

"I'm not tired, even though you wouldn't let me hang up."

He chuckled. "I like talking to you."

"You like making fun of me because that's all you do the entire time," I retorted, feigning annoyance because my insides were tingling at his casual admission.

"Just because I like your little laugh. You sound like a little baby hyena."

My mouth dropped open and I punched him the shoulder. He held onto the spot I'd hit, laughing as I glared at him.

"If you're trying to look mean right now, it ain't workin, Bambi."

"Who?"

He grinned, eyes glinting with amusement, but didn't answer. Really, Devin was so cool. Way more insightful and perceptive than most people probably realized. He was smart too- I had no idea that like Jersey, he was at South Texas on partial academic scholarship. Gia said the fact that he'd called every day for the past week and half meant he was into me. But I wasn't at all convinced. For one, he never acted as though he was interested in me beyond just friendly conversation. I'd even told him about Jaden and after he teased me for being named "Willow" and dating a guy named "Jaden," like the Smith siblings, he just listened, even offered advice.

"If he doesn't support, you, he's not about you," he said when I told him Jaden wasn't sure if he was going to be able to make it to my performance.

"But he has to..."

"If he doesn't support you, he's not about you," he interrupted me. "And you'd be stupid to be about him if that's the case."

"Wait. Did you just call me stupid!?"

"If you keep messin' with ol' boy and he can't be bothered to show up for you."

I'd laughed because Devin was always so forthright, it was hard not to like that about him. And last night, even though it was late and most guys would've started dropping hints about sex, or subtly trying to steer the conversation in that direction, Devin never did. He talked to me like an older, protective brother. Which is what made that whole exchange with Jaden weird. Maybe he was just looking out for me?

I looked up at him now. Devin twisted his ball cap around to the back, eyeing me, his gaze dropping to the bouquet of flowers I was still holding.

"I see your brother-boyfriend showed up."

My mouth dropped open again, and I pushed at his hard chest.

"Stop calling him that! It's so nasty!"

I glanced back toward the building, where a few more people had spilled outside, talking. The air was still hot, even though it was evening, sticking to my already sweaty skin. I lifted my hair off my shoulders and neck, quickly tying it up in a sloppy top knot, acutely aware that Devin was watching me. Our dance outfits were kinda skimpy—basically a glittery sports bra and boy shorts, like the Dallas Cowboys, only with Kinte patterns. I shifted my weight, aware of my body in a new way under Devin's stare.

"I got something for you." His baritone was low, intimate.

My tiny shorts actually had back-pockets and I stuffed my hands inside, looking up at him curiously. He dug in his pocket and pulled out an individual package of chocolate chip cookies.

"The way you owned that stage tonight definitely earned you a cookie," he deadpanned.

Realization dawned on me and I burst into laughter, tilting my head up toward the sky, where the sun was setting in a blast of deep orange and pinks. When I calmed down enough to look at him, he was smiling too. But it was different from the ones I'd gotten before. It felt personal. His eyes were lower, his gaze more intense. I touched my tongue to my bottom lip, accepting the package from him, my fingers brushing against his, sending goosebumps crawling up my arms.

"Got you this too."

He reached into his pocket, then took my wrist since I was still holding the cookies, pulling me a little closer, so that I was nearly standing in between his legs. My heart was about to beat out my chest and I tried to control my breathing without being obvious. He smelled familiar, like linen and his subtle cologne, intoxicating. I looked down when he spread his thumb over the inside of my wrist. I smiled again, shaking my head at the sticker he'd pressed against my skin—a literal gold star.

"Where did you even find an actual gold star?" I asked, still looking down at the sticker because if I looked up at him I might actually dissolve.

"I got connections, baby," he teased playfully.

"This is literally the best gift ever."

I finally met his eyes, and for a second, we just stared at each other. His brown eyes were concentrated on me, a half-grin on his full lips. In that moment, the embarrassment, the nerves, all of it faded away, as a new feeling, one that was unidentifiable but far more potent coursed through me.

I could see when he took a deep breath, releasing it slowly, his broad chest expanding.

"You're still coming to the show tonight right?" His voice was still low and unbearably sexy and I nodded my head. "I'll be by for y'all at 10."

"Thank you again, for coming to see me," I felt my body flush and I looked down at the gravel lot. "Or, you know, for coming and supporting the community."

He chuckled again, looking at me amusedly. His back was still against the truck and he hadn't released my hand yet. He tugged on it, just barely, and I swayed a few centimeters closer to him, so that I could almost feel the heat from his body.

"I'll see you in a few hours."

He reached and tucked a strand of hair behind my ear, his fingers grazing my skin and my eyes drifted closed for a second. I opened them as he released another breath, then pushed off the truck, causing me to take a step back. He pushed out a humorless chuckle and shook his head.

"I'll see you in a few," he repeated, yanking open his truck door. "Good luck with the kids."

I nodded again, heading back toward the backstage entrance, willing myself to walk normally. He waited until I pulled the door open before he drove off, allowing me to exhale.

6

DEVIN

THE CROWD WAS way thicker than I expected. The bar we were playing, The Spot, was packed, with people who were there for *us*. There were a couple of other bands on the bill, but the mid-sized bar was filled with Prototype fans wearing the t-shirts I'd picked up. Hopefully, Jimmy would recognize that we were pulling in more people than he did on a regular Friday night and give us the residency Trav and I had been pushing for. He'd just bought the place and was planning on changing the name to "Jimmy's"—real clever. I didn't care what he called it. If we could perform every Friday here, it'd not only help us build our base, but it'd give us live practice and a steady check. And I definitely needed the bread. All in all, this was a huge come up from the chitlin-circuit hole in wall spots we'd been playing around Tyler and in small town Texas and Louisiana over the past few months.

"Aye, fam. Some girl named Nicki is out there lookin' for you."

I looked up as Zay approached, pushing his way through the backstage door unhurriedly. That's how both he and Travis moved—like they had all the time in the world. I had a homeboy from back home that moved the same way and he was originally from New Orleans too, so I figured maybe that was their thing.

"Who?" I asked Zay. I didn't know any Nicki's and wasn't trying to meet any when I still had business to handle. Travis and I were just back in Jimmy's office, getting everything squared away.

"Nicki?" Zay said again, frowning because he obviously didn't remember who the hell he was talking about. "Nicole? Natasha? Ni-something."

"*Nikitta*?"

"Yeah," he nodded, "that's it." He accepted a pound from Travis in greeting.

"Got the gig," he told him. "Good looking out on that. They said I can start Monday."

"Told you they'd be cool," Travis said, taking a drag from his cigarette. "You didn't try to holler at the manager's woman."

Travis looked at me pointedly and I rolled my eyes.

"How the hell was I supposed to know that was his girl? She was not behaving like a woman who was taken," I smirked.

I went to get a job up with Trav about a month ago but ended up getting into it with his bullshit manager instead. Punk ass. If his woman was choosin' that didn't have nothin' to do with me. Fightin' over disrespectful women was never my shit.

The noise beyond backstage got louder and I glanced at the door. Travis took another drag from his cigarette, eyeing the door too. He didn't smoke often, just before shows or when he was drunk. It was one of his tells and I knew he was nervous. I was too. This was probably the biggest crowd we'd ever played for.

"It's thick out there," I said. He inhaled again, blowing smoke out of the side of his mouth, his face not giving away his nerves.

"Is this what your regular crowd is lookin' like these days?" Zay asked Travis, before swinging his gaze to me. They were first cousins but looked more like brothers, though Zay sounded like he should've been the smoker, not the other way around.

"Nah, this is a bigger crowd than usual."

"But I think it's about to be our regular crowd," I added.

Zay nodded, looking around the backstage area, which was still basically empty.

"You seen Jersey?" The question was directed at both me and Trav but I didn't say anything. She'd just gotten into it with her punk ass Pops on the way over here and I was still hot about it. That was my girl. She seemed tough but she was actually sensitive as hell, and she'd been dealt a shitty hand. Her mom committed suicide when she was just a baby and her dad was a loud mouth alcoholic who took his shit out on her.

I stared at Zay, ignoring Trav's glance. Hell yeah I was protective. Jersey needed protecting, and nobody else was around to do it. Zay seemed cool but I ain't know buddy like that. I only knew he'd been through some real shit. Bam didn't even need to tell me his story. I peeped that from the way he showed up, just out of the blue on some "I'm here" type shit. He was either trying to catch a break, or running from something he still needed to handle—in which case, nah. Jersey wasn't emotionally equipped to anyone's baggage.

Zay stuffed his hands in his pockets, nodding his head toward me, still determined.

"She rode with you, right?"

"She's out front. By the bar, I think," Travis finally spoke up, albeit reluctantly. I already knew where his head was—if Zay joined Prototype, it wouldn't be cool for him to be messing around with Jersey because it'd screw with the dynamics of the band. I wasn't as worried about that I was about her.

"Cool," Zay said, ignoring both of our warning looks. He smirked at me a little, then took off toward the backstage door, which led into the bar.

I cocked my head at Trav, brows arched.

"Man, cut that shit out," Travis said, chuckling a little. "Hothead ass," he mumbled, shaking his head, fixing a look on me. "He's my family and he's good peoples."

"I ain't even say nothin'. But you need to let him know what's up, or I will. Jersey—"

"Is your heart. I know. She's my family too, D. And Zay is more like my brother than my cousin," he paused and looked at me. "I know Bam told you about his brother and sister." They'd both died in a car crash. It was fucked up. Unimaginable. "He could use a break."

"I hear you. But as far as Jersey goes... he needs to be easy with that."

Travis frowned and shook his head, just as my phone buzzed in my pocket. *Shit.* I'd forgotten about Nikitta that fast, which wasn't cool because she was working the door and would be handling our money.

"Imma go holler at 'Kitta," I told Travis, who nodded, and put his cigarette out on the ashtray that was sitting on the table pushed closest to the wall, leaving a drift of tangy smoke in his wake.

"She's really cool to work the door?" Travis raised his brow, falling in step with me as I headed toward the door.

"Yeah, she got it." I glanced at him. I knew he was asking because he knew me and 'Kitta messed around sometimes and neither one of us normally mixed business with anyone we were fooling with. It wasn't smart.

"Her girl Maya was buggin' me about finding you earlier."

"She hit me up." I couldn't tell if that was good or not, with Trav I never could. Not that I cared either way.

We were immediately greeted by the hum of the crowd and the sound of Eightball & MJG pumping through the speakers, when we entered the main area. Everyone playing tonight was soul, so the set, even when it was hip-hop was laid-back, classic.

"There she goes," Travis said, watching as 'Kitta made her way toward us, weaving her way through the crowd. Automatically, my gaze skirted over her. Tight jeans, a little shirt that showed off her cleavage and heels. That was the uniform in this bar and 'Kitta was no different but she did wear with a little more swag. My gaze lingered on her hips for a minute, remembering the last time we'd hooked up just over a week ago, the way she'd just laid there for a full minute after I made come so hard she claimed she saw fireworks. She hopped up and cooked a fajita for me afterwards. Shit was delicious too.

"Devin, I've been looking for you for twenty minutes."

She waved her fingers at Travis and he nodded at her. "What's up, Kitta," he greeted her.

She shifted her weight, placing a hand on her hip for extra emphasis, before looking at me again. "Do you still need me or what?"

"Stop trippin," I said grinning at her antics. 'Kitta was a cutie. "I thought you said you were good."

"I am. But that guy, the owner Jimmy or whoever, was telling me—"

"We got him straight." I paused. "He wasn't talking to you crazy was he?"

'Kitta shook her head, which was good. "He came back and told me you handled things," she said.

"Then what's the issue?" I widened my eyes, grinning at her.

She smiled stepping closer to me, running her fingers down the front of my shirt.

"You coming through later?" she asked, her voice soft, so that only I could hear it. "You know we got things to do," she sang, smiling.

"We'll see what's up," I said chuckling at her singing corny Drake lyrics. She stared at me for a second, trying to hide her disappointment.

"Right now we're about this paper, right?" I asked, nodding my head toward the door, running a hand down her arm. We were giving her a little something to hold the door down, and it was time for her to refocus.

"Right." She smiled at me, backing up.

"I'll check you later, okay? And you know I appreciate you, right?"

She smiled. "You better."

I grinned, watching her saunter off toward the door. Trav exchanged another look with me.

"We're good," I reiterated. "She has an 'A' in math."

He laughed. "Okay, man."

He turned, assessing the crowd. It was mostly college kids—urban hipster types— but there were locals scattered throughout and folks who probably came from out of town--- most likely Dallas, maybe even Shreveport.

"Ain't that Jersey's lil' roommate over there?"

Travis nodded toward the side of the room, where couches were situated against the concrete wall. I followed his gaze, my stomach tightening immediately at the sight of Low. I couldn't shake her. She was like a new *force* in my life. Everything, almost every thought was coming back to her. Her smile. Her laugh. The way she walked. Her brown eyes that were pooled with emotion she didn't have enough game to try to hide. The smoothness of her skin, and the way it looked like honey in the sunlight. The way she'd dominated the stage tonight, dancing circles around everyone else— sometimes literally. She looked free up there, in a way I recognized because I was the same way on stage.

I couldn't take my eyes off her, and nobody else could either, including ol' dude, Jaden. For second, I can't front, I was lightweight embarrassed, because I couldn't afford to get her flowers for her performance like I wanted to. I had to send most of my refund check back home to moms. My little cousin Tanya was staying at the house now, and her momma couldn't help out so it was all on moms... again. But that was my moms--- the caregiver, even when she had nothing to give except her love and a beat up living room couch.

So, I had to get creative for Low. And the way she'd looked at me when I gave her that gold star—damn, it took everything in me not to pull her into my truck and let out the feelings I had for her, show her the way she'd been dominating my thoughts lately. Find out what she knew and if I could teach her a little bit more.

I was dancing on tightrope with Low. Showing up at her performance only solidified that I was easing past that gray area with her. *I wanted her.* I wanted to get her out of my system. Or get her into it. I hadn't figured out which one yet.

I let myself take my time looking at her now. She was always pretty —more than pretty, actually. She was like a flower- bright and not just innocent, more like, *pure*. Low changed the energy of whatever space she was in—made it happier. But tonight was something else. When I picked her and Jersey up, I wasn't expecting her to look like that. She'd dressed up—the way girls did, with the eye make-up and all that. She'd changed out of that barely-there dance outfit she had on earlier into a black dress that showed off the curve of her ass, the dip of her small waist and her breasts.

As if feeling my eyes on her, she looked up at me. Our gazes connected, and my pulse sped up a little. Her eyes narrowed before she turned away, pushing a lock of hair behind her ear. *Damn, did she just roll her eyes at me?* I tilted my head, watching her as she talked to her little group of friends, most of them from her dance troupe. And standing next to her now, was Jaden. *Did she invite him to my show, like as a date or some shit?* I'd picked her and Jersey up earlier but did she tell dude to meet her here?

"Hi, Devin." I was momentarily distracted from Willow by a skinny girl I didn't really recognize.

"What's up, girl," I greeted her anyway, accepting her brief hug, before she thankfully kept it moving through the dense crowd.

Willow glanced over her shoulder at me again, like she was making sure I was still staring, before turning away, obviously satisfied that I was.

Oh yeah, she definitely rolled her eyes.

I frowned. Maybe she was mad because I'd left her with her friends. She wanted to see our backstage after her and Jersey kicked it for a while, talking about Low's performance earlier, but really trying to avoid mentioning Jersey's crazy argument with her dad. I was down to show Low whatever she wanted, but I needed to get things straight with Jimmy first, so when she ran into her friends—that girl Gia and buddy with the blue hair— on our way back there, I told her to chill with them for a second. That wasn't any reason for her to be trippin', I didn't think anyway.

"She's lookin' grown tonight," Travis observed, tilting his head a little as he eyed her. "I'm surprised Jersey ain't hovering."

Jaden grabbed Willow's hand and was whispering some shit in her ear that made her lean toward him and smile. *Fuck that.*

"I'll be back." I didn't wait for Trav to respond as I maneuvered through the crowd, nodding a quick what's up to one of the homies from campus.

Willow looked up right as I stepped to her.

"Sorry that took so long."

"It's fine." She rolled her tongue in her mouth, refusing to look at me. She was so damn cute, her little features bunched into a scowl.

"You still wanna come check it out?" I asked, stepping closer to her. I could smell her honey scent, soft and inviting, and my groin tightened.

She looked up at me.

"Come on," I said, before she worked up a rejection. I put a hand on her hip, subtly pulling her toward me, ignoring dude. He didn't want it with me—he knew it and so did I. Willow's brown eyes were round when she looked up at me.

"Come on." I grabbed her hand without letting her answer, leading her away from her group of friends and ol' boy.

WILLOW

"You mad at me?"

I looked up at Devin, all of my irritation threatening to melt away under the sound of his baritone. His voice was low but the music backstage wasn't as loud as it was up front. I could only hear the steady pounding of the bass; the rest of the noise was muted.

"No," I finally lied, turning away from him.

I walked over to the table that was pushed against the far wall and climbed up on it, letting my legs dangle off the edge. The room was fairly small, with white brick walls, as opposed to the concrete walls that were up front. The floor was concrete as well, worn and decorated with cracks and dents that showed the building's age, and it smelled of stale cigarette smoke and sweat. Me and Devin were the only ones back here and it felt secluded, even a little exclusive, especially since the place was so packed.

Devin was eyeing me but I looked away, down at my toes again. I'd painted them pink earlier. I was so thrilled at the prospect of spending more time with him before. But now I was so pissed at him, my insides were literally hot. He asked me to come backstage with him, then basically abandoned me before we even made it, only to pop up thirty minutes later, flirting with some other girl. And then another girl. And *another*.

I sighed, staring down into the shot glass he'd just handed me after we made a quick stop by the bar. Really, I was mad at me for being so obvious. It wasn't even like I had a right to be upset. Devin didn't like me in that way anyhow. Which made me even more upset because I was being silly. Jaden was here, and he was nice, and he liked me, and he hadn't ditched me to flirt with other women— but all I could think about was Devin.

"I really didn't think it was gonna take that long."

He'd leaned against the wall perpendicular to the table where I was sitting, just a few feet away. He was wearing all black like the rest of the band, his short sleeved black button up stretching tight against his hard chest, his defined biceps and forearms revealing two colorful tattoos— one of drum sticks encased by flames, the other with the words "*wait expectantly*" written small but in all caps that was on the inside of his left arm. His black Falcon's hat was perched backwards on his head. He looked like everything I wanted but wasn't supposed to have.

"I said it's fine," I managed, tearing my eyes away from his tattoos and looking down at my feet again. "I saw you were busy. It's not a big deal."

"Your face is tellin' me something different."

I looked up at him.

"What's it telling you?"

"You got a little attitude." He bit the inside of his lip, suppressing his grin, but his dimples were peeking out. I couldn't help it, I grinned too, looking down at my swinging legs.

"I don't."

"It's cute on you." He was grinning as his gaze skated over my face. "But I can't have you upset with me, messin' with my concentration when I'm on stage tonight."

I chewed on the inside of my lip for a second before releasing it, meeting his gaze because he hadn't looked away.

"Just me being mad at you would mess with your concentration." I cocked a brow at him.

"Why wouldn't it? I'd be on stage and I'd feel you out in the crowd rolling your eyes at me like you were earlier—"

"I was *not* rolling my eyes at you!"

He cocked his head to the side, nodding as he grinned.

"You did. That shit hurt me deep in my soul too."

I rolled my eyes, suppressing a smile. "Oh whatever. You were barely even paying attention to me."

"Nah. Have you ever been in a room and *not* felt me lookin' at you, Willow?"

My gaze flew to his, the warmth in my belly spreading all over my entire body.

"Let's do this shot," he suggested, holding up his glass and nodding his head toward mine as he closed the space between us. "To forgiveness."

I rolled my eyes but held up my glass and tapped it against his. I downed the clear liquid, like he did, wincing, and then frantically fanning my face. It burned its way down my throat, to my chest, landing like lava in my stomach. I started hacking as I held my throat.

"You follow the shot with the chaser, baby. Here, Bambi," he offered, laughter in his voice when he handed me the cranberry juice he'd brought from the bar. I immediately took a large swallow from the small glass, my face finally relaxing as the sweet taste hit my tongue, giving me a bit of a relief.

"Why do you keep saying 'Bambi'?" I managed, taking another large swallow of juice, soothing myself with another blast of tart sweetness.

"You straight?" he asked ignoring my question, his gaze amused as he narrowed his eyes. I nodded quickly.

"That was vodka? I think I like red Jell-O shots better," I told him, blinking heavily. He eyed me, measuring my well-being, I guess.

"You ain't gonna fall out on me or nothin' are you? Your cheeks are flushed," Devin observed, running the back of his fingers against my skin, sending chill bumps dancing over parts of my body that he hadn't even touched.

His eyes were bedroom sleepy, low but alert, his lashes almost skating over his cheekbones. He was standing close, his legs brushing against my exposed toes in my heeled sandals. He was so close that I couldn't help but to subtly breathe in, expanding my lungs so that I could fill it with his clean scent, which fogged my brain almost as much as the potent alcohol I'd just downed. He was so close that if I tilted my head up and pulled him down by the shirt, I could reach his lips. I pulled mine between my teeth, biting it before lifting the juice to my lips again, taking a cooling swallow of the sweet liquid.

"It was just one shot. I think I can handle that," I somehow murmured, looking up into his brown eyes.

"What else do you think you can handle?"

He tilted his head, his brown eyes low, as his gaze touched my lips before moving down to my chest and back up. My heart began pounding, my breaths shallow.

"More than you probably think." The words came out like a whisper, unexpectedly.

And then his mouth was on mine. And I was melting. And I was floating. And I was *aching* everywhere, from the tips of my fingers to my belly and lower. The soft sound that left my lips coming from deep inside me, drifting between us, calling Devin closer.

My lips parted, making way for Devin's warm, demanding tongue, which I immediately met with my own, without any reservation. He tasted like the potent alcohol and mint, his clean scent invading my nostrils, the combination making me lightheaded and high, especially when I could taste the tangy sweet juice from my own lips on his.

As hungry as the kiss was, it was languid and thorough, a complete contrast to the way he was always moving—as if all his focus, all his talent and *skill* was being applied here, to this moment, to me. My heart was pumping hard, the throbbing moving to the pit of my stomach and lower, beating there was hungry intention I'd never experienced before. I hadn't even realized how it happened but he was standing between my parted legs now, my already short dress was hiked up to the top of my thighs.

He slid his rough palm up my forearm slowly, up over my bare shoulder, until he reached the back of my neck, palming it beneath my hair, bringing me closer to him, making a noise from deep in his throat, that turned me on even more, as he tilted his head in the other direction, tasting me from a different angle. But just as I was about to drown in him, in his taste, the heat of his mouth, he pulled back, bumping his nose against mine, breathing heavily against my lips.

"You're gonna get me into all kinds of trouble, Low-Low." He met my eyes then, his gaze heavy with desire, and the tightness in the pit of my stomach only increased. My phone buzzed and it took me a second to register that I needed to pull it out of my small purse. Finally, I blinked and broke Devin's gaze.

"Hey, where'd you go?"

Shoot. Jaden. I closed my eyes briefly, feeling guilty. I hadn't invited him but hadn't discouraged him from showing up when he said he was coming earlier. Things had shifted between us. It was never that serious in the first place, we just hung out when it was convenient mostly, but he was acting weird lately. Ever since Devin popped up in my life. Gia said that's the way it worked though. Guys always want you when they sense they can't have you. Maybe Jaden sensed the electric pull I had toward Devin. I could still taste him on my lips when I wet them.

"You good?" Devin asked, watching as I tucked the phone back into my purse after sending a quick text that said I'd be back. I hesitated for second, touching my tongue to my bottom lip.

"Jaden was just asking where I was."

Devin cocked his head a little, looking me directly in the eyes. "You ain't worried about him."

His voice was quiet but he said it with such confidence, no *authority*, my heart started racing again and my lips parted slightly. He didn't release my gaze. I bit my lip, staring into his eyes, those eyes that held so much passion and soul and fire. No, I wasn't thinking about Jaden. At all.

As if sensing where my head was, without even requiring my confirmation, Devin leaned forward. His warm breath brushed against my parted lips, which were tingling because I wanted more. I bit my lip hard, to keep from touching his again, as he breathed against my mouth, his thumb rubbing back and forth over the base of my neck, up to my hairline, as his other hand rested on my outer hip. I could feel his erection pushing into me intimately with him standing between my open legs and I tried not to wiggle against it.

I didn't have a lot of experience. Hadn't gone much further than hot kisses and a few underclothes feels. But my body completely awakened under Devin's touch, like it was natural. Like his touch is what it'd been waiting for to react the way it was always supposed to. He brushed his nose against mine again, barely touching his lips to mine, and grinned. He was so *sexy*. I was breathing heavily, my gaze focused on his mouth before I met his eyes.

I released my lower lip, the action causing my mouth to brush against his again. His grip on my hip tightened and low sound left his chest when he leaned in again, this time kissing me with a raw urgency that literally left me breathless. My hands, which had been dangling useless at my sides, reached up and snaked around his neck, pulling him more firmly against my mouth, my fingers gliding through the tight, soft curls on the back of his head.

He sucked on my bottom lip, releasing a hot, heavy breath against my mouth, a low, deep noise escaping him as he moved both hands to my hips, his grip tightening. Before I processed what he was doing, his lips were on my neck.

A rush of air flew out of my parted lips at the touch, my entire body breaking out in goosebumps as my heart pumped frantically. I allowed my head to fall back and to the side, giving him whatever access he wanted.

My head was swimming; my body was pulsing all over when he rained hot kisses against my skin, before dragging his lips to the front of my throat, his facial hair gently scratching me as I held the back of his head. He bit the sensitive skin there, then kissed and licked his way to the underside of my jaw, and I gasped, and then whimpered, my body automatically arching toward him. He pulled me tighter against him, into his erection, kissing his way down my collarbone to my shoulder, and I gasped softly again when he pushed the thin straps of my dress down over my shoulders, nipping my skin. The material slipped even further, exposing the top of my breasts, the combination of Devin's hot mouth tasting me there, just above my nipple which was so hard it hurt, making me lightheaded. The sound that escaped me was foreign and Devin paused against my skin, his breathing labored.

"My bad, love," he murmured almost inaudibly, his facial hair scratching my collarbone when he shook his head slightly. "I'm trippin'."

He lifted his head, his gaze heavy and hot when he met my eyes. Slowly I unwound my arms from his neck.

"I didn't mean to get all carried away with you," he grinned, pulling my straps back up on my shoulders. "Back here actin' like a savage."

He backed up a few millimeters and I began to straighten my dress, heat flooding my cheeks. When I looked up, Devin was already watching me, as he straightened out his own shirt. I couldn't help but wonder how many other women he'd brought back here, how far he went with them. Was this a regular thing for him?

"You okay?" He dipped his head to meet my eyes when I looked away, his brown eyes almost apologetic but still heavy with arousal.

I nodded stiffly because I could still feel him everywhere, smell his scent in my skin. "Yes. No," I shook my head. "I'm just confused, I guess," I admitted, just as someone barged through the door.

"Yo, D..." a deep voice bellowed. "Need to holler at you."

Devin nodded, glancing back over his shoulder, but still blocking me with his body so that whoever it was wouldn't get a glimpse of my hiked up dress and strap which was still falling off my shoulder.

"A'ight."

Whoever it was left but Devin still hadn't moved. I didn't look at him as I adjusted my straps and ran my fingers through my tousled hair. He didn't speak again until I met his eyes. His gaze was discerning, curious.

"What're you confused about?"

I wet my lips and shrugged. "This," I waved a hand between us, my heart thumping in my chest but this time for a different reason. "Why did you kiss me?"

His gaze fell to my mouth before he met eyes, a half-grin playing on his lips.

"Because it was getting too hard not to."

"But you act like my friend. Or like you think I'm 'cute'." His eyes were glinting with amusement now, which was embarrassing.

"Because I am. And I do," he answered.

I sighed, touching my tongue to the corner of my mouth.

"Getting to know you for real, just gettin' to vibe with you is the highlight of my day lately."

I blinked up at him, unable to hide my surprise, or pleasure, as heat flowed through my body at his admission.

"I thought music was the highlight of your day." My voice was quiet when I spoke, barely carrying over the muffled music coming from beyond backstage.

He grinned. "Music is like my air. Or water. A necessity. It's gonna be there regardless for survival. But you? You're like... my cookie." A spurt of laughter escaped me and he grinned that same smile that made that girl run into the light pole. "Every time I get to talk to you or be around you—whenever you give me your time, it's like, I'm gettin' a treat that nobody else gets."

I laughed, tugging at a strand of my hair. An easy half grin was still on his face and he stepped closer.

"I didn't expect you. But I like you in my space, Willow Elizabeth." His baritone was low and deep, and he bumped his nose against mine, his breath warm against my lips, the hair on his face tickling my skin. He pulled back a little, forcing me to meet his eyes. "Is that cool?"

I smiled and nodded.

"I like your energy. I think you're dope." I smiled. "Hell yeah, I wanna kiss you," he said emphatically, his baritone low and deep. "All the damn time. Every time you let me."

I smiled and he bit his bottom lip, grinning. "So you gonna keep lettin' me, or what's up?"

I laughed and looked down at my feet, unable to stop my wide smile. I was buzzed from the shot, from Devin's words, from his presence.

"I'm not that girl." The words felt forced from my lips.

He tilted his head and looked at me but his eyes were no longer curious. It almost looked like he already knew the words I was having trouble formulating.

"The girl who will just be whatever you need at your convenience." I clarified. I shook my head. "I mean I can be what you need." *Oh God.* My ears were burning they were so hot. Devin only smiled, biting on the corner of his lip. "I just want you to know I'm not like other girls."

I stopped talking. I was a bumbling cliché at this point—giving Devin Walker the "I'm special" talk.

He chuckled as if reading my mind, amusement dancing in his eyes now. "I hear you. And trust me, I already know. For one, you have absolutely no filter."

He grinned at my stricken expression. "Which means you're not about that bullshit like most people. I like that. I like *you*."

His phone buzzed and he pulled it out of his pocket, his eyes suddenly narrowing as he read the text, his expression shifting, hardening.

"What's wrong?"

"Jersey just got into it with some dude." He was still staring at his phone, and he scratched the back of his head.

"What? With a *guy*? Like in a physical fight?!"

"I don't know what the hell," he shook his head again, his eyes worried. "She's alright though. Bam said Zay handled it. Said he broke the dude's nose or somethin'."

My mouth dropped open and Devin shook his head, pushing out a breath as he slid his phone back into his pocket.

"We should go check on her. Especially after what happened in the truck on the way over with her dad," I said. Her dad was drunk when he called. And verbally abusive. I thought Devin was going to reach through the phone and punch him he was so mad.

"I keep tryin' to tell her, man..." Devin shook his head again. "She's not gonna find what she lookin' for out there. She's gotta look in here first." He tapped his heart.

I gripped the edge of the table, inhaling as I looked at him.

"Can I ask you a question?"

He looked up at me and I could tell he already knew what I was going to ask.

"Do you have feelings for Jersey beyond friendship?" The words tumbled out of my mouth in a rush, and my face was burning, partly because it was already way too late for me to finally ask such an obvious question. My heart was thudding in my chest when I looked up at him.

"No." His answer was stark, his gaze unwavering.

"Did you ever?"

He released and breath and glanced over at the backstage door, rolling his tongue in his mouth. The music beyond the door was getting louder, almost as if deliberately adding to the tension.

"Back in the day."

"For like... a long time?"

He expelled another breath with his eyes still locked with mine. "It took me a minute but I realized that being anything more than friends wasn't our lane. Music is."

How long was "a minute"? I chewed on the inside of my lip, the alcohol weighing down my thoughts as I stared at my feet. My head was spinning. I shouldn't have taken that shot. I needed all my brain cells because clearly, I didn't use them properly whenever Devin and his lips, and his eyes and his dimples, and his hypnotic voice were around.

"Low."

I blinked and looked up at him.

"I know we're just getting to know each other but I ain't no foul-ass dude. If I was feeling Jersey like that, even a little bit, I wouldn't be back here with you."

He eyes were serious. "I wouldn't be making up reasons to call you, just to hear your voice," baritone was quiet and chill bumps covered my arms, when he ran his fingertips over mine, which were flat on the table.

He ran his fingertip up to my wrist, back down over my knuckles and my lips parted, my lungs fighting for air. His voice was low and unbearably sexy when he spoke again. "I like you and I'm already feelin' you *way* more than I probably should be. So no, I don't want Jersey like that. She's my girl but that's as far as it goes."

I inhaled, looking into his eyes, and nodded.

"We done with this? With the Jersey thing?"

I nodded again.

"Cool. Because I don't want you over here thinkin' a bunch of wrong shit."

I couldn't help but smile, looking down at my toes. "Okay."

"The first set is about to start in about 10 minutes," his voice was softer, deeper. "You ready?"

I nodded, his rich baritone pulling me out of my obviously vodka infused thoughts. Devin still hadn't moved, so he was basically in between my legs. His gaze fell to my swollen lips, hungry and hot, before he looked at me. For a long second, we just stared at each other, weighing what had just happened. He leaned forward, placing his palms flat on the table trapping me between his arms. He bit the inside of his lip and grinned that alluring half grin of his, his face just inches from mine.

"You enjoy backstage?"

I laughed, nodding my head, "Immensely," I said, my nose nearly brushing against his.

"You're so damn *cute*," he murmured.

He closed the space between us and I tilted my head up, meeting his lips, like it was natural. He dipped his tongue into my mouth, holding me at the nape of my neck again, but this time the kiss was unhurried and sweet, but no less stimulating. I wrapped my arms around his neck again, my heart thrumming in my chest, and he smiled against my mouth. He pulled my bottom lip between his, sucking it gently before he pulled away with a low hum.

"I'm not gonna be able to leave you alone," he confessed, his voice barely above a whisper.

"I don't want you to."

He smiled against my lips.

8

DEVIN

I TRIED to leave her alone.

For two full days, I fell back. All the way back. No calls. No texts. She didn't call or text either. After that kiss backstage, and the one when I dropped her off at her dorms later that night—the one where I got way too carried away with her... *again,* right there in the parking lot, I needed the head space.

"I'm a virgin," she blurted out, as if I wasn't well aware. She was on my lap in my truck, her face flushed, her hair mused because I couldn't keep my hands out of it. It was thick and soft. Her full lips were swollen from my kisses, her red lipstick long gone. I liked the color of her natural lips better.

"Thanks for the update," I teased her, so her cheeks would turn all black girl pink again.

"I ain't trippin, Low Low," I told her when she didn't smile. She just looked at me, her brown eyes round, chest heaving.

But her outburst did cool me out a little. Once again, I was going too far, too quick with this girl and I needed to slow my ass down. I let her out of the truck after that, and walked her up to her room.

Everything I felt about Low still stood, even more so after that damn kiss. I'd never been as messed up as I was over just kissing a girl before, but our chemistry was crazy. Her boldness, her skill was almost erotic, the way she used her tongue, the little noises she made. Low was an innocent but she was *sensual*. I vibed with her like I did the drums. Naturally. Instinctively. Nothing about my attraction to her was cerebral because if it was, I would've left her alone. She was still too Bambi.

I needed to focus on my music and I didn't have time to put in the work to deal with a girl like her. I couldn't get away with a few phone calls here and there, no texts asking her to come through at midnight. Hell, that was part of the intrigue. I didn't even *want* to do that with her. And I sure didn't want anyone else trying her like that either, the way I'd done with 'Kitta the other night.

The entire time I was with her, I felt, *guilty*. And I wasn't even committed to Willow, hadn't made any promises. It felt wrong in a way that messed me up. I felt like an asshole, to both 'Kitta and Low. I liked 'Kitta a lot. But Low... I dunno. She was something else entirely. She wasn't like other girls, just like she'd told me backstage. She was... all in my head.

So here I was, after only two days of not talking to her, standing outside of her dance practice because when I did start calling her again, yesterday, she wouldn't answer. I called twice. She answered the last time, to tell me she was on the phone with a 'friend' and she'd call me back. I didn't even need to hear her voice to know what was up. That 'friend' was Jaden. I felt it in my gut. And it was confirmed when she never called back. Shit was driving me crazy. I was tempted to stop by her room but I didn't want Jersey all up in our business.

The heavy doors to Warren Hall, where Low practiced, pushed open and I looked up from my spot on the bench that sat across from the sidewalk, a little to the left of building. My gaze automatically slid over her spandex clad legs, up to the tank top she was wearing. One strap was hanging off her smooth shoulder as she exited the building, talking animatedly with that girl Gia and some other chick from the team I didn't know. Buddy with the blue hair was behind them and Low turned when he said something to her, then paused as she looked over at me. My heart beat sped up when our gazes connected—which was wild because she was wearing sunglasses and I couldn't even see her eyes. Her lips parted, barely.

I could almost feel her hesitation when I stood, making my way over to her. She stopped walking and so did Gia and buddy, though the other girl kept it chugging.

"What up, Willow Elizabeth."

Her sunglasses were still covering her eyes but I could feel the energy coming off her in waves.

"Hi, Devin." I stuffed my hands in my pockets to keep from touching her.

"What's goin on, Gia," I said, nodding at her and then greeting buddy.

"Can I steal you for a minute?" I asked, refocusing on Willow.

"We were actually about to go grab a bite and then we had plans." Gia spoke up, stepping closer to Low. Low chewed on her lip and looked over at Gia, before staring at the ground.

I nodded, twisting my lips.

"Think maybe you could call me when you're done then?"

Willow looked up at me. I still couldn't see her eyes but my stomach dipped a little anyway. I stepped closer to her, ignoring Gia, close enough to feel the heat emitting from her body, close enough to inhale her clean scent, even though she'd just finished sweating. It was even better, actually because she just smelled like Low.

"Call me okay?" I asked, my lips brushing the shell of her ear, causing her chest to rise and fall more quickly.

She nodded and hastily stepped away from me.

"Devin?"

"Yeah, hey, what's up?" I ran a hand down my face then opened my eyes and stared at the phone. It was after 1 in the morning.

"You good?" I asked, furrowing my brow. Willow sighed.

"Yes. Sorry for calling so late."

"All good," I told her. "I was waitin' to hear from you."

I was silent for a minute, giving her space to talk since she was obviously wanting to get something off her chest. She hadn't called after I stopped her coming out of her rehearsal. That was yesterday. I'd texted and called a few times today but again... nothing. I didn't know what to think.

"I was thinking about you," she admitted softly. I shifted in the bed, my stomach tightening at the sound of her sleepy voice. *This girl, man.*

"I've been thinkin' about you too. Nonstop."

"Even when you didn't contact me at all? After what happened backstage and... in the truck?"

I bit the inside of my lip, staring up at my darkened ceiling.

"Yeah. Even then. Especially then."

She was quiet and I heard shuffling in the background.

"I wasn't supposed to..." She trailed off, and sighed.

"Supposed to what?" I asked after a long second when it was obvious she wasn't going to finish her thought.

"Nothing." I narrowed my eyes and looked up at the ceiling.

"Low."

"Yes?"

"I wanna see you."

Silence.

"Can I see you?"

I heard her soft inhale. "Okay."

"Tonight?"

"*Tonight?*" she repeated, surprised. "It's 1 in the morning."

"I know. Can I see you? I need to— I really wanna see you, Low."

A few seconds ticked by as I waited. "Please? I have a hot pocket."

She laughed and I bit the inside of my lip, tripping at how the sound actually made me hard.

"Did you just try to bribe me with a hot pocket?"

"Whatever works," I said, and she laughed again.

I ran my hand down my chest to my stomach, listening to her breathe.

"Yes," she finally said softly. "Okay."

I sat up in the bed, kicking out of the sheets.

"I'll be there in 10 minutes," I said before she could change her mind, making a mental note to stop by the corner store to pick up a damn hot pocket.

An hour and half later we were seated in the bed of my truck. I'd parked not far from campus, near a bike trail that was connected to a park, and I brought a blanket, which we were sitting on. We listened to The Isley Brothers, ate hot pockets I'd warmed in the corner store's microwave, and talked. And talked some more. And I realized that nagging in my chest was at ease because I was with her. Like she was my fix.

"I should probably get back," Willow yawned, turning her head to look at me as we rested our back against the truck's rear window. "It's super late."

"I appreciate you lettin' me kidnap you."

She smiled up at me and I wanted to lean in and kiss her so bad, it was crawling through my stomach. But I chilled. Low was still looking wary and I didn't want her pulling that not-answering charade again. So, instead, I reached and brushed my finger over nose, then tucked her hair behind her ear, just because I needed to touch her in some way. Her eyes flitted closed and I leaned in, pressing my forehead to hers. For long seconds we just breathed each other's air, before I finally made myself take her home.

When I walked her to her dorm, we hesitated in the entrance way. Her hair was pulled up in a bun, showing off her features, and her eyes were heavy with sleep, her lips more pouty. I tried not to focus on them.

"Can I see you tomorrow?"

She looked up at me, her brown eyes surprised, as she smiled biting the inside of her cheek.

"Morning?"

She giggled then and I stepped closer.

"And can I see you the next day? And the day after that?"

"Are you just saying things again, or is that what you really want?" she asked, blinking up at me, the smile fading from her lips. Her voice was quiet, vulnerable.

"I ain't know how far to take things with you," I told her honestly.

"Why?"

"Because you're not like anyone else I've ever dealt with."

"And now you do... know how far to take things with me?"

She bit her lip and my gaze landed there, my groin tightening at the inquiry in her eyes.

"I know I can't leave you alone. And I know I don't want to either. And I know I hope you feel the same way."

She shivered a little when I stepped closer, brushing my lips against the shell of her ear.

"So, can I see you tomorrow?"

Her head dropped to the side when I pressed a light kiss against her neck, inhaling her honey scent. "Is that cool?"

She looked up at me and for a long second, we just stared at each other until she responded.

"Yes."

BACK THEN: 6 MONTHS LATER

9

DEVIN

"RUN IT AGAIN."

The beat picked up once more at my direction, and I bobbed my head in rhythm, trying to find the center, the place in the middle of the sound that let me know what we were doing was gelling. It wasn't.

"We need to scrap this," Zay spoke up, lifting his Saints fitted and turning it backward on his head.

"For real, dude," Jersey added. Because that's what they did lately. Zay said something and Jersey added to it. Or she said something and Zay co-signed. I looked over at Travis, who just scratched his head and raised his brows. We'd been working on a few new songs, something to add to our live shows, possibly record, but this song, "Certain Truth" wasn't living up to its title. Something was just... off.

"We shoulda called this shit 'Unpredictable Lie'," Bam piped up, grinning. Travis chuckled along with Zay.

"Wack-ass Fallacy," Jersey tagged on, giggling.

"Questionable Inaccuracy." Bam laughed.

"Y'all got jokes but does anyone have suggestions?" I asked, picking at my hair, eying Bam, then Jersey, who were still laughing. "We got studio time lined up and the shit ain't cheap. We need to go in there ready to lay at least two, preferably three songs. This was supposed to be one of 'em."

"We all know what needs to happen, Devin," Jersey huffed. "You have to stop stressin' all the time. It messes up the energy down here."

"Time is money, Kincaid." She rolled her eyes again, and I heaved a breath, willing my irritation away because she was right, it wasn't productive.

"We can't force it if it's not there, D." Zay was talking to me, but mostly taking up for Jersey, as usual.

I shook my head, tapping my stick against my leg. I was frustrated. We needed this song to work. I was ready to start recording. We had two songs that we were floating around but they were old, made right when Zay joined the group, six months ago. He'd changed the dynamic of the band completely, like I'd predicted. What I hadn't figured, was that he'd change Jersey's life too—for the better. Trav was right. Zay was a good dude. Cool, laid-back, thoughtful. He calmed her wild ass down. She was even playing better, which is saying a lot because she was dope as hell before—all natural talent and instinct. She stopped running around looking for something she wasn't ever gonna find, started focusing more on loving herself. But right now she needed to be focusing on this damn song. We all did.

I stared at the large vanilla candle that was burning on a saucer that was sitting on top of an overturned crate next to Bam's keyboard. I wondered how much heat it was generating. It was mid-April but it was already hot as shit in the basement. I'd pulled off my t-shirt a long time ago and pulled off my black undershirt too, tossing it next to me. I pushed out an audible breath. Bam and Jersey continued their back and forth, but my eyes were on the OutKast poster hovering over the worn blue couch where Willow was currently sprawled, typing her public policy paper. Zay brought the couch to the house a few months ago, said some woman was about to throw it away when he was moving her. It fit perfectly in the basement.

My gaze distractedly dropped to Low, crawling up her bare legs to her thighs, which were partially exposed beneath her orange dress. The color complemented her skin, made it look richer and smoother. What I really wanted to do was go upstairs with her, lay my head in her lap and let her rub on my head the way she liked to. That shit felt *good*—her touch, her smell, her *vibe*. I needed a break—shit was getting to be too much between school, the time I needed to give to Low, and the side hustle I had going, slanging beats to wanna be rappers around town.

A big box of promo materials was pushed against the wall next to the couch—flyers and t-shirts which Low had rode to Dallas with her girl Gia to pick up for us just last week because we didn't have the time between soundcheck for an art show were playing, plus our regular gig at Jimmy's. That was Low. She *always* held me down.

Willow looked up at me now, her eyes almost apologetic. Like it was her fault the song wasn't working. I broke eye contact and bent down, pulling a joint from the green ashtray that was setting on the rug next to my foot petal. I lit it and inhaled, watching the bulb burn bright orange, filling my lungs and holding it for a long second, trying to figure out what we needed to do to make the song work. It was there. But it wasn't. I let out the breath, filling the air with the weed's sweet, herbal scent, and handed it to Jersey, who stood directly in front of me, just to the left.

"It's good but it's not really our sound," Jersey offered, reading my mind as she took a quick hit. "We're in here pulling a Whitely and a Byron."

Willow giggled, and I exchanged a look with Zay, who shook his head and rolled his eyes. Damn near every time either one of us were in their dorm room, they had a rerun of the show on. Even I had the episodes memorized at this point.

"Who?" Travis asked, taking a hit of the weed before passing it to Bam because Zay didn't smoke.

"From A Different World," Bam supplied, blowing smoke out the side of his mouth. "I don't know what that has to do with anything that's happening here though."

"When Byron and Whitley were going to get married," Jersey prompted, eyes wide.

"And then Dewayne had to break that terrible mess up because *he* was the one that was supposed to marry Whitley," Willow tacked on.

"'*Baby please'!*" Jersey and Willow said that last part in unison and Zay and I exchanged another glance.

Travis looked at them blankly.

"Young Low, you gonna partake?" Bam teased her extending the joint in her direction.

Willow shook her head frantically, her cheeks turning pink, eyes wide. She looked over at me guiltily and I chuckled, shaking my head at her cute ass, as Bam laughed.

"You sure?" he prodded playfully, passing it back to me, I took another hit, meeting her eyes, grinning.

He was here when she tried to smoke for the first time a month ago, and witnessed her paranoia in person. I finally ended up feeding her a turkey sandwich and making her ass go to sleep in my room. I took another hit and put it out in the ashtray, bobbing my knee up and down, as I tried to work out another rhythm in my head.

"Trav, no!" Willow suddenly exclaimed, her cheeks reddened, eyes wide. I looked over at Travis, wondering what the hell happened that fast. He was seated on his metal stool; a cigarette was dangling from his lips. He was reaching into his pocket for a lighter but froze.

His chest heaved with his sigh and he twisted his lips, casting a sidelong glance at me. I shrugged.

"I ain't got nothin' to do with that," I told him, grinning as I glanced at Low. She met my eyes, biting on the corner of her lip and the pit of my stomach tightened when she shifted on the couch, pulling at her dress. Sometimes it was enough to look at her to feel centered again. Because that's what Willow had become—my middle, that feeling in the center of my gut that was both heavy and light. The thing everything else circled around.

Even my music was better with her around—she was inspiration, in more ways than one. She was more than my muse. She was my rhythm. I felt better when she was in my space. We were only **six** months in but I could admit, she had me from the beginning, from the very first time she gave me half of her burger at the Pancake Shack. She'd proven herself over and over. How many other girls would be cool doing homework in a hot ass basement, just because I had to work? She could be a lot but at the end of the day, *my baby was a rider*.

"I told you the cigarette smoke messes up the equipment," Bam was telling Travis.

"Man, get outta here with that bullshit. And weed smoke doesn't?"

"Herb is natural, homes."

Travis rolled his eyes as Jersey giggled.

"We just don't like the smoke form of cancer entering our lungs," Jersey piped up, running her hand through her hair, before adjusting the strap on her bass. "I enjoy certain things in life. You know, like *breathing*."

Travis pulled a toothpick out of his pocket and stuffed in his mouth, casting a deliberate glance at Jersey then Willow, raising his brows.

"Better?" he asked her.

"Much better," she smiled.

Travis chuckled and nodded his head toward me. "So what's up. What you wanna do, D?"

"We'll hold off on it for now," I caved, picking at my hair. "Let's run through 'Come Undone' one more time though."

I'd just come up with the beat the other day, and told Zay the concept. Together, we were able to get out lyrics that matched what I had in mind. It was a song about Low, what I felt for her, shit that she made me realize, just by being in her presence. By being her. It was easily one of best songs we had, one that I wanted to record, once we got it down right.

I looked over at Low again. Her feet were curled under her and she was typing fast now, satisfied Travis wasn't working his way toward a slow death. I knew she was finishing the public policy paper she had due tomorrow. Her brow was furrowed, her bottom lip between her teeth, like she was trying to focus but didn't really want to. She was stressing about declaring a major next year because she'd be a junior. For a while, she was leaning toward a degree in fine arts with a focus in theater but thought something in mass communications would be more practical. But she liked her public policy class too and was talking about making that her major just the other day. Basically, she had no idea what she wanted to do, and it was eating at her.

"Hey-yo! The article is up."

I looked over at Bam, whose eyes were on his phone. *Hell yeah.* I dug my phone out of my pocket, as Willow looked up at me, her eyes bright with excitement.

"Yay!" she squealed, clapping her hands, practically bouncing on the couch, her fingers flying over the keyboard once more, probably pulling up the article.

A site based out of Atlanta was doing a review on one of our recent shows there. They weren't national but had a good reputation, and it'd be one of the first times we were featured somewhere other than college sites. It was a good look. I pulled up the article on my phone and read the first few sentences. My heart dropped.

What the...

"*Fuck*," Bam muttered, his eyes on his own phone, his face crumpled into a grimace.

I frowned, scanning it quickly, my stomach knotting the more I read. *Shit.* I ran a hand over my head, then pushed the phone back into my sweat pockets. Then pulled it back out two seconds later, re-reading to make sure it said what I thought it did. *Shit.* When I looked up at Low, her eyes were already on me, widened in shock.

"This is *bullshit*!" Willow rarely cursed and Jersey looked up at her, then glanced at me, her surprise momentarily covering up her agitation.

"What is this Trevor Carmichael person even talking about?" Willow continued, sitting up on the couch and swinging her legs to the floor, planting her bare feet on the turquoise rug that was underneath the couch.

"Some bullshit," Bam answered her, still scowling with his eyes on his phone.

"*The band sounds like they're reaching for something they haven't quite obtained... while obviously individually talented, The Prototype together sounds as though they are split, each searching for their own validation while subtly neglecting the cohesiveness of the band.*"

Hearing Willow say it aloud made it even worse. I turned, leaning forward with my elbows on my knees, heaving a sigh as I stared at the floor. Normally, criticism didn't affect me like that. I'm a creative. If I put what I create out into the world for public consumption, critique is part of the game. But this... it was our first big review. And the writer basically shitted on us.

"But then he says, '*The Prototype is skilled but almost too deliberate, too polished.*' That doesn't make sense!" Willow's voice was shrill, her gaze bouncing from me to Bam then to Zay. "He contradicts himself in the very next paragraph!"

Willow continued reading silently, her brows furrowed. I was getting a dull headache.

"What show was he at?" Jersey asked, she was mad but she also sounded deflated. "Was he even really there?"

"It ain't all bad. He had some positive things to say." Zay offered. He scratched his chin, his eyes red rimmed probably because his eclectic ass woke up at the crack of dawn daily, like he was a ninja warrior or some shit.

Jersey looked up at him, her eyes narrowed in disbelief but laced with disappointment she couldn't hide.

"It's one review from one website. It's not *Rolling Stone*, Kitten. Who cares what one writer from one bullshit website thinks?"

"It wasn't bullshit when we thought they were gonna show us some love," Bam countered. "This is a respected paper."

Zay shook his head and sighed. Jersey only rolled her eyes, still studying her screen, tugging agitatedly at a lock of her hair. She took her bass off and all but slammed it onto the stand.

"It's like he didn't even listen to the music. He was just trying to sound smart or something," Willow said, glancing at Jersey, her soft gaze landing on me.

"I'm about to leave a comment and tell him this article is wack, and he's wack for writing a wack ass piece of wack-crap article," Jersey said, her fingers already tapping on her screen.

"Pop Tart, don't leave a comment," Travis interjected, still perched on his stool, squinting at his phone in frustration before sliding it back into his pocket. "We're better than that. It's one article. Who cares if he didn't say what we wanted him to? It's publicity. And even if one person reads this and decides to check us out, it's a win."

"Yeah but Trav, he's attacking everything about us," Jersey countered, hurt creeping into her voice. "And it's not even accurate! It'd be different these criticisms were valid."

"I hear you but Trav's right, baby doll," Zay said, raspy voice quiet when he looked at her. "Yeah, he's wrong but exposure is exposure. Our music speaks for itself."

"Which is why we gotta get 'Come Undone' recorded." I spoke up. "Music can't speak if it's not available."

Zay nodded, his eyes on Jersey, probably weighing her mood. I sighed as I ran my hand up and down my chest, my eyes falling on Low again, who was still reading the review, her face scrunched up in anger. We needed to record. And we *did* need to tighten up in some spots, the writer wasn't lying about that. And we needed to work on—

"Fuck this review." I forced myself to stop mid-thought. *Speak the truth until it becomes the truth*. "We need to be focused on the right shit and this ain't it."

We all fell silent for long minutes, lost in the disappointment that was clogging the poorly circulated basement air. I met Low's eyes for several seconds, pushing out a slow breath. Maybe we'd just call it a night.

"What y'all think about this?" Bam suddenly spoke up.

He started playing the chords to "Certain Truth," but changed the rhythm up. Immediately, *instantly* some of the tension in the room began to dissolve. Travis bobbed his head, joining in on guitar after Bam ran through a few bars, but at a slower pace than before. Zay picked up the rhythm too, and glanced at Trav, a smile on his face.

"Yeah," Bam, nodded. "That's it, Jersey Belle," he said when Jersey grabbed her bass again and started picking out a different bass line, smoother with more drop to it, adding to the bobbing rhythm. Normally, she played off me, but what she was doing worked. I'd build the drums around her this time.

"*Hell yeah*. Let's run it from the top," I directed, my adrenaline spiking the way it always did when we were creating and it was flowing the way it was supposed to.

I looked up at Low as everyone picked up the beat one more time. She'd started gathering her books and laptop, stuffing them into her bag. I beckoned her over to me with a short head nod, signaling to Travis to keep the music going, though I momentarily stopped playing.

She hesitated for a second before finally leaving her bag on the couch and making her way toward me, in the far corner of the room. Her dress swished as she moved, and her hair fell over her left eye before she distractedly pushed it behind her ear. She'd recently cut it, so that it fell just to her jaw line, framing her pretty face, accenting her large brown eyes, which right now were full of disappointment she was trying to hide.

Jersey touched her arm, and she paused, listening as she said something quietly in her ear that made her tip her head back and laugh, her eyes on me. Finally, she stepped over the equipment wires, putting her directly in front of me, and I pulled her down on my lap because she just stood there, acting like she didn't know what to do. She smelled like coconut today, and something else edible and sweet that made me want to keep her as close as possible. The music was swelling around us and I kept my voice quiet, so that only she could hear me.

"I didn't forget. I'm gonna be up in a minute. So don't leave yet."

My lips brushed against her neck, and nuzzled my nose against her soft skin, inhaling her. I pulled at the underside of her thigh and she turned, so that she was straddling my lap, pulling her dress down in the process so that her butt wasn't exposed. Her palm-sized breasts were directly in front of me and my gaze dropped there for a second, gliding over her cleavage before I met her eyes again.

"You promised, Devin." She met my eyes and blinked, pouting, her voice quiet.

"Come on, baby, don't—"

"Everyone is flaking on me today. First my parents, now you..."

"What're you talkin' about?"

"They said they're cutting me off." I arched a brow.

"Well, not cutting me off," she amended, shifting her weight on me, "but they're harassing me to get a job. They said next year they're cutting it 'significantly'." She used air quotes, heaving a breath and rolling her eyes as she did so. "They just don't understand that I'm too busy to get a job with all of the other commitments that I have. They can't expect me to be involved on campus, maintain a good GPA and *work*. It's unfair."

"You went over your stipend again?" It felt weird saying that shit. Willow's parents actually gave her a monthly stipend.

"You don't have to say *again* as if it's a regular thing"

She frowned and I bit the inside of my lip, eyeing her. As down to earth and generous as she was, Low was also unconcerned with money to a fault, and she spent it with little regard for how regular folk had to deal in the real world. It wasn't that she was ungrateful, or even deliberately ambivalent. She was just... brand new. Used to things being a certain way for her, with little effort on her part.

"You're not saying anything." She frowned in disappointment and shook her head. "I know it's because you agree with them, right? You think I need to 'improve my life skills' too, right? Like I'm just some completely unaware person who just goes through life all in 'la-la-la land' and whatnot."

"I ain't say that."

"You didn't have to. Your lack of response says everything."

Her brows bunched together and she blinked. "Just forget it then. Just like you forgot about the movies."

I fixed a look on her. She was getting herself worked up, talking crazy. She rolled her eyes and moved like she was going to get up from my lap, but I put my arms around her waist, tightening my hold on her. She glared at me.

"Your ass is spoiled."

Her mouth dropped open, like she didn't already know that shit.

"I am *not.*"

Her denial bounced off me, because I was speaking the truth. Low always wanted what she wanted, right when she wanted it, regardless of what else was going on around her. When it was her who had things going on—stuff with her sorority, or her dance team, or the kids she worked with, or school—I let her be, even though free time didn't come often for me. I still didn't sweat her. But not Low. If the tables were reversed she was all up in my ear about it.

"You're the one who said we could go to the movies, and so I rearranged my schedule and cancelled my study group with Gia, but now *I'm* spoiled for expecting you to stick to what you promised?" she retorted quietly.

She glanced around to make sure no one was paying attention. I wouldn't've cared if they were. But they were working on the breakdown of the song, and Zay was playing around with a few different riffs. The music was climbing up the walls around us, filling the space as Jersey worked out the languid, wavy bassline. My gaze dropped to Low's thighs and I ran my hand up over the material of her dress, then back down. It's like sometimes I forgot how thick her thighs were, until she was sitting on me again. And they were all smooth—

"Devin, are you even listening?"

"I hear you," I lied, meeting her eyes.

"I miss you," she said quietly, her gaze darting around the room before she looked at me again. I couldn't help but laugh at her wide-eyed expression, which earned me another eye roll. I cocked my head to the side, unable to keep the grin off my face.

"How you miss me when we see each other every day?"

It was true. She was usually here but when she wasn't, I was at her and Jersey's too small dorm room, helping her study or laying around with her, eating ice cream and shit.

"I mean *really* see you, Devin."

I widened my eyes and touched my forehead to hers, staring directly into her pupils. "Like this?"

Her eyes were gorgeous. Dark brown with traces of hazel and even gray in them if you stared hard enough. She was doing her Bambi glare again and I struggled not to smile because that would only piss her off more. But she was so damn *cute*.

"Stop bein' all dramatic," I said quietly. "I told you we can still go," I said, pulling her closer, inhaling her soft scent, getting a momentary high. Yeah, she was spoiled but she was also adorable. And she held me down. And if there was ever anyone that I wanted to go out of my way to do shit for, it was her.

I kissed her chin and met her eyes. "It's 8:45. We can still make the late show."

My thumb trailed slowly along her lower back, over the soft material of her dress. She shifted her weight on me, probably feeling the start of my erection, and I brushed my nose along her jaw line, trying to ignore it. I basically kept a semi whenever Low was around. I couldn't ever remember being so attracted to a girl before. Low made everyone else I'd ever entertained dim in comparison, made every other encounter I had with other women before her feel elementary. With every other girl, it'd felt like I was just doing somethin' to pass the time—because they were cool, but mostly because it was convenient and I enjoyed women.

But not with Low. Our shit was *intentional*. From the very beginning.

My moms said we fought and argued like a married couple, when Low came home with me a few months ago when we were doing a show in Atlanta. Like we'd been together forever. It kinda felt like that. I'd gone to her parents' in Houston, a couple of days after Christmas, and hung out until the new year. It was mostly because I needed to gain ground with Willow after I had to bail on going home with her for Thanksgiving. We had a show in Atlanta, a show that was important and came up last minute. Willow was pissed but I had to handle business.

When I went to Houston for Christmas, it was the first time I'd ever gone home with a girl before, and it was cool. Her folks were older, in their late 60s, and explained that Low was a "change of life baby," I think as a way of letting me know why she was so spoiled. She was a "beautiful surprise" her mom told me when she showed me Low's baby books, pictures of her as a chubby-cheeked baby and a little girl with a huge smile and bright eyes. She looked like an Old Navy ad, all cheery and bright. Low was the type of person you *wanted* to look after, to give everything she ever wanted because she was so sweet and just *loveable*.

What was wild about it all was we weren't even having sex. And Low and I kicked it *a lot*—hanging out in her room, watching movies, studying together—she'd come to our shows every Friday at Jimmy's and chilled at some of our rehearsals. But I didn't want to push her. I told her early on it wasn't just about sex with her, and I meant it. If she wasn't ready for us to take it there yet, I'd wait because I for damn sure didn't want her doing something just because she felt pressured. I never understood that shit, coercing women into sex. Either they wanted it or they didn't—the end. How do you even get off being with a woman who is half-ass committed to having sex with you? I get off on my woman getting off. That other shit is weird.

Willow was worth the patience, worth the blue balls I'd gotten a couple of times when we were messing around and I let it go too far, when I knew better.

"I know you, Devin," she said, shifting her weight on me. "You'll be down here all night like the last time we were supposed to hang out together. And the time before that. And the time before that."

She was gnawing on her lip now, and I leaned in and kissed the corner of her mouth, feeling a little guilty, which was bullshit because I wasn't supposed to be feeling bad about giving my music the time it needed. I'd already ended rehearsal earlier than I should've twice this month so we could hang, and I didn't want it becoming a habit. Especially with that bullshit review we'd just got.

"Thirty minutes, okay?" I told her again, as I brushed my nose against hers. "We gotta get this done."

She pulled back, heaving another breath as she stared into my eyes. "That writer didn't know what he was talking about." Her voice was barely audible but her eyes were serious. "You can't take it to heart, baby."

"I know. But this is a priority."

"Believe me, you make it super clear what your priorities are all of the time."

She tilted her head looked at me, sighing in resignation at my expression.

"Come 'ere." I pulled her toward me, sliding my hands down to her thighs, but she stiffened in my arms.

"Oh, for real?" I smirked. "You don't even wanna kiss me now?"

She was holding back a smile, trying hard to maintain her attitude. Her gaze dropped to my mouth and she shifted her weight.

"You are so annoying," she murmured, her lips twitching as she attempted to contain her grin but she gave in anyway, holding my biceps as she leaned toward me, pressing her soft mouth to mine. I captured her bottom lip, sucking on it gently and she closed her eyes, her breath warm against my mouth.

"Thirty minutes," I repeated, for me as much as her.

After a few long seconds, she pulled away and wiggled off me, not acknowledging my words. I tapped her on the ass as she stepped away from me, which earned me an eye roll. I moved on the stool, trying to subtly adjust myself.

"You outta here, Young Low?" Bam called out, looking up from his keyboard.

"Yep, going upstairs to finish my paper," she returned loudly, her voice barely carrying over the music. "And then I'm going home to take care of my *priorities*."

Low made sure she glared at me before waving to everyone else and disappearing up the stairs. Jersey tossed me a look, which I ignored, as I rolled my eyes, picked up the sticks, and let myself get lost in sound.

WILLOW

"Do you have a highlighter?" Jersey peeked her head around Devin's door before stepping all the way in.

"Devin has one on the dresser."

I watched as Jersey made her way around the blue record crate, which sat next to his plastic drawers. The first time I'd come back to his room, I was surprised by how little there was in it. Plastic drawers stacked on top of each other, a box spring and mattress, and records, tapes and CDS lined along his wall. To me, it smelled like corn chips but Jersey said it smelled like "late night shenanigans with low self-esteemed girls." After that I brought candles and Lysol.

"I thought you were going home," Jersey smirked.

I rolled my eyes and sat up on his rumpled bed glancing at the time on my phone. One of Devin's flat pillows was squished behind my back, where a headboard should've been. *Two hours* had passed since I came upstairs. Obviously, we weren't making the movie.

"Where's Devin?"

"Downstairs, getting the beat down, I think," Jersey answered, rifling through the contents on the top his dresser before finding what she was looking for. "You know he's a perfectionist."

"He's probably gonna be down there for *another* two hours."

Jersey looked up at me, twirling the yellow highlighter between her fingers, her gaze sympathetic. Devin's extreme focus was both incredibly attractive and endlessly frustrating. Even now, he'd given up eating meat for the past month because he'd read it could increase his stamina.

"I think he was almost finished. You know he's worried about—"

"Who's worried about what?" Devin interrupted, pushing through the door, barefooted. A chocolate chip cookie from the batch that I baked earlier was in his hand and he took a bite, chewing as he looked between the two of us. Without a conscious thought on my part, my gaze travelled over his chest to his flat abs. He'd put back on the black undershirt that stretched across his chest and showed off his biceps and tats, and his gray sweats were hanging low on his hips. He was so *good-looking*. Devin's body, his face was like... joy personified, or something.

"Those cookies are official, right?" Jersey asked him, grinning.

"Have the whole house smelling like peace and joy on earth," Bam said out of nowhere, poking his head inside the doorway, his mouth full of cookie.

"Man, get those crumbs outta your beard," Jersey frowned. Bam shrugged and bushed his face. I couldn't help but laugh as Devin eyed him.

"You didn't eat em' all did you?"

"There's maybe two left," Bam said quickly, edging his way back out of the room as Devin rolled his eyes.

"Man, your greedy ass—"

"Kitten," Zay suddenly yelled from the room next door, his raspy voice calm even though he was yelling. "Hurry up, I need you."

Devin smirked and raised a brow. Jersey actually looked mildly embarrassed. The walls were thick because the house was old but the music in Zay's bedroom was turned up, blasting Marvin Gaye. We all knew what that meant.

"The highlighter," she clarified, holding up. "He needs it."

"Yeah, okay," Devin smirked, stuffing another bite of cookie into his mouth.

"Baby doll," Zay appeared suddenly in the doorway. He'd stripped out of his t-shirt to his white undershirt with a pair of basketball shorts. I'm sure if the hoards of women who chanted his name that their shows could see him now they'd go into cardiac arrest.

"What're you in here doin, baby?"

"Dang, Isaiah! I said I was coming. Impatient." She was pretending to be annoyed but the way she was looking at him gave her away.

Zay stepped close and murmured something in her ear that made her cheeks turn all red. She shook her head, shooting me an exasperated glance.

"I'm out. Good night, loves," Jersey said, pushing at Devin's shoulder, as Zay pulled her out of the room by the bottom of her tank top.

"Low Low, you got the macro notes I sent you?" Zay asked, poking his head back around the door. I nodded. "You're the best."

"No worries," he said, throwing up two fingers at Devin before leaving the room.

Devin looked at me once they were gone, closing the door behind him. I tried to ignore him by staring down at my phone. He sighed audibly and I looked up to see him chewing on the inside of his lip, the way he did when he was trying to think of how to pacify me. His left dimple showed when he did that, which meant he didn't have to say much.

He made his way toward the bed, and moved the stack of his books that were sitting on the edge of the mattress to the floor, before climbing on and crawling toward me. I glared at him, or tried to.

"What's up, Sweet N Low," he asked, meeting my eyes, cocking his head to the side. He put the cookie in his mouth, holding it with his teeth then pulled at the underside of my thighs, causing me to fall flat onto the bed.

"Devin!"

He climbed on top of me, straddling my hips without putting his weight on me, balancing on his elbows. Instantly, my body softened under his, no matter what my brain told it to do.

"I know we missed the movie," he started, staring down into my eyes, holding his cookie with one hand. "My fault."

"It's whatever," I managed, trying not to sound affected by his closeness. "I knew we weren't going two hours ago when you lied and said we were."

He bit the inside of his lip again and sighed. I shifted under him, trying hard not to focus on his lips, or his eyes, or his chest and arms.

"I know. I'm sorry."

His voice was barely audible, low and affecting. As if he couldn't help it, he leaned down and kissed my mouth, pressing his forehead against mine before pecking my lips again, lingering longer this time. He tasted like the cookie he'd been eating, warm and sweet. He kissed the corner of my mouth, then my bottom lip before brushing his nose against mine. My heart was racing, my breath coming quicker as my nipples hardened, pressing into his firm chest.

"You forgive me?" he asked, kissing my mouth again. I could feel his erection against my stomach and I shifted beneath him, my body warm, compliant, as it always was when Devin was near.

"You know I can't deal with you bein' mad at me."

"I just wish you wouldn't commit to doing things with me when you know you're not gonna be able to."

"I'm sorry."

He kissed me again. This time, I couldn't help but wrap my arms around his neck. I nipped his bottom lip. He kissed my mouth again, dropping kisses along my jaw line, down to my neck, then paused.

"What?" I asked, sensing he was about to say something I didn't want to hear. I could feel it in his breathing, weird as that sounds.

"Don't get mad... but I gotta go make a run right quick," he said against my neck, the hair on his face brushing the sensitive skin there.

"What? *Now?*"

He nodded, raising his head to look into my eyes.

"Devin, it's almost eleven. Where are you going?"

"PNC's."

"The rapper guy?"

He grinned at me amusedly and nodded.

"I need to take him these beats so he can finally pick one. He's actin' like he needs me there to do it."

I knew selling beats to wanna be rappers was how Devin made

money. And if he was leaving this late at night on a Wednesday, he must've really needed it.

"I'll be back in an hour." He leaned down, brushing his nose against mine. "I don't want you to leave tonight," he told me, his baritone low.

I bit my lip staring up into his brown eyes. I didn't stay the night often. It was too tempting for both of us.

"I'll just come with you."

Immediately, he shook his head. "Nah."

"*Nah?*"

Devin didn't say anything, just pushed up from me, and stood, stuffing the rest of the cookie in his mouth. He made his way toward the dresser, grabbing his wallet and stuffing it in his back sweat pocket.

"Why not?" I pressed, sitting up on my knees, my dress swishing around my thighs with the movement.

"I'm only gonna be gone for about forty-five minutes." He turned and looked at me before pulling a t-shirt out of his drawer.

"Even more reason for me to go with you."

He shook his head again, pushing out a breath, when he looked at me again.

"Low, I'm not gonna be able to... look after you like that. I'm gonna be handling business."

"I don't need you to *look after me*, Devin. I'm grown."

His gaze dipped from my thighs up to my chest before he met my eyes again, chewing on the corner of his lip. I tilted my head to the side, and because he was near enough, grabbed the bottom hem of his black undershirt, pulling him toward me. His eyes were low and curious when he let me pull him, stopping when his knees hit the edge of the mattress. His gaze skirted over my face, and my entire body warmed. His chest was rising a little bit faster beneath my fingertips.

"I wanna ride."

For a second he just stared down at me, and I let my eyes roam from his full lips, to his nose, which was pierced with a small gold stud, to his ridiculously long eyelashes that framed toffee-colored eyes. I turned my head and pressed my nose to his bicep, brushing it there before kissing it and looking up at him again.

"Please?"

"You know you ain't right," he said, his voice husky.

I bit my lip, blinking up at him. He touched his tongue to the corner of his mouth and groaned.

"A'ight," he murmured resignedly, still staring into my eyes.

I smiled and clapped my hands and he blew out a breath and shook his head before turning to put on his shirt. He mumbled something about "spoiled" which I gamely ignored.

WILLOW

"SO, THIS IS HIS HOUSE?" I asked Devin when we pulled up in front of a house with cars lined in front of it a few minutes later. We were about 10 minutes from campus, in an old residential neighborhood. Bass was pumping from the ranch style house and a few people were hovering out on the porch. I knew that rapper guy went to our school, but this didn't seem like a college crowd.

He nodded, his gaze on the front porch where the group was gathered, as he turned off the dead prez that was blasting from the boombox.

"We're gonna be in and out, okay?" he told me, glancing in my direction.

"Okay. I have to be up early to finish my paper anyway."

"I thought you only had a couple of pages left?" He looked over at me, brow furrowed.

"I didn't get it done."

"Did you look at the article I sent you? That shoulda helped."

Devin's business ethics class was studying the history of redlining in the housing market so he'd sent me an article by Ta-Nehisi Coates to look at for my paper too.

"I did but that article was *so* long. The information was good but there's so much to take from it. It was a lot. It was depressing."

"As hell," Devin agreed, shaking his head. "It was real. And the worst part is, we don't learn about anything about housing discrimination against black people in history class. They don't want us to understand how systems really work. They know we'd be ready to riot."

He shook his head once more. "Did you at least finish reading it? It shoulda helped," he said again.

"School work doesn't come as easily for me as it does for you, Devin," I admitted quietly. "I can't study for like, 20 seconds and get passing grades."

He stared at me, his expression flat. "You coulda finished that paper if you weren't up in the room on your phone watching *A Different World* reruns."

"How do you even know that's what I was doing?"

He only eyed me and shook his head, then slid his phone back into his pocket as he cut his loud engine. The door creaked when he pushed it open and hopped out, without bothering to answer me. A few seconds later he yanked open my door, filling the cab with the damp night air, and held out his hand. I grabbed it, sliding down the front of his chest until my feet hit the pavement. Devin stepped forward, backing me against the truck with his body, dropping a quick kiss on my mouth.

"This is gonna be real quick," he told me.

I nodded. It seemed like he didn't want to go inside.

"C'mon," he said, grabbing my hand and interlacing our fingers before leading us up the cracked sidewalk toward the house.

Forty minutes later we were inside of the stuffy backroom that I could tell was supposed to be the master bedroom but was set up to look like a makeshift studio. It was full of guys—nothing but guys—and the music was blaring all around us. It was almost as if the loud music made the smoke that lingered in the air even thicker. The walls were covered in dull white foam, the same as it was in Travis' basement, only this looked cheaper, like whoever hung it up wasn't sure where to put it, and had therefore just tacked it up anywhere there was space on the wall. And it didn't match anything.

Devin was seated at the controls bobbing his head to the beat he'd just put on. That guy, PNC was bobbing his head so hard, I know his neck had to hurt.

"Everybody think they're the next Future," Devin mumbled to me, as we'd made our way into the house earlier, passing by random guys were in the living room, playing video games and drinking. *"But if these cornball college dudes wanna give me their refund checks, I'mma take it."*

"What's up, lil mama?" A snaggle-toothed guy with a full beard sauntered into the hot room, nodding his head at me. I was seated on a chair pulled from the dining room, across from the control board where Devin was.

"Hi."

He grinned, extending a Fanta bottle toward me.

I eyed the bottle before looking up at him.

"Um," I shook my head. "I'm okay... thanks." I glanced at Devin. I knew he couldn't hear us because he was right next to the speakers and the music was playing so loud.

The guy leaned against the wall next to me. He smelled like cigarette smoke, strong and stale. I sniffed, subtly wiping at my nose.

"Smile, baby girl. Why you lookin' all mean?"

I almost rolled my eyes. There were few things less irritating in life than some guy you've never met insisting that you smile at him.

"I'm not mean."

"No? You're *nice?*"

Oh God. I crossed my legs, glancing over at Devin, as I bobbed my head to the music.

"This is a good beat," I offered, trying to distract him.

I also wanted to show Devin that I could hang. That he didn't need to keep an eye on me the way he seemed to think he needed to.

"It sounds a little like J Dilla production, right? With the drum breaks and the soulful keys?" I asked referencing one of the legendary producers Devin told me he studied to learn how to make beats. I smiled a little. Hanging around Devin and Jersey so much, I used words like "drum break" in actual sentences.

The guy shrugged disinterestedly, his gaze skirting over my legs.

"You like rap?" he asked. I nodded.

He cocked his head, running his tongue along his bottom lip, which was stained black. "What else you like, baby girl?"

I shifted in my seat, glancing over at Devin. He met my eyes, then looked over at the guy who was hovering.

"Low Low," he said, standing, his voice carrying over the whirling beat. "You ready, baby?"

I nodded, and stood too, pulling at my dress, because the guy was still staring uncomfortably hard at my legs.

"We need to wrap this up," Devin told PNC, who was still seated and bobbing his head.

"You ain't gotta go nowhere, baby girl," the guy told me, more loudly than necessary, eyeing Devin. *Oh no.*

"The fuck you call yourself doin, dawg?" Devin said, brow furrowed as he cocked his head, stepping forward.

My eyes widened but Devin wasn't even looking at me. I crossed the room toward him, grabbing the bottom edge of his t-shirt, my heart thudding. Devin looked at PNC, and widened his eyes in an expression that clearly said he needed to get his friend.

"Man, Leonard shut the *hell up*," PNC breathed exasperatedly. He stood too, rolling his eyes. He was lanky and almost looked like he could've played basketball because he was at least 6'6, but he didn't really have the body mass. "Always gotta be sayin' some shit. D, ignore his drunk ass."

"Ain't nobody drunk," Leonard mumbled. "I hope that's your girl, cuz. You cuffin' hella hard."

"He's fucked up— ignore his ass," PNC interjected.

But Devin wasn't looking at him.

"You can get fucked up for real tryin' to show out," Devin warned, his eyes still on Leonard. His face was hardened, almost unrecognizable, and my palms got sweaty as I shifted my weight.

Leonard stepped forward and Devin, pushed me behind his back, with a hand on my hip, not breaking eye contact with him. I exchanged a look with PNC, who was shaking his head, as he moved to stand between Devin and the guy. This was the Devin I hadn't seen much of. The one with the temper. My heart was still racing. I felt a little crazy because seeing Devin like this was kind of...sexy.

"D, man," PNC said, tapping his shoulder. "C'mon, I'mma get you your money." Devin stared at the guy for a second longer, and I looked around for something I could grab in case a fight broke out because Devin would be outnumbered. There was an empty beer bottle sitting on the control board.

"C'mon, man," PNC urged again. "Man, Leonard, cool the fuck out," he said pushing lightly at his chest.

"Whatever," he mumbled.

We finally all pushed out of the room, past Leonard who plopped into the chair I was just occupying, and started bobbing his head to the beat Devin made.

12

DEVIN

I WAS *HOT*. I clenched my jaw together, trying to cool down, my grip on the steering wheel tight. That punk ass muthafu–

"...and the one that sound like the one beat on that one album, I can't remember which one..." Willow was rambling nervously next to me, as I drove with one hand on the wheel.

I knew some shit was gonna go down at PNC's. And the fact that Low was there, in that environment because my dumbass could never say 'no' to her.

".... I think it was the second one from the..." Low was still talking and I shook my head, irritation bubbling in my chest.

"*Low*."

My tone was rougher than I intended and she looked over at me, eyes wide, and snapped her mouth closed. I sighed. I ain't mean to snap at her but *damn*. I hated that she was even around that shit. And I was frustrated because even though I sold four beats to PNC, it wasn't enough. No matter how much money I made, it was never *enough*. Because as soon as I got one thing handled, like buying an extra book at the end of the semester for my bullshit civics class, it was something else, like my little brother Omar telling me he needed soccer cleats, and knowing moms couldn't afford it. Or my truck, which was always one day away from breaking down. The engine light was on and it was making noises. I thought it might be my wheel bearings going bad. Buddy who worked with Trav and Zay, Aaron, said he could look at it but I needed to be able to slide him something. Every dime I'd made from PNC was already gone. And no one was hiring.

I couldn't even take Low to the movie, I was so broke. The truth was, I'd checked my account right after we finished rehearsing and it was almost overdrawn. After that, I just stayed downstairs for an extra hour, working, trying to kill some of my frustration. Low wouldn't've tripped if I told her didn't have the money. She never did. Ever. But I was tired of having to tell her that shit. She was used to being treated a certain way—the way she deserved to be treated. I knew motherfuckers like Jaden, with the means to date her, and take her places, and give her things were there, waiting for their opportunity.

So, I deliberately messed up our plans, hoping that the extra work I was putting in would pay off in the long run. Everything in my life felt like that lately—like it was off in the horizon somewhere, far away.

I glanced over at Willow again. I could feel the energy coming off her in waves. She was chewing on the corner of her lip, her head turned toward the passenger side window. My chest tightened, and I picked at my hair.

"Hey." I touched her hand, which was lying on the seat, running my fingers up the inside of her wrist. She looked over at me, and even though it was dark in the truck cab, I could see that her eyes were guarded but mostly hurt. "I'm sorry."

She inhaled and nodded.

"I shouldn't be snappin' at you like that. That shit's not cool."

She nodded again, releasing her lip from between her teeth, turning her hand over and interlacing her soft fingers with my rougher ones. That was the thing about Low. Her forgiveness never capped her anger. She slid into it easily, never held a grudge, like a lot of girls I'd dealt with in the past.

The Isley Brothers' "Groove With Me" was playing from the boombox sitting on the floor, a contrast to the harder tracks I'd been listening to for the past thirty minutes. I blew out a silent breath, trying to let the music affect my shitty mood.

"That was pretty cool," Willow ventured softly, as I maneuvered through the residential streets, my truck's engine rumbling loudly, threatening to drown out her voice.

My brow furrowed and I turned to look at her incredulously. She actually thought that shit was *cool*?

"No, it wasn't 'cool'," I informed her. "By any definition of the word."

"I mean, it's pretty cool that you made money, not that you almost beat that poor, drunk guy up," she clarified, running her finger over my Twin tattoo, her small touch, soothing.

"His hoe-ass wasn't drunk."

"He definitely had liquor in that bottle he was drinking from."

"That was *lean* in that Fanta bottle." Her eyes widened. "And who knows what pills them nig—" I stopped and shook my head, glaring at the road. "Who knows what they were poppin before we got there. PNC is cool but he's a dumbass. I keep tryin' to tell him to stop lettin' them stupid ass dudes hang around him, but he don't wanna listen. Lettin' them tear up the house his auntie left him. It's always the folks who have shit who don't appreciate it. Tryin' to prove he's not just a college boy to a bunch of people who don't really give a shit about him."

"So, *lean* is what that guy offered me to—" Willow started before snapping her mouth closed, as if just realizing what she'd said.

I looked at her, eyes wide. "He did *what* now?"

"Don't flip out, Devin," she said in a rush. "It was no big deal."

"It's a big deal, Low. What if you would've..." I bit my lip, shaking my head. "Don't ever accept anything from a dude you don't know, *ever*."

"I know."

"I mean it."

"I know," she said emphatically.

I bit my lip to keep from saying anything else. I was gonna have to deal with dude and PNC both. That's all there was to it.

"Do you think PNC needs an *intervention*?" Low's eyes were round and concerned, and she'd sat forward in her seat, looking at me. So damn *Bambi*. I chuckled a little.

"Nah, baby. He's just dumb as hell, mostly. Doing stupid shit to fit in."

"Is that really why you didn't want me to go, because you knew there'd be a lot of guys and... whatever there?" She asked after a few seconds.

I glanced over at her. "There's dudes everywhere and they're gonna try you—and me— because you're so pretty."

She blinked, as if she was surprised. She didn't have low self-esteem but she was still more concerned with how the girls she hung out with saw her than men. She didn't seem to be that aware of how men viewed her, beyond the obvious. She didn't get that it wasn't just her looks—it was the way she carried herself, the intelligence in her eyes, the pureness of her energy that made her so attractive.

"You're the type of girl that dudes... aspire to," I told her. "Like, the *goal*. Beautiful, talented, smart, sweet, fine as hell." My gaze dropped to her legs, where her dress had ridden up, exposing most of her thighs. I met her eyes, noting her blush. "You're the prototype, Willow. It ain't just me that recognizes that."

She furrowed her brow, biting the corner of her lip.

"But that is what it is. Really, I just don't want you around certain elements."

"You make it sound like I'm some innocent."

I smirked my eyes, on the road. "You are."

She looked as though I'd offended her. "I'm not *that* innocent," she mumbled. "I stole a pair of earrings from Target once."

I laughed. "*Why?*"

She shrugged. "To say I did it."

I rolled my eyes, still smirking.

"There's nothing wrong with you being how you are, Low. Trust me. It's actually attractive. Refreshing. You ain't about an agenda."

"I've never been in a real fight before," I glanced over at her brows raised, wondering what she was talking about now.

"Well, I had one once with this girl named Amber in the seventh grade because she thought I was talking about her behind her back, even though I *wasn't*," she continued. "But, if those guys would've tried to jump you, I had your back. I saw a beer bottle I could've used as weapon."

"*What?*" I whipped my head to face her so fast; I actually heard it crack a little.

"I said, if those guys would've tried to jump you I saw a beer bott—"

"Don't say no shit like that again." I interrupted roughly, running a hand over my head. *This damn girl*. "I wouldn't've— I'm not putting you in a position to use a damn *beer bottle* on a room full of dudes."

I shook my head, trying to erase the thought of my baby picking up a beer bottle to bust some dude's head open. Some dudes mighta thought that shit was cute, but not me. It actually made me sick to my stomach that she thought she even needed to think like that when she was with me. She was looking at me like she was trying to understand my reaction.

"If anything ever goes down, don't be in there trying to fight, Willow." I shook my head again. "*The hell?*"

"Jersey would've."

"You ain't Jersey."

She'd lost her mind. I glanced at her again and she shrugged, looking down at her pink nail polish.

"Isn't being around rappers like PNC kind of the life of a musician?"

I chuckled humorlessly. "What I've been doing lately— being at PNC's, that's *hustling*. What I do with Prototype—that's musicianship. We all live and breathe this music, so our sound is... *alive*."

I thought about how they were probably about to mess my music up with their wack ass rapping and shook my head. PNC called me a music snob but fuck that. I have taste. And an ear for music. There's a difference.

"I can't wait 'til I reach the level where I can pick and choose who to give my music to, ya know? They don't really know what to do with it." I glanced over at her. "You know he tried to get me to 'thin the beat out' because he thought I had too many 'sounds' in it? He didn't even know there were live instruments on that track, and doesn't care because he doesn't appreciate it. No musicality. He can't tell that I actually played the drums live and the part that sounds like a sample—"

I hummed it and Low nodded, recognizing what I was talking about.

"That was really live instruments that I chopped up and recorded back down to the beat."

I spent too much time doing it. Bam was always on me about putting so much time and effort into the beats I sold to these local rappers but I couldn't help it. If my name was on it, it had to be right.

"But I need the paper," I said aloud. "That's the compromise. Give my music away to people who don't even have the capacity to appreciate it, or I don't eat."

"At least you're making some money doing what you love in the meantime," she said helpfully. "At least kinda, right?"

"True."

I grinned at her, ever the optimist. It's one of the reasons she was so addicting. If I was ever feeling a way, all Low had to do was smile, or say something cheery, or read me one of her happy scripture affirmations and I felt a little lighter.

"Are we going back to my dorm?" Low asked, looking out of the window, her brow furrowed.

"My truck is acting up. You hear that noise it's been making when I turn the wheel?"

She nodded as I turned onto the street that led to campus, trying to push down the tightness in my chest, knowing I'd disappointed her.

"I'm gonna have to get up early and take it to Aaron so he can look at it. I'm supposed to be helping Zay and Trav out with a moving job after class and I gotta have the truck."

"If you need to use my car for anything, you know you can," she said quietly when I pulled into the side parking lot at her dorms. The darkened lot was half way full of cars, and silent. "I have classes all day tomorrow and I don't have practice so I won't even need it."

I didn't say anything as I cut the engine.

"I mean it."

"I know you do, baby," I finally looked over at her. "I appreciate it."

"Did your mom get that job?"

I shook my head, frowning.

"Why not?" Low sat up a little, her brow creased. She helped moms rewrite her resume after she got laid off from her customer service job. She'd worked there for seven years, and then—boom. No more.

"They ran a credit check on her. After it came back they said they couldn't offer her the gig."

"A credit check?"

Willow's eyes widened and I knew she probably wasn't even aware that jobs did things like that. Both of her parents had careers, not jobs. Moms had just enrolled at a technical college this semester, to get certified as a dialysis technician. I was happy for her. She was making temporary sacrifices to improve her end game, applying to her own life what she was always trying to get across to me and my little brother, Omar. But this setback was messing things up.

"I can't believe you need good credit to get a job," Willow said.

"Ain't that some shit?" I shook my head. "You gotta have good credit to get a job but you can't get good credit without having a job. It's an endless, bullshit cycle." I shook my head, gazing out over the parking lot. "I need for this music to take off, man. I need for this to work so I can make moves outside of the bullshit systems they have set up for us to fail."

"Like in that article," she supplied.

"Exactly. I wanna be able to do for my family, you know? Stop this check-to-check bullshit."

She leaned her head against the passenger's side window, her feet propped up on the boombox which was sitting on the passenger floor as she stared at me, tugging on a lock of her hair.

"It's gonna happen for you, Devin. You have the vision and you work really hard. I think God will honor that."

I nodded, wanting to believe her. I knew we had the talent to make it. But I also knew a lot of talented people who it didn't work out for, and now did shit like work at Jiffy Lube, even with a degree. I didn't want that to be me. That *couldn't* be me. The thought made me sick to my stomach. It was crazy because all the people who flocked around us, hanging on after our shows didn't know shit about my actual life, and didn't care to know.

I could feel my mood slipping and I inhaled trying to focus on better things. I looked over at Low. The light from the parking lot was dancing over her skin, giving it an orange glow. Even under that harsh light she was gorgeous. Reluctantly, I pushed open the door and hopped out of the truck, moving around the front to let her out.

"What's on your mind?" I asked when she just kept looking at me as if she had something to get off her chest as we made our way toward her building. The air was cooler now, and Willow zipped up my hoodie she'd just taken from my truck.

"I did something."

She looked nervous and I narrowed my eyes curiously, stopping just outside of the entrance. She leaned against the brick wall, and licked her lips.

"I replied to that review of your show. The one from earlier."

I raised a brow, and leaned against the wall next to her, watching as she reached into her huge bag and pulled out her phone. She slid her finger over it then handed it to me. My gaze immediately dropped to the comments section of the review. She'd broken down, point by point, why the writer was wrong. She was staring at me anxiously when I looked up at her.

"I know you and Trav said to leave it alone but I just felt really compelled to explain to him why he was so wrong." The words tumbled out of her mouth in a rush.

"You felt 'really compelled'?" I grinned and handed the phone back to her. She smiled and looked down at her toes.

"*Aquemini* though?" I asked, arching a brow, referencing the name she used when she left her reply. Her cheeks flushed and I felt my chest tighten.

"Are you mad?"

"Hell no." She smiled.

"I just can't believe you used the word 'antithetical' in an actual sentence."

She laughed then, the warm sound hitting me right in the groin.

"It was appropriate."

I grinned, as I studied her features. The way her eyelashes were so long, they curled and tangled at the ends. The sensual curve of her lips. The three freckles that dotted her chin.

"I think you're *so* dope."

"Only because I like your music," she teased, her voice soft and sleepy because it was after 1.

"Because you ain't all about you, and what you think you can get from me," I corrected, stepping in front of her, pushing her fully against the wall as I pressed my forehead to hers. "I need you to keep being that way."

She ran her hands up my sides, and I pecked her lips, enjoying the feel of warm hands, when she pushed them under my t-shirt.

"I thought you said I was spoiled," she tilted her head up, her lips barely touching mine again before pulling back. I bit my lip, grinning at her teasing.

"You're that too."

She frowned and pushed playfully at my shoulder, "Get away then."

"Can't do that," I said, grinning, grabbing her hips. "I *wanna* spoil you."

I kissed her lips, and she held onto my sides, pressing up on her tip toes to get closer. I slid my hands to her butt, pulling her up and into me, losing myself for a second in the sweetness of her mouth, her breathy little noises, when I pulled her even tighter against me.

"Are you coming inside?" she breathed, looking up at me. I sure as hell didn't want to leave her. I wanted to wrap myself in her, breathe her until shit felt right again. But I couldn't.

"Nah. Not tonight."

"Why not?" She was pouting again.

"I just told you my truck is running funny. I gotta get up early to get it handled."

I didn't speak the other reason aloud—I was too horny to be in the bed with her tonight and just sleep. I *wanted* her. Every part of her. I wanted to bury myself inside of her and release some tension, let her fill me up. But Low wasn't ready for that, not for the way I needed her tonight. She wasn't even ready for sex at all, and I was only frustrating myself thinking about it.

"I'll call you tomorrow, alright?" I told her, kissing the tip of her nose as I pushed off the wall, and pulled the door open to her dorms.

I held it open for her, my mind already on the stuff I needed to get handled. She looked up at me, tugging at a strand of her hair before tucking it behind her ear.

"It feels like... you're not mad at me, right?"

I frowned and shook my head, looking off over the empty patch of grass that led to the quad. She asked me that shit at least twice a day.

"Why would I be mad at you?" I was struggling to keep the irritation out of my voice.

"You just seem weird all of a sudden."

I bit the inside of my lip and sighed. Had she not just heard any of the shit I'd told her over the past 20 minutes? Sometimes she was so oblivious to actual life issues, it was stressful explaining the shit over and over.

"I'm not mad," I said instead of telling her that. I pulled her toward me again, and kissed her lips. "I love you, Low Low."

"I love you too," she whispered, blinking up at me, her eyes searching mine before she drew in a breath, pressing her forehead to my chest. For a long second, she stood there, holding my sides.

Finally, I pulled back and kissed her forehead. She offered me a small smile before I turned and headed back to my truck, wondering how long I could keep everything up before something broke.

13

WILLOW

DEVIN DIDN'T CALL the next day. Not until 11:21 at night. The conversation was short too. Sometimes we spent hours on the phone, even after just leaving each other, talking about everything and nothing. But yesterday it'd been quick, and stilted. I asked him about his truck and he said it was "kinda fixed"—whatever that meant. I tried not to read much into how short he was being with me. But I had started to notice a pattern—whenever he was stressed, it was like he pulled away from me.

"I think Tre is stealing money from the team."

I jerked my head up from the psychology notes I wasn't really even reading and looked at Gia. We were in my room, studying and she was seated at the desk. The room was mid-sized, with twin beds pushed against either side of the wall. Our two desks were in opposite corners, facing each other. Jersey hated the set up and so did I but I'd done the best I could with limited design options.

"You think Tre's stealing money?" I repeated, just to make sure I heard her correctly. She nodded, twisting her faux-locs into a bun that sat high on her head.

"Why are you saying that?"

"Okay, so you know how we each had to pay $110 for our outfits for the last show we did in Monroe?"

I nodded, smiling at the memory of the six-hour drive to the small Louisiana town. Me, Devin, Jersey and Zay all rode down together, and they watched me perform. We had so much fun.

"Why are you smiling so hard?" Gia asked, her brow wrinkled.

I shook my head, embarrassed. "Nothing. Go on."

Gia eyed me but kept talking. "Well, so Lauren said when she asked for the receipts, he couldn't ever find them. And so she asked him what website he bought them from and he gave her some name that didn't even exist."

Gia said the last part slowly, her eyes round. She could be so dramatic.

"Okaaay..."

"So, she Googled it herself and found out that the outfits were really only sixty-dollars each online. What happened to the rest of that money?"

I twisted my lips, thinking.

"Isn't that *crazy*?" Gia asked obviously excited to be relaying the information, even though our dance team could be in big trouble if he really was stealing money because we had to maintain an ethics code to keep our school endorsement. "And on top of that, you know how we have a budget at the beginning of the year, right? Well, he hasn't kept track of spending, and can't provide documentation for anything but we've already spent the entire budget, supposedly."

"I guess that means..."

"That Lauren is going to run for captain," Gia finished for me. I nodded. She was going to be a senior next year and was already vying for the spot.

"Devin thinks I should run."

Gia rolled her eyes. "I thought we were going to go an entire thirty minutes without you bringing up Devin. Obviously, I was mistaken."

I frowned. "I don't talk about Devin all the time."

Gia rolled her eyes. "Every other word out of your mouth is 'Devin thinks this' or 'Devin told me that'," she said, rolling her eyes again and stared at me without blinking. "You're way too wrapped up in him. It's almost... *regressive*."

"Regressive?"

"As women, we don't have to be under the thumb of some man any more, succumbing to their beauty standards, bending to their will. We don't have to subscribe to old, patriarchal relationship standards."

"Are you quoting bell hooks again?"

Gia rolled her eyes.

"That's not what my relationship with Devin is about."

"I'm telling you what I see as your friend, who cares about you. Just think about it, Willow. What happened just the other day? We were supposed to hang out and study for a class that you say you're having a hard time in, and then Devin called and it was over, just like that," she snapped her fingers. "It's like; he sucks up all of your time. Everything you do has to revolve around him and *his* schedule. I mean, he has you hanging out in a sweaty basement half the time."

I picked at my pinky as I thought about what happened at PNC's. But Devin didn't drag me there, I'd practically begged him to go.

"It's not like that."

Gia ignored me.

"And you're not even getting any?"

"I told you I wanted to wait. There's nothing wrong with that. And Devin is really sweet about it."

My mom didn't talk to me a lot about sex. But when she did, it was in gentle warnings. When you gave guys sex too early, they lost interest. Once you had sex with a man, the dynamics of the relationship changed, so it was important to be ready. God doesn't enjoy fornicators, even though He loves you anyway.

"Okay," Gia said, sarcasm dripping from her tone. "You're entitled to do whatever you want to with your body. It's your body. But guys like sex. That's just the truth. And it's been six months and you two still haven't done it? And you're not even giving him head? And he's *Devin Walker*."

I pressed my lips together, my cheeks heating. Maybe Jersey was right. Maybe I did talk to Gia too much. But the other part of me was wondering how true her words were. Women flocked around Devin like vultures. But he didn't seem to be that bothered by us not having sex, or me not giving him head. This one guy that I dated at the beginning of freshman year, before I met Jaden, tried to push my head down when we were making out. Like, literally palmed the back of my head and tried to push it toward his penis. I stopped seeing him after the second time he did that. I refocused on Gia, sighing. Devin was nothing like that.

"You just finished going all feminist but now you're saying I need to have sex with him to keep him? You're contradicting yourself."

"No, I'm pointing out the obvious and trying to make you think."

I rolled my eyes.

"I'm not trying to be harsh but I just had to say something, Willow. What are you getting from this thing with Devin? Besides being able to say that you're with the popular guy on campus?"

I shook my head. "I don't care about that. I love *him*."

"We all know that. He's all over all everything you do, but how many pictures of you two together does *he* have up?"

My heart was thudding, and I willed it calm as I looked out of the small window, just above Gia's head. We couldn't see much but the tops of the trees, which were just sprouting leaves. I'd asked Devin about that, and his answer was simple—his social media was for branding, not personal stuff. None of the band members shared things that were actually personal online, even when it appeared that they were. Everything was deliberate, they were careful when crafting their persona. They even had meetings about it. But then... Jersey and Zay were all over each other's pages, together. When I asked Devin about that his answer was, again, simple—they're both in the band and it adds intrigue. Another branding technique.

"That doesn't matter. I know what's real," I told her. I didn't sound convincing and Gia's face told me as much.

"Okay, just don't forget about you," Gia warned, brows raised. "That's how women get caught up all the time."

"Why are guys so stupid?!"

Jersey burst into the room, before I could formulate a real response to everything Gia had just said. Her bag was slipping off her shoulder, lips curled into a frown.

She glanced up at Gia as if seeing her for the first time. "Oh hey."

"Hi, Jersey." Gia began gathering up her books. Gia and Jersey never cared for each other. Neither one of them ever directly said it, but whenever one was around, the other usually left, and the air was always uncomfortable when they were together.

"What's wrong? Did Zay do something?" I asked, watching as Jersey pulled off her baggy sweats, leaving on a pair of boxers. She was the only girl I knew in real life who could wear baggy sweats and a tank top and still look feminine and sexy.

Jersey flung her bag onto her bed and plopped down on it, kicking off her shoes and lying flat on her back.

"No Zay is... good." She grinned her eyes kind of dreamy and I smiled because it was so weird to see her so obviously in love. "It's this guy from business administration class who will *not leave me alone*. He texts me non-stop, he went through and liked every single one of my pictures for the past *three years*, he always tries to sit next to me in class. And I literally told him, 'dude, it's not happening,' but I think he thinks he's wearing me down. He even showed up at our show last Friday."

"He sounds like a stalker," I told her, as she stared up at the ceiling, holding her phone over her face as she swiped.

"Why does he have your number if you hate him so much?" Gia asked standing.

Jersey's gaze skated over Gia, and this time the mild annoyance was evident in her eyes, like she was wondering why she was still in the room, or chose to speak.

"Because I don't work for the CIA. It's not hard to get."

They stared at each other for a second and I fidgeted in my seat.

"I'll see you later, Willow," Gia finally said, making her way over to me and stooping to give me a hug, engulfing me in her apple scent.

Once she was gone, Jersey looked over at me.

"She smells like a bowl of fruit."

I covered my laughter with my hand.

"Stop that. She's nice."

"She smells like a freakin' blueberry farm," Jersey said, causing me to laugh again as I stood. "And she's not 'nice,' Willow. She's shady."

"No, she isn't. Gia is my friend."

"Of course she is. You like everyone who pays you attention."

I frowned and looked over at her. "What does that mean?"

"Nothing," she sighed, setting her phone on the bed next to her. "Just, everyone who wants to be around you doesn't have good intentions. Sometimes they're leeching off your energy and what they think you can give them." She shook her head. "Something is just off about her."

"So, did you tell Zay about your stalker?" I asked changing the subject because I was tired of everyone offering me unsolicited advice today.

"Yeah, right. Are you freakin' kidding?" Jersey laughed, sitting up and crossing her legs, pulling at her Spider-Man boxers. "I never tell Zay about stuff like that, ever. I value his freedom too much. You've seen how he can get. He'd go to jail if I told him some guy was harassing me.

"That's true," I admitted. "I wish I could've seen him break that guy's nose," I said, referencing the now infamous incident.

Jersey shook her head. "He's crazy."

"About you."

Jersey rolled her eyes, the way she did when she thought I was going "Full Willow," her way of calling me corny.

"What are you gonna do about the guy?"

She shrugged. "Nothing. He's just being annoying right now. If he gets too crazy I'll tell my professor or something."

"Or report him to Dean Winslow. I think she's the one who handles harassment and stuff like that."

"Oh, your mom called earlier while you were in class," she said abruptly as she grabbed the remote from her nightstand and clicked on the TV.

We still had a land line in the dorms, which my mom only used when she couldn't reach my cell. I was kind of avoiding her. And my parents were disappointed in me, which I didn't get. They didn't actually come right out and say it, but our conversation from the other day was bothering me. They acted as if I was in Tyler doing drugs, or acting out, or flunking out of school or something. So I occasionally overspent—there were worse things.

"She says I need to get a job," I told her, my eyes on the TV screen.

"I told you Cheyenne'll hire you at Aroma," Jersey said, glancing at me. She'd been working at the coffee shop near campus since freshman year. "She thinks you're cute and perky."

I laughed. "You should go in there," Jersey urged, smiling. "You won't be making stripper money or anything but she'll work with your class schedule and it's laid back."

I nodded, sighing, watching as Jersey reached onto her night stand and opened up a box of strawberry Pop Tarts. She tossed me a pack and I caught it, ripping the package open and taking a bite.

"Plus, we'll be able to work together," Jersey offered as she chewed, "which means I'd *finally* have someone who I actually like to hang out with." Jersey grinned and wiggled her brows and I laughed.

"Oh shoot!" she suddenly exclaimed, snapping her fingers. "I totally forgot to call that venue in Dallas about gigging there next weekend. I hate doing that kind of stuff. But it's my turn."

The band took turns booking gigs, even though I told Devin it should just be one person to avoid confusion. He didn't listen to my suggestion, obviously.

"I'll do it," I told her, grabbing my laptop off the end of the bed and opening it. "What's it called?"

"Blue Lounge in Irving," she said, swallowing.

"I think it's smart to just call all of the similar venues in that area and try to book them so you guys don't have to worry about it every week."

Jersey nodded. "I so love you. That totally makes sense. Anything to get Devin's bossy ass off my back."

At the mention of Devin's name my heart started beating a little faster, though I kept my eyes focused on the screen.

"I think he's mad at me."

"Why?"

I shrugged.

Jersey rolled her eyes. "He's not mad at you. Even when you guys do your arguing routine I've never seen him *actually* mad at you. He thinks everything you do is adorable. Every time you walk into the room he gets the goo-goo eyes."

I laughed. "He does not."

"Please. You snap your fingers, he jumps."

"That's not true. Devin doesn't listen to anyone except Devin."

"Usually. But all you have to do is that blinking thing you do," she looked up at the ceiling and flapped her eyelids dramatically, "and it's a wrap for the homie," Jersey said, as I shook my head in denial, laughing loudly. "You're like that cat from Shrek. The one that hypnotizes everyone with its eyes," she laughed.

"Shut up," I laughed. "I have *never* made that face."

"You have him so sprung, Willow. And you're doing it all with like... your personality."

She shook her head, her eyes faraway before sighing. "I wish I would've been more like you."

I blinked, surprised, crossing my legs under me as I faced her.

"Not with Zay," she immediately clarified. "He's the only one I did do things the right way with. Well... I mean, I did things wrong with him at *first* but thank God he has the patience of Yoda to deal with my shenanigans. And with him it was never just about sex, that was just the icing on an already very delicious cake."

I laughed again.

"But before him, having sex with people I gave two craps about, it drained me. Took away from *me*. I think it's great that you took the time to get to know Devin and see what you two are about for real before hopping into bed with him. And when you do decide to do it, it'll be about love, you know? I think that's beautiful."

Jersey looked at the TV screen, stuffing more pop tart into her mouth, almost as though she was trying to shut herself up.

"He's being... like, distant. Or something."

She looked up at me.

'You know he's moody and rude," covering her mouth as she chewed. "It's that Gemini thing."

"He's ignoring me."

Jersey rolled her eyes. "I literally heard you on the phone with him last night," just as my phone buzzed. I smiled automatically when I saw his text, like he'd read my mind.

"*Wanna take a ride with me?*" It was already past 10 but it was the first I'd heard from him all day.

"See, that's him, right?" I looked up to see Jersey staring at me, smirking, and I grinned, my pulse racing, just from his text.

On the day I left Houston for South Texas, my mom gave me *The Rules* book. She handed it to me when my dad stopped for gas on our ride up here. While he was outside pumping gas, she told me there was life advice in it that I could use, and she wanted me to have it, as a guide. I read it the first week I was on campus. I'd since broken practically every single rule written in the book with Devin, especially the one about not accepting an invitation to hang out with a guy if he can't be bothered to call you and ask at least a day in advance. Jersey's words, Gia's words, my mom's words, all whirled in my brain. But it was my heart I listened to, always with Devin.

"*Okay*." I typed. I just wanted to be anywhere he was, that never changed.

"*I'll be there in an hour.*"

I smiled.

WILLOW

IT WAS a little after midnight when Devin drove me to the park around the corner from Travis'—the same one he'd taken me to that night that seemed so long ago now, when we decided to be serious with each other.

The park was small but pretty, with weeping willows and cotton trees dotting the stretches of grass that lined the long, winding walking path that cut through the park. A tiny playground was on the left edge of the park, covered in darkness because it was almost midnight.

We'd had a lot of make-out sessions in Devin's truck. Devin's kisses were like everything else he did—better than everyone else's. In fact, the ancient worn out cab had quickly become one of my favorite places. We'd find a spot here, at the park and talk, and kiss and listen to music on his boombox, and kiss some more. Sometimes while we were making out, his hands beneath my clothes, his mouth all over my chest and neck, he'd groan low and deep, biting hard on the fleshy part of his lip, his frustration evident when he pulled away from me. When he did that it made me want to give him everything, every single of piece of me.

Right now, his tablet was sitting up on the cracked dashboard of his truck, playing *Love Jones* from the small screen. He wanted to sit in the back of the truck bed like we often did, but it was drizzling.

"I know this ain't the same but..." he said when we first arrived, gauging my reaction to his make-shift movie theater.

"It's perfect," I'd assured him, kissing his lips. He'd even stopped at the corner store and bought ice cream.

I knew Devin was tight on money. Jersey told me she'd overheard him talking to his mom about it. She said he was probably embarrassed, which hurt my feelings because I hated for him to feel that way. I didn't want him feeling that way with me. I felt his eyes on me and I looked up at him. He grinned, his dimples peeking out.

"What?" I asked, dipping my spoon into the melting carton of ice cream that was next to me. "Why are you looking at me like that?"

"Because you're beautiful and I don't really know how else to look at you."

I laughed, my entire body warming, as I snuggled against his chest, stuffing the spoon in my mouth.

"What's been up with you today?" he asked, leaning and kissing me behind the ear.

"Nothing, really. Well, except I found out Tre is probably stealing money from the team," I told him, goose bumps breaking out on my arms when he slid his lips to my neck.

"Who?"

"Tre... 'buddy with the blue hair.'" Devin laughed against my neck.

"Told you he was on one," he said, before I launched into the full story. He just listened, his fingers pushing through my hair as he rubbed slow circles on my scalp, relaxing me as I talked and watch the tiny drops of rain splatter against the windshield.

"You gonna take over as captain then?" he asked when I finished.

I shrugged, taking another bite of ice cream, before absently feeding the rest to him. "Do you *want* to take over as captain?" he asked, swallowing.

"I think I'd be good at it. But if I were to do it, I'd change a lot. Like, for one, we'd be way more involved with the kids in the community."

"How so?" Devin was still running his fingers through my hair and I closed my eyes, envisioning what I was saying as I talked.

"I'd just do more workshops with the kids who want to dance. And maybe do some kind of mentoring program." I was getting more excited as I talked. "Maybe we could connect with the elementary and middle schools and set up some programs where we meet once a month or something, and work on routines."

"You should do it, baby," Devin said, looking down at me.

I nodded. "I think I will run, if I can beat out Lauren."

"Fuck Lauren."

"Devin!" I dropped the spoon back into the carton and stared at him wide-eyed.

"I mean, I'm sayin. She's not more qualified than you," he looked at me as if daring me to deny it. "That's the one with the short hair, right?" I nodded. "Yeah, nah. You need to take what's yours. Know your worth. Know that every time you enter a room, it's better because you're there. God gave you a gift, and you dishonor Him when you don't use it."

I was silent for a moment, watching the rain trickle down the windshield before fixing my gaze on the tablet's screen.

"You ever think about what your obituary will look like?" I wondered aloud. "Like, what people will say about you when you die?"

Devin looked down at me, his brow wrinkled. His eyes were a little exasperated but beneath that, there were traces of humor.

"No."

I rolled my eyes. "We were talking about it in class today. It made me think. Like, what are people going to say about me when I'm gone?"

"Probably that you were always on some random shit."

I rolled my eyes, shifting against Devin's firm chest. My brain was in a million places lately but also focused on the same one thing. *What was I doing?* All of that talk about being the captain had made me think. What *was* I passionate about? I loved dance. Loved it. But I didn't want to be on Broadway or in videos anything like that. And I didn't know what I could realistically do with it beyond college. I just loved movement, which isn't really a thing. At 20, my mom already knew she was going to be a nurse because she wanted to help people. My daddy already knew he was going to be an engineer because he loved numbers.

Devin knew what he was here for too. He had purpose, and that purpose shaped almost everything he did. Everyone kept telling me that I had "time" to figure things out. But it didn't feel that way. I was living my life *now*. Wandering through spaces that didn't seem to fit.

"I used to be hyper-paranoid about my parents dying, since they're older." Devin looked at me, his brow furrowed.

"Like, when I was in kindergarten my mom was like, 50, and my dad was 56. My dad is old school, so you know how he still gets the paper every morning?" I waited for Devin's nod before continuing. "From the time I was in the second grade, and realized how much older they were than everyone else's parents, until middle school, I read the obituary section, just to see if anyone who died was the same age as them."

Devin shook his head, his brown eyes full of compassion. "Damn, baby."

"I know, right."

"Your parents are in great shape, even now."

"I mean, I know. But that fear was there anyway. I guess just aware of living life to the fullest, maybe." I shrugged. "I want people to say I lived with intention," I murmured aloud, as Devin resumed running his fingers through my hair. "The intent God put in me, I want it to be obvious I'm giving it over to the world. And that I added to people's lives. But I can't add if I don't know what to give. You're so lucky that you *know* without a doubt what you were put here for. So does Jersey. And Zay. And Travis. And Bam."

It worried me sometimes. I was the only one in Devin's immediate circle who wasn't living out my intention.

"You'll figure it out," Devin offered after a few long seconds. "You need to stop stressing yourself about it. It'll come to you when it's 'posed to. Just living your life—being proactive is putting you on a path, and you just might not realize it yet."

I stared out at the darkened tree, inhaling the damp air that was slowly circulating through the truck since the window was cracked.

"Anyway. What have you been doing today?" I asked him.

"Running around. Class. Debating on whether or not we're gonna check out this dude who wants to manage the group, Jay Little. Wishin' I coulda been kickin' it with you. You been heavy on my mind all day."

I looked up at him. "You didn't call or text."

"I forgot my phone at the house this morning. I didn't have a chance to go back to get it either because I've been running nonstop."

I bit my lip and released it and his gaze dropped there.

"I've been thinking about you all day too."

"Yeah?"

I nodded, my eyes on his mouth, my body already pulsing in anticipation of his touch. His eyes were low when he looked at my lips again, still fingering strands of my hair.

"What are you gonna do about it?" I teased, touching my tongue to the corner of my mouth.

He chuckled and leaned toward me but I pulled out of his reach, grinning.

"You better stop playin'," he warned, pulling me back toward him, brushing his lips against mine lightly, before pressing more firmly against my mouth.

We kissed slowly, our lips and tongues meeting in an unhurried rhythm, matching the steady pulsing between my legs. Devin tasted sweet like ice cream, and himself, and I was addicted to it, to the way he always kissed me, as if it was the only thing he wanted to be doing. His thumb was brushing across my nape, as he kissed, then sucked gently on my lower lip. I pressed closer, and Devin made a noise from deep within his throat, angling his head the other way against my mouth, sweeping his tongue against mine, tasting and then pulling back, before dipping in again.

"You okay?" he asked, his voice low and gruff, when I grimaced, shifting myself because the seatbelt buckle was poking into my upper thigh.

"I'm okay. The stupid seatbelt—"

"Here."

He shifted, pulling me so that I was almost sitting on his lap, his erection poking me. The position was sort of awkward but neither of us cared. I just wanted his mouth again, and I turned my head, eagerly meeting his lips. He smelled so good, like cedar and spice and laundry detergent.

I slid my palm up his firm chest over his shirt, then back down, my fingers brushing against his tight abdomen. A low hum left his lips, and he kissed my neck, sending shivers throughout my body, when I traced my fingers over the top of his waistband tempted to push my hand lower. I pressed my mouth against his neck, tasting his warm skin there with my tongue, the pulsing between my legs increasing with his low hums of pleasure, and I slid my hand lower, my pulse racing double time when I made contact with his hardness.

Devin met my eyes and bit his lower lip, humming low in his throat as he slid his hand under my dress, palming my butt, then squeezing it, before finding my mouth again and kissing me with hungry intentions, his tongue meeting, demanding mine as he squeezed my butt.

The kiss was getting hotter, more intense, and I felt Devin growing harder in my hand, even through his sweats. He slid his rough hand beneath my panties, still palming my butt, as I moved against his erection, liquid desire coursing through my body, landing in the pit of my stomach, when I licked his bottom lip, then pulled lightly at it with my teeth.

Devin pulled at my hair with his other hand, making me tilt my head back so he could kiss his way down the front of my throat, just as his phone buzzed against my hip then buzzed again two short seconds later, and again. Devin's fingers were in my hair, and he kissed my collar bone, groaning in disappointment when I finally pulled away from his mouth, nuzzling my nose into his neck, heart racing as I inhaled him.

"Nuh-uh, don't move," he breathed gruffly, when I attempted to shift off him. He leaned in and pecked my lips again, his chest still heaving when he lifted his hips so that he could pull the phone from his pocket. He quickly texted whoever it was back, his arm still wrapped around my waist. I could feel his erection, insistent against my hip, and I wiggled against it as I shifted myself in his arms. The light from the screen was illuminating his features and he grinned slightly.

"Who's that?"

"Someone wanting to know when our next show is."

"Who is 'someone'?"

Devin looked at me. He got annoyed when I asked him those kinds of questions because he's "grown" and doesn't like answering to anyone. But I didn't care.

"Ol' girl whose party we went to last week. The one who's redesigning the site for us."

"Brianna."

"Yeah."

I rolled my eyes. The entire time we were at her party, which we really went to so Devin could handle business with her, she ignored me, as if *I* was the groupie. That happened a lot. People just wanted to be in Devin's space. If we were out, even on a date, Devin belonged to *everyone*. Women chasing after him nonstop was also apparently part of his "brand." He literally told me that. I slid off his lap, putting space between us, and he didn't even notice. I felt anger gathering in my chest as I glared at his handsome profile. He was still on his phone.

"Devin." I said his name more forcefully than I intended to.

He looked up, brow furrowed.

"Why is she texting you this late?"

Devin shrugged his eyes on me as he dropped his phone onto the seat next to him

"It ain't that late. She's prolly up smokin', tryin' to get some ideas out."

I rolled my eyes because that was a load of crap and I didn't care what the heck she was doing before she felt empowered enough to text him at midnight.

"I told her to hit Jersey though," Devin continued. "She's better at the visual stuff."

"I don't like her texting—" I started, just as he said, "Stop trippin'."

"Why is it always okay for women to contact you at whatever time they feel like it?" My voice was getting louder, bouncing around the small confines of the truck.

"Why are you always *trippin*, Willow?" He had the nerve to sound exhausted.

"Stop saying that," I snapped, rolling my eyes. "I'm not 'trippin' every time I say something you don't like. And it's not just her. It's Nikitta too."

He rolled his eyes. "Here we go." He didn't even look mad, just annoyed.

"I'm serious. You don't like that I'm still friends with Jaden, who I *never* slept with, but it's totally fine for you to keep her around and use her help when I know you two have been together, repeatedly."

He shook his head, looking out across the parking lot. "That's business." He looked at me. "You know what's up. You know what I'm about, what I'm trying to accomplish. And you said you didn't want to work the door."

"Because—"

"You wanted to see the show," he finished for me. "Which I was cool with because I'd rather have you near, and I didn't want you doin' that shit anyway. But I let you because you asked. And now, what? You're mad again that Nikitta is doin' it? Why are you trying to find things to be upset about?"

"I'm tired of being the only person in your life who isn't properly acknowledged. Everyone in the band, random women who don't even *know you* get the spotlight on your page and pose with you, but not me. I'm like, nowhere to be found."

"I do that to protect you, Low. I've told you that 100 times. You're the one whose important to me and I don't want anyone feeling like they have the right to comment about us or come at you any kind of way, which is exactly what would happen."

"You do that to protect *you*."

He rolled his eyes. "You ain't even makin' sense right now. Like you're looking for reasons to be mad."

"I can't be in a regressive relationship."

"In a *what*?" He was staring at me as if I'd sprouted two heads. "A *regressive relationship*? The hell does that even mean? Who've you been talking to?"

I frowned, glaring at him.

"I'm tired of being second to everything else in your life, Devin. If all of those other people are so much more important to your 'brand' than I am, then maybe you should be with them instead, because I'm over it."

"You're *over it?*" His voice had dropped an octave and he leaned forward in his seat, his brown eyes on me, sending chill bumps crawling over my body. He reached for me but I pulled away.

"Take me home."

He pushed out a humorless chuckle and shook his head. "Hell no. I'm not takin' you home, Low. We were fine until—"

"Then I'll walk."

I scowled at him before turning and pushing my shoulder against his door a little harder than was probably necessary because it hurt. It creaked loudly and swung open and I hopped out of the truck into the night air, ignoring Devin's bass voice calling my name. My sandaled feet touched the wet asphalt, as I slammed the door shut behind me, grabbing my sore shoulder. I knew I wasn't walking anywhere in the dark but I was so *mad.* I wasn't the crazy one here. I hated that I always felt like I was sharing him when he'd owned every single piece of me, from day one.

My emotions were all over the place and I inhaled the wet air, thankful that it'd stopped drizzling. I felt like crying or punching something or... I didn't even know.

I heard the truck door slam and I braced myself, crossing my arms in front of my chest, watching as Devin made his way around the front of the truck.

His worn jeans were low on his hips, his white t-shirt showing off the expanse of his chest. The hair on his face was thicker, almost a full beard and his ball cap was sitting backwards on his head. But it was his eyes. His gaze was hot when he made his way over to me, not stopping until he was directly in front me, and I was backed against the wet truck. I struggled to remain angry, but it was hard because he was so close, and he smelled so good, he was making me light headed. He put his hands on the hood of the truck, trapping me. For long seconds, he just stared down into my eyes, and I couldn't deny the desire, the love I saw there, which stirred in my own chest, moving to my stomach and lower. I was so confused. But I *wanted* him.

"Why you do this, huh?" he asked, his baritone low.

"I'm not doing anything," I somehow managed.

He pressed closer so that we were touching. I tried to think.

"*Stop* it," he said, as if reading my mind. "Because you know what's real."

He looked down at me, and I inhaled when his gaze dropped to my mouth before he met my eyes again.

"It's me and you. Right?"

I couldn't move. I didn't want to.

"I don't need a bunch of 'likes' to validate what you are to me. That's not reality. *This* is reality. The way I love you... that's what's real."

My eyes were trained on his, my body warming at his words. I blinked and he bit his lip and shook his head.

"You drive me crazy," he murmured, leaning close and pressing his forehead to mine.

"Then we're crazy together," I admitted.

He kissed me then, all but demanding that I open for him, invading my mouth with his warm tongue. My back pressed into the cool truck and of their own accord, my arms wrapped around his neck, pulling him closer.

"I'm sorry," I whispered against his mouth just as he murmured that he loved me.

Our kiss wasn't slow this time. It was urgent and a little wild. He bit my bottom lip, holding it between his teeth, and I pushed my fingers through his hair, nearly knocking off his cap. He released it, focusing on my neck, murmuring that he loved me again. It was drizzling again and I looked up at the darkened sky as tiny drops of rain hit my eyelids, the coolness of the light rain contrasting Devin's hot mouth on my skin.

He bent low, lifting me and I wrapped my legs around his waist, kissing him hungrily. He got the creaky door open and pushed me inside, then climbed in right after me, slamming the door shut so that we were enclosed in the small space once more. The tablet playing on the dashboard was long forgotten.

I reached for him and he dragged me closer. Our touches were hurried and electric, and I couldn't get close enough, fast enough. I turned and climbed onto his lap, my leg sliding against the warm, cracked leather seats as Devin held me at the hips. He slid his arms around me, grabbing my butt and I rolled my hips into his erection, a soft moan escaping me as I wrapped my arms around his neck and angled my head the other way against his mouth, his facial hair brushing roughly against my skin, contrasting the feel of his tongue.

My back arched, brushing against the leather dashboard when he kissed his way down my sternum, between my breasts, impatiently pushing my dress down over my shoulders, exposing my pink lacey bra. My skin was still damp from the rain, and my heart rate doubled, along with the pulsing between my thighs. It wasn't the first time he'd seen me in my bra, especially over the past month. Everything we did together seemed to be more intense lately. His breath was hot against my already warm skin, when he kissed between my breasts and I moaned quietly, running my fingers over the back of his head.

"Let me take this off?" His voice low and strained as he reached around me and slid his fingers up my spine to my bra hook. His gaze was intense as he waited for an answer, his lashes practically brushing his cheek bones. He was so *sexy*. His fingers brushed against my bra hook again.

"I—" I stopped myself and nodded quickly, staring into his eyes as he expertly unhooked my bra, then slowly pulled it off, pushing one strap down over my shoulder, then the other, his rough fingers brushing over my skin. He tossed the cotton material onto the seat of the truck unseeingly as his gaze roamed from my lips, over my neck, to my breasts, heating me everywhere his eyes touched.

My heart felt as if it was about to pump out of my chest. We were shaded by the thick trees but I nervously looked out of the rain splattered window anyway, then back to Devin who was smiling, barely as he bit the corner of his lip.

"No one can see you except me."

He shook his head, his gaze on my exposed breasts. My nipples hardened under his attention, and I fought the urge to cover myself.

"*You're so beautiful,*" he murmured darkly, meeting my eyes, as he ran his thumb over my hip bones, and up, circling my pelvis, the small touch setting my already hot skin on fire. "I could just stare at you all night, no bullshit. And in this light too?" He shook his head, his eyes roaming freely over me in the dark truck cab.

I could feel his erection pressing against me intimately, even as my body heated, then softened at his words. The window was cracked, allowing the cool night air to circulate in the stuffy cab, filling it with its dewy, after nighttime scent, and I inhaled it through parted lips when Devin pulled the spoon from the nearly empty carton of ice cream.

I watched, wide-eyed as he touched the spoon to my left breast, circling my nipple. I jumped in his lap and my body jerked in response when the cold cream hit my skin. My nipple peaked painfully, and the air rushed from my lungs. Devin bit his lower lip, gauging my reaction as I met his eyes, then training his gaze on my breast, as he continued drawing on my skin with the spoon. My back arched and my breaths were coming rapidly, the moan that left my lips unfamiliar. Just as the ice cream threatened to drip, Devin dipped his head and his warm mouth was on me, sucking gently then harder, a low groan leaving his lips. *Oh my goodness.*

"*Devin...*" I gasped his name because it's the only thing I could think to say. My heart was racing so fast, my breath coming so quickly, the throbbing between my legs so fluid, I thought I might break apart.

I was moving now, rocking and grinding on his erection as he released my nipple before focusing his attention on the other one, his grip on my hips tight, his erection impossibly hard. I slid my arms up his defined biceps, over the tattoos that covered them, to his neck, running my fingers over the back of his head. My fingers threaded through his kinky curls as he flicked his tongue over my nipple. He groaned, low and deep, and it matched my moan. My dress was hiked up around my waist, the only barrier between us was my thin panties and Devin's sweats and I could *feel* him. I could only imagine what it would it be like when he was inside of me as I worked myself against his erection, especially when he slid his hand to my butt and squeezed.

"*Low, you're too much sometimes,*" he murmured, his voice strained, barely audible.

I had my first orgasm with Devin less than a week ago when we were messing around downstairs after his show at Jimmy's. Usually, I stopped us before things went too far but when Devin slid his fingers into my panties, I couldn't stop him and before I knew it, it felt like I was exploding from the inside out.

That time he'd groaned in my ear, "I wanna be inside you so bad, love," like he was tortured. I'd sat up on the couch, chest heaving, tempted to tell him okay, but he shook his head, biting on his lip as he sat up too.

"I'm gonna hop in the shower before I take you home," he'd told me.

I didn't get why. I was worried that maybe he could smell me, or something. But then when I told Jersey later, she'd laughed and shook her head at me. "You don't stink, Low, sheesh. Think about it." I furrowed my brow. "All I know is, I'm scrubbing the shower before I use it again. Gross." I figured it out then, and I felt stupid and naïve and very turned on at the thought of Devin imagining me in the shower.

I could feel another orgasm building now, coiling tight in the bottom of my stomach, stretching downward. My panties slipped to the side with my rocking and I could really feel him now. He grabbed my butt again, kneading it as he turned to bury his face in my neck, tonguing then kissing the skin there, his moans low but affecting. I pushed my nose into his skin, holding on tightly to his neck, my breathing ragged. I wanted him. I wanted *this*. I wanted—

"Willow?"

Mom?

"Willow?" It was a louder this time and we both stilled. "Willow, are you there?" It was definitely my mother's voice.

"Oh my gosh!" I mouthed, eyes wide.

"Shit," he whispered, his voice panicked. "*Shit*! Where's the phone, baby?"

"I dunno!" I whisper-screamed, looking around frantically.

I slapped at Devin's shoulder, trying to get him to move. "You're probably sitting on it!"

"Willow, are you okay? What's going on?" My mom's voice was muffled but I could tell she was about to get panicky.

Devin finally raised up and I grabbed the phone from under him, nearly dropping it before I caught it.

"Hey, mom!"

"What on earth is going on? It's almost 1 in the morning."

"Nothing, I just… I must've accidentally called you. On accident." I looked around frantically for my bra, as if my mom could see me through the phone, tapping Devin's shoulder again and pointing to where he'd thrown it on the seat. He shook his head and reached for it, handing it to me.

"Oh," my mom breathed, as I struggled to slip my arms back through the bra straps. "I thought something had happened. And then when I heard all of that noise in the background—where are you?"

"I'm at the park—"

"*The park*? This late?"

"I mean, I'm in the truck," I closed my eyes, trying to get my brain to work properly. "I'm with Devin. Hanging out."

"Oh," She grew quiet and I opened my eyes to see Devin shaking his head.

"How are you, Mrs. Harden?" Devin called out, sounding a lot less affected than me.

"I'm good, Devin. Y'all scared me for a minute with the late night call."

"I know, our fault." He shook his head again, his eyes on the phone. "Didn't mean to wake you."

"Okay, well now that I know Willow's alright, I'm going back to sleep."

"Tell Mr. Harden I said hello."

My mom let out a small laugh. "I'll do that. In the morning," she tacked on pointedly. Devin bit his lip and shook his head again, when he looked at me.

"Night, mom."

"Goodnight, daughter," she hesitated and I chewed on the corner of my lip. "Y'all be safe."

"Sorry," I whispered once I'd hung up with my mom, absolutely mortified.

Devin ran a hand over his head. "Your parents are gonna think I'm up here corrupting you."

I shook my head, burying my nose in his neck, inhaling him.

"They don't think that."

He shook his head again, looking out of the window.

"You ready to go? It's really starting to come down anyway."

How embarrassing. I nodded. "Okay."

15

WILLOW

BY THE TIME we pulled up to Travis' house, it was pouring rain.

"Ready to make a run for it?" Devin grinned at me and I nodded. We pushed out of the truck and I yelped, running to the protection of front porch as Devin fiddled with the keys. The house was quiet when we pushed inside, except for the low hum of the TV which was on in the living room, though nobody was there.

I felt Devin pressing against my back as I stepped further into the living room. He kissed the back of my neck. "You want anything from the kitchen?"

I shook my head, leaning back into him, instantly aroused again, especially when I felt him hard against my butt as he wrapped an arm around my belly.

"C'mon," he breathed against my neck, urging me toward his bedroom. I turned in his arms once I pushed open the door and he shut it behind us, locking it. We kissed our way to the bed, falling unceremoniously onto the rumpled sheets.

"Devin, wait." He stopped, lifting his head from my jaw, his chest heaving.

"I need the bathroom. And can I get a t-shirt?" He bit his lip, and released a breath, nodding.

"Yup."

I slid off the bed and he did too, walking to his dresser and pulling a t-shirt from his drawer for me, running a hand over his head.

"Thank you," I said, my fingers brushing his when I took the shirt from him. I slipped through the door and hurried across the hall to the bathroom. I closed the door, quickly pulling my dress off and slipping on his t-shirt after I used the toilet. I'd cleaned it the last time I was over so it didn't smell like pee and I felt comfortable sitting on the seat. I washed my face, staring at myself in the mirror for a long moment, when the sky suddenly crackled loudly and the lights went off, my reflection disappearing completely as the room was engulfed in darkness.

I hurried back across the hall, feeling in the dark for Devin's door knob and pushed it open just as he lit a candle. He looked up at me and grinned, his gaze roaming over me in his t-shirt.

"Power went out."

"I know. I couldn't see anything in the bathroom. I almost fell in the toilet."

He shook his head, laughing at me. His shirt was off now but I could see even in the dim light that his shoulders were really wet now.

"Why are you wet?"

"Ran back out to get the boombox," he answered, nodding toward where it was sitting on top of his dresser.

"Good call," I smiled, walking over to it and pressing play on the cassette, since it was battery powered. We'd been listening to The Isley Brothers and the music came drifting softly out of the speakers.

"It's hot in here already," he said, as he moved to crack open the bedroom window, his muscles flexing with the effort because sometimes it got stuck. It was still raining, though it had slowed down and I could instantly smell it, sweet and wet, floating into the room, pushed in by the gentle breeze outside.

I crossed the room and climbed into the bed, watching as he ran a hand over his head, before he pulled off his black undershirt, leaving on only his basketball shorts. He yawned, climbing into the bed and sliding under the blue sheets I'd bought him from Target last month because he literally didn't have one matching pair.

He reached for me, as I scooted toward him into his arms.

"Wait. Where's your phone? Make sure it's nowhere near here," he said, smirking so that his dimples peeked out.

"It's on your dresser."

"Good," he said, laughing as I hid my face in his chest, shaking my head.

"How do you always smell so good?" he asked, running his nose along my skin, to my collarbone. "You smell like coconuts and flowers and... life."

"Life?" I laughed again and shrugged, my eyes drifting closed, when he kept nuzzling his nose into my neck.

"My life," he clarified.

God, when he said things like that to me... I shifted even closer, sliding my leg between his and he wrapped his arms around me, running his fingers down my rib cage to my hip, before he slipped his hands under my t-shirt.

He paused and looked up at me when his hands grazed my butt. I wasn't wearing panties. His eyes were locked on mine when he squeezed my butt again, as if testing to see if underwear would magically appear.

I didn't say anything. We just stared at each other, the breath leaving my lungs in short spurts when Devin released a breath, somehow pulling me even closer against him. I tilted my head upward, pressing my lips to his.

The kiss was different. It felt heavier, more intense and meaningful. Devin kept his hands on my butt, almost as if he was afraid underwear was going to appear, running his hands from my lower back to just under my cheeks, as he kissed me, his tongue meeting mine in a hungry rhythm. I just wanted to be closer, and I rolled on top of him. He threaded his fingers through my hair, as he licked and nipped my lips, still holding on to my butt with his other hand.

I loved it when Devin kissed me like this, like he wasn't really in control any more, like he couldn't get enough of me. He tugged at my hair, making me angle my head the other way against his mouth, squeezing my butt as he pushed his body closer to mine, his groan low and deep when our pelvis' pressed together.

My heart was racing, the pulsing between my legs heavy and acute as I worked my hips against his erection, craving the friction. I felt his tongue against my neck, sending chill bumps across my skin, as he made a noise from deep in his throat.

He dipped his head, working his way down my jaw, to the underside of my chin, to my neck, biting then licking the skin there. He reached between us, sliding a finger against me.

My body constricted, jerked and then arched into his fingers. I gasped, biting Devin's shoulder when he slid his fingers up into me. I stilled, and he waited, his breaths heavy against my skin as he watched me adjusting to his fingers inside of me. My body relaxed and automatically, I rocked against his fingers. I could feel myself tensing, as he licked and kissed my neck.

"*Devin...*" I breathed his name on moan. I didn't know what I wanted beyond him. My breathing was coming in quick succession, like my muddled thoughts.

I started to push at the waistband of his shorts, without even thinking. It just felt like the natural thing to do. Devin slipped out, heavy and rigid, and I felt him, hard and warm against me as I worked my hips against his him.

"Damn, Low," he murmured closing his eyes, turning his face into my neck.

"Take them off," I whispered. He pushed his shorts all the way off, flinging them over the side of the bed.

I pulled at the bottom edge of my t-shirt, trying to take it off too, but he took over for me, sliding it up over my belly and chest slowly, his fingers grazing my skin. I moved my hips against his erection once it was off, he dipped his head, sucking hard on my left nipple, causing me to moan loudly, the sound forming its own rhythm around the music already playing. But I couldn't care less about how loud I was being. The only thing I could focus on was Devin, as I arched my body into his hot mouth. Abruptly, he rolled us over, the mattress denting with our shifting weight.

He lifted a little, his biceps flexing, his gaze traveling the length of my naked body. It was the first time a man had ever seen me naked and I willed myself not to fidget, because it was Devin looking at me, and I wanted him to. He ran his rough fingers down my side, over my rib cage to my hips, his touch reverent but possessive.

"You're so beautiful, Willow," he said, almost to himself, his words hitting my heart. He met my eyes, shaking his head. "You're like every fantasy I've ever had, times a hundred."

I could still feel him hard and insistent between my legs. My lips parted and I arched my hips up, reaching for him and guiding him toward my entrance. His eyes widened slightly and he chuckled a little, moving my hand from him, putting it around his neck instead. He stared down at me, his chest rising and falling quickly.

"You sure?" he asked, his voice deep and strained, affecting every part of me, as he hovered over me, balancing his weight on his forearms so he wouldn't crush me.

"Yes."

He reached over the side of the bed and grabbed his wallet, extracting a condom. I honestly wasn't even thinking about that, and my cheeks warmed a little at the thought that I'd been so careless. He was watching me as I lifted my head from the pillow so that I could see him roll it on. My heart was thudding when he lowered himself between my legs again.

I bit my lip and looked up at him and he touched his tongue to the corner of his mouth, his gaze hot. I tilted my head up and his mouth was on mine immediately. But instead of working his way down my body or pushing into me as I expected, he just... kissed me, languidly. Like he was communicating things with the kiss, our love, his intent for us.

His fingers were in my hair and he rubbed my scalp in slow circles, the motions almost mimicking our tongues. I feel could myself relaxing, even as my heart rate sped up, my body melting into his. Before long, we were starting to rock together, seeking friction from each other's bodies. Devin was cradling my head and I felt, desirable and protected, sexy and aware; of every touch, every breath as the rain pounded against the window outside, the music flowed through the hot bedroom, the strength in Devin's body, in his touch.

His mouth was on my neck now, teasing his favorite spot, just above my collar bone, his erection slick from the wetness between my legs. It felt different, incredibly arousing being completely naked with him. Natural. He whispered something I couldn't make out in my ear, his voice impossibly low, his hips rocking into me.

"*Devin*," I hummed pleadingly against his skin, so turned on I thought I might combust. He groaned, biting my neck, then kissing it, his body slick with perspiration because the air had cut off with the storm.

He raised up, meeting my eyes, positioning himself to enter me, his mouth pressed against mine, his breath hot against my lips. And I held my breath, wanting him so badly it was almost painful.

"I love you," he told me as he pushed into me.

"I love you too."

My body automatically tensed at the invasion. It was foreign and painful and I couldn't stop the whimper from leaving my lips as I squeezed my eyes closed, my entire body tensing.

"You okay?"

I opened my eyes.

"You want me to stop?" His voice was strained, his lids so low I could barely see his eyes.

"No, don't stop." I shook my head quickly.

His gaze was locked on mine and he waited, his chest heaving, giving me time to adjust to him inside of my body. The light from the candle was flickering over his handsome face and I saw him inhale, biting on his lower lip. He pressed a little further and I closed my eyes, grabbing his muscled back, tilting my head up toward the ceiling, trying to breathe. The fullness, the stretching *hurt* and I bit hard on my lip.

"Is it... Are you in?"

He shook his head, his lips brushing against mine. "No. It's just the tip, baby."

Good Lord.

"You want me to stop?"

I shook my head again.

"You have to relax, love. Relax your legs."

I wet my lips and nodded again, doing as he said, letting my legs fall open further, eyes on the ceiling. Perspiration was forming on my brow and Devin's muscled back was slick as I held it. I blinked and re-focused on his tattoo, the one that said "wait expectantly" noting the swirls and the lines there, trying to will myself calm.

"Hey," he whispered, drawing my gaze to his.

He brushed his nose against my mine, back and forth, as his thumbs worked slow circles against my scalp. His tongue dipped into my mouth and he kissed me unhurriedly, as if he weren't halfway inside of me, as if we had all the time in the world and he couldn't help *not* to. He pulled back a little, angling his head the other way, capturing my lips again, his tongue flicking against my lower lip, teasing but sensual, as he moved his hand down, palming my breast, lightly rubbing my nipple with his thumb.

I felt my muscles growing soft, felt myself getting even wetter, as I held onto Devin's broad shoulders, lifting my head off his flattened pillow so that I could better reach his mouth. He tasted so good, he was so *everything.* Our breaths were shallow but connected as we breathed together in the same rhythm as our tongues. The soft moan that left my lips connected with his deeper one. He sucked on my lower lip, and at the same time, pushed all the way inside of me.

At first I tensed at the full invasion, at the *pressure*. I could feel his chest heaving against my breasts as he stilled, his forehead pressed against mine, allowing me to adjust, pecking my lips over and over through the pain.

I moved a little and it hurt but not as badly. Devin took his cue from me, rocking into me slowly, and I tilted my head up again, my eyes drifting closed as I concentrated on our joining, gripping his back muscles tightly.

"*Ah, baby*," his voice was low and deep, the tone foreign, almost tortured, sending goosebumps scattering across my arms.

"I love you, Devin," I breathed.

The pain was subsiding, and Devin inside of me, *knowing* that he was inside of me... it was all melding together, and starting to feel good. Devin's strokes were slow and I could tell he was trying to control himself, from the tortured way he was biting his lip, the heaviness in his gaze. He kissed my neck, tasting my damp skin with his tongue. The breeze from the open window as soft, the light flickering calming orange in the distance, and my body softened even more as I ran my fingers through his hair, our bodies slick with perspiration.

My lips parted and I turned my head, seeking his mouth again. He touched his tongue to my bottom lip, sucking it gently, and I pulled at his back. He groaned, dropping his forehead against mine, and the deep sound that left his lips was different.

"I'm tryin' to make this good for you but you feel way too good," he breathed tightly shaking his head, his deep voice barely audible. "I can't believe how good you feel, Willow."

"I like the way you feel inside of me," I whispered.

He shook his head, pressing lips into my neck, emitting a low moan and I felt him jerk inside of me. He lifted his head, kissing me hungrily, as he moved just his hips, maintaining a leisurely, steady rhythm. It was starting to feel good. Really, really good.

Devin was whispering low and deep in my ear, and I felt my body began to pulse, pressure building low in my belly and spiraling downward. I was catching onto his languid rhythm and the pleasure was acute where we were joined.

Wow. I didn't realize I breathed the word aloud until he looked down at me, his eyes full of love and desire.

"I love you," he murmured.

I could feel wave upon wave building, gliding over my body.

"Devin," I breathed, eyes wide. I was coming out of nowhere, gripping his shoulders hard as I buried my face in his neck, then lifted my chin, eyes shut tightly as my body began to unravel, my moans loud, uncontrollable.

Devin moaned loudly too, his lips pressed to my ear, his grip on my hips strong as his body tightened and jerked with his release. I held onto his back, absorbing him, loving the feeling of him losing complete control inside of me.

For a while we just laid together, sweaty and spent, wrapped in each other. I turned my head and looked up into his eyes. He smiled at me and I felt it in my heart.

"I can't believe I actually had an orgasm my first time."

Devin opened his eyes and grinned at me lazily. "I can't believe I didn't come two seconds after I got inside of you."

He bit his lip and shook his head, running a rough hand absently down my bare hip as I giggled.

"I read that rarely happens for women. Like, one in a hundred. Everyone I know said it definitely didn't happen for them. Some women can't even orgasm while having sex period."

He looked at me, his eyes low. "I don't know any of those women."

"Devin!" I slapped at his shoulder and he grinned.

"For real. You read all that? Like, you sat there at your laptop with your little nose scrunched up and researched it?"

My cheeks warmed at the amusement in his eyes. "Shut up."

He grinned a little, and kissed my nose. "Know what I think?"

"What?" I asked warily.

"It was so good because it's *us*."

"Aquemini," I offered, matching his grin.

I slid my thigh between his and tilted my head up for a kiss. We were silent for a few seconds as I watched the light dancing off the walls before I looked at Devin again. His arm was folded underneath is head and he was lying on his back. The sheets were mismatched again because we'd pulled the others off. There was a little blood on them and I was embarrassed but Devin was so sweet about it, I almost felt silly being worried about it.

We'd showered together, in the middle of the night, with the power off, the only light coming from the candle we'd carried into the bathroom with us. When we showered together, it was the first time I'd ever done that too. The tub was really too small for both of us but we made it work. It was so sensual, as Devin let his fingers glide over my soapy skin in between kisses. Then later, we shared a turkey sandwich in bed.

We were lying in bed now, me in one of his undershirts and him in a pair of gray boxer briefs. It had to be at least four in the morning and my eyelids were growing heavy, but the question popped into my mind, so I had to ask.

"How old were you when you lost your virginity?"

Devin opened his eyes and looked at me.

"I know you said you were young—and you told me all about Angel Jackson with the 'big breasts' from your ninth grade geometry class—"

"I said 'big titties' not 'breasts,'" he corrected, mimicking me. I rolled my eyes and he chuckled.

"Seriously. How old were you exactly?

"Why does it matter?"

"I'm just curious."

He bit his lip then released it, expelling a breath. "Eight."

My eyes rounded and I lifted my head from the pillow. *"Eight?"*

"Lay back down, baby." He said, reaching and pushing his fingers through my hair.

"With who? How is that possible?"

"My babysitter." My mouth dropped open.

"How old was she?" I asked the question tentatively and he shrugged, as if it were no biggie.

"I dunno. Thirteen, fourteen maybe."

I stared at him, aghast.

"Devin... that's like, it's... sexual abuse."

He shook his head, smirking.

"Nah. It wasn't like that. I didn't know what the hell was going on, obviously. But... nah," he shook his head again. "It wasn't like *abuse*."

The room was quiet as I tried to even out my breaths, to keep the alarm I felt at bay.

"Baby, you were eight," I said quietly. "Too young to give consent. You couldn't have even known what the word 'consent' even meant."

"I'm not messed up about it," he said calmly, probably reading my horrified expression. "It was what it was. I didn't even completely get what really went down until later. I just knew we weren't supposed to be doing it because she kept looking at the bedroom door. I remember I had this huge poster of wolverine hanging on the back of the door. One of those floor to wall joints." His eyes were far away as he talked and I studied his profile. "I kept looking at his claws. That's what I remember most. His claws."

He bit the inside of his lip, his eyes narrowed. I sat in stunned silence for a long second.

"Did you keep the poster?"

He grinned. "Nah. Got into Black Panther a little while after that."

"What'd your mom say about what happened?"

"Nothin." He reached for the water sitting on the floor next to the mattress. "I ain't tell her no shit like that," he said, swallowing, before handing the glass for me to drink. "She woulda flipped."

"Did it... did it ever happen again?" I gave him the glass and he sat it back on the floor.

"Nah. Just that one time."

I released another slow breath, trying to digest the information he'd just shared. I looked up at him and he pressed a wet kiss to my temple, offering me a lopsided grin.

"I'm not messed up about it, Low. I get it... I get what it means now. But I'm good. I actually haven't even thought about her in years."

"Something like that happened to me before," I admitted.

"Something like what?" He stilled completely. His voice was alarmed and his brow was furrowed, eyes suddenly alert.

"Not *that*. Just... my older cousin. He was like, a teenager, maybe 17. But this one time, when I was maybe six, he sat me on his lap and he..." I shook my head; memories had me fidgeting the sheets. "I don't remember much. I just remember the *feeling* more than anything. That something bad was happening. He just kind of humped me while I was sitting on his lap."

"You tell anyone?" Devin asked, his eyes on me, voice gruff.

"I told my dad. I don't know what he did—they say he roughed him up or something. You know my dad was way older so I don't know how true that is. I just know I barely saw my cousin after that. I always felt a little bad. Like, I divided the family or something. My dad's side of the family was small and we didn't see them a lot anyway. Even less after that."

Devin kissed my forehead heaving a sigh.

"That ain't on you, Low. I'm just glad you actually told."

I lay still, staring at the candle bouncing off the walls.

"That was not good after love-making talk," I said after a few seconds.

"Messin' with you, I know to expect some random shit," Devin returned, grinning as he pulled me closer.

I was quiet for long minutes, sleeping hovering over me but not pulling me under completely.

"I feel different," I murmured, my lips brushing his skin when I talked. He was running his finger lightly up and down my spine. "Not more connected to you but different connected to you. Is that normal?"

"Normal is relative," Devin answered without opening his eyes, his baritone husky with sleep. "But this is new for me too."

I opened my eyes then, and arched a brow, smirking. "It's 'new' for you?"

His eyes were low when he opened them.

"I ain't ever been with anyone I was in love with before."

I smiled up at him and he pressed a kiss to the bridge of my nose, pulling me even closer, so that I was completely wrapped in him.

"I wonder if—"

"*Shhh....*" He whispered. "Wonder it tomorrow and take your ass to sleep, baby."

"Don't 'shhh' me, Devin! That's so rude!"

He laughed, opening his eyes. I sighed, twisting my lips and he rolled his eyes.

"What, Low Low? What do you wonder, baby?"

"How long we have to wait to do it again."

His grin was slow and he bit the corner of his lip. "You're too much. You know that?"

I looked up at him.

"I'm not gonna be able to leave you alone," I whispered, pressing a kiss to his neck, sliding my hand up his chest, even as a sleepy haze finally descended on me.

"I hope you never do."

BACK THEN: 6 MONTHS LATER

16

DEVIN

"LOW LOW, YOU GOTTA GET UP."

Nothing. The lump in the bed didn't move.

"Willow." I touched her shoulder, partly because I couldn't see her head. It was buried underneath my comforter.

"Baby, you gotta get up." I shook her shoulder this time, and she finally stirred, blinking up at me sleepily. I smiled, even with tired eyes and her hair wrapped in up in a red sleep rag thing, she was gorgeous. Just stupid pretty. My gaze dropped to her full lips before meeting her eyes.

"It's almost 3:30."

She blinked heavily again. "Already? Shoot."

The fact that she was wearing her nighttime hair tie meant she was serious as hell about that nap. "You're gonna be late."

I sat down on the edge of the rumpled bed, searching for my shoes. It was mid-afternoon but it'd been cloudy all day. The light trying to stretch its way through the window was muted, casting a soft blue-ish glow over the room because Low insisted on buying me blue curtains a couple of months ago.

"It adds dimension to the room," she told me. I didn't care about curtains but they did make the room look more relaxing, I couldn't lie.

Marvin Gaye was playing on my record player and I grinned because Low had finally really gotten into the warm sound of vinyl after fighting me about being "old school."

She yawned and rolled onto her back and tucked her arm underneath her head, like she didn't need to be at the airport in Dallas by 5:30 to catch her flight home.

"I have a little time. It only takes an hour and half to get to Dallas and my flight doesn't leave until seven."

I shook my head, eyeing my shoe underneath her backpack. Other than her bag in the floor, the room was clean and airy, because of Low. It was so comfortable, I felt like crawling into bed with her and crashing too.

"You're pushing it," I told her instead. "You still gotta get dressed and you know what an event that is." She wasn't wearing anything except my old red Hawks t-shirt. "I don't want your dad thinking I'm the reason you missed your flight home."

Willow sighed audibly when her phone buzzed on the bed next the pillow. She picked it up, squinted at the screen, and tossed it back onto the blue comforter.

"My mom," she answered my unspoken question. "I just didn't want to talk to her while I was over here."

"What's up with that?" I met her eyes, brow furrowed.

"She thinks I'm 'playing house' with you because I'm over here so much."

"Since when did she say that?"

Willow shrugged, pulling off her hair thing and tossing it onto the bed. "The other week. She says she doesn't know why they pay for me to live on campus when I really live over here."

I bit the inside of lip, my gaze scanning the room. Willow's books were on the small desk she insisted on getting for me. Her clothes took up practically half of my closet space. One of my dresser drawers now belonged to her and her soaps and girly whatnots were in the bathroom shower rack. But I liked it that way. I wanted her near, all the time.

We hadn't spent a single day apart in months and I was kinda tripping because I really didn't want her to leave now, even though I knew she needed to see her fam for the Thanksgiving holiday. She was flying in to Houston a little earlier though, since she'd be coming into Atlanta the day after Thanksgiving to be with me. Our new manager, Jay Little, had three shows lined up out there--- Friday, Saturday and Sunday. Trav was still hesitant about buddy but these gigs proved he was ready to handle us, in my opinion. Plus, I was looking at what he was doing with another band out of Atlanta, Black Bottom. They were blowing up and had just brought him on as their manager a few months before.

Doing the gigs in Atlanta was big but I also wanted to check for my moms and Omar, see how they were doing. Moms finally landed a job, not where she wanted, but it was something at least, working in the cafeteria at Omar's middle school. But the gap between unemployment and her finding work left them in a tight spot. And her punk ass landlord went up on her rent. I'd been sending money when I could but my paper was low too.

"Can you give Kennedy back her headphones for me?" I looked down at Willow, who yawned and stretched again. She worked the early shift at Aroma today, the coffee shop near campus where she started at the beginning of the semester.

"Where are they?"

"On your dresser somewhere I think. Or maybe in your truck?"

She twisted her lips, thinking. "You're bad as Jersey, losing other people's stuff."

"They're not lost!

"But you don't know where they are."

"They're somewhere near here. I do know that." She smiled, as I absently rubbed her calf, since she still hadn't made a move to get up. "Oh my gosh, last night she was *amazing*, right?"

Kennedy joined the band as a singer at the beginning of the semester, when she moved to Tyler to stay with her grandma Pepper, Trav's neighbor from the down the street. Kennedy changed everything when she joined Prototype. Zay elevated the band when he'd joined. But Kennedy *completed* it. She'd changed Travis too, because dude was in love with her on some "alter my entire existence" type shit. Buddy actually told me that the other day, and was dead ass serious.

"She's next level. She's startin' to get why she's dope, which is the key. You can't just be good. You need to know what separates you from everyone else so that you can lean into it."

Willow's eyes were lowered when she looked at me and she tugged at the bottom hem of my t-shirt.

"I love it when you talk like that."

"Like what?"

"Like all..." she shrugged grinning. "Devin-y. I'm gonna get t-shirts made with your quotes."

She bit her lip, still smiling at me. I knew that look in her eyes and I grinned, my groin tightening because that look, coming from Willow Elizabeth Harden, was better than any high I'd ever known.

"What's up?" I asked, letting her pull me toward her by the hem of my shirt, wrapping me in her coconut scent.

"We have a few minutes," she breathed, against my lips. She bit hers, then released it.

"Nah, we don't, love."

She nodded against my mouth, "We do," she whispered, reaching and wrapping her arms around my neck, pressing her mouth against mine, her tongue tracing the seam of my lips, making me uncomfortably hard.

She pulled back suddenly, and in one quick motion, pulled her t-shirt over her head. Her eyes were still on me, her cheeks flushed because she was still brand new and getting used to her body, and to me looking at her body. But she liked it.

"We do," she said again, as she kneeled on the bed in nothing but a pair of purple underwear. The afternoon light creeping through the blinds left a zigzag pattern on her belly that I traced with my fingertips. I bit my lip shaking my head as I took her in. *Damn.*

"You better look and see what time the next flight is."

She wasn't going to miss her flight, because I sped the entire way into Dallas. We were driving her car, because I knew my truck wouldn't make it. I really wanted to stay in the bed and play around with her for the rest of the day. See how many times, and how many different ways I could get her to moan my name.

We didn't get to do that a lot—just kick it—between our schedules. Willow took over the dance team back in August, at the beginning of the semester, when they ousted buddy with the blue hair. They had try-outs and I made a beat for her to dance to—a socca rhythm with a little bit of jazz flavor- crazy as that sounds. It worked for what she did though—really she brought the music to life, she was so dope. But now between dance, working at the coffee shop and school, her schedule was tight like mine.

"So, I'll see you in a few days," she was saying as she dug through her oversized bag that was sitting on the floor in between her spandex clad legs. She'd put on a long-sleeved dress and boots that stretched up her legs and made her thighs look thicker. I couldn't help but reach and put a hand there, and she looked up and smiled at my touch.

"My performance isn't until six in the evening and if you drive down by like four, you'll be good."

I drew in a breath, as I switched lanes, trying to figure out how I was going to hit her with the news I'd been dodging telling her for the past few hours.

"What's wrong?" I hadn't realized her eyes were even on me as I glanced over at her, touching my tongue to the corner of my mouth. It was almost like I could still taste her there from earlier. I sighed inaudibly.

"I'm not gonna be able to make your performance, baby."

She inhaled sharply and the sound hit me hard in the chest.

"We gotta gig Thanksgiving night at Jimmy's."

For a long second, she was silent, which was way worse than when she got all squeaky loud and started talking double-time.

"What do you—" She shook her head. "This performance has been planned for weeks, Devin."

"I know. But Jimmy wants us Thanksgiving night."

She shook her head, biting her lip as she turned toward the window before looking at me again.

"You know how big this is for me, how hard I worked on it." I glanced at her, picking at my hair. "I didn't just choreograph our group's performance. I planned the entire program."

"I know, love."

She turned to look at me, her gaze defeated, angry. "You don't even *like* Jimmy. You've been complaining about performing there forever, about how it's a waste of your time because you've outgrown the venue."

"The crowd is probably gonna be at capacity. It's more exposure."

She shook her head again. "It's not just me that's gonna be disappointed. This is the second Thanksgiving in a row you've missed. My mom and dad are expecting you and—"

"I talked to your dad earlier already and told him."

Her head snapped up. "What?"

I switched lanes, pulling off the exit to the airport.

"So, my dad knew about this before I did? Unbelievable," she muttered to herself. "And I guess I'm the immature and spoiled one for giving a crap about you being there for me and supporting *me*."

"You know I support you, Low. Every show I can make I'm there."

"Yeah, and how many has that been this year, Devin? Two?"

I bit my lip, eyes on the road.

"You know things are picking up for us now, since Kennedy joined the band. That means more gigs. We ain't in the position to turn opportunities down."

"And what you do is more important than what I do."

"I ain't say that," I glanced at her, one hand on the wheel. "But you don't even know what you want to do for real, still. I do. And I'm doing it...so..."

Her lips parted and I heard her sharp intake of breath. "You can be such an *asshole* sometimes."

"An asshole?"

She was glaring at me when I looked over at her.

"I declared a major this year. Theater arts with a minor in communications. You don't have to throw it up in my face that my life isn't perfectly mapped out like yours."

"What are you talking about? That ain't what I said or meant, and you know it. And my shit isn't mapped out. I have a vision that I have to work and sacrifice for otherwise I won't have *shit*—nothing real to fall back on. My parents don't give me a monthly stipend."

She gasped but I didn't stop.

"I don't have 'spending money' or a house to go home to in case this shit fails. My moms just moved into a *one bedroom* apartment and is sleeping on the damn living room couch, working two jobs and going to school." Willow's cheeks were red when I took my eyes off traffic to look at her. "It's all on me. So, if I gotta miss one of your shows to get to this money, to get to the level I need to be at, then that's what has to happen."

I glared at the passing traffic. There was still so much shit she just *didn't get*. Low's mouth was fixed in a tight line, her hands clutched in her lap when I looked at her. I shook my head.

We'd made it to the airport parking and I was barely able to put the car into park before she hopped out, slamming the door shut. I sighed and took her heavy bag from her when she acted like she was going to carry it herself. We were silent the entire way into the airport, watching harried passengers lug bags to the check-in counters or kiosks. Low stayed typing on her phone the entire time, refusing to look at me.

"I'll see you later. Have a good show," she said, barely looking at me when she was checked in and it was time for her to go through security.

"Low." I grabbed her elbow.

"*What?*" She turned to face me, her eyes full of disappointment and hurt, making my chest feel like someone was squeezing it with a vice.

"C'mon. Don't leave like this." She shook her head and looked at the ground, stepping aside for a family that passed by her in the security line.

I stepped closer to her, pulling her by the bottom hem of her jacket. I pushed a strand of her curly hair behind her ear, pressing my forehead to hers.

"You know I would be there if I could. I love you."

She closed her eyes, shaking head against mine.

"Can you tell you me you love me too?"

"You know I do," she breathed as I pressed my lips against hers. She pulled away, heaving a breath.

"Call me when you land."

She said nothing.

"Low."

"Okay, alright. I will."

She nodded, staring at me for a long second before releasing another breath, and making her way through the crowd.

Sweat dripped down my forehead. I pulled a towel from my back pocket and wiped my face with it. We'd just finished our set at Jimmy's and it was one of our best shows in a while. But the agitation I felt before I got on stage and drowned in the music returned the second I released the sticks. And then I had to deal with Jimmy about our money, again. It was time for us to bounce. We'd outgrown the club, that was more obvious every time we performed.

"What's up with you?" Bam asked, opening his water bottle and taking a long swallow.

"This is some bullshit," I told him irritably, nodding at a girl who passed by and waved. I was leaning against the bar, not really wanting to be there but I didn't want to go home to an empty house either. "Nobody wants to be dealing with Jimmy's shit every time we're here. We shoulda just skipped this shit and just did the Atlanta shows like I said."

I thought about Willow, who had her performance a couple of nights before. The one I missed to be here for this bullshit. Our crowd was thick and responsive but Jimmy's dumb ass made it not worth it, making us hound him about getting our money right.

"We're done with this as soon as our residency is up," I told Bam. "You need to talk to Trav because he ain't hearin' me."

"Trav is dealin' with a lot. He ain't hearin' nobody right now."

"Except..." I nodded my head toward Kennedy, who was talking with Jersey and her sister, Cassie, who'd just come in town the day before. Travis thought his ex, Maya, was pregnant, or pretending to be pregnant until she wasn't. And Kennedy was mad at him, and then she wasn't and then she was again, and it was just a bunch of fuckery he needed to handle.

"This ain't an episode of *Unsung*. He's on that bullshit right now."

Bam looked at me and shook his head. "You need to cool out, D. We'll be finished with this spot soon enough. Have some patience, my dude."

"There's a difference between having patience and sitting around waiting for more dumb shit to happen, like you ain't got control over your life."

"Why you be so charged all the time?"

I rolled my eyes because Bam was as annoying as Zay with that Yoda-shit.

"Whatever. I'm out man," I said giving him dap. I grinned. "You better pull up on Cassie before one of these corn balls in here gets to her."

He laughed, and I nodded toward where she was standing toward the middle of the dance floor, before pushing my way through the crowd, head down, because I didn't feel like being bothered.

"You leaving?"

I almost made it. It was Nikitta, hovering by the entrance of the club. She looked up when she saw me and stepped away from the girl she was talking to. She didn't work the door for us any more really but still popped up at our shows occasionally. I knew she was still in town over the break because she was from Tyler.

"Yep. About to lay it down."

Her eyes flickered when I said that, and I pulled in a breath.

"You guys were awesome tonight. I love your new sound, since you added the other singer."

"Kennedy. Yeah, she's dope."

"You're still my favorite though." She smiled, her eyes saying more than her words.

I ran a hand over my head. "You been good though?"

She nodded, offering me one of those forced smiles you give someone when you have shit to get off your chest but the time isn't right to do it. I hoped that time never came around. Nikitta was good peoples and when I fell back from her, I did it with no real explanation, though she figured out what was up when Low started showing up at our shows all the time, and it was obvious I was with her. 'Kitta didn't even trip. Didn't call me out, ask what was up, she just... adjusted.

"Thanksgiving was cool?" I asked.

"Oh yeah, I was extra greedy. I ate until I couldn't anymore." She patted her flat belly and I grinned.

"How was yours?"

"It was cool. Chilled out with Kennedy's grandma and everyone before heading up here."

She nodded, looking down at the ground, the silence awkward.

"I'mma catch up with you later though," I told her. She nodded quickly, shifting her weight, offering me another forced smile.

"Bye, Devin."

I pushed open the door into the night air. The blast of cold didn't do anything for my attitude and I shrugged into my hoodie, making my way toward my truck, happy as hell I drove tonight. I was tempted to call Low again but I'd just talked to her less than an hour ago, after I saw a picture of her posted up with Jaden like they were going to the prom or some shit. He was home for the holiday too and I knew Low posted that shit to get under my skin.

"He wanted to come to my show to support. What was I supposed to tell him?" She'd asked me indignantly. *"Besides we're just friends. He brought his girlfriend too."*

I knew buddy supposedly having a "girlfriend" ain't mean shit. But I wasn't trippin' on ol' dude. Not really. His Poindexter ass was standing too close to her, looking too happy to be there, but it was really *us* that had me messed up. We talked everyday she was in Houston, but it wasn't enough. I missed my baby.

I called her again after I got the house and took a shower. I pretended like I was gonna be able to make some music happen downstairs but gave up on that and lit a joint instead, falling into the empty bed as I dialed Willow. My sheets smelled like her.

"Devin?"

Who else would it be?

"You sleep?"

"A little bit." Her voice was low and sexy and I rubbed my hand down my chest, grazing the top of my waist band. I closed my eyes, imagining her close, pressed against me, and took a pull from the joint.

"How're you little bit sleep?"

"Are you calling to yell at me again?"

"I never yell at you."

"Well, fuss with me?"

I grinned. So adorable. "Nah. Just needed to hear you." I blew out the smoke silently. "Wish you was here. Wish I was there."

"You had priorities." Her voice was soft but she was still mad. I sighed.

"You still comin' to Atlanta tomorrow, right?"

There was a long pause and I opened my eyes, staring up at the darkened ceiling fan.

"Yes, Devin," she finally answered. "Because *I'm always* there for *you*."

"Baby..."

"I'm going to sleep now." I shook my head.

"Aight." At least she answered and was talking to me without squealing. I looked up at the ceiling fan again. "I love you, Low Low."

"Yeah, okay. Thanks." She hung up.

I laid there, staring at the phone for a minute, before pushing out a humorless chuckle. I took another pull from my joint, put it out and took my ass to sleep.

I half-expected her not to show up. When she came up the long escalator to baggage claim at Hartsfield-Jackson Airport, I felt a wave of relief. She spotted me and her face broke into a wide grin, and instantly all that shit that was between us was squashed, right there in her smile.

She was still smiling when she half-jogged over to me, and jumped into my arms, like one of those corny movies she was always watching. She dropped her shoulder bag to the ground, wrapping both arms around my neck and I caught her, like always.

"What up, Sweet N low," I asked her, grinning and pecking her lips, inhaling her sweet scent. She tasted like sunshine and honey too. She kissed my mouth over and over again, and that space in between my chest in my heart got a little relief because she was with me again. She pulled back from my mouth.

"I'm still mad at you," she warned me, biting her lip, giving me her Bambi glare. I smiled.

"I can deal with that, long as you're here."

She rolled her eyes, and grinned, and I kissed her again.

17

WILLOW

"THEY'RE FEELIN' it tonight, huh?"

I glanced over at Jay Little, The Prototype's new manager, who was sitting next to me, beer in hand. He'd just started working with the group a couple of months ago, and booked the weekend of shows in Atlanta. We'd become fast friends, partly because I handled a lot of their schedule before. He said he was impressed that I'd handled all of that for them. But I did it for Devin because it helped him not be so stressed, and he already had a lot on his plate.

"They feel it every night, I think. But yes, this is... the music *feels* different."

He bobbed his head in agreement. Jay Little was handsome, though not in an obvious way. His hair was grown out into kinky curls and he dressed like he belonged in the music industry— his outfits always cool but casual. The sleeves on his black Henley were rolled up, revealing tattoos up and down his forearms. But he was smart, I could tell that right off the bat. And he believed in Prototype, whole heartedly, I could tell that too.

I was seated at a bar table near the front of the stage, choosing to be out in the crowd for once, instead of backstage while Prototype performed. Devin's overprotective self wouldn't have went for that if

Cassie and Jay weren't here too, especially since we were in Atlanta and not Tyler.

Cassie had just excused herself for backstage but I wanted to stay out in the crowd and experience the show. It was their last one of the weekend, in Star Bar, and even though the small venue wasn't at capacity, the energy in the crowd was infectious, electric, and alive. Some people were mouthing the words as they sang "Come Undone". Even the people who didn't know it had their eyes closed, as they bobbed along to the mellow, wavy bassline, vibing with the song's energy.

My eyes fell on Devin again. He was in the zone tonight, even though his t-shirt was still on, for once. His eyes were closed and he was biting his lower lip, his entire body moving to the rhythm, his hands moving in sequence that was nothing less than brilliant. I *loved* watching Devin play, especially when he was feeling it the way he was tonight. He made me feel high too, just watching him. He was the core of Prototype. The foundation of the band, setting the tempo—deciding whether the energy was going to be smooth and infectious or aggressive and affecting.

I took another sip of my drink, a peach margarita that Devin ordered for me before they went on.

"Their *sound,*" Jay shook his head, taking a swig of his beer. We had to yell to be heard over the music. "First time I ever heard them on one of those YouTube videos, I knew I had to hear more. I got chill bumps watching them. Same way I felt the first time I heard Prince 'Controversy' or Amy Winehouse 'Back to Black' or Erykah Badu's 'Didn't Cha Know.' It's old school but not. It's new but familiar. This is what music should be about."

He leaned in and nodded toward the crowd that was gathered in front of the stage, wholly engaged in the show.

"Look at them, Low. Look at their reaction. They're completely absorbed." I did as he said, my gaze falling on individuals who were completely wrapped up in the music that was filling the space, affecting everything. "And they don't even have a full album out yet. This is... I dunno. We're watching something special here, Low Low."

I nodded, my heart racing as Devin tapped in the final song, ready to end the show. Jay was right and it was exciting to witness.

Thirty minutes later the show was wrapped and the band was standing around, talking to the people who'd flocked to them. Devin was the center of attention. It wasn't just me he drew like a magnet. He just had that thing that famous people had. They all did, really. I watched as a couple of girls approached him, gawking. He flashed them his dimpled grin and one of them laughed, throwing her head back, in a way that made her boobs push out more.

"C'mon," Jay spoke up, climbing off the stool where we'd been talking. "Lemme get you another drink."

I eyed Devin for a second longer, then nodded, following Jay toward the bar area, which was lit up with a string of soft yellow lights lining the counter tops, deep blues and yellows illuminating the liquor behind the bar. I was happy to hang with Jay.

"Gotta have tough skin to deal with a personality like Devin, huh?" Jay said conversationally, once the bartender, a beefy guy with long locs that hung to his waist, gave us our drinks.

I shrugged and grinned. "He's always telling me that, actually. 'You gotta be tougher than some girl liking a picture on Instagram, Low Low'," I mimicked.

Jay laughed. "I tell my girl the same. This music business, it's just a completely different lifestyle," he said. "So many of our business interactions are in social settings—it can get easy to blur that line, you know? That's what my girl struggles with the most. And she's gorgeous, like you." My face warmed but he said it matter-of-factly. "I know there's people all up in her ear. People that don't know anything about us and what we have going on."

I nodded and sighed, eyes on Devin. Sometimes picking through everything, all the advice and opinions was too much. Jay was right, there were always people telling me this and that. But when I was with Devin, when it was just me and him, I knew what I felt in my heart was right. There's just no way we could feel so real together and it *not* be right.

"That's that artist charisma," Jay supplied, accepting another beer from the bartender, nodding toward Devin as he talked animatedly to some dude. "It's a gift when he wants the attention. A curse when he doesn't wanna be bothered."

I laughed because that was Devin. His moods switched like lightening. One second he was loving the attention, the next he was ready to go and isolate himself with his music or just lay in complete silence while I rubbed his head. I loved those moments with him. The ones where it felt like I was his solace, like I was the one thing in his life besides music that made him feel like himself.

"But I see it..." I told Jay, turning away from Devin. "I see them doing shows in Paris and arena tours, and the Grammys. But staying connected to their core base. The people who love *real* music." I thought about our argument on the way to the airport. Devin's constant talk about "sacrifices," and took another sip of my drink.

"You got the vision," Jay said, nodding, grinning at me appreciatively. "That's what I see for them too. Them and Black Bottom. Two young black bands with completely different sounds, pushing the culture forward."

I smiled. Music people, the ones who thought beyond the money aspect were always using phrases like "push the culture forward." Everything was about "the culture." All I ever had to do to fit in was say something about "the culture" and their eyes lit up.

"What's good with you?" Devin slid up out of nowhere, wrapping a hand around my waist from behind, pressing his body into mine. I looked up at him and he smiled down at me, pecking my lips. He eyed my drink and raised his brows.

"I'm not drunk, I'm nice," I offered, using Devin's catch phrase. He shook his head and Jay laughed, giving Devin dap and congratulating him on the show.

We all hung out for another hour so before everyone else went to the house that Jay rented for his artists. We were leaving early in the morning to get back to Tyler because me, Devin and Zay had class. Well, Zay and I had class. Devin probably wouldn't go.

"You sure you don't wanna stay at the house again with everyone else?" he asked again, as we made our way into the cold night air to Devin's mom's car, which she was letting him use while she was in town.

"Moms' spot..."

"Only has one bedroom, I know, you've told me that like, a

hundred and three times. But Omar is at his dad's so your mom will take his room and we can pow wow in the living room."

We'd stayed the last night at Jay Little's but Devin understandably wanted to spend some more time with his mom before he headed back to Texas. We'd dropped our stuff of over there earlier, but we'd only stayed for like, five minutes before Devin pushed me back out of the door.

"Unless..." I frowned, looking up at him, as we made our way across the parking lot. "Do you not want me to stay with you?"

"Nah, it ain't that."

"Okay then. Stop trippin." I smiled up at him, blinking hard because he was a little blurry.

He grinned but I could tell even through the liquor in my system that it didn't meet his eyes, so I grabbed his hand, running my thumb over his Gemini tattoo in between his thumb and pointer finger.

"You should get this changed," I suggested as we paused so that he could open the passenger door for me.

"Oh yeah?" he asked, looking down at me, grinning a little, probably because he thought I was endlessly amusing when I'd been drinking.

"You should make it the Aquemini symbol."

He smirked and leaned down, pecking my lips before helping me into the car.

The apartment was quiet when we entered it twenty minutes later, and it smelled a little like bug spray that was covered up by candles and air freshener. I overheard Devin's mom telling him that the neighbors had roaches, so they had roaches, earlier. She said she was going to bomb the house again after we left.

"I'm so tired of this, man," Devin said, his voice low as they talked in the kitchen and I pretended to be engrossed in my phone in the living room. The sound of his voice, the *defeat* in his voice, was so unlike him, so foreign I had to sit on my hands and make myself not go into the kitchen, or cry. I *hated* for him to feel that way.

"It's temporary," his mom said. Devin said something else but his voice was low and I couldn't make out the words, only the rumble of his baritone. After that, they both came out acting like nothing was wrong, though I did notice that Devin picked my bag up off the living room floor and sat it on the dining room table.

I sat down on the worn beige and blue couch now, and Devin flicked on the small end table lamp, pulling his wallet out of his pocket and setting it next to it. Nothing in the small apartment matched and I knew that his mom was only able to bring less than half of their stuff from the house they'd moved out of after their landlord went up on the rent.

"Did you wanna use the shower first?"

His baritone was quiet, so as not to wake his mom. She'd come to the show yesterday and danced the entire time with Omar, who they snuck in even though he was only 14. His mom knew all the lyrics to every single song too. But she had to work early in the morning so she had to skip tonight.

"You can go ahead," I said nodding toward the food we'd stopped and got on the way over. "I'm starving."

He grinned, making his way over to our bags that were sitting on the small, square dining room table and pulling out some clothes, as I unwrapped my burger and sat down in the chair next to the table, digging in.

"It ain't goin nowhere, baby," he said, laughter in his voice as he looked down at me, brows raised.

I smiled as I chewed, wiping my mouth with a napkin I pulled out of the paper bag, too hungry and buzzed to care about how greedy I looked. I held up the burger for him to have a bite, still grinning.

His gaze skirted over my face as he chewed.

"You're a cool ass chick."

"Duh."

He chuckled and shook his head, brushing a finger over my nose before heading to the bathroom and shutting the door.

An hour later I stepped out of the steaming bathroom, peering down the dark hallway. The apartment was small, to the left of the bathroom was the bedroom and to the right was the living room which was connected to a small boxed shaped dining room, with a small patio. To the right of that was the rectangular kitchen.

I crept into the living room, which was now dark, except for the light of the TV. I looked around, finally spotting Devin sitting in a chair on the patio. I pulled the sliding glass door open and was immediately greeted by the cold, November air. He looked up, smiling at me, nodding his head for me to join him. I was wearing his Prototype hoodie, and I pulled it up over my head, sliding the door shut behind me. He pulled me down onto his lap and grabbed a blanket, which was sitting in the empty chair next to him.

For a while we just sat quietly, watching the nighttime activity of the parking lot. There wasn't much, only a few cars occasionally pulling in and out of the small spaces. Devin took a hit of the joint he'd just lit and I felt him exhale against my back, as I turned my head into his neck, nuzzling my lips against his skin, inhaling the fragrant smell of the weed. I felt a little floaty and relaxed. Maybe I had a contact high.

"The Maldives," he said, his baritone deep. He exhaled, the smoking lingering in the air, then licked the tip of his finger and put the joint out.

"Santorini, Greece," I said, smiling, resting my head against his shoulder, looking up at the dark, cloudless sky.

"Cape Town," he said, his facial hair scratching the side of my jaw, when he pressed a light kiss there, his thumb beating a rhythm against my thigh.

"Lagos, Nigeria," I offered.

We were naming things or places on our bucket list, a game we played sometimes, usually when we were lying in bed together, our brains quiet, breathing and feeling each other. Last summer, when they did a six-date west coast tour, was the first time Devin had been anywhere other than Georgia or Texas.

"Colombia."

"Fiji," I said. "Maybe I can help Jay book a show for y'all there."

He grinned, pressing a kiss to my jaw, his hand sliding under the blanket and my hoodie, until his rough fingers grazed my abdomen, drawing slow circles on my skin that I felt everywhere.

"Italy," I said, inhaling when his thumb skated under my breast.

"Jamaica," he said, his voice low in my ear. His had dipped further down, and my lips parted, eyelids growing heavy as he touched me over my cotton shorts.

"Where the water is so clear you can see the white sand on the bottom of the ocean floor," I said, breathlessly as Devin touched me, his fingers moving in slow, arousing circles. I opened my legs a little more, unable to help myself, his erection pressing insistently against my butt.

"That's where I wanna go on our honeymoon," I admitted lazily, all my feelings focused on the pleasure he was bringing with his hands on me.

"And we can chill and not do shit, except each other," he said, his baritone low and calm, contrasting how quickly he had my pulse racing. I hissed out a tight breath, closing my eyes when he slipped his hand into my shorts, so he could touch me without any barriers.

He hummed his approval when he felt me, kissing my neck, his fingers still working deliberately against me. His erection was hard against my butt and he pressed up into me when I arched into his hand, only mildly aware that we were still outside on the patio, even if it was dark. My breaths were labored, eyes closed, lips pressed into his neck as he continued working his finger against my wetness. I was whimpering now, my orgasm building, desire spiraling languidly through my body as I arched into his hand even farther, breathing his name as I came, squeezing my eyes shut, but still seeing nothing but light.

He groaned against my ear with me, his facial hair scratching my skin.

"I'mma sample that sound you make one day," he murmured in my ear, giving me goosebumps. "The one you make right when you're about to come. It has a rhythm."

I was still too foggy to adequately respond. I could only barely meet his tongue with mine when he turned his head and kissed me, slowly, thoroughly, like he had all the time in the world contrasting my racing heart. For a while he only kissed me, pulling back then dipping in, playing with my breasts, one then the other. Devin always kissed me like he had nothing else to do, like he was *savoring* me, and the time we had together when he didn't have to be on the go. This kiss was growing hotter, more insistent, his erection pressing more firmly into my butt.

"Raise up," he said, tapping my thigh, his deep voice barely audible.

My breathing was labored, my mind foggy and I did what he said without thinking. He pushed my shorts down over my hips. I was still blocked by the blanket and I quickly stepped out of them, my heart racing.

"Sit down like this," he murmured. He slid down a little in the chair, pulling at my thigh, so that I'd straddle him.

We were outside, and his mom was right inside of the house—

"You know I got you," he said, reading my mind.

He lifted me again, effortlessly, biceps flexing beneath my fingers when he pulled himself out and showed me how to sit down again, positioning me to take him inside of me. I gasped aloud at the sensation of him filling me, my eyes falling closed because he felt *so good.*

"You feel *so* good," he murmured at the same I thought it, breathing hard. I blinked my eyes open.

"We didn't use..."

"I'll pull out," he said, his baritone strained.

He still had me by the hips and he started guiding my movements, showing me what to do, how to move in this position.

I looked down at our joining, then back into his eyes, which were heavy, full of possessive desire that turned me on even more. I couldn't believe I was doing this, right outside on the patio.

The combination of the night air, the soft fabric of the blanket covering me, Devin's rough hands on my hips, the feel of him inside of me—I don't know, I just wanted to *move*, get more of him. I grinded my hips on him before switching rhythm, lifting and sliding back down on him, taking him further inside of me, my eyes drifting closed.

"*Fu— Low,*" he breathed, squeezing my butt.

I was working my hips faster, finding a rhythm that had me breathless, quietly moaning his name, before biting my lip to stop myself because I couldn't be loud, especially when headlights briefly flashed over the patio. The blanket was covering us though, so I trusted that they couldn't see anything, way in the back of my mind because mostly, I could only concentrate on how good Devin felt inside of me.

Devin's grip on my hips tightened and he wasn't moving me

anymore, as much as just holding me loosely so that he could watch me move the way I wanted to.

"I wish I could take this hoodie off so I could see you," he murmured, eyes on me. My brain wasn't even registering the cold air. I only felt hot all over, under Devin's touch, the way he was looking at me.

"I promise, I'mma wife you," he breathed as I rocked on him.

He slid one hand up under my hoodie, to my nape, pulling me down to his mouth, meeting me in a demanding kiss, thrusting his warm tongue into my mouth. That was Devin's thing, I'd learned. He liked to kiss me when he came, and knowing that he was close only amplified my feeling, and my movements got faster, wilder, less controlled. I was coming again. This one wasn't slow rolling like the other, it was hard and fast, the explosion racking my entire body as Devin, grabbed me at the hips, thrusting up and into me. He came then too, groaning my name in my ear.

It took a full five minutes for us to start breathing normal again.

"Wow," I breathed.

"I don't even know what my life was before you. Real talk," he said, against my neck, which was perspiring, despite the November chill.

I smiled, then it dawned on me.

I wet my lips and looked up at him, and I saw the same thing in his eyes.

He didn't pull out.

WILLOW

"MS. HARDEN. What can I do for you?"

Professor Bandele wasn't looking at me. She was still writing on one of the many sheets of paper scattered on her desk. I tore my gaze away from the mess because it was distracting, my eyes falling instead to the pictures of her family on her desk, before roaming to the pictures of Fela Kuti and Nina Simone hanging on her walls.

"I had spent many years pursuing excellence, because that is what classical music is all about... Now it was dedicated to freedom, and that was far more important," the quote underneath Nina's photo read.

"I can't fail your class." I blurted it out, something I'd been doing more of lately, and felt an immediate rush of heat when she looked up at me over the rim of her glasses, her expression blank.

"You made a statement. I remain unclear about what I can do for you."

Her sing-songy Nigerian accent was full of life, although she was trying to suck mine away. If I failed this class—I didn't even want to think about it. She was focused on her disorganized stack of papers once more, as if I weren't even standing there.

"Is there something I can do to salvage my grade? An extra assignment, or three?"

"There are two weeks left in the semester, Ms. Harden."

She didn't even look up at me over the rim of her glasses this time. "There's been an active study group for this class taking place since the start of the semester. Have you attended?"

Shoot. I was tempted to lie but Bandele knew everything, sometime before it even happened, like a South Texas version of John the Baptist. She was the appointed liaison between campus security and students, taking the position after the rash of police shootings and an incident between campus cops and a student last semester, where the cop broke the student's nose and ribs for no reason, other than him "not being respectful." Bandele was a force on campus with connections and influence and eyes everywhere, even in small study groups.

I shifted my weight, switching my massive communication strategies book to my other arm.

"I attended one session."

"Yet, here you stand, with the expectation that I can, and will do something for you when you've done nothing for yourself." She looked up at me and quirked a brow.

Guilt flooded me and I looked at the ground, inhaling. The cleaning staff was fantastic because there wasn't a speck of dust on the gray carpet. Opening my mouth to tell her that the study group regularly interfered with the time I spent with my boyfriend, attending his gigs and helping out where I could with his music, didn't seem like a wise communication strategy. I'd learned that much in her class. I was really going to *fail*. Not one but *two* classes because I was failing microeconomics too.

I could just imagine what my dad's face would look like when he heard the news. His eyes would get crinkly at the corners and he'd get that *look*. That look broke me down more than any word he could say.

I felt like crying. Or disappearing. Or *something* other than existing in this space. My juggling act, the one where my life circled around Devin because my heart did, was faltering.

"Thank you for your time," I said, clearing my throat because it felt like the office walls were closing in on me.

She looked up again just as I was about to turn around.

"Your final is worth thirty percent of your grade. If you manage to score a 90 percent or higher, you'll come away with a passing mark."

"Thank you." I nodded my head, and dipped out of the office.

Bandele knew without looking up my file what I needed to score on my test to pass. I'd already done the math, which is what led me to her office because scoring a 90 percent on her difficult exams was an extreme long shot.

I stepped out of the mass media arts building into the blinding sunlight, wishing it had the ability to shine clarity into my life.

19

WILLOW

I WAS CRAMPING LIKE CRAZY. Kennedy's grandma Pepper says that the dreams you have when you're on your period are really your subconscious manifesting themselves when you're sleep and not aware enough to rationalize your thoughts away. I told my mom that and she laughed and told me I just need to stop eating before I go to bed. Pepper and my mom aren't *that* far apart in age for their ideologies to be so different. My mom is spiritual but grounded and practical. Sometimes when I'm talking to Pepper I feel like she might literally just start floating or might go poof and explode into a purple ball of magic glitter.

I rolled onto my side, and stared at Jersey's posters hanging on the wall, my dream still heavy on my mind. I couldn't really remember it fully, just the feeling. I only know it was about Devin. *What* about him, I had no clue.

All I know is, I already missed him. The band was blowing up and Jay arranged for them to tour with Black Bottom, starting in three weeks. He'd called me and asked how it coordinated with some of the dates I already had set up for them. His excitement was infectious.

In between their tour they'd record their album in Atlanta. Their schedule was about to be packed—so packed; Devin was talking about possibly dropping out of school. It felt like I was losing him. Like we were falling away from each other, slowly, so that it was hard to notice until one day it'd just be done.

Everything was changing. Everyone was moving on, into their lives, except me. I had a major but still didn't really know what I wanted to do. I had another internship offer in Houston, which one of my professors—*not* Bandele—hooked up for me. I'd be teaching elementary aged kids dance and movement through this new program, Moving Life, that a small dance company was launching. But I turned it down because I'm going on the road with Devin and the band. My mom is disappointed in me over it. She says there's plenty of time for me to go on the road with Devin. My dad says I have to make my own decisions and live with them, which is his way of saying he's disappointed in me too.

I sighed and rolled onto my back, grabbing my phone when it rang.

"Hey, Gia."

"Girl, I need a favor." She didn't even bother with a hello. I hadn't been hanging with her as much lately for that reason. Gia was always needing favors.

"I need to use your car tonight, please?"

I frowned. The last time I let Gia use my car, it came back dirtied with fast food bags and it smelled like she'd sprayed strawberry air freshener over funk.

"She was having sex in your car, Low," Jersey told me. "Ugh, I would kick her nasty *ass*."

"I don't think she was doing that," I'd said half-heartedly. "Why would she do that?"

"Because her ass is nasty!" Jersey exclaimed, eyes wide.

I didn't tell Devin anything because he told me not to let her use the car in the first place.

"I need it," I told Gia, feeling bad for half lying. I wasn't going anywhere but I did need it. I needed it to be with me, in my possession.

"You mean you're not with Devin, using his truck? Where is he?"

"I don't know."

"Are you guys fighting again?"

"Not really."

"It's all in your voice, Willow. I don't know why you put up with his shit. Devin is about Devin. I keep telling you that. What'd he do this time?"

"Nothing, really."

I'd slowed down telling Gia a lot of things about my relationship with Devin. She liked to bring up the things I told her in later conversations, after I'd moved on, and it just muddled and confused things all over again. It was almost like she got excited when Devin and I had drama. And Lyssa, one of the girls from the dance team, told me that Gia was talking about me behind my back. Nothing really *bad* but making snide remarks about my commitment to the team, even though I never missed a practice and we'd secured more performances since I took over. It sorta reminded me of the girls from middle school, and that girl Amber that I got into a fight with in seventh grade.

One day, they were my friends, the next I was like a pariah. They tortured me for an entire six months, making fun of my braces and crooked teeth, calling me a 'ho' even though I hadn't even kissed a boy at that point, saying I thought I was better than everyone else because I had good grades. They even made up songs and chants about me, which they'd sing when I walked down the halls. I'd go home crying every other day. Until one day, Amber actually hit me and I just finally snapped. Gia was reminding me more and more of them. I valued my friendships and I thought she was really my friend. It hurt, finding out little by little that maybe she wasn't really. Yet another fail. Another obvious thing that I didn't see coming.

I ended our conversation and turned back onto my side, restless and still cramping. I stared at my phone, then finally picked it up and called Devin. He let it ring five times before he answered.

"Hey."

"What's up," he said, distractedly. I could tell he was still irritated with me but the sound of his baritone still hit me, every time.

"What are you doing?"

"Oh, you talkin' to me now?"

I rolled my eyes.

"Can you come over?"

"Nah."

I blinked. "No?"

"That's a foreign concept for you, huh?"

"Devin."

"You just finished throwin' a fit three hours ago, talkin 'bout you wanted to leave, made me drop you off at your dorm, and then stomped your ass off."

He sounded a little hurt.

"Because you were being all moody and snappy and I was tired of your attitude."

"Nah, because you were bein' all spoiled and irritable and nobody was in the mood to hear all that."

We'd gotten into another petty argument that I couldn't even remember the details of earlier, and I did tell him I wanted him to bring me to my dorm. And I *was* really irritable, stressing out about getting a 90 percent on my final, which seemed impossible. But now I wanted him.

"I need you to rub my stomach. I'm cramping and it hurts."

"Then you shoulda stayed your ass here."

I rolled my eyes. "Fine. Whatever, Devin."

I hung up, and flopped onto my back, glaring at the ceiling. My period was on my nerves but I was glad to have it, especially after my almost- pregnancy scare back at Thanksgiving time when Devin and I were careless on his mom's balcony. I took the morning after pill when we got back to Tyler.

"What do you wanna do?" Devin asked me, sitting on the edge of his mattress.

"I can't handle a baby. And neither can you."

He didn't say anything, just chewed on the corner of his lip, eyes on me.

"It's on you, Low. Whatever you want."

I knew he wanted to mean that. I tried not to think about it a lot after I took the pill. Tried not to think about *what if.*

I grabbed the remote off the nightstand and flicked on the TV, pressing my heating pad to my stomach, prepared to get lost in *A Different World* when there was a knock at the door. I frowned and got up, pulling at my spaghetti tank, adjusting my spandex. I cracked the door open, before opening it all the way, smiling at Devin, who was standing there with that familiar look in his brown eyes. The one that said he was tired of me but loved me anyway.

"You even brought ice cream!" I exclaimed, bouncing on my toes and clapping as he stepped all the way into the room. He shook his head as I shut the door and pushed the carton into my hands.

"You're so damn spoiled."

I stepped to him, pressing on my toes and kissing his lips. He just stared down at me, looking all sexy and annoyed.

"But you wanna spoil me?"

He rolled his eyes, expression still angry but resigned.

"Your ass, man."

"I love you, baby," I told him.

"Yeah, yeah."

He grabbed me by the waist, as he plopped down onto my bed, pulling me with him as I yelped.

"What are you studying for?"

The sudden sound of Devin's sleepy voice made me jump. He'd been snoring for the past two hours, lulled to sleep when I started rubbing his scalp when he laid his head on my thigh.

He looked up at me and my hand stilled in his head. I'd been absently fingering it while I poured over my crappy notes from Bandele's class. There was no way I was going to pass this test at this rate.

"My communications strategies class," I answered, sighing and pushing my purple notebook to the edge of the bed.

Devin hummed his response, already uninterested in his own question, tapping on his phone. I swallowed my irritation at his lack of interest.

"You're making a beat?" I questioned instead.

"Had a sound. Had to get it out of my head," he answered, groggily. His eyes were low and red with fatigue because he'd been going non-stop.

My phone buzzed next to me and he turned his head then looked up at me, brows raised. The text popped up on the screen from Jaden.

"You up? Wanted to go over these notes with you..."

It was after 11.

"Word?" Devin tilted his head, his eyes daring me to say anything he didn't like.

"Don't start," I said wearily, rolling my eyes. "You saw what the text said. He wants to *study*. Not look at my boobs like the women who text you."

"I don't have boobs."

"Ugh, you know what I mean Devin."

Devin blew out a breath, his gaze hot when he looked up at me.

"Every time I go in Aroma, there he is. I guess y'all are 'studying' while you're at work too?" Devin rolled his eyes, lifting his head from my lap.

"I'm about to be out."

"What? You're leaving?"

"I have shit to do, Willow. I didn't have time to come over here in the first place."

I scowled at him and his gaze softened but only a little.

"Come with me."

"It doesn't make sense for me to do that. I have an eight a.m. You should just stay—"

"I just finished tellin' you I have shit to do," he interrupted, speaking the words slowly, like he'd lost his mind.

"Don't talk to me like that, Devin."

He rolled his eyes in the air again and grabbed his hat from the bed, just as my phone buzzed again. I picked it up as he stood, grabbing his t-shirt which he'd taken off earlier, from the rumpled bed.

"Oh my God!" I jumped, my hand flying in to my heart, then covering my mouth as I stared at what popped up on my screen.

"What?" Devin stopped what he was doing and walked back toward the bed, eyes on high alert.

My eyes were trained on my screen though, and I felt like I'd be sick.

"What Low?" he asked as tears welled in my eyes. He sat down next to me on the bed, and took my phone from me. He stilled as he watched the screen, and I watched his eyes harden with *rage*.

"These *motherfuckers*." His jaw clenched and for a second he just sat there shaking his head. I took the phone back from him, watching the video of a boy named Jamal Waters being shot in the head by campus police in Colorado at point blank rage. The article said he was unarmed, pulled over for an expired tag. An officer approached and within less than two minutes he was dead.

I rubbed my stomach, vision blurred as I stared at the screen.

"Don't keep watching it, baby." Devin said, taking the phone from me.

"*Fuck*. They can't keep doing this to us. But they *fuckin' can*."

He stood, pacing to the other side of the room, near Jersey's bed. "Fuck," he mumbled again, looking as though he wanted to hit something.

"Are you okay?" he asked, turning toward me, tossing my phone next to me again.

I nodded, wiping my cheeks. It was a lie, and he knew it. How okay could you be after watching someone get their head blown off by a cop at point blank range for doing nothing more than existing? People were already making up excuses for the cop, saying Jamal shouldn't've been driving alone with only a learner's permit, like that was reason for him to be shot in the head.

For a while, we just stood there, lost in time. I was tired, and still crampy and confused about *my* life. Now I was confused about what my life meant outside of the confines of my personal world too. It was all... too much.

"I'm gonna go," Devin suddenly said, swiping his wallet off the bed, pressing a quick kiss to my forehead. Even his lips felt enraged. Suddenly, it was like a bubble burst in my chest.

"No!" It came out louder than I intended, and I stood up, my pillow dropping to the floor. But it was the only thing I could think of to say.

"You can't leave. Not now. It's not safe... it's late and you're mad so you might drive reckless and if you get pulled over..." I shook my head. "You can't leave. Wait until the morning."

"Baby, nothing..."

"You can't leave!" I all but shouted. Devin blinked shocked. I was crying again, hormonal, in shock, in a rage, defeated, just a mess. "You can't leave." I said again, pleadingly as I sat down on the bed again.

"Okay," he said, sitting down next to me on the edge of the bed. "Aight? I'll stay, okay?"

He pulled me against his firm chest and I nodded, wrapping my arms around his middle. He laid us down on top of the comforter and reached and shut off the lamp, shrouding the room in darkness, his grip on me tight.

"It's okay," he murmured in my ear again. And it felt like he was talking about more than just tonight. I nodded, because it was what I was supposed to do, even if I didn't feel it in my heart.

Finally, I closed my eyes, and I said a prayer in my head for the classes I was failing, for clarity in my life, for Devin, and for Jamal Waters.

20
DEVIN

"It's *crazy* out there."

Kennedy's eyes were wide and you could practically see the energy dripping from her. Just beyond backstage, the crowd was chanting "Prototype" over and over, so loudly, it sounded like the floor might cave in because they had to be stomping too.

It was our final show at Jimmy's—a send-off bringing an end to our residency. The end of an era. The audience felt it too, and the air was peaked and charged, crackling with our day ones—the fans who'd held us down before "Space" got picked up by radio, before we started getting national press, before the tours, like the one we were about to head out on in a couple of days with Black Bottom.

But I wasn't expecting this kind of response.

We were just about to start our final set at the club, and the place was at capacity. Jimmy actually had to turn people away at the door, and they were still hovering outside in the early May heat, so thick, Neil, the head of security was outside arguing with the fire department, because they were threatening to shut it down.

People were there for us, but they also just needed a release. It was two weeks after the murder of Jamal Waters and it just felt as if the air had changed—it was tight and thick, like it might explode at any given second. This show tonight was about more than the music; it was about having the opportunity to be free and let go, if only for a few hours.

"Where's Low?" Zay asked, eyeing the backstage door.

"She was supposed to be here by now," I said pulling out my phone and checking it again. She was closing at Aroma tonight, so she wasn't getting off until 9:00. But she should've been here by now. It was close to 10 and we were about to go on. I frowned and called her.

"Baby, where are you?" I asked when she picked up. I could barely hear her, there was so much noise in the background.

"I'm here, but it's so crowded..." the phone was muffled and I pressed it against my ear.

"I can't hear you."

"I said it's so crowded I don't think I can get backstage. They have it blocked off."

She was irritable.

"You see Neil?"

I glanced at Travis. "Aye, text Neil and tell him to look for Low outside," I told him.

"You see him?" I asked her, frowning because I could barely hear her. This is why I didn't like her rolling up here by herself.

"Okay, here he is," she said. "See you in a second."

She hung up and I scrolled through my messages again, frowning when I read the most recent one. It was from a number that I didn't recognize, but then, I didn't recognize half the numbers from the people that texted me, especially these days.

"Hey. It's Gia. Have a good show tonight! I'll be cheering for you! My friend lives in Miami and I wanted to see if you could get her three tickets to the show? I asked Willow but she hasn't responded."

I frowned again. *The hell? Tickets to the show?* I ain't know ol' girl like that and wasn't trying to. She was Willow's people, for whatever reason that was. I was gonna have to talk to Low about giving random tag-alongs my number. I stuffed my phone back in my pocket, checking the door, just as Neil pushed through, Low tucked underneath his arm.

At the sight of her, my pulse sped up a little, as usual. Looking at her never got old. She was wearing jeans tonight, and a simple top that still showed her cleavage. My gaze, as usual, lingered on her thighs. The thighs I stayed buried between as often as I could. Losing myself. Finding myself. Keeping myself grounded. Discovering new things, building on what was and what would be.

Her gaze landed on me and she bit her lip, her expression unreadable before she heaved a breath, and turned, saying something to Neil before lifting on her toes and pecking Neil's cheek. He saluted me with two fingers before pushing back through the door to deal with the crowd.

"You guys, there's like a *million* people out there!" Willow exclaimed when she reached us, eyes round as saucers. "Thank Jesus Neil saw me. I never would've even made it inside. Neil literally broke up a fight right in front me."

"You okay?" I asked, grabbing her hand, pulling her close.

She nodded, not really looking at me.

"What's up?"

"Nothing."

When she finally did look up at me, her eyes were a mix of emotions that I couldn't really get a handle on because *she* didn't have a handle on them. It'd been that way for the past month. Everything was changing. *Fast.* Including us... because we had to.

After "Space" got picked up by radio, it was like things were moving at lightning speed. First came the summer tour offer with Black Bottom. They'd taken off in the past year—were even getting Grammy talk— so touring with them was big. We were doing 36 cities in six weeks. In between, we'd be recording our album.

Out of nowhere, our schedule was packed. I was ready for the change but preparing for it was something different. Me and Low had been off for the past month. It was weird because this was probably the best time in my life—I was starting to see all the sacrifices I'd made for the music paying off. It was *right there*.

We heard the DJ announcing us and the crowd reached a fever pitch. I grinned, my adrenaline spiking. We'd outgrown Jimmy's a while ago but tonight, we drew a crowd from all over the region because it'd be our last for a long time, possibly ever, in the club that helped break us. The crowd was chanting our names now and I exchanged a glance with Jersey, who was smiling. *Hell yeah.* This is what we'd been working for over the past three years, and it was just the tip of the iceberg.

"We're on in three minutes," Travis said, bobbing his head toward Jimmy, who'd just entered backstage.

We all gathered in a circle as he led us in our customary prayer, but my eyes were on Willow. I pulled her close again when Trav finished and everyone moved toward the stage steps.

"You know I can't get on stage with you looking like that."

"I'm not looking like anything," she said, her voice quiet.

I sighed, staring into her eyes. Her gaze softened and she exhaled, then pressed up on her tippy toes, kissing my lips, holding on to my sides. I closed my eyes breathing against her mouth, craving her, her energy in ways I couldn't even articulate.

"Go Bruce Banner, baby," she whispered, touching her mouth to mine again.

"You already know."

She smiled and released my hand as I headed on stage, the crowd's chants increasing to deafening levels.

21

DEVIN

"Willow and Jersey just left."

Zay leaned in to shout the update to me because the spot was so loud. We'd been off stage for about an hour. Now we were hanging out at the bar still because people kept us surrounded the entire time, wishing us well, asking for autographs and pictures. Zay and I got hounded the most. Kennedy would too if she could handle it, because she had that same innocent sensual energy that Low did. But she didn't deal well with the extra attention, which was alright. Her disappearing act added mystique to the band.

"You said they bounced already?"

"Jersey wasn't trying to hang around tonight so she left with Low."

He didn't need to say they were probably into it if she left him. And I already knew Low was on one. Her attitude was back when I stepped off stage. She'd been up and down all week. One second practically bouncing with excitement about everything that was happening, the next, snapping my head off for no reason.

I looked up from the autograph I was signing for Brianna, who was wearing one of our old t-shirts, the very first ones that Jersey designed our sophomore year, probably to show off that she'd been rocking with us since the beginning.

"Appreciate it, love," I told her, nodding my head in her direction.

"I figured I better get your signature after all this time," she said, smiling. "I can't believe this was really your last show here." Her eyes were wide and a little glassy and she pressed close, making sure her titties brushed against my arm when she smiled up at me. "You know I need a picture too. I might need the money one day."

She pulled her phone out without waiting for a response, hugging me around the waist. I put an arm around her waist and threw up two fingers as she snapped the picture, kissing my cheek. She smiled when I released her.

"You have to stay in touch, Devin."

I grinned. "No doubt."

"Let me get one with you both," she said pointing at Zay. We exchanged and glance and he gamely got into the picture as she stood between us.

"We have to do shots!" her drunk friend volunteered, sliding up to us, ass jiggling all over the place. She didn't wait for an answer, just signaled the bartender, Kenny.

"You game?" I asked Zay. Being real, I wasn't into it. I was down to celebrate but it shoulda been *Low* here, not Brianna. Zay shrugged, accepting the shot from Brianna's thick friend.

"To the next level," Brianna said smiling widely.

"To the next level," we repeated, downing the shot.

Forty-five minutes later, I was bored. Brianna and her girls bought two more rounds of shots for themselves and watching drunk girls fall all over themselves, over emphasizing their drunkenness wasn't my shit. I could tell Zay was ready to go, and so was I because I wasn't trying to get caught up foolin' around with Brianna.

She was already practically in between my legs, talkin' shit in my ear. My gaze slid down to her ass, which she kept deliberately backing against my crotch, whenever she turned to talk to her girl.

Zay leaned back against the bar, shooting a look in my direction, and I nodded.

"We're about to be out," I told Brianna.

"Aw, it's early," she whined, touching her tongue to the corner of her mouth so I could see her tongue piercing.

I ignored her, nodding my head at Kenny to take care of the tab for me.

"Which way are you going? Toward campus?"

I looked at her.

"Can you give us a ride back to the dorms? I'm *way* too drunk to function right now." She widened her eyes.

"Y'all can't call a car?"

"I can! But I lost my phone earlier and she forgot hers." Brianna leaned against the bar and looked up at me.

I glanced at Zay, who smirked. I looked at Brianna and her girl and sighed.

"Aight. Let's go."

Their goofy-asses giggled the entire way to the dorms, making slick comments about my truck. It was a tight squeeze because Zay was riding with me and the four of us had to share the truck's bench seat. I drove as fast as I could without getting stopped, and when we reached the dorms, the same as Low's because that's where Brianna's girl stayed, I didn't cut the engine. I just wanted them out of my truck. Brianna was cute and all but drunk Brianna was annoying as fuck.

I hopped out so that she could slide out on my side.

The air was still warm and it smelled like growing grass. I wanted to get back to the crib, open the window and feel the breeze while I handled Low, since it'd be our last night together for a couple of weeks. Lately, she'd been handling *me*. Being all cute and aggressive, acting like she was really gonna miss me when I left. Well, when she wasn't trippin' and being all overly emotional, stompin' away and shit.

"Thanks for the ride," Brianna said, staring up at me after I helped her out.

"It's all good," I told her, forcing patience.

"Wanna come up?" She bit her lip and blinked up at me, sliding her hand down my chest, hesitating at the waistband of my jeans.

"I'm good." I moved her hand away but she stepped closer. I could smell the tequila on her, and whatever fruity lip gloss she'd reapplied in the truck on the way over here, probably preparing herself for this moment.

"You should come up." She put her hand back on my chest but this time moved it to my crotch, giggling.

"What's up Zay and Devin?"

It was Jersey's accusatory voice breaking through the night air, just as I was moving Brianna's hand away again. I turned, but it wasn't Jersey my gaze landed on, it was Willow, standing next to her, face crumpled, chest heaving. Her eyes dropped to my crotch and she looked back up at me, standing in the middle of the parking lot. She made a noise that sounded like, *pain*, coming from her diaphragm. *Ah, baby. Shit.*

"Willow—"

Brianna looked over at Willow, then back up to me.

"So, you're still comin up, right?" Brianna interrupted. She broke into giggles and looked over at Willow again.

"Yo, move—" I moved Brianna aside, trying to get around her to get to Low.

I looked up just in time to see Low flying toward us, her pretty features twisted into a furious mask that I didn't even recognize, and I knew all of Low's expressions. *Oh shit.*

Willow was swinging, wildly, hitting anything her little fists could connect with, including me, but mostly Brianna, who caught a clean one to the jaw. *Gotdamn.*

"Low!" I snapped out of it, my adrenaline kicking in but she'd lost it.

She gotten a hold of Brianna, and had her pressed up against the side of the truck, wailing on her.

"Willow!" Jersey's voice came out of nowhere and she ran toward Willow, eyes wide, as I tried to pry Low off the damn girl. I grabbed Low by the waist, dodging her wild fists, swinging her away from Brianna who was covering her head. Brianna's friend rounded the front of the truck, screaming like a lunatic. Jersey pushed her just for the hell of it, probably, and girl staggered against the truck, still yelling like someone got shot. It was late but it was Friday night and with all the racket people were starting to gather around. They were gonna call the damn cops. But I focused on Willow, who was still screaming out of control, her cheeks red, as she struggled to get out my hold.

"*Stop it, baby*!" I said in her ear, tightening my grip. "Low! *Stop!*"

"*I hate you!* Let me go, I hate you! I hate you, Devin!" she screamed at the top of her lungs.

Her words hit me in the chest but I kept a hold on her anyway. Brianna and her friend were still drunkenly talking shit, staggering around in front of the truck, pretending like they still wanted to fight.

"Come on y'all," Zay urged, his eyes darting from the crowd to Low and Jersey. "Let's go before the fake ass campus cops roll up."

Brianna and her friend was still yelping but Jersey grabbed Low's arm, yelling a "fuck you" over her shoulder to Brianna, pushing Low into the truck.

22

WILLOW

"I COULD'VE GOTTEN SUSPENDED. I could've gotten *arrested.*"

I looked around Kennedy's tiny room. The bedspread was lavender and the curtains were sheer white and it looked like a doll lived there, souring my mood further.

I dropped my face into my hands and shook my head, tears spilling out of my eyes. There was a dull ache in the back of my head that wouldn't leave. What had I done? Getting into a fight with a girl over my man like a Real Basketball Wife? In the public parking lot of my dorm? It was embarrassing. It was crazy. I shook my head again, pushing out a long breath.

"Things happen, Willow." It was Kennedy who spoke up. "Remember when me and Maya got into it?"

We were sitting in her room at her grandma's house because I had to get away from Devin. I couldn't even look at him. Thank God Zay pulled him away so I wouldn't have to.

"That was different," I answered Kennedy.

"Not really," Kennedy said, shrugging her small shoulders.

"*I* started that fight tonight," I said looking up at her. "Not her. Who does that?" I shook my head again. "I don't even know who I am right now. Or who that person was."

"Hold up. Have you never been in a fight before?" Cassie asked, looking up from painting her toenails.

"Once, in middle school. But I'm a grown ass woman."

She glanced at Kennedy, and I had the feeling she was barely managing to not roll her eyes. "You're not the first 'grown ass woman' to get into a fight, dude. VH1 has made millions off of that realization. And I don't know your situation like that but it sounds like ol' girl needed to be slapped."

"She did. And she definitely caught it. I didn't know you had it in you, gangster." It was Jersey speaking up this time. She held her fist out for me to bump but I only stared at her.

"That's not funny."

She rolled her eyes and dropped her hand.

"Not right now because you're in it. But it was a little funny, Low. She was being super disrespectful and she caught one." Jersey shrugged.

"Yeah but disrespectful women come a dime a dozen in y'all's lifestyle."

"What am I going to do? Fight them all? What is *wrong* with me?"

"Sounds like you're putting a lot of blame on yourself. Devin is the homie but he shoulda played that a little different," Cassie said.

I closed my mouth, running a hand down my face. The hand I used to hit anything I could just two hours ago. My parents wouldn't even know me if they saw me earlier.

"And hadn't you two been drinking?" Kennedy asked, rolling onto her stomach, making the bed shift.

"Hennessey," Jersey supplied matter-of-factly.

"Oh well, *hell*," Cassie piped up from the chair with the yellow lace pillow that had "live and love" etched onto the front of it. "You left that part out. Of course you wanted to fight messin' with that brown."

"Or gin," Kennedy said, grinning. "I've had a moment or two drinking gin."

I sighed again, and bit my pinky nail, then sipped my "calming" ginger tea, which Kennedy made for me when I came into her house looking like a bad reality show character.

Yes, I'd been drinking with Jersey at the bar after their show, and then later in our dorm room with Jersey. She was upset with Zay and I was... I didn't even know what I was. Trying to escape for a while, I guess. I found out today that passed Professor Bandele's test with a 79 —which was better than I'd ever scored on any of her tests but meant I failed anyway. For the first time ever, I failed not one but two classes.

My dance team was in disarray too because I found out that Lauren pulled a Tre and was stealing money after I made her treasurer. I had a meeting with the dean about that earlier today too—he threatened to pull our endorsement next year. In the meantime, we were on probation. It didn't look good. And a few of the dancers were trying to get me removed as president. Lyssa told me it was Gia who put the bug in their ear. Gia who I thought was my friend. I approached her about it and she denied it but I could tell she was lying.

On top of all that, Devin was leaving tomorrow. And it was no longer a possibility; he was definitely dropping out of school.

"J. Cole finished school." It was the only thing I could think to say when Devin told me the other day.

"J. Cole didn't have a deal from Jay-Z his senior year either," he'd said. *"He finished school because the music wasn't happening for him yet. We have an opportunity here, baby. Recording this album? Hopping on a tour with Black Bottom, when they're hitting the charts as hard as they are, selling out all of their venues? This is our time. This is what I've been working for. The school thing was always gonna come second to the music, you know that. And now that things are moving for us... it's time to make some real decisions. This is my life. The business degree will be here when I want to come back and get it. This though? It can be gone just like that."* He snapped his fingers in front of his face, illustrating his point. *"And if that happens what am I gonna do? What is my family gonna do?"*

He was right. I knew it with everything in me.

We all attended Zay, Travis and Bam's graduation a few days ago. It's why Cassie came into town, after her own graduation. Jersey, Kennedy and Devin were all leaving South Texas because they were headed out on tour with Black Bottom tomorrow—36 cities in six weeks. It was huge. They were going to be in Atlanta, finishing up recording their album in between dates. I couldn't go on the first two weeks of the tour—because they were using a van, not a bus and there wasn't room. But Jay Little worked it out for me to be able to join them in two weeks, at their Atlanta show, where they could switch to a bus. I was supposed to go on the rest of the tour with them from there.

But everything felt wrong now. Everything felt wrong *before* tonight, honestly. This was the most important time in Devin's life. I knew that. And I was proud and happy for him—everything that he'd worked hard for and sacrificed was coming to light now. But we were so off. My heart hurt, all of the time lately because I didn't know what to do to fix it. I sipped my tea again then stared into the cup.

"You know he wasn't going to do anything with her." Jersey's words hit my ears and my heart but not my stomach. I still felt like I wanted to hurl thinking about that girl's hand on Devin's crotch and the way she acted as if she owned him. He was *mine*. And I was his. I'd been his.

I was studying Kennedy's lavender comforter. "What's going to happen when you all go on tour?"

I looked up at her and she sighed.

"Zay told me what happened. I believe him." Her gaze was pointed. "Devin gave them a ride, ol' girl pushed up on him and he shut it down."

I felt Kennedy's discerning eyes on me. "Are you gonna be alright, Willow?"

I nodded just as Pepper came into the room. It was late, after 1 a.m. but she was still awake, her eyes bright and alert as if it were the afternoon.

"Willow, Devin is here."

My stomach immediately lurched again, along with my heart and I inhaled. He called twice in the past hour. Cassie eyed me, giving me a look that said there better not be any drama in her grandma's house. I stood, readjusting my ponytail and took a breath, heading for the door. Kennedy smiled at me, Jersey threw up a fist and Cassie just looked at me curiously.

"Thank you, Ms. Pepper," I told her as I followed her into the hallway.

"Trust your heart—it beats for a reason," she told me softly, taking my tea from me.

I felt him even before I saw him. Devin was leaning on the back of the couch, hands in his pockets and he looked up when I entered the room. I wet my lip and his gaze dropped there before he met my eyes again.

"Can we talk?"

I nodded. He held out his hand and I bit my lip, before crossing the room and taking it.

23
DEVIN

I CLOSED my bedroom door and leaned against it, my eyes on Willow. She was sitting on my bed, her eyes red rimmed and puffy because she'd been crying. For long seconds, we just stared at each other.

"I'm tired of feeling like this." Her voice was thick and hoarse.

"That makes two of us."

Her eyes flickered but she kept them trained on me. I was tired of proving myself over and over to her. It was the first time we'd spoke since I went over Pepper's house and got her. Zay and Trav told me to chill, give her time. But an hour was enough. I was leaving in the morning and I couldn't leave shit up in the air with us.

I didn't even know what to think about tonight. I'd never seen Willow like that before, so outside of herself. I didn't give a fuck about her molly-whopping ol' girl. On another day, with anyone else, the shit would've been hilarious. But I did care about Willow. And I know that wasn't her, and there wasn't nothing funny about this situation. The look in her eyes then, the look in her eyes *now*, it made me want to punch some shit because she was my baby, my *love* and I didn't know that new look in her eyes. That light that was always there, that *thing* that illuminated everyone and everything around her was replaced with something else that was unidentifiable.

I wanted to ask her what was going on with her, but I didn't even know how to approach it for real because we'd end up stuck on stupid shit again, like Brianna, or some other girl I wasn't even thinking about. After all this time, Low still didn't get it.

"You're getting on the road tomorrow, Devin."

"Exactly. And look at us." I shook my head, shifting my weight against the dresser as I leaned against it.

"So this is all *my* fault?" Her eyes widened. "It's my fault Brianna had her hands down your pants? It's my fault you have pictures with her practically sitting on your lap with her herpes-lips on your cheek?! That's my fault, Devin?"

"See, that right there? That's what you're *not* gonna do."

"What?" She stared at me defiantly.

"You're not gonna act like you don't know what's up. Like you don't know it's you, all day, every day."

"Then why was she touching all over you?"

"Because she was tryin' to fuck!"

Willow's mouth dropped open and I ran a hand over the back my neck, too exasperated to sugarcoat my words.

"You don't think I know Brianna ain't about anything real? She doesn't want me. She wants the lifestyle she thinks I'm about to have. Or the attention of the lifestyle she thinks I'm about to have."

Willow's eyes flickered, as if she was finally hearing me, though her mouth remained in a tight line.

"You know how many of these hoes throw it at me on the regular? And there's only gonna be more once we really start poppin'. But you know what I do? I fall back. Every single time. And you know why? One, nobody's worried about runnin' up in some thirsty broad who doesn't want anything but to get me caught up or waste my time when my life right now is about this music. And two, because I have *Willow Elizabeth Harden*. There's nothin' out there like you. I already know. I don't need any reminders."

She looked down at the rumpled bed shaking her head. When she looked up at me, her gaze was fiery.

"Remember a couple of months ago after you finished getting into with Travis over that Maya and Kennedy pregnancy thing? You said if you were ever feeling yourself too much, or it seemed like you were getting 'caught up,'" she raised her arms using air quotes, "you wanted me to let you know? Well, this is it. You're caught up."

She held up her phone with the picture I took earlier as evidence. She shook her head. "You never claim me. You're not the only one with options. Jaden was just on my phone again today, asking me to the movies."

She stared at me defiantly and my jaw clenched. She was trying to be cute but she was taking the conversation somewhere it didn't need to go.

"You're talkin' reckless," I told her. She blinked and looked away. "When have I ever not claimed you, Willow? You talkin' about social media again? Because I put pictures of us up after you kept talkin' about it and what happened? Huh?"

She bit her lip, her cheeks turning pink.

"Exactly... people started saying way out, disrespectful shit. You ended up with your feelings hurt, we put people in our relationship that had no business being there, and it was bullshit all around."

She glared at me, like I was lying.

"It feels like I'm the only one ever making sacrifices. I changed my entire schedule for you last summer, Devin. I turned down a great internship in *New York* to stay in Dallas so that we could be together as much as possible."

What? She was throwing that in my face now?

"And now here I am doing it again, turning down *another* internship in Houston to go on the road with you. And for what? For this?"

I looked out of my open window where the box fan was sitting, attempting to circulate air. This was supposed to be a happy, celebratory time for me but here I was, arguing in my fuckin' room with my girl, my heart, at two in the morning instead. I was *so* tired of this high school shit.

"I feel like sayin' fuck it."

She blinked, blanching.

"All I wanna do is *keep* you, Willow. All I be wantin' to do is come back here and be with you and chill. But nah, you ain't about that."

I shook my head. "I shoulda just went ahead and fucked Brianna."

The words slipped out of my mouth, loose, out of control. I felt her move before I saw her, felt the words hit me in the gut; the way I knew they hit her. Willow sprung from the bed, headed for the door but I moved quicker to block her.

"Move, Devin!" She pushed at my chest, her cheeks red, chest heaving. She pushed my chest again, but I grabbed her arms, pulling her close.

"If you want her than have her!"

"I'm *sorry.*"

"*Get out of my way*," she grated out, struggling against my chest as I held her.

"I'm sorry," I said again in her ear, inhaling her sweet scent, tasting the salt of her tears. "I'm sorry, Low. Don't leave. I didn't mean that."

I kissed her ear, the side of her face, her nose, anywhere I could find skin. Her chest was heaving, her cheeks flushed, eyes still puffy.

"I love you," I murmured against her skin. Her body was softening and she stopped struggling in my arms, her chest rising and falling quickly.

"I'm sorry. Don't leave," I whispered. I felt the fight leaving her body, the moment her emotion flipped the other way, the moment she started to feel the kisses I was pressing into her skin. Her head fell back and her grip tightened on my arms. A small whimper escaped her, turning into a moan as I kissed and sucked on warm skin, just below her jaw.

"I'm sorry too," she breathed, turning her head and finding my lips.

"I love you," I told her again, pressing her hard against the bedroom door as I pulled at her hips, fitting her soft curves against me.

I could taste her tears on her lips when I kissed her and I swiped them with my tongue, delving into the sweetness of her mouth. The kiss was furious, a little crazy but that's how I felt with Low sometimes. *Fucking crazy.* The push and the pull with this girl was too much at times. But never enough. I could never get enough of her.

"I love you," I said again.

She didn't answer, just made a small noise in the back of her throat that had my hands sliding over her ass, then to front of her jeans, unbuttoning them, dipping low to slide them over hips. Her warm hands were on the back of my head, when I stood again pulling me closer as she arched herself against me, her nipples hard, pressing against my chest.

I bent low and lifted her easily moving us to the bed. Because I needed her. I needed the connection. I needed to know I wasn't losing her. Or us. She ran her fingers over my scalp as I kissed her eagerly, pulling her bottom lip between mine, her breathing frantic, matching the heavy breaths leaving my lungs.

I pulled her tank up, over her belly, her breasts, grazing her smooth skin as I went, before pulling off her underwear. And once it was off, my gaze slid over her body as she lay there naked, dried tears on her face, chest heaving. She was everything. Everything I wanted. *Needed.* She blinked up at me, looking like she did that very first time we were together.

"No one else matters to me," I told her, staring into her eyes, sliding my hands possessively over her hips. "It's me and you."

I spread her legs, my gaze fixed between her thighs and I dipped low, breathing against her wetness. She nearly bucked off the bed on the first swipe, calling out my name.

I held her thighs apart as she moaned, not allowing her to move, to not feel anything but me.

And when I slid into her warmth, forehead pressed against hers, I couldn't stop the low noise from leaving my chest at the feel of her, slick and warm, pulsing, for me.

She lifted her head, kissing me eagerly, panting against my mouth as I thrust into her, again and again, trying to get deeper, closer, so that the space between us lately faded away completely.

"Devin?"

I was laying in the dark, waiting for her breaths to even out and tell me she was sleep. I hadn't been able to get enough of her. Two more times we made love, moving off emotion only because we were exhausted. That was how we were communicating right now. That was our rhythm while we worked out the rest.

Even now, I wanted her again. But she was fatigued and so was I. Our fingers were interlaced over her heart, her back pressed to my chest.

"What, baby?"

"Why do you love me?"

I blinked in the darkness.

"It just *is*. Like the way that I love sound and rhythm. I feel you whenever I breathe."

She snuggled closer against my chest and I felt the long breath she released. Minutes later, her breathing evened out and I knew she was finally asleep, so I could drift off too.

I slept so hard I didn't hear her get up the next morning. Didn't hear her pack up all of her things. Didn't hear her leave.

I just woke up, and she was gone, without a word.

PRESENT DAY

24

WILLOW

I STRETCHED TOWARD THE SUN, reaching my fingertips up to the sky inhaling before I hinged forward from my waist on my exhale. Yoga was my thing lately, but this morning, it wasn't doing what I wanted it to do. It wasn't giving me release from my thoughts. I wasn't centered. I was off balance. Again.

I barely slept last night after I left Devin's room when we all got back from the Progressive Union Rally. In Houston, I slept a lot. So much, the first week back home, my mom thought I might be depressed.

Last night, my first night back in Tyler after two months, I slept maybe four hours max, even though Kennedy's grandma Pepper gave me herbal tea to "soothe my soul" when I pushed through the door with Kennedy, after leaving Devin's bedroom. I guess I looked like I needed my soul soothed.

I couldn't get Devin out of my head. His voice. The way he looked at me when we were in his bedroom last night when I left again. The hurt in his eyes. The desire. The *anger*. The love.

Every conclusion that I'd come to over the past eight weeks we were apart was being tested and after just a day in his presence.

Kennedy didn't question me last night when I left Devin's room after the rally. That's one of the things I liked so much about her. She let people talk when they were ready—though usually one of her perceptive stares would be enough for me to spill my guts. Jersey, on the other hand, wanted to know everything right then.

"What are you doing, Willow?" she'd asked me last night when she walked with Kennedy and I back over to Pepper's. *"Did you guys even talk? Or are you guys still being stupid?"*

I didn't know what to say because I *was* still being stupid and I didn't need Jersey to tell me that. I was in love with Devin Walker and had been for years. I couldn't deny Devin any more than I could my own heartbeat. I didn't need two months to figure that out. But I did need that time to figure *me* out. After the parking lot incident, I needed to get my head on straight and I knew I couldn't do that in Devin's space because so much in my world revolved around him. I needed to find me. All this time though, I still couldn't figure out how to tell him that. I couldn't figure out how to tell him why I left the way I did and why I risked destroying our bond by not speaking to him for that long, with no real explanation.

I opened my eyes, automatically peering down the street toward Travis' house when I heard a door slam. As if I'd conjured him, I watched as Devin came out of the house. He reached his SUV, which was parked in front of the house, and put it in the backseat. Immediately, my heart started beating faster. Even from afar, he looked good. He was wearing basketball shorts that hung low on his hips, and a black ribbed tank top. And from four houses down, I still was able to make out his defined biceps, strong jaw, and those lips. Those lips that teased me, taught me, exhausted and uplifted me.

I don't even know when my feet started moving toward him. They just did. He looked up, and spotted me, surprise crossing his handsome features before he cleared his expression. I willed my feet to keep moving over the worn sidewalk, passing Mrs. Johnson's house as I made my way toward him. It smelled like early morning—fresh and dewy, the sun barely risen the sky, only offering a faint glimpse of the heat that would certainly greet the day later.

"Morning," I said as I approached him, pausing on the curb just at the end of his SUV.

"Morning."

His voice was early morning husky and it hit me in my belly because it was so familiar. His gaze skirted over me, from my sports bra to my shorts before meeting my eyes again. My twists were secured in a high top knot, and I instinctually reached for a strand to twist before dropping my hands to my sides. Devin had bulked up a lot over the past eight weeks. His arms and wash board abs were already out of control but now they were even further defined, like a ball player or an underwear model, or someone who should never, ever wear shirts.

He was staring at me, maybe waiting for me to speak and my face heated.

"I was up early doing sun salutations," I quickly explained, gesturing toward Pepper's house. "Yoga is kinda my thing now."

He didn't say anything, just sort of hummed, the way you do when someone is talking about something completely boring but you're being polite. His freckles were visible in the early sunlight, his ball cap backwards on his head, his brown eyes tired but alert.

"You're leaving? I thought you guys didn't go back on the road for a couple of days?"

"Gotta make a run home right quick."

"To Atlanta?"

"That's home."

I bit the inside of my lip, my heart suddenly racing at the thought of him leaving, which was insane. I looked off, across the street, shifting my weight.

"Aight, well, I'll holler at you later," he said, dismissing me, just as I blurted, "Can I come?"

He stilled, staring at me for a long second, his gaze surprised before becoming hard, dissecting. I wondered if he was still seeing me, or the girl who'd left him without a word two months ago.

"You wanna come with me." He said it like it was unfathomable.

"I just feel like I need to get out of town."

"You been outta town for two months." The anger was back, as was the hard edge to his voice.

"You know what I mean," I said, gnawing on my lower lip.

"Nah. I don't."

I blinked up at him, releasing a pent up a breath and he narrowed his eyes, shaking his head as he looked away.

"Don't you have class tomorrow?"

I shook my head. "It starts Tuesday for me and I can miss the first day."

I held my breath, waiting for his response.

"I don't think that's a good idea," he said, finally, staring off somewhere over my head before finally meeting my eyes.

I nodded, chewing on my bottom lip, feeling like I wanted to melt into the ground. Stupid. What did I really expect for him to say?

"Okay. I'll see you, I guess," I said, staring down at my bare toes. At least I had the presence of mind to put on sandals before I wondered over here like a crazy person.

"Drive safely, Devin."

I turned and started walking briskly back down the worn sidewalk toward Pepper and Kennedy's.

"Low." I stopped when he called my name and hesitated for a second before turning around.

He walked toward me, closing the space between us. He rolled his tongue in his mouth, the way he did when he was debating. He looked down at me and I stared up into his eyes. He shook his head.

"I'm pulling out in fifteen."

I nodded quickly.

"Okay."

"I mean it, Willow," he said, eyeing me, making my heart beat faster. "I'm leaving in fifteen minutes."

"I'll be ready."

25

DEVIN

THIS WAS A MISTAKE.

I glanced over at Willow, who was sleeping peacefully. Like everything inside her body wasn't awake and jumping all around because we were in each other's space again, the way it was in mine.

All that talk about not being under her spell any more, about her not affecting me, all those pep talks I gave myself when she bounced on me without a word— out the window.

And all she had to do was blink her damn Bambi eyes.

I spent way too much time staring at her while she slept. Her pouty lips, her long eyelashes, her honey-colored skin which was darkened from the summer sun. Looking at her was like a salve. Healing in ways I didn't even know I needed. It was also like someone gutted me.

I tapped my thumb against the steering wheel, glaring out at the road, feeling like a punk because even though it was some bullshit, I *wanted* her with me. Breathing her again, having her in my space again, it was like a hole being filled up with her smiles and her laugh and voice and *her*.

When I glanced at her again, she was awake and looking at me, her eyes sleepy. She'd been doing that for the past five hours. Looking at me when she thought I wasn't. But I felt her. Two months hadn't changed that. I doubted anything would. Willow was in my skin.

"Kennedy told me you changed your album cover."

Her warm, sleepy voice broke the silence because for once, I didn't need any sound. She asked it like a question and I glanced over at her, as she yawned then stretched her arms above her head, her nipples hard and straining against her tank top. I tore my gaze away and met her eyes. She bit her lip, heat spreading to her cheeks in awareness. Her voice was softer when she spoke.

"You decided on a completely different concept?"

"Yeah."

"So you guys changed the album completely too from the last I heard or...?"

I kept my eyes on the road. She already knew the answer to that question because I knew she kept in touch with both Kennedy and Jersey when she was dodging me for eight weeks.

"We moved some things around. Added a couple of new songs you haven't heard yet," I finally answered, watching the passing scenery. I don't know why I was trying not to look at her. I could still smell her sweet honey scent, could still feel her energy, could hear her little sighs.

"Can you play them? Jersey said she didn't have the completed tracks yet."

Jay and I were the only one with them. I glanced over at her, before nodding my head toward the stereo.

"The unmastered version is in there. You can hit play."

She looked at the stereo and I knew her thoughts were aligned with mine, especially when she met my eyes, a tiny smile playing on her lips.

"I'm glad you got something new but I kinda miss your truck and the boombox."

She glanced at me, the look in her eyes making my stomach tighten. All of the memories of us in that old truck, listening to that boombox stacked up, toppling over in the space between us.

"It finally gave out on you?"

"It was just time for something new."

I stared at her, watching her cheeks flush. Finally, she sighed, looking out of the window. I bought a used Tahoe with our summer tour money. It wasn't fancy but it felt good to have something reliable for once.

"Well, I like this too. It's you. It's dope."

I looked at her and she exhaled and turned her attention to the stereo, turning on the album.

"Twelve tracks right?"

"Yep." I grinned a little because I couldn't help it. She remembered my album theory—the one that said unless you're Stevie Wonder, there's no need for an album to ever be more than 12 tracks long, max. You get in, and get out. Helps it sound more cohesive, eliminates filler.

She closed her eyes, as if she was meditating as the music poured through the speakers, filling the space. Even unmastered it sounded good. Better than good. I was proud as hell of this record. It sounded like fate. Like jazz made in dirty nightclubs and soul made in blue-light basements. Like the sweat of hard work and the sweat from love making in stuffy bedrooms with OutKast posters on the wall and blue curtains. It sounded like our love. Like us. High and Low.

I watched Low inhaling the music. Her eyes were closed and she bobbed her head just barely, the way she did before she got into the zone when she was choreographing. When she got to the three new songs she hadn't heard yet, she smiled. We'd reworked "Come Undone" and "Certain Truth."

But I knew the second she heard it. The air shifted and she opened her eyes and looked at me. Hers were wide, expressive, because even after all this time, she couldn't help but show me what she was thinking.

"What's this one called?" she asked, her chest moving more rapidly under the weight of her breaths. I wondered what her face would look like when she heard the song. And so, I stared at her, probably longer than I should've, taking it in.

"Her and I."

"Aquemini..." she murmured. I'd left that part off the title but she didn't need it to get the meaning.

"Devin this is..." she shook her head, the music climbing around the truck, bouncing back to us because there was nowhere else for it to go. "I don't even know..."

"*I don't want to leave you alone/ I hope you never do...*" Kennedy and Zay were singing my lyrics—our lyrics. It was the standout record on the album. The entire project was tight, woven together to follow—

"A *theme*," Willow said aloud, finishing my thought. She'd fallen silent, listening to the words. "This album has a theme."

I bit the inside of my lip, watching the sign whip by that told me we were just approaching the midway point, Jackson, Mississippi.

"Her and I," I offered, glancing at her. "That's the theme. And that's the title track. We're pushing it as our main single."

She bit her lip, her gaze intense, chest heaving before blinking, looking out of the window. I don't know why she was acting so surprised. How could the album not be based on us? She was my love. Music was my love. It was inevitable— natural and instinctive for them to intertwine in the most meaningful way I knew how to connect them.

"This entire album... it's just... *wow*." She breathed it again, "wow" and looked at me this time. Her eyes were bright and she inhaled a shaky breath. "I'm so proud of you, Devin. Like... this is *amazing*. Better than I even imagined it would be, which is saying a lot because I know your talent."

The sincerity in her eyes, her nearness was messing with my head, again.

"Thank you."

She bit her lip, hesitating.

"Can I see the cover? You said you just got it back this morning?"

She shifted in her seat and my gaze automatically dropped to her thighs. She changed out her skimpy yoga outfit into a pair of shorts and an orange tank that made her skin look brighter. I didn't even have to knock on Pepper's door when I went to pick her up fifteen minutes later. I told myself if she was even a minute late, I was bouncing. My punk-ass way of trying to control the situation. But Kennedy opened the door, grinned sleepily at me and told me Willow was coming just as she rounded the corner, looking like sunlight, her smile bright, even though her eyes were hesitant.

I exhaled now and looked at the passing scenery.

"That's actually what I was callin' you about a couple of weeks ago. The album cover."

Her cheeks turned red and she looked out the window. That knot that lingered in my chest since she left, tightened back into a heavy ball. I called her at least 10 times, all unreturned. All my texts and voice mails, unreturned.

"Devin I..."

"Here."

I cut her off, not wanting to hear her excuses, sliding my finger over my phone until I came to the album cover. I passed her my phone, my fingertips brushing against hers, sending goosebumps dancing across my skin. She inhaled inaudibly but I still saw it, and dropped her gaze to the phone.

Her eyes widened and this time her gasp was audible.

"This is..." she studied the picture. "This is us."

I didn't say anything. I kept my eyes on the road. It was a picture I took of us a while back, when we were in bed, just lounging, watching movies, eating and ice cream and just... feeling each other. No one else could really tell it was me but if you knew Low then you could tell it was her. It was a close up of me kissing the corner of her mouth, an artistic shot that happened accidentally. It was my screensaver for months and now it was probably gonna be our album cover. The graphic designer Jay Little hired did her thing. It was sensual but artistic. Bare but it spoke volumes, like our sound.

"I need your permission to use the picture."

She nodded immediately, still staring at the art work, before finally looking up at me.

"Of course," she said. "I can't believe you..." She stopped and shook her head and I stared at her, anger balling in my chest.

"Can't believe I what, Low?" She blinked.

"Did this."

"Loved you? Love you?"

I shook my head, my thumb tapping against the steering wheel again.

"You were my world," I told her, the words leaving my lips on their own accord. "My everything."

I looked at her and she blinked heavily, her eyes bright. My chest tightened to the point of pain and I shook my head. This was a mistake.

"I never could leave you alone," I said aloud.

"I never wanted you to."

"But you left anyway."

"Not because I don't love you."

"Then why?" I couldn't keep the emotion out of my voice and Willow swallowed hard, inhaling.

I stared at her, hard and long, watching her struggle to think of what to say. The silence crept through the space until finally, Low reached and turned back up the volume, replaying the album from the beginning. I pushed out a humorless chuckle and refocused on the road.

This was some bullshit.

26

WILLOW

ATLANTA'S AIR WAS STIFLING. Thick and slow moving through my lungs, clogged by the heat and humidity like its never-ending traffic. But that hadn't stopped me from talking. My mouth had been moving for what felt like at least two hours. After I listened to Prototype's album two more times, after I got over the shock that he'd named his entire *album* after us, Devin seemed to loosen up a little. Maybe that was an exaggeration but he'd stopped responding to me in grunts, which was refreshing.

I told him what I'd been doing in Houston. That, in an extraordinary showing of God's grace, I'd still been able to take the internship I passed on because my replacement dropped out at the last minute. I told him about the kids I worked with, how I didn't enjoy the administrative part of running the dance program but I could literally see the effects of what we were doing had on them. I saw them become bolder, empowered, braver, more confident, and that was amazing because as they were morphing into a better version of themselves, so was I.

I told him about the woman who ran the program, Monique, and how she'd sort of become my mentor and helped spark the idea of creating a floating program, that I could implement wherever I was, instead of having a static building.

Devin mostly just listened, his eyes on the road, one hand on the wheel. Occasionally, he'd push out a long breath that I only saw, but couldn't hear. Sometimes, he'd glance over at me, his gaze pensive, like in the early days when it seemed like he was trying to figure me out, or realizing something new about me.

"You think working with kids, teaching them dance is something you want to do as a career?"

I nodded and smiled. "Maybe even open my own studio. But I'd incorporate both dance and yoga. I might even think about starting an after school program, or in-school program so that the kids can practice yoga during their day. It'd be an amazing resource as an alternative disciplinary tactic."

"Yoga, huh?"

He arched a brow, a slight grin on his face that my stomach tingle.

"The breathing techniques are calming. The movement and stretching into poses focuses your mind, even for little ones. I just think it could be a first alternative, especially in predominantly black schools where the only thing they seem to think works is criminalizing our kids."

Devin grinned a little again, his eyes still on the road.

"Like even with you, think about when you were in elementary school. The first thing that the responsible, active adults in your lives suggested was to put you on drugs strong enough for a grown man. Think about how *insane* that is."

He glanced over at me.

"I'm not suggesting yoga or movement is the cure for everything. But it's one viable method to addressing so-called behavior issues in kid's lives that don't include pumping drugs into their still-developing systems."

"That makes sense," he said, eyes on the road. "That concept is dope. I could see you doing that."

I didn't realize how much I needed to hear those words until right then, the second that he said them.

"I used some of your music for my classes, both the yoga and the dance class."

"You had kids doing yoga to trap music?"

"No," I laughed and he smiled. I felt it to my toes. "The bouncier beats I choreographed routines too. The smoother ones like the one I used to audition with that time… that I used for yoga. And I developed a new component to the dance program, where instead of just teaching the kids dance, we study the origins, and try to give them some real connectivity to our history."

He glanced at me again. "That's dope, Low. Sounds like you were really doin' it out there."

"I was just focused, and inspired, I guess."

He didn't say anything, just exhaled as he switched lanes. I wasn't really used to this version of Devin. He wasn't withdrawn but reserved. His thumb was tapping a rhythm on the steering wheel, and for a while I just looked at him. *I missed him*.

The thought reverberated through every part of my being. I wanted him. Even though this summer was what I needed, and I loved being able to spend time with my mom and dad, being away from Devin was like a constant hole in my chest that was never filled. I missed his smiles and his deep voice and his teasing and the way he listened when I talked and his patience and his passion, as well as his bluntness. I missed the way he only had to look at me with his brown eyes and I immediately felt safe.

"I gotta make a couple of runs," he said as we pulled further into the city, up I-85. His driving, as usual whenever we hit Atlanta, had become more aggressive, whipping front of slow-moving cars, cursing under his breath at people who braked on the interstate. "I can drop you off at my moms or you can roll."

"I wanna be with you."

He looked over at me, his gaze indecipherable when I said that.

"You said something about a house?" I asked tentatively after a few long minutes of watching cars on the interstate.

"I gotta go sign some paperwork. I'm renting a house here now. Moms is gonna stay there with Omar since I'm gonna be in and out anyway."

I blinked, my heart suddenly racing. "You're gonna..." I stopped, focusing on at one thing at time. Something I picked up in yoga.

"You're renting your mom a house?"

Devin nodded, "On the east side, near Grant Park. Probably near where you said your grandma used to live. She's pretty much moved in, but I gotta go sign the paperwork."

"They let her move in without the paperwork being signed?"

He grinned though there was no humor in it. "When you got the paper, it's funny how things change. I paid six months in advance. He let moms move in."

"Wow, I know she's happy to be out of the apartment."

He didn't say anything.

"That's so cool, Devin. I know that has to feel so good that you're able to do that for them."

I remembered our long conversations in the dead of night. The things he told me about wanting to buy his mom and brother a house. This wasn't that exactly but it was a step in that direction that I know he had to feel good about.

"And you'll be... living here?"

He looked over at me. "Somethin' like that."

My heart was beating triple time as I processed his words. Devin was moving to Atlanta.

I looked out of the window, at the passing traffic, willing the bile back down my throat, so that I wouldn't get sick in Devin's truck.

27
DEVIN

SHE WAS DIFFERENT.

Nothing huge. Nothing world-changing, but I noticed. I knew everything about Willow Elizabeth and... she was different. She talked different. She even moved different. I took a hit of the joint that Jay Little passed to me, bobbing my head to some new music that he was playing for me from a new rapper dude from the west side that he was working with and wanted me to help produce. But mostly I was watching Willow.

She was sitting on the leather couch across from the console, engrossed in conversation with Chad, the lead singer from Black Bottom. He was talking about Atlanta's ever-changing music scene and its burgeoning film and arts communities. Buddy talked about it non-stop while we were on the road, so I didn't even need to hear the conversation to know what was being said.

Mostly, it was Willow's body language. She was relaxed. She was always gorgeous but even that was different. She was more magnetic. The twists she was rocking framed her features, making her eyes stand out more, and her lips. She crossed her legs, her sundress riding up a little on her thighs, and looked up at me. I inhaled again, and blew the smoke out, not breaking eye contact. Her gaze dropped to my lips before she met my eyes again, biting her lip then releasing it before turning her attention back to Chad, who was now breaking down Atlanta's bounce era. It was obvious buddy was completely under her spell. Low just had that effect on people, without even trying. Everyone genuinely liked her. She was different, but her energy, her sweet, accepting vibe was the same— that was still love.

"So what do you think?" Jay asked me about the music. "Got something that will work for him?"

I nodded. "Definitely. Dude has the type of sound I've been wanting to work with."

"That's what I thought too."

"I'll send you some tracks tomorrow to check out. What's up with the mastering?" I asked, switching the conversation to our album.

"We can have it done in a couple of weeks. Thinking we'll drop the album around October or November," he said, throwing on some new beats I'd recently made, bobbing his head.

Jay started his own label, NDE over the summer with some startup money from one of his old college roommates who was heavy in the Afrotech scene out in California, and Prototype and Black Bottom had signed with him because we believed in his vision. We had a couple of small label deals on the table, so did Black Bottom—but it wasn't just about the quick check. It was about the vision, the long-term and Jay understood that. Now, we were looking for a distribution deal. We'd put the record out either way but a distributor had more money and access.

"The album is *flames,*" Chad said, eyes wide. "Y'all poured your heart into that."

"No doubt, folk," I said nodding my head in appreciation at him. I glanced at Low who was looking at me.

"I did put my heart in it," I said, looking at her, as I inhaled from the joint once more. Her cheeks turned red and she shifted on the couch.

"It's been a minute Low Low," Jay said, looking at her, smiling. "How you been?"

"Good." She smiled and it was genuine, and it was messing with my head, again.

"Heard you were home in Houston? We missed you on the road. But it was a good time?"

She glanced at me. I put the joint out in the ashtray but didn't say anything.

"It was. I took an internship there." She filled him in about the internship, her eyes animated and bright. That pull, that tug in my chest was active again.

"Ganja yoga?" Jay repeated now, after she'd told him about some new yoga trend where you got high and stretched. It sounded like some white hippie shit but she was so damn cute telling the story, everyone just listened anyway.

"It's supposed to help you relax deeper into the meditative qualities of the practice," Willow shrugged.

"You tried it?" Chad asked, grinning, glancing over at me.

"Once."

I raised a brow and her gaze fell on me. "I think you'd like it, Devin."

She turned back to Chad.

"I just took one hit and it was... interesting. Not something I'd do regularly but... interesting. I did feel a little more relaxed."

"You can teach yoga to some of my artists while they're on the road, help calm their asses down sometimes."

Willow laughed. "That actually might be cool."

"I'm serious," Jay said grinning. "Chad is all over the place when we're on the road, he could use the focus." Chad looked up from his phone, exchanging a look with me. He was just an eccentric dude, put me in mind of Zay that way.

"And your boy barely slept the entire time." Jay nodded his head toward me.

Willow's eyes widened in obvious concern when she looked at me.

"He'd come off stage at 1, and be up until six or seven in the morning, working. Sleep a couple of hours and be right back at it."

"Here you go. You stay exaggerating," I said.

"Chad." Jay leaned forward, eyes wide and trying to get Chad to co-sign.

"We started calling him No Doze because he never slept."

I felt Willow's eyes on me but I ignored her.

"No one slept like that," I corrected. "Until we got the bus."

"Remember that night in Memphis, when the damn bus ran out of gas." Chad shook his head. Willow was just listening as Chad launched into one of his elaborate stories.

Her eyes were a little wistful.

"Next time, you need to come with us when you get out of school, keep this dude sane," Jay said.

"Bein' on the road is tough. Don't know if that's Low Low's vibe," I said, watching as her cheeks turned pink again. She met my gaze directly a bit of challenge in hers.

"I've always been good at adjusting, Devin. You know that."

She cocked her head to the side a little, and I almost grinned at her little display of aggressiveness. But she didn't have any ground to stand on. Not anymore.

Jay glanced between us. I didn't have to tell him anything for him to pick up something was off with us, especially when she dipped on the tour. We spent too much time together for him to not know something was up. He just didn't know what. Neither did I.

After we ran and got the house stuff handled for moms, we had dinner with her. Moms wasn't much of a cook but she was in a good mood and threw one of those frozen lasagnas in the oven for us, laughing and talking with Low like old times. She told her about the new gig she'd just landed, working as a dialysis technician since she'd just graduated from school about a month ago, and Low eagerly peppered her with questions, since her mom was a nurse and she knew what to ask about. But moms really spent a lot of time asking Willow questions about her summer spent in Houston, like she was trying to fish something out of Willow that she wanted me to hear.

All that wasn't necessary though. I got it. Willow being away, no matter how it affected me, was good for her. It was all over her, in her spirit.

But she just didn't have to leave the way she did. That was the part I couldn't wrap my head around. She just fuckin' left. Talked to me *one time* in eight weeks. How is that love?

"Hey, what's up, man."

Jay looked up, greeting some dude who walked into the studio, greeting Chad with a broad smile.

"Been a minute," he said, exchanging dap with him.

"What up," the dude greeted Jay, heading to the console to slap his hand in greeting. "What's good with you, Jay?"

"What's up, man," I greeted dude because he was lingering next to me. I ain't know buddy like that and glanced at Jay. We normally didn't have anyone we didn't know in the studio.

"This is Trevor Carmichael." Immediately I looked up at him, watching as he seated himself on the edge of the couch next to Low, bobbing his head in greeting when Jay introduced us all.

Willow eyes grew wide. She recognized the name too.

"Trevor, Devin Walker, who I was telling you about. The rest of the band isn't here today but we want you to sit down with everyone soon."

"I dig y'all's stuff, man. A lot. Jay let me hear the new album too," Trevor said.

He bobbed his head up and down, brows raised. "Shit is dope." I had the feeling that was high praise from buddy and nodded my head at him.

"'Preciate it, man. Glad we earned your approval with this one."

He cocked his head a little, tossing a look at Jay before meeting my eyes again.

"You shitted on us last time you wrote about Prototype."

Dude widened his eyes chuckled a little, scratching his chin. "You remember that piece, huh?"

"Hell yeah I remember it. It was our first big review. Shit stung."

He laughed again. "I didn't shit on you, for the record. I knew the band was dope from the beginning. I offered a critical observation. And listening to what you're workin' with now—with the new singer, Kennedy, playing off Zay's vocals, and the improvements you've made — I'd say it was accurate."

I pushed out a chuckle. We'd started getting more press over the past few months and most of them were ass kissers or didn't know the music for real. This dude wasn't afraid to speak his real mind and he knew his stuff.

"It's all good, man. I'm actually a fan... *now*."

He laughed. "I appreciate that. I did a little write up on that rally you did out in Texas yesterday."

"Oh word?"

Trevor nodded. "Saw the footage online," he shook his head. "I thought that crowd was gonna lose it when you started with N.W.A. You plan on doing a lot of those kinds of rallies?"

I shrugged, glancing at Jay. He followed our lead when it came to those kinds of decisions.

"We're down to do more, whenever it makes sense. But to be real, I'm tired of the marching shit. I'm damn near feelin' like we need another revolution or somethin.'"

"Like war?" Willow asked.

"I mean... *somethin'* gotta give at some point," I said, as Chad bobbed his head. "It's like America doesn't understand anything except war and money."

"This is all off the record. Don't be putting any of this shit in any stories, have the Feds running up on us," Jay warned, grinning at Trevor, who laughed.

"Nah, man. I ain't working. I feel where you're comin' from," he told me. "It's messed up but the best music comes out of times like these. Look at the music that was coming out of the sixties and seventies— Nina Simone, Marvin Gaye, Funkadelic, Stevie Wonder..."

"Isley Brothers," Willow spoke up, glancing at me, earning a head nod from Trevor.

"Look at the *drugs* that were coming out of the sixties and seventies," Chad laughed. "And then they wonder why everyone is poppin' pills and whatever else now. It's a sign of the times we're in, the music shows that."

"It's like even if the music wasn't directly about politics or social change, it just had *soul* because of everything that was going on," Willow agreed, redirecting her attention to Trevor. "That's what Prototype is about... the *love*. That's the core of it. That's why the music speaks to you the way it does."

Trevor grinned at her, still bobbing his head up and down.

"I agree." He tilted his head, listening to the tracks I'd made playing the background.

"This you?" he asked, pointing at Chad.

"Nope," Chad bobbed his head toward me.

"Dope," Trevor said, appreciatively. "Haven't heard your music sound like this."

The music had a little more of an edge, was a little more raw. Stuff I'd made when I was up all not on the road, trying not to think about the woman who was sitting across from me, looking and feeling like light.

"Thanks, man," I said, tearing my gaze away from her.

"Read the piece you wrote on Zo," Jay told Trevor, leaning forward with his elbows on his knees. "Crazy how he's gotten big, so fast."

Trevor nodded. "Yeah, man. Getting ready to head on European tour." He glanced at me. "I actually was hollerin' at him the other day, telling him that his shows would work better with a live band. He's down with it, so I let him hear some of your stuff."

He bobbed his head toward me. "He loves Prototype. Y'all may be able to work something out."

"Word?" I asked.

Low sat up on the couch a little straighter.

Trevor nodded, turning to Jay. "I'll shoot you his manager's info now. He said somethin' about being his band but opening with your own stuff, if y'all can get it worked out."

Trevor took out his phone and started texting. I glanced at Jay before my gaze landed on Willow. Her eyes were wide, her lips slightly parted. I kept my face straight even though I wanted to jump out of my chair. Zo was a rapper out of Cali, who'd bum-rushed the industry a couple of years ago because he'd blown up independently. His style was dope, heavily influenced by Kendrick Lamar but he sang too, and the combo was ill. He was easily the biggest dude in hip-hop right now, and one of the biggest acts in music period. Opening for him would be a *game-changer*. I kept my cool though and so did Jay. Chad grinned, nodding his head.

"Look at you. Out here about to put me out of a job," Jay joked.

"Nah, you can keep the business side of music," Trevor replied, eyes still on his phone. "That isn't what moves me."

"Seriously, man. That's what's up," Jay said, bobbing his head up down. "D, wanna hit Trav and everyone else, see what's good?"

"Hell yeah. Appreciate that, man."

"It's all love, homie," Trevor replied. "Hope y'all can get something worked out."

"I think this is cause for a celebration," Chad said. "Low, you down?"

Her eyes fell on me, her smile making my heart beat faster. "I'm down for whatever Devin wants."

She held my gaze, almost as though daring me to look away. As usual, I couldn't.

28

WILLOW

THE LOUNGE CHAD took us to in Old Fourth Ward was black hipster central. Prince's "Dorothy Parker" was pouring from the speakers and everyone there looked cool without appearing that they were trying to look cool, which takes effort. The energy was low key but alive. All the women were rocking naturals— fros and twist outs, locs or twists like mine— and the guys were just as creative with their hair and dress. There was a hookah corner in one section of the rectangular space, where groups were gathered around funky colored pipes. I'd been dancing around with Chad on the dance floor, getting introduced to all his friends who were there. He called me "Devin's girl" and I never corrected him.

I turned and looked at Devin, who was sitting next to me at the bar after I told Chad I needed a drink break. It was the first free moment Devin had because everyone in Atlanta knew him too.

"Can I buy you a drink?"

He stared at me. "I have one." He lifted his beer toward me.

I released a silent breath.

"I can't believe you're about to go on tour with *Zo*. I'm so excited for you, Devin."

"It's not in concrete yet."

"It'll happen," I said confidently. He didn't say anything, just looked away, out over the crowd. I took a small sip of my drink. I studied his profile, his long eyelashes, the shape of his jaw beneath his 5 o'clock shadow, his lips before letting my gaze drop to his arms.

"You have new tattoos."

He looked over at me.

"You have new hair." His gaze trailed over my face. "It suits you."

"Thanks," I said, my face warming.

He met my eyes when without thought, I traced the lines of the new Chinese symbol on his arm, just above his tat that said, "wait expectantly." Goosebumps broke out where my finger trailed over his skin but his expression didn't change. It was bored, unaffected, like he was waiting to see what else I was going to do just so that he could show me how deeply unconcerned he was with me.

"What's it mean?" I asked ignoring the twisted knot in my belly, my fingers still tracing the mark, because I wanted to touch him.

"Live in truth. Live free."

He looked at me pointedly before subtly moving his arm out of my reach by grabbing his beer, redirecting his attention to the girl who was sitting next to him, the engineer who was going to be mastering their album. They had an easy rapport and it was obvious they knew each other pretty well. Maybe they'd even been together back in the day. Or maybe they'd been together recently. I tried not to spend a lot of time thinking about if Devin was with other women while I was in Houston. I knew it was a possibility and I knew if he had, I couldn't say anything. That was the risk I took in leaving the way I did.

I shifted on my bar stool, feeling anxious. I wanted to be alone with him. I wanted to reconnect with him. I wanted him.

But he didn't want to touch me. Every time our arms bumped accidentally, he'd pull it away, or when our legs brushed against each other's at the bar, he shifted in his seat, away from me. He didn't want to be alone with me either. I knew Devin. He was extremely social until he wasn't. I'd sorta figured out his moodiness that way. It was like a sugar high, and when he crashed he didn't feel like being bothered with anyone. He should've been crashing right now and I could tell he was getting agitated, being in a crowded lounge in

Atlanta's Old Fourth Ward, but he didn't seem to be in a hurry to leave.

I took another sip of my drink, biting my lip when the girl laughed loudly at something Devin said. I felt like crying. He was basically ignoring me. I felt stupid and guilty, and horny because I was near him, and confused and hurt. I knew in my heart I made the right decision to go to Houston for a while but this new space Devin and I were in was unbearable. I took a deep breath and slid off my stool. I was about to push through the crowd when I felt a hand on my waist.

"Where you goin?" Devin asked. His touch was so hot it felt as though someone was burning a hole into my skin.

"To the restroom." *To get myself together*.

His eyes were low and relaxed, effects of the weed he'd been smoking. "You comin' back?"

My stomach rolled at the aloof accusation in his eyes. I wet my lips and nodded.

"Were you ready to leave or something?" I asked.

"Nah, not yet."

I nodded again, watching as he pressed his beer to his lips, eyeing me over the bottle.

"I'll be right back." I slipped away from him and pushed through the crowd, talking to myself the entire time, telling myself to keep it together.

I returned from the restroom after fixing my make-up, and staring at myself for a minute in the wide, dirty mirror which was lined with dim white lights until another group of girls came in, talking loudly and it was obvious I was hogging the mirror space staring at my reflection like a dork. But when I exited I halted in my steps, nearly causing a girl coming in to bump into me. I muttered a "sorry," my heart racing. They were playing Prototype's song, "Space" one of three single's they'd released ahead o the album. It was the first time I'd heard the song in public, while I was actually with Devin.

I rushed my way through the dense crowd of hipsters, grinning ear to ear, searching for Devin at the bar. I paused in my steps when I saw him though. The engineer girl was on her tip-toes, whispering something in his ear and Devin was laughing, bobbing his head up and down. I touched my tongue to the corner of my mouth and exhaled, as I made my way back to the bar, this time more slowly. I stood at the bar counter and picked up my half-full drink, downing it quickly.

"Word?" Devin asked, turning toward me and quirking a brow. I didn't know he was paying me any attention. I leaned my arms against the bar counter, my back turned to the crowd.

"I'm good. The drink wasn't very strong."

"Hey, so I'm gonna catch you guys later." I looked up to see the engineer girl standing in front of Devin, texting on her phone. She looked back up and grinned at Devin, stepping forward and giving him a long hug, saying something in his ear that made him smirk sexily. I looked away.

"Aight, be easy, girl," Devin said when she stepped away from his chest. She waved her fingers at him then me, pushing her way through the crowd toward the doors.

"Where'd Chad go?" I asked, after a few seconds of us standing there silently, like strangers.

Devin bobbed his head toward the hookah section, where some woman was sitting on his lap. The DJ went into another Prototype song, "Certain Truth," mixing the two seamlessly. And people brightened up again, dancing around to the smooth beat. I remembered the night they'd made that, and I smiled, then looked up at Devin.

"This is *so* cool. Do you still get excited when you hear them playing your music while you're out?"

He nodded, grinning, and my belly tingled. "I can't front. It feels good."

"You worked hard for it. It feels surreal to be out with you while your song is playing, seeing the crowd reaction."

I'd obviously seen him countless times live but this was different. He gave dap to a guy who passed by him, nodding, thanking him for the compliment he'd just delivered. The guy nodded at me too and I smiled and waved.

I glanced around the lounge, where more people were dancing on the small dance floor because security moved the bar tables to the back a few minutes ago, to clear the space.

"You shoulda seen entire venues rockin' with us. Places twice the size of Jimmy's and other places we've played." His tone and gaze was pointed when he looked at me.

"I did, kinda. I watched snippets of your shows that fans uploaded online."

Devin shook his head, taking a sip of his beer, and looked away. I stepped closer, brushing my nose against his bicep because I couldn't help it. I inhaled his clean scent, and closed my eyes, heart thudding, moving so that I was directly in front of him, standing in between his legs. He exhaled, biting on the corner of his lip as he looked down at me but didn't touch me otherwise.

"I'm sorry." The words came out like a whisper. I pressed my forehead against his chest, and he inhaled, releasing the breath slowly. When looked up at him, everything around us faded into the background as I stared into his brown eyes.

"Now ain't the time, Low." He arched a brow, taking another swig of his beer and swallowing as he eyed me. "We had an eleven-hour ride to get into us."

"I know. But—"

"You thought you were gonna come back and, what? It was just gonna be whatever? It was gonna be all good?"

"No."

"Then what?" I could feel the rapid rising and falling of his chest. I bit my lip then released it.

"I just... I'm sorry that things happened the way that they did. That I handled everything that way—that we're so broken now."

Tears gathered in my eyes that I willed not to fall. He broke eye contact, looking off over my head.

"We *were* broken."

"What are we now?"

He looked into my eyes.

"Done."

29

DEVIN

THE RIDE back to the house was silent and tense. Low was biting on her pinky nail, staring out of the window and when she did look at me, her eyes were bright with tears she was holding back.

I felt like an asshole. Then the next minute I felt vindicated because she was hurt too. But that would last for about .5 seconds because when she hurt, I hurt.

I gripped the wheel, making the block to the house. The street was quiet, lined with cars that were marked with nighttime dew. Moms driveway was empty because she was chaperoning an overnight trip to Lake Lanier—some bonding thing with Omar's high school soccer team.

When we pushed inside of the dark house, a renovated bungalow that moms called "charming and cute," and I turned on the living room lamp, Low immediately asked if she could use the shower and had been there for the past thirty minutes. I took my shower quickly in the master bedroom, and was on the couch in the living room with the TV on, stuffing lukewarm lasagna in my mouth, pretending I wasn't craving Willow when I hadn't had her in eight weeks. Hadn't heard the rhythm of her soft moans, felt her breath against my ear when she breathed my name, or her fingers digging into my back.

I heard the bathroom door open and a few minutes later, Willow walked into the living room, wearing one of my old Hawks' t-shirts, just as I sat my plate down on the end table. It hit her mid-thigh and I wondered if she had on anything underneath it as I stared at her legs before meeting her eyes. They were puffy and red like she'd been crying in the shower, and that rock in the center of my chest got heavier.

"I love you, Devin. I've loved you for so long I can't even remember what it feels like to *not* love you." Her voice was quiet.

"I was falling apart."

I looked at her and she twisted her lips.

"I know that sounds melodramatic. Maybe more like..." She bit the inside of her lip and shrugged. "I dunno. I needed to get to my middle, you know? My core. I had to find me. It was like, I had stuff going on with dance and school but my only real passion and focus was *you* and that wasn't healthy for either of us."

I leaned forward, putting my elbows on my knees, staring at the hardwood floor.

"Ain't that what we were about?" I looked up at her. "I hold you down, you hold me down? You weren't just my girl. You were my best friend, Low. My *love.*"

I looked down at the floor.

"You were, *are*, mine too," she pressed, heaving a breath. "I just got to a point where I didn't know what *my* life was about. You have music. You've had it forever. You've been working toward it. And even when things got bad or difficult, you still had your end goal in mind. For me, it felt like I was just floating along. Getting swept up by whatever breeze knocked me in a new direction. I wasn't happy with *me* and that put all these unrealistic, unfair expectations on you to fulfill that emptiness."

I looked up at her when she moved to sit down on the edge of the couch, bringing her sweet coconut scent with her.

"I feel you on that but—"

"And then the whole thing with Gia," she interrupted, turning and crossing her legs underneath her on the couch, pulling her t-shirt over her knees, so that we were only a few feet apart.

"I never told you everything I was dealing with, between her and the dance team," she said, tugging at one of her twists. She'd let them down, and they were hanging to the middle of her back. "And I failed my communications strategy and microeconomics classes," she was talking double-time now. "I've been doing summer school online too, so that I can still graduate on time, which my parents made me pay for, and they should have," she tacked on. "But it was just so much coming all at once... and I know I didn't really tell you—"

"No, you didn't tell me," I interrupted. "I had to find out everything that was going on with you from Jersey, after you left."

"Devin, you were so busy. And I didn't know for sure if I was gonna fail or not. I didn't want to burden you with a what if."

That was bullshit.

"Low, when have you ever had an issue tellin' me what's goin' on with you? I know things were moving fast that last month and we weren't seeing each other like that. We weren't connecting. But I'm thinking, aight, we'll get on the road, where some of the extra noise will die down a little and it'll be cool."

She got up and paced toward the TV. "There was only going to be more noise on tour, Devin. More rushing and less time."

"You don't know that."

She shook her head, biting her lip and sat back down on the couch.

"I know after how things went down that last night... we weren't in the best place," I admitted. I watched her inhale, her gaze dropping to her pinky nail as she picked at it. "I accept my part in that. I shoulda just left Brianna's ass at the club. But we got to a place where we couldn't even talk? You couldn't holler at me about what was up? And then you just *dip*? Just up and leave at six in the morning with no explanation? You know how that felt? After everything we've been through that you could just leave me like that, that easily?"

"It wasn't easy," she countered, her eyes filled with tears. A tear dripped down her cheek, and she quickly wiped it with the back of her hand. "I love you. And if I would've said something to you, I wouldn't have left. If I would've been talking to you the whole time, I wouldn't have been able to focus on getting my head together."

I rolled my tongue in my mouth, staring unseeingly at the TV.

"I hear what you're saying and all but..." I shook my head. "I don't know how to... you *left*, Low. Without a word. That had me questioning *everything*. Two years of me and you and then just...bam. *Nothin'*? A couple of texts talking about you needed space? I don't hear your voice *at all* in eight weeks? What were we even about for real? Some college shit? Because that's not where my head was. I was thinkin' about *wifin'* you. I thought *that* was the path we were on, where we were headed eventually..."

"I did too, Devin." The look in her eyes was desperate, matching the yearning in my chest. "Our relationship, everything about it, was, *is* real. It's the most real thing I know."

"That makes it even worse, if that's how you treat the people who mean somethin' to you."

I shook my head again, watching her as she chewed on her lip, her gaze heavy, eyes still puffy. "I'm *sorry*. That whole Brianna thing, Devin... and then what you said afterwards..."

"You know I didn't mean that. You know Brianna was never, and could never be a 'thing' for us. And I wasn't the only one talkin' reckless that night."

Low touched her tongue to the corner of her mouth, looking away.

"I think if I wouldn't have left, we would have been messed up for good, Devin. We needed that time."

I rolled my tongue in my mouth, staring blankly at the TV screen, her words bouncing around in my head, my heart.

"*Nah*." I ran a hand over my face. "Even if that was true, I don't know how to move past you just bouncing on me like that."

"I'm *sorry*," she whispered again.

"Let's just drop it, Low. I'm tired as hell and we're talkin' in circles."

She heaved a breath, eyes on me, and leaned her head against the couch cushion. Finally, she looked toward the TV, the light bouncing off her pretty features.

"Why did you let me come with you?" she asked quietly, after a few minutes of us both staring at the television.

"You asked. Sayin' 'no' to you ain't ever been my shit."

She blinked and looked down at her hands.

I sat there in silence, watching the light from the TV more than what was actually on the screen, my mind in so many different places I knew that if hadn't smoked earlier, I wouldn't've been able to sit still. Willow was off in her own world too, her eyes distant whenever I glanced at her.

"I'm gonna go to bed," she said. "Are you sure you don't want me to take the couch?"

I fixed a look on her and she sighed softly, standing. She hesitated for a second, tugging at the hem of her t-shirt.

"G'nite."

"Night."

I watched her make her way toward the spare bedroom, where there was a black futon made up like a bed. I stayed on the couch for another forty-five minutes, idly flicking through the channels before I finally decided to try to shut off my brain, and my thoughts.

I headed to the bathroom, rounding the corner back into the living room, just as Willow exited the spare bedroom and rammed into me.

"Sorry," she breathed, looking up at me, rubbing her forehead where she'd hit my shoulder.

"You aight?" I brushed a thumb over the spot she was just rubbing.

She nodded. "All that muscle you've put on over the summer. It felt like running into a wall." She smiled a little, shifting her weight.

"Thought you were sleep."

"I couldn't." She looked up at me. "I was about to snoop and see if your mom had any ice cream," she admitted, smiling sheepishly.

I grinned. "I doubt it. They ain't been here long."

She exhaled, one of those stuttering breaths like when you've been crying for a while. She was still standing too close to me in the darkened, narrow hallway. There were a few boxes backed against the wall that still needed to be unpacked, making the space even tighter. Her eyes were on my chest now, which was bare because I'd pulled of my shirt. She hadn't backed up and I hadn't moved either. The way she smelled, the heat that was coming off her in waves, all of it was messing with my head.

"Are you hungry?" I asked, my gaze on her lips. I could barely make out the details of her features because it was dark and the only light was coming from the TV in the living room. But I heard her intake of breath, felt her sway a little closer to me.

"I just wanted ice cream."

The words came out breathy and her chest was rising and falling fast, her nipples peaked beneath her cotton t-shirt. *I can't go there with her.*

Her lips parted, and she blinked up me, as if reading my mind. She reached down and pulled her shirt over her head in one quick motion, her long twists shaking free, hanging down her back. Her breasts were full, and my gaze slid over her darkened areolas to her hardened nipples before traveling down her flat belly to her thick thighs. She looked like an Ethiopian goddess. Like how Eden probably looked before Adam did whatever she told him to do in that African garden. She stared up at me, in just tiny pink panties, her expression vulnerable and wide open like it was that first time when we hung out at the Pancake Shack and I dropped her off at her dorms. Her chest was heaving in her nervousness. She was asking.

Like a puppet on a string, I reached out and ran my hands over her smooth hips. She shuddered and literally moaned, a short, desperate sound, when I touched her. I stepped closer, backing her against the wall, the back of her head hitting it with a soft thud. She arched her back, pushing her hips toward me and she made a soft noise that made me even harder. It'd been too long.

I wasn't thinking any more, I slid her panties off and pushed my sweats down enough to free myself, bent low and lifted her, thrusting up into her and at the same time, pressed my mouth to hers, kissing her like I hadn't seen her months. She didn't hesitate for even a second. She just opened for me, eager and ready, her tongue clashing and dancing with mine, as I pumped into her, all the thoughts about us sliding in and out of my brain every time I pushed deeper into her tight warmth, harder, faster.

Our kiss was desperate, frantic, a clashing of lips, teeth and tongues, mingled with Willow's soft whimpers, as she struggled to push herself closer to me, her legs locked possessively around my waist, her heels digging into my ass.

I bit her neck hard, not trying to leave a mark, but maybe I was. Trying not to be too rough with her, but maybe I was.

"Devin," she breathed my name in her familiar way, so it sounded like my name was the only the only thought in her head worth speaking.

Within seconds I was coming, grunting deeply as I thrust into her harder, faster, gripping her thighs so tightly I hoped she wasn't bruised.

"*Low,*" her name tore from my lips as an unintelligible groan as I came hard, my entire body tightening, nearly dropping her as she held tightly onto my neck. My breathing was harsh, and I struggled to blink my way back to reality because my ears were still buzzing from how hard I came. I didn't even know if she finished. I let her go and she slid down the wall, her breathing labored, as I held her loosely at the waist, her face buried in my chest.

When I was able to move, I walked her back to the spare bedroom, before leaving for the bathroom. I relieved myself and cleaned up a little, dodging my reflection in the small oval mirror because I'd have to square with what I was doing, versus what my head was telling me to do, which was to back up off her, and not take my ass back into that bedroom. But I knew that wasn't happening. I wanted Willow. I always did. I wanted her close. Everything was up in the air with us, and it was still raw but I loved her. And for now, in this moment, that trumped all the other shit I felt.

She was under the striped yellow and green sheets when I came back into the room.

"I used your mom's bathroom. Hope that's okay."

I nodded, pushing my sweats off and sliding onto the futon with her. It reminded me of all those nights we made love on my shitty mattress in my too hot bedroom back in Tyler, the times she slept with me on the living room couch at my moms' tiny apartment, or the times she watched movies with me on a cracked tablet screen in a beat up old truck that smelled like oil because no amount of air freshener could get it out.

Willow was on me immediately, rolling on top of me pressing her naked curves against me, her hair forming a curtain around her face, brushing against my shoulders. I was hard again, and I grabbed at her thighs, because I couldn't not touch her. The moonlight was stretching through the cracks of the closed blinds, dancing over her skin. She was *beautiful*.

She lifted her head, her gaze connecting with mine, then leaned down slowly, kissing my lips over and over. Light touches, like she never wanted to stop.

"I missed you," she murmured against my mouth, pecking my lips again. "I love you... *so much*."

She pressed her forehead to mine, interlacing our fingers, at my sides, and slid down onto me, closing her eyes in relief when we were connected again. She slowly began working her hips, eyes trained on me and I shook my head. *This girl.*

"Can you tell me you love me to?" she whispered.

"You know I do."

I closed my eyes, gripping her hips, thrusting up and into her so that she moaned aloud, and let everything that wasn't Willow, go.

30

WILLOW

When I woke up, he wasn't there. I blinked to clear my vision, my gaze falling on the empty, wrinkled space next to me, and my heart dropped. I sat up, running a hand over my face. My ears registered the faint sound of OutKast playing beyond the room. Of course, he hadn't left. He couldn't leave me at his mom's house in Atlanta. I pulled on my t-shirt, which was now lying next to me on the bed because Devin had obviously retrieved it from the hallway at some point last night and headed out of the room for the bathroom.

The living room was empty except for the sound of OutKast's "Elevators" playing when I walked in. I turned the corner into the kitchen and spotted Devin. He was leaned against the counter next to the sink, texting, wearing nothing but sweats. There was a mug and a green teabag sitting next to him on the counter.

"Good morning," I greeted him. He looked up from his phone, his eyes unreadable.

"Morning." He returned his attention to his phone.

"You drink green tea now?"

"Found out it works for me over the summer. Gives me an energy boost." He glanced at me briefly before resuming his typing. "Want some?"

He extended the cup toward me and I took it, sipping a little, wondering if that was snide remark about how many times we'd made love last night. Three.

"You're like a drug to me, Willow," he'd murmured that last time that he slid inside of me in the early hours of the morning. But the way he said it wasn't cute. Or good. It was like I had side effects that he didn't want. A bad addiction.

"Do you want breakfast? I saw your mom had eggs and some bacon in the fridge."

He shook his head. "I was about to wake you up. We gotta push out in about twenty minutes. We can grab something fast on the way. I gotta make it back to Tyler before eight."

"Okay."

He looked up at me, his gaze sliding to my legs. He frowned.

"Are those my briefs?"

I blushed looking down at his gray boxer briefs. "I forgot to pack underwear and I saw you had like three pair..."

He raised his brows and shook his head, returning his attention to his phone. He was still so mad at me. I wasn't stupid. I didn't think a night of making love would solve our issues. I just wanted to be close to him again. But I did hope that maybe the closeness we'd shared last night would chip at the wall he had up. That wasn't the case this morning. If anything, he seemed even angrier. I heaved a breath, heading out of the kitchen.

"Low."

I stopped and turned to look at him.

"You still takin' the pill?"

Heat spread through my body and I nodded. We hadn't used condoms last night. After that maybe pregnancy scare, I got on the pill and we did away with them completely. It was so weird for him to be asking that now, so foreign. So, indicative of the distance between us, even after last night.

"Can you be ready in twenty?"

I nodded again and left out of the kitchen.

31

WILLOW

I STARED out of the passenger window, the scenery whipping by so quickly, it almost seemed as though it was in slow motion. We were just hitting Mississippi, nearing the halfway mark of the eleven-hour drive that Devin would probably cut to ten with the way that he was driving. I'd offered to take over but Devin frowned, and said nothing, so I took that as a "no."

I popped more sunflower seeds into my mouth, enjoying the saltiness, listening as Devin talked to Travis about their travel plans. They were leaving from Tyler tonight to head to Dallas to catch a red eye to New York to play a show at B.B. King's. These were the kinds of gigs they were getting now. He'd been talking to Jay Little on and off all morning, getting things set up for the European tour with Zo, which was definitely going to happen. That Trevor guy was also interviewing them soon, not for the paper where he worked, but for a small feature in *Rolling Stone*, in their "artists to watch" section. I smiled every time I thought about it.

I opened my tablet, popping more sunflower seeds into my mouth, pulling up my syllabus for the survey of media and society class I had with Professor Bandele tomorrow, trying to push down the lingering doom in my stomach that picked up full speed after our last gas stop.

My phone rang next to me and I turned it off. It buzzed a minute later, indicating I had a text.

Devin was off his call with Trav now and glanced over at me.

"It was my mom," I volunteered.

"You dodgin' her calls now too?"

I pushed out a breath and shook my head.

"No, Devin. I just didn't want to answer while—"

"You were with me?" He glanced over at me again, the muscle in his jaw working, because he was struggling to keep his expression casual.

"No. Well, yeah. I just know she's worried about me staying focused while I'm back."

"And she thinks I keep you unfocused now." He glanced at me.

"No. The opposite. She thinks you keep me 'grounded' and I could use more of your confidence when it comes to my work."

I used air quotes because she'd said that to me verbatim. We'd had a lot of talks over the summer. Nothing dramatic but we spent a lot of time in the sunroom, getting to know each other again, or actually, getting to know one another as adults. My mom was cool and wise, and way more understanding than I gave her credit for. I was happy to have that time with her and my dad. I saw the value in it, in a way I hadn't previously. Before, a lot of the time we spent was because I loved them but also about fear because they're older. Now, I was more so appreciative of them, their easygoing wisdom, their love for me.

"I just know she'd have something to say about me going out of town on a whim when I just got back," I told Devin now. "She just thinks that I sometimes get too caught up with... I dunno. Pleasing other people, and that I sometimes lose focus of my own goals in the process."

I focused on the semi in front of us, who was slowing traffic down as he tried to pass by a U-Haul. "And what do you think?"

"I think some of what she's saying is right. But that some of her fear is just because I'm growing up. I'm graduating this year and she's having a hard time letting go of her 'baby'."

"You'll always be her baby, Low."

The way he said it made me look up at him, but his eyes were on the road. He heaved a silent breath. His phone rang and he glanced at me before answering.

"What's up. All good. Yep..." He continued speaking, using a handful of words, and a knot formed in my stomach. "I'll call you when I get back." He was talking to a woman. He hung up a few seconds later, and I bit hard on my lip, staring without seeing at my syllabus.

"I saw Nikitta took the pictures at the rally the other day."

I'd also seen his phone, when he left it in the truck while he pumped gas. She called, and then left a text message.

"Miss you. Hope things are cool in Atlanta. Holla at playa when you can, lol."

Devin said nothing, just kept his eyes on the road. We were listening to Prototype's album again, and it wasn't lost on me that an album about us was playing while another woman lingered in the space between us.

"Did you... were you with her while I was...."

"Gone? Gettin' your space and 'exploring'?"

I bit my lip, trying to keep cool, trying to push down the bile that was gathering my stomach at the thought of them together.

"Did you sleep with her, Devin?"

"No, I didn't," he said, glancing at me. "Even though if I woulda took it there it woulda been well within my rights."

"But you were... seeing her?"

"I saw her, yeah."

"Like, you were dating her?"

"C'mon, Low. I was on the road non-stop. When would I've had time to date somebody?"

His jaw was tight. "Saw you were hanging tight with ol' boy though."

"He came to *one show* because his little cousin was in my class. And then he asked to take me to dinner to celebrate."

Devin's jaw was working, his eyes narrowed.

"He tried you?"

I bit my lip. "He tried to kiss me. I made him take me home."

He released a breath, his thumb tapping against the wheel. "He's still your 'friend' though right?"

"Wrong," I said quietly. "I needed to focus on me. And Jaden wasn't helping with that. He was just drama. And... I dunno. Being around him, even for that little bit time felt *foreign*, and not real. Especially when me and you..."

I trailed off and Devin sighed again.

"We gotta get this shit together," he said, his voice low, causing my heart to beat faster in my chest because other than last night, it was the first glimmer of hope I'd gotten from him.

"What do you want, Willow?"

"You." My answer was instant, no hesitation.

His gaze roamed over my face, discerning, thumb still tapping against the wheel.

"What do you want?"

He bit the bottom corner of his lip, eyes back on the road. "You."

He met my eyes and shook his head again then reached to turn the music back up. I looked back down at my syllabus and tried to concentrate, ignoring my pounding heart.

It was just after seven when we pulled into Tyler, winding our way through the residential streets back to Trav's house. Devin finally let me take over for the three hour stretch between Jackson and Shreveport, so that he could get some sleep. He snored lightly while I played the Isley Brothers and planned out my school week, thinking about rehearsals and the program I was planning on implementing with the local elementary schools this year. I thought about the time Devin would be spending on the road, how his life was about to get even more demanding. I wanted him to be in a good head space when he left tonight because I knew he wasn't going to really get a break, or time to deal with his feelings and emotions and whatever else he'd have to wade through, dealing with us.

Devin pulled into Trav's driveway and cut the ignition, heaving a breath.

"Well, that was an eventful trip," I joked.

He cocked a half-grin in my direction, chuckling. He pushed the door open and I did the same, sliding out of the truck and stretching after the long ride. Devin made his way around the front of the truck, and passed me my back pack.

"C'mon. I'll walk you to Pepper's."

I followed him and we stopped next to my car, leaning against the passenger side.

"I thought we were ready," I said, staring out across the street toward Mrs. Johnson's house. "I hoped we were."

"Maybe we were never ready."

My heart dropped to my stomach and I looked down at the ground.

"That can't be true." The words came out like a whisper. "My heart doesn't recognize that as truth."

I kicked at a pebble and he stuffed his hands in his pockets.

"I dunno, Low Low. You messed me up this summer. *All the way up*."

I looked down at the ground. "I never wanted to be that person to you."

"Maybe we need a minute." He pushed out a laugh. "I'm soundin' like you now."

"Maybe we need to go slow, no pressure," I suggested, looking up at him. "So we can figure out how to be 'us' again."

"Maybe we don't need to be 'us' any more," he said.

"Maybe we can be something better."

He sighed, following my gaze to Mrs. Johnson's manicured lawn.

"My life is just gonna get more hectic. And you're falling back into your thing here..." He shook his head.

I stared down at the ground. It felt almost like we were back at square one. But maybe not, because I felt different. Clearer-eyed. And at least we were communicating, for real now.

I tilted my head to the sky, then dropped my gaze to Devin again, who was watching me. I offered him a smile and he reached, grabbing my hand and pulling me in front of him, resting his arms on my shoulders.

"I already miss you though," he admitted, his voice low, staring into my eyes. His were weary, with dark circles under them. "Feels like all I do lately is miss you."

I rested my forehead against his chest, breathing him as I held onto his sides. I knew it would be at least three weeks before I saw him again.

"Aw, y'all back on your cute shit?" Bam's voice came booming out of nowhere, as the front door slammed shut. He came bounding down the porch stairs, ignoring Devin's middle finger, and sliding up to drop a kiss on my cheek.

"I told D we're puttin' you in the suitcase next time, Young Low," he said, making his way down the sidewalk to Trav's house.

"I wish," I called out, not moving my head from Devin's chest.

"We're leaving in twenty, D," Bam yelled. "Later, baby girl."

"Aight," Devin acknowledged. "I do gotta go. Still need to pack for this trip."

I nodded again.

"Okay."

He met my eyes, pulling me closer by the waist. He leaned down slowly, brushing his nose against mine before kissing my mouth, releasing a sigh against my lips, pressing his forehead against mine.

"Try to get some sleep on the plane," I said. He let me go and I willed myself to back away.

"I'll holler at you."

I nodded, exhaling as I watched him walk away.

32

DEVIN

SHE CALLED AND TEXTED, but I didn't talk to Low for four days.

One, I was busy—I barely had any time to breathe in between the three shows we had in New York, Jersey and then Connecticut, and the local press runs we had. Folks were buzzing about the upcoming album, more than they had been in the early summer. And we were back and forth on the contract with MUSE, one of the largest indie distributors in music. If they could get it right, it'd be *it* for us. The thing we'd been waiting for.

Two, I had to deal with Nikitta.

"I'm in love with you, Devin. You were just using me for a stand-in for Willow. Again."

I'd been talking to her those last two weeks we were on the road, when Low was avoiding me, more than I should've been since I did know she had feelings for me and I knew my head wasn't there.

When we had a two-day break and I was back in Tyler, she was there. Not at the house because Jersey and Kennedy would've skinned me. But I did go to her spot. And I was tempted to take it there with her again, especially after I saw Low posted up with ol' boy. She didn't post it, he did and tagged her in it, but it messed me up just the same.

'Kitta was there, and down. Rubbing on my head the way Low used to, telling me how she's always had my back, the way Low used to. Then kissing on my neck and sliding downward, her eyes telling me she wanted to please me and take control, the way Low used to. I ran my fingers through her hair, contrasting it bouncy softness with Willow's full softness.

But as sweet and cool as 'Kitta was, I couldn't get into it. As much as I wanted to, I couldn't let myself take advantage of what she was offering, because she was offering me her heart and mine belonged to someone else, even if she was way in Houston, on some "the hell with you, Devin" vibe. I wasn't no foul ass dude, so I told 'Kitta to get up, kissed her cheek, made up some shit about why I had to leave, and got the hell on, wondering if I was making a mistake the whole time. But women's intuition was somethin' I didn't fool with. If Low came back, and found out me and 'Kitta were together, it'd be a wrap, and I wasn't ready for the finality of that, even then. I had to let 'Kitta know that I couldn't be that dude for her. She said she couldn't talk to me anymore and I was relieved she's the one who said it first.

So, here I was, back feeling like I was playing head games with my heart. Some backwards mess.

We'd just got off the stage in Hartford and I was exhausted but wired, already falling into the same routine as when we were touring this summer. I needed to go to sleep. But more than that, I needed to hear her voice. I sat down on the edge of the bed and called Low, taking a sip of whiskey Trav stopped by with earlier. We were now "influencers" which meant free shit everywhere we went. It wasn't a bad problem to have.

"Hello?"

I smiled at the sound of her voice. Whenever Willow answered the phone she always seemed genuinely curious about who was on the other end, as if she couldn't see who it was on the screen.

"What's up."

"Hi." I could hear the smile in her voice, and I took a drink of the whiskey, letting it warm its way down my throat.

"How was the show?" she asked.

"It was cool."

"Just cool?"

"It was dope."

"You didn't break your sticks?"

I chuckled. "Nah, not tonight."

"But you killed it. I saw little snippets on Instagram your devoted fans posted. You went Bruce Banner."

I chuckled, staring down into my glass.

"Where are you now?" she asked.

"In the room." I glanced around the boxy interior. We were still on a tight budget, so it was mid-scale hotel with flowers and framed pictures of stripes and whatnot on the wall, because hotel people apparently thought that was art.

"Did you get to see any of the city?"

"Nah, baby. We landed at three, went and did a quick radio interview, had sound check, grabbed something to eat, then played the show."

Low was quiet. "You said 'baby'." I shook my head. Trust her not to let that get by.

"You are my baby. Even when you're not."

"I don't know what that means," she said softly.

"Neither do I. I'm just talkin'. A little delirious, I guess. Been on the phone with Jay a lot, tryin to see what's up with this distribution deal."

"The strategy is still the same?"

"Yep, hold out til someone comes right. Jay's out here thinkin' he's Jimmy Iovine."

Willow laughed. "He just wants what's best for everyone."

"I ain't mad at it. I'm just restless. Tryin' not to get impatient."

"It'll all be handled sooner than you think. And then you'll look back on this period of feeling impatient and barely remember it. Jay and I were talking about that at the studio in Atlanta. How these music industry people gamble on you being a starving artist, willing to settle for whatever crap they offer."

I smiled, because she sounded so passionate. I missed her. "You're right," I offered.

I stared at the ugly striped picture, and took another swallow of my drink.

"You sound tired," Willow ventured after few seconds of silence.

"I am. I just wanted to holler at you." I was readying myself for her to complain about me not calling her for four days.

"Jersey said everyone was going out tonight," she said instead.

"I stopped through for a minute," I took another swallow of whiskey. "Wasn't feeling it." I didn't add that everyone was coupled up because Cassie met us in New York, and I didn't feel like lookin' at all that.

"Your dreams, the ones we always talked about? You're living them now, Devin. You should savor these moments, you know?"

"I feel you." I wished she was here though, experiencing everything with me.

"You know what I was thinking?" I heard shuffling and it sounded like she was laying down.

"What?" I leaned against the pillows.

"Well, not really thinking but discovering and really, really praying about?"

I chuckled. "What?"

"Your love language. It's words of affirmation."

"My what?"

"Love language. The way you communicate best in your relationships." "And you say mine is what?"

"Words of affirmation."

I laughed. "That sounds real feminine."

"No," she interrupted, laughing, the sound arousing and soothing. "It just means it's important for people to speak positively to you, not nag you and always talk about what you're *not* doing."

"That's human nature. Nobody likes that."

"Well, no. But it means even more for you. That's what I think, anyway."

"And what's yours?"

I swallowed more whiskey, enjoying the buzz from the liquor and Willow's voice.

"Can you guess?"

"What are they? This sounds like that new age, yoga life you're on," I teased her. "I thought you loved Jesus."

She laughed again, light and airy, and I grinned.

"*Anyway,* They're words of affirmation, quality time, physical touch, gift giving, acts of service." I could tell she was really excited about this.

"I think mine is physical touch," she said before I could guess.

"Sounds accurate. You are a lightweight nympho."

"Devin!"

"You said it."

"Only because it's you," she said, her voice soft teasing. "So, if that's true it's your fault since you're the only one I've ever been with."

I bit the corner of my lip, wishing she was here for the tenth time in the past 10 minutes.

"Anyway, it doesn't mean just sex. It means when you touch me, like hold my hand, or play in my hair like you do... I need those kinds of touches to feel loved."

I hummed my response.

"I think that's where we messed up."

"Love languages, Willow?" I frowned and rolled my eyes.

"No but... getting to know each other."

"Nah, I *know* you, Low."

"I *know* you too, Devin." I chuckled because she tried to echo my voice and she sounded crazy. "But I mean, there's a difference between knowing someone and doing the things that actively show that you *know* them," she pressed, her words falling together the more amped she became. "I know that when I speak negatively to you, even if I think I'm just expressing myself or whatever, it makes you feel bad so you get defensive. If I *know* that, why would I keep doing it? It's selfish, really. I need to find another way to communicate, that doesn't include starting with what you're *not* doing."

"I'm enjoyin' this little epiphany you're havin."

She laughed, soft and light.

I rolled my tongue in my mouth, grinning before taking another sip of whiskey.

"So, you're sayin' you need me to come physically touch you?"

She sighed loudly and I laughed.

"Nah, I hear you. I coulda did some things different too. I know I can zone out and tune out. I've heard I'm moody."

She laughed long and hard at that and I stared at the phone.

"I think I just left before you could." She said it quickly and quietly after her laughter died down.

"That was my insecurity. Not yours. I need to own that," she said.

"You know you had me from day one, Willow. I wasn't goin' nowhere."

"You're literally going everywhere."

I looked down into my glass, narrowing my eyes.

"And I saw you before you saw me, Devin."

"I always saw you. But I fell back for a long time because you were too new," I sat up and pulled my shirt off. "I didn't want to corrupt you," I said, grinning as she murmured "whatever."

"So tomorrow... it's back to Atlanta for two more weeks?"

"Yeah, back to the A to learn Zo's songs and rehearsals, then we have a two-day break and we'll fly overseas for six weeks."

"I'm so excited for you, Devin. I know I keep saying that but this is just beyond amazing. You should hear everyone on campus talking about you all. Everyone is claiming to know you. And everyone is still talking about the rally. They're gonna maybe have another one tomorrow. I think I'm gonna go."

"You need to be careful while you're out there fightin' the power."

"I got this," she said, and I know she was probably wearing one of her silly, adorable grins.

I closed my eyes, running a hand down my chest.

"I wanna see you."

"Now?"

"Yeah, get online right fast." A few minutes later we were connected and I was staring into her brown eyes, which might've been a mistake because instead of easing the tightness in my chest, it increased it.

"What?" she asked when I just shook my head.

"Lookin' at you..." I shook my head. "Makes my day better."

Even though my tablet screen I could see her blush.

"I think you're wrong about physical touch."

She blinked, scrunching up her nose cutely. "What do you think it is then?"

"Quality time."

She smiled, staring away from the tablet before shrugging her shoulders.

"Maybe so. I could see that."

"Tell me about your classes," I said, studying her pretty face. "Was Professor Bandele bein' cool?"

She nodded and smiled, free and open.

"Oh my gosh, Devin, we got into this discussion about black women in film and ..." I listened as she talked about school and how she was laying the law down this year with her dance group, and the programs she was working to implement in the local elementary schools. I listened to her words but really, I was enjoying the hum of her voice, it's cadence.

"I'm not sleep," she insisted an hour later, when it was obvious she was about to pass out on me.

It felt like it did back when I was in Tyler, when we were first really getting know each other, and I'd be on the phone with her all night, sometimes not even realizing I'd fallen asleep until I heard her heavy breaths in the phone.

"Stay on with me?" she asked sleepily. "Please?"

So, I did, drifting to sleep to the sound Willow's breathing for the first time in months.

33

WILLOW

"LET'S take it from the top."

I stood and watched my dance team get into formation to run through the new routine we were performing the day after tomorrow. The small theater where we practiced was empty, save for the dancers who didn't make the cut this go around, observing from the audience chairs because I wanted their eyes too, to see issues with the routine I may've missed.

But the dancers were tight and on point, I'd made sure of it. This year I wasn't playing any games. I cut two people from the team already and I was willing to trim more, and everyone knew it. There would be no embezzling money or no slacking off this year. We were also going to be more involved with the community. I was already working with Professor Bandele to set up volunteer sessions with the elementary and junior high schools closest to South Texas. Her John the Baptist influence came in handy this year, probably because I wasn't on the wrong side of her omnipotence.

"Gia, pick it up," I directed, bobbing my head to the music. She nodded, picking up the tempo. We weren't friends any more but we weren't enemies either. She apologized for her shadiness, and I accepted it. That's as far as it went for me though. We were done with everything out side of dance.

I focused on my choreography, proud at how good it looked. The music was a mix Devin made for me, not of Prototype songs because they wouldn't work but songs from other artists, mixed in with his own beats that he'd put together during his down time. He surprised me with the email a few days ago, after I told him how frustrated I was with the mix I had, because it sucked. He was on the road, super busy but still took time to do that for me.

Even though after our conversation a couple of weeks ago, things were a *lot* better between us, I still didn't know where we stood, or if we were together. I didn't want to pressure him so I didn't ask. But I missed him, so much.

I saw my phone buzzing in my bag, which was sitting at the edge of the stage and signaled to everyone to run through the routine as I went to grab it.

"Hey," I said, unable to keep the smile out of my voice.

"What's up," My smile increased when Devin's baritone came through the speaker. "What you into?"

"Practice. We're running through the routine."

"I thought it was over at nine?"

"They were sloppy so I made them stay until they tightened up."

He chuckled. "Look at you, bein all aggressive."

I shook my head, watching as they picked up the routine again without me telling them.

"Where are you?" I could hear voices in the background.

"At rehearsal. But I got some news. We signed the deal with MUSE."

"*What!?*" I screamed way louder than I intended to and I looked over my shoulder at the team. "Lyssa, can you take over?" I asked quickly. She nodded, wiping her brow and signaling them to start from the middle, as I walked out of the theater's side door, into the lobby so I could have some privacy.

"You're *kidding*, Devin!"

"Nope." There was a smile in his voice. "Signed it less than an hour ago. I wanted you to be the first person I told."

A tear leaked down my cheek and I wiped it with the back of my hand.

"This is *amazing*. I don't even know what to say."

"Are you crying?" His voice got quiet.

"No," I lied.

"Baby..." His deep voice rumbled in my ear, making my heart ache because I missed him so much.

"I'm so happy for you is all." I wished I was there celebrating with him, with everyone.

"But *wow,*" I said, trying not to linger in my disappointment and screw up the moment for him. "You gotta take a picture of the pen you signed the contract with."

He laughed.

"No, seriously. I hope you kept it."

"I kept it," he said, amusement in his voice, as if he was indulging me.

"So now that you're all rich, what's the first thing you're gonna buy? A yacht? A mansion?" I teased.

He laughed. "I signed the deal. We didn't take an advance though. I think someone told me something about having patience and making smart moves. I listened."

I smiled, biting my lip.

"I wish you were here, Low Low," he said after a few seconds. "I wanna celebrate with you. You're a part of this too. A *huge* part of why this is happening."

My stomach tightened at the sound of his voice and I ran a hand over my chest, silently exhaling.

"But I'll see you in a few days, right?" I said, struggling to keep my voice bright. "We can celebrate then."

He was quiet and I bit the inside of my lip, holding my breath.

"I'm not gonna be able to make it, baby. We signed this deal and now we have to be here to do marketing stuff. Photo shoots, interviews, a bunch of stuff before we head to London on the tour."

I looked down at the floor, my eyes filling with tears again, this time for a different reason. That would mean six more weeks until I saw him again, on top of the two and half he'd already been gone.

"If there was a way for me to work around this I would but I just don't see how I can make it work."

"Okay." I nodded my head, closing my eyes. "Okay."

He sighed. "I'm sorry."

"It's not your fault. And it's not like something bad is happening... everything going on with you is something we should be celebrating. I just wish..."

"Me too," he said, his voice deep and intimate in my ear, giving me chill bumps. "I miss you like crazy."

"I miss you too."

I heard his name being called in the background and I leaned against the brick wall in the lobby, closing my eyes.

"I gotta go. They're calling for me."

"Okay. Congratulations, Devin. For real, I'm so proud of you."

I hung up after he promised to call later tonight but stayed pressed against the wall, staring down at the laminate floor.

"Willow?"

"Hey Lyssa," I smiled through my tears, sniffing, quickly wiping them with the back of my hand. "I'll be in, just give me a quick sec."

"Are you okay?" Her eyes were wide and concerned.

"I will be."

She nodded, giving me my space. I blew out a breath and wiped my tears, then headed back inside to finish practice.

34

DEVIN

"HEY."

Kennedy plopped down on the couch next to me, careful not to spill the tea in the big mug she was holding. She pulled her legs under as she stretched her arms above her head and yawned.

"They need to hurry up and get back. I'm *starving*," she said, eyes wide.

"The spot is right around the corner. They should be back soon."

Everyone else was out getting wings while we took a break from rehearsal. My stomach was acting funny so I wasn't messin' with any wings. Kennedy just didn't feel like riding, so she'd stayed behind to keep practicing. The studio where we were rehearsing was miles away from the basement, literally and figuratively. It was state of the art, probably the best in the city, which was saying a lot.

We were chilling in the break room, which was bigger than most people's entire houses. Huge flat screens, a pool table, a couple of arcade games and a mini-bar were all inside of the room. The real draw was the huge, colorful mural that covered one wall, featuring the best musicians of the past 40 years—that was the kind of thing I'd have inside of my crib, whenever I bought one. After this tour, with the bank we'd make, and after the album dropped, I'd be buying... soon.

Probably could even find something where I could have a dance studio built for Low and... I stopped mid-thought and exhaled.

"Your throat sore?" I asked, focusing on Kennedy, as she sipped her tea, wincing.

She shook her head. "It's just tired."

"You need to rest it."

"I am."

"You're not," I countered, raising a brow. "All that extra practicing isn't rest, Kennedy."

She frowned. "I'm just trying to make sure I'm prepared."

"You got it already. Just relax into what you already know."

She nodded, and smiled at me, her eyes tired but perceptive, as usual.

"You okay?" she asked.

"I'm chillin'."

She glanced at my phone in my hand before looking at me again. Willow had just posted a picture of her and a couple of girls from her dance team. She looked so damn *pretty*, and happy, it made miss her energy even more.

"You're missing Willow?" It didn't sound like a question as much as an observation.

I did miss her, maybe more now than even over the summer, which I thought was impossible. I wanted to hear her voice but she was in rehearsal right now.

"I think your bond is so sweet," Kennedy offered when I didn't respond.

I stared at her and she chuckled.

"I'm serious though, Devin. The way you two just *love* each other. You're like... family. You can physically see that you're better when you're together."

I leaned my head back against the soft leather cushions, running a hand over my head. We *were* like family. And then she left and now, I wasn't sure what we were like. I loved her. That was always there. I wanted her. That was always there too. She was still my heart. And knowing I wasn't going to get to see her for *another* two months wasn't cool, at all.

'You're still mad at her?" Kennedy asked. There wasn't any judgment in her eyes, or even curiosity, just discernment.

"We're good. I get why she left. I get why she left the way she left too. I'm not... it still ain't cool but I get it."

"People deal with pressure in different ways." She shrugged, her eyes faraway. "Sometimes you need a jolt to find your way back to yourself when life gets overwhelming."

She looked at me. "Look at the way I came to Tyler. I didn't tell *anyone* I was leaving, not even Cassie. I didn't talk to my mom for a while after I left either. Sometimes you need solitude to find yourself. And if I wouldn't have left, none of this would be happening. You never know why God has you move the way He does. You should just listen when He tells you to."

I exhaled, eyes on the ceiling, Low's words from our conversation the other night echoing in my mind. It was a couple of days after we signed the deal, and we were having another one of the middle of the night conversations we'd been having a lot of lately because our schedules were so packed during the day it was the only time we had to talk. I was feeling a way about her being gone, about her having left, about her not being close enough to hold.

"I can't make you trust me," she'd sighed, her voice soft and sleepy. "I just have to show you that you can. The truth is, you can't control what another person is gonna do. Like, how I was hyper-paranoid about you cheating. I could never control that. If you wanted to cheat, you would have, no matter how much I harassed you about it. I just have trust that you won't—either that or not be with you. And I wanna be with you." She sounded so matter-of-fact when she said it, I realized how much she'd matured in those weeks she was away. She was more thoughtful than reactive.

"This doesn't even feel like my *life* sometimes, man," Kennedy said after a while, pulling me out of my thoughts. That was the thing about Kennedy, she was so quiet sometimes, so in her own head, it was almost like being alone. "Whoever thought we'd be here, doing this at this level?" She swept her hand around the huge room.

"We had the vision. The Creator honored it," I told her, thinking of when Willow told me that. It seemed like a lifetime ago.

"And Zo is *so* cool, huh?" Kennedy pressed, seeming a little star-struck.

I chuckled. "Calm down, Nebraska, cheesin' all hard. He's aight."

She smacked her lips and rolled her eyes and I laughed. "I'm from *Denver*, thank you," she retorted.

"Nah, he's a good dude. Just wonder how long he's gonna have us here tonight."

"He's sort of like another perfectionist I know."

"Who Trav?"

She laughed and I smirked. I really wondered if we'd be finished early enough for me to call Low. We'd been rehearsing until one or two in the morning lately.

"Oh, *yes*, you guys are back," Kennedy exclaimed suddenly, clapping her hands as everyone else pushed through the door, bringing the smell of chicken with them.

"Did you remember..."

"Ketchup?" Trav said wiggling a packet in front of her, seating himself on the arm of the couch.

"Got you some ginger ale, homie," Jersey said dropping the bottle in my lap, plopping next to me, smacking loudly on a celery stick.

"Right on." I twisted the top off, and took a long swallow, just as my phone buzzed. It was Low, sending me one of those weird faces with the tongue out. I still didn't know what it meant but my grin was automatic, as the chatter around me dimmed.

"Hey, Bruce Banner. I'm still at rehearsal but I'll be up late studying if you feel like talking whenever you finish rehearsing..." she wrote a few seconds later.

"Cool. Have a good rehearsal. I holler at you later," I replied, before pushing my phone in my pocket.

Kennedy looked over at me.

"Now who's cheesy?" she asked, grinning.

"Shut up." I shook my head, taking another long swallow of ginger ale to hide my smile.

35

WILLOW

"Willow, you have mail."

I looked up from my homework at Pepper, who was sitting at the kitchen table, sorting through her mail. I furrowed my brow.

"From Devin, looks like. Came out of Pearl's mailbox."

Even though she'd passed almost five years ago now, Pepper still referred to Travis' house as his grandma, "Pearl's house." She was checking in on the house, collecting the mail while they'd been gone.

Pepper passed the certified mail envelope to me and resumed her sorting, peering over her glasses as she went. I spent as much time at Pepper's as I could. Her house made me feel like home. It was bright and airy, the way my mom kept our house in Houston, full of pastels and yellows, and all the curtains were wide open so the light could shine through with its full power. It was the kind of house that made you want to smile as soon as you entered.

Being here also made me feel closer to Kennedy and Jersey, and even Devin and the guys. Kennedy was a lot like her. Pepper didn't pry. She just listened and when she did speak, it was usually to say something profound, even if I had to decode it because she sometimes talked like a walking affirmation book. She'd become one of my closest friends in Tyler, weird as it sounds.

"I didn't realize people your age knew how to use stamps," Pepper teased, sipping from her tea cup as she eyed my letter.

I curled my legs under me on the wooden chair and grinned. "I didn't either. I have no idea what this is."

I opened the letter and peered inside the cardboard envelope. I didn't immediately see anything so I shook it upside down, then gasped.

"Oh my gosh." I knew better than to take the Lord's name in vain in Pepper's house. A velvet box fell onto the table with a muted thud. I could feel Pepper's eyes on me but I was still staring at the box.

"I know this isn't what I think it is," I breathed, glancing at Pepper, who looked amused.

"I must really be out of the loop if people are proposing through the united parcel service these days."

I was too shocked to even laugh. I finally grabbed the blue velvet box and popped open the top, then frowned. *What the—* I pulled out a necklace, my heart thudding when I looked at the pendant. It was an "Aquemini" symbol, beautifully cut. I ran my fingertips over it, then opened the folded paper that fell out with the box.

"'Got the hottest chick in the game wearin' my chain.' You are the Prototype."

"The 'hottest chick in the game'?" Pepper's brow was arched, as she peered to read my note. She winked at me.

I laughed. "It's a quote from a rapper named Jay-Z."

"Beautiful necklace. He has good taste... In more than just jewelry."

I smiled and got up, the chair scraping against the hardwood floor and kissed Pepper's cheek, swiping my phone off the table.

"Dinner will be ready in an hour," she called as I practically skipped to Kennedy's room. "Ida Lee and Bertha are coming by so be ready for Tonk."

"I will," I called out, laughing as I quickly dialed Devin after snapping a quick picture.

"Check your messages," I immediately told him when he picked up.

"How am I gonna check my messages with you on the phone?"

"Just do it," I sighed, rolling my eyes and smiling.

"You got it," he said a few seconds later. I sent him a picture of me wearing the chain.

"I did."

"That's a lot of cleavage you're showin'. Nobody else better see this picture."

"It is *not*. And thank you, Devin. I *love* this. Love, love, love it."

"I love, love, love you," he replied his baritone deep and sexy.

I got quiet. Most days Devin and I felt closer than we'd ever been before. We were more connected and... calm. But there were moments still, when I knew he was holding back with me. And even though I knew he loved me, he hadn't said it in a while.

"You there?"

"Yes. I love you too."

There was noise in the background and he told me to hold on while he talked to someone. He came back a few seconds later.

"What were you up to?" he asked.

"Hanging out over Pepper's."

He chuckled. "Kennedy said y'all are best friends now."

"She's the homie."

"Pepper is cool as shit." He laughed again before telling me to hold on when more noise swelled in the background.

"Do you need to go because—"

"Nah," he said sounding irritable and authoritative. "They can wait. Let me hear about your day."

I smiled and did as he asked.

36 WILLOW

"YOU'RE GOING TO HOMECOMING RIGHT?"

Lyssa looked over at me as she filled her coffee order.

I accepted cash from the customer I was waiting on at Aroma, before passing him his coffee.

"Yep. It'll be fun, and plus, this is my senior year. Gotta enjoy the entire college experience before I graduate."

"Are you sure you're not gonna be globe-trotting around the world with your *fine* famous boyfriend?" Lyssa teased.

I grinned, shaking my head. Lyssa hadn't stopped teasing me about the pictures Devin recently posted of us. They were from a while ago, last semester, but there was no mistaking we were together in them. In one, I was sitting on his lap and he was kissing my neck, looking like a Billboard ad for "men whose bathwater I'd like to drink." In another he was standing behind me, arms wrapped possessively around my center, flipping off the camera, with his sexy Devin-smirk. He tagged the pictures with "#HerAndI." Technically, it could still be viewed as promo for the album but I knew what it meant, what it signified. It meant us.

"I can't globe-trot right now," I smiled. "I have classes that I can't fail. He actually leaves out for London tomorrow for a month."

"I know you knew him before, but what is it like dating a famous person?"

I grinned, stacking the coffee cups neatly behind the counter.

"It's like dating someone I knew before he was a famous person," I said, laughing as Lyssa rolled her eyes and smiled before resuming her work, rambling on about this guy she was dating and their plans for the game and tailgating. She stopped mid-sentence and gasped.

I looked up from wiping the counter, following her gaze to the front door. My lips parted and I drew in a breath. *Devin.*

I didn't realize I said his name aloud until the people who were seated closest to the counter in the cozy little shop turned to look at me and then him. But I didn't care what they were looking at. All I saw was him, as I flew around the counter, weaving my way through tables to get to him. I jumped into his arms and he caught me, as usual.

"What up, Sweet N Low?" he smiled.

"I thought you had to be on a plane to London in the morning!?"

He grinned, his eyes tired.

"I do. But I couldn't go another six weeks without seeing you."

He leaned forward and pecked my lips, again and again, then again. I opened for his kiss, melding my tongue with his, kissing him like I hadn't seen him in weeks, because I hadn't. He pulled back with a low hum, his brown eyes low and full of desire, before releasing me so that I could stand. I looked around the coffee shop, face hot. I'm sure the owner, Cheyenne, would not approve of our display.

"Let me go tell, Lyssa I'm leaving," I told him, reluctantly releasing his fingers. I only had an hour left to my shift anyway.

"Go!" Lyssa said, waving her hands, when I reached the counter. "I'll cover for you. It's slow anyway."

I took off my "Coffee Makes Me Happy" button and slid it too her, unable to keep the wide smile off my face, as I made my way back to Devin, who was leaning against one of the empty tables, Braves fitted on backwards, t-shirt tight against his chest. Devin grabbed my hand, smiling down at me and interlaced our fingers when I reached him, leading me out of the shop to Bam's van, which was parked illegally in front of the building. He'd left his truck in Atlanta with his mom.

"What's gonna happen?" I asked, leaning against the passenger door. "With Zo and the band?" I didn't want him to get in trouble or mess up the biggest thing in his life to see me.

"Nothin. It's handled." His baritone was tired, and he ran a hand down his face. "I'll fly out from Dallas instead of Atlanta at seven in the morning. I'll layover in Atlanta but it'll put me in London a few hours after everyone else lands."

That meant he needed to leave by around 2 a.m. Which meant he'd get no sleep.

"Baby," I shook my head. "You're gonna be exhausted."

"I needed to see you," he said simply, his voice low, pulling me to stand in between his legs as he leaned against the truck.

"Does this mean your officially my boyfriend again?"

He chuckled a little. "I'm yours. You're mine. Exclusively. Is that cool?"

I stood on my tip toes and kissed him again, sighing against his mouth, inhaling his energy, *him*.

"We only have a few hours. What do you wanna do?" I asked.

"You."

"Devin!" I smacked his shoulder and he grinned that sexy half-smile that made want to do whatever he wanted, whenever he wanted to.

"We're definitely gonna get to that later," he promised, his low baritone making my stomach tingle. "I'm hungry, actually. Kinda feel like hittin' The Pancake Shack."

I kissed his lips, wrapping my arms around his neck. "And getting ice cream? The glittery boo-boo kind?"

He chuckled against my mouth, nipping my bottom lip.

"It's whatever you want, Low Low. Whenever you want it. However you want it."

"Because I'm spoiled?"

"Because you're you."

I grinned and he kissed me again, slowly, one hand threading through my hair, the other on my hip, pulling me closer. He pressed his forehead to mine, pecking my lips again.

"You," I said against his mouth. "What I always want is you."

He smiled. "I never could leave you alone."

"I hope you never do."

EPILOGUE: DEVIN

THE DAY WAS nothing like I'd imagined it. All those years fantasizing about how my album release party would look, and feel, nothing prepared me for the reality. The studio where the release was taking place was packed, according to Jay. We had one of the most buzzed about debut albums of the past couple of years.

It was *surreal*. But also super real because I visualized it, grinded for it and The Creator brought it to pass.

The event had started an hour before we arrived, but we were expected to be fashionably late, it was part of business, stupid as it was, so we were on the patio of a local taco joint near the East Side, where my moms' place was, enjoying the cool, fall air, tossing back margaritas.

"You ready to roll?" I nodded at Zay's question, but I wasn't looking at him.

My eyes were on Willow. Her head was tipped back to the sky, her smile like a summer time breeze on a hot day, rejuvenating, refreshing and free, as she talked to Jersey, Kennedy and Cassie. Bam no doubt said something else goofy and she laughed again, covering her mouth with her hand. That pull I always felt in my chest when she smiled that way was there, and I grinned too. Zay followed my gaze and grinned knowingly, tipping his head at me.

"How long is she here again?"

"A week."

It wasn't long enough. It never was. She was on fall break and was in good enough shape to miss a day of class. Once we got off tour with Zo we had about two weeks of down time and instead of being in Atlanta, I headed back to Tyler to connect with Low. It was probably one of the best times of our lives, let alone our relationship. We were clicking now, on all cylinders. Even when things got off track, we fell back in sync quicker.

I always loved her, maybe even from that first time she gave me half of her burger. But the way I loved her now was more mature, more solid. I knew circumstances, or situations or people, none of that silliness was getting between us because both of us were committed to not allowing it to. Not even Continents could separate us.

Feeling my eyes on her she looked over at me and smiled. For a second, we just stared at each other, as she absently fingered her Aquemini chain.

We had a plan. She'd be finished with school in May and then she was moving to Atlanta with me. If things kept moving the way The Creator had blessed us so far, we'd probably be on the road again and if that was the case, she was coming with me this time, for real. I wanted her to be able to travel with me, see the world. It felt good, better than good to be able to give her that.

The dance program she wanted to start could be developed logistically, at least, while we were on the road, and I'd have the paper to fund it when she wanted to really get it rolling. Even if those plans changed, one thing was definite—we'd be together.

Fifteen minutes later we all pulled up to the studio with the driver. Everyone else headed toward the side entrance, but I pulled at Willow's waist halting her on the side of the brick building that was private because it was hidden from the street.

She was gorgeous tonight, her hair pulled up into a bun, her eyes smoky and seductive. She was wearing a dress, showing off most of her thighs and a short-cropped leather jacket.

"Know what I was thinkin' about today?" I asked as I stepped close, backing her against the stucco wall, inhaling her sweet scent.

"What?" she asked, biting then releasing her lower lip. I leaned in and brushed my nose against hers as she grabbed at the sides of my leather jacket.

"Jamaica."

She furrowed her brow and looked up at me.

"Where the water is so clear we can see the white sand on the bottom of the ocean floor. And we can chill and not do anything, except each other."

I stared into her eyes, watching the moment she caught on, the second her pupils dilated and her lips parted in realization. I brushed my lips against the side of her neck, loving that her pulse was racing.

"You're my high, Low. My future. My love. My rider. My baby. My everything. Will you go there with me?" I asked, pulling the ring out of my jacket pocket as I met her eyes, my pulse racing.

She bit her lip and nodded, tears gathering in her eyes, as I slid the diamond on her finger.

"Yes," she nodded again, pressing her forehead to mine, as I finally allowed myself to exhale. "Yes. I'll go wherever with you, Devin. Always."

AFTERWORD

Thank you so much for reading *Keeping Willow*!

I'm so excited to *finally* share their story with y'all. Thank you guys for being patient and riding with me on this one.

I think more than anything, this book is about growth. What does love look like when you experience inevitable personal growth, and can that sometimes painful growth ultimately strengthen you and your relationship?

Love isn't always easy but that's okay. The rough patches, the growing pains make you appreciate it all the more. You come out on the other side of pain stronger, more discerning, and with more empathy. I think that's the case with Willow and Devin.

I don't think I've ever been as immersed in my characters as I was in the lives of Devin and Willow, maybe because their book was a long time coming. Or maybe, because so many pieces of both of their lives mirrored mine.

But I'm happy with their story and I hope you enjoyed it too.

Until next time.

Love & Peace,

Jacinta

ACKNOWLEDGEMENTS

To my mom, thank you. You're the coolest ever. To my daughter, who is the awesomest child on planet Earth, thank you for making me smile every single day. To my husband, thank you. To Natalie Cummings and Kanisha Rose, thank you—y'all are the best. To Tina V., thank you. To the awesome cover designer of The Prototype Series who, by request, shall not be named, thank you. You're one talented individual. To the indie author community, the bloggers, authors, event planners and book clubs, thank you— you all are *so, so* awesome. Your support is so instrumental to my work and the successes I've experienced in my journey. I appreciate you so much. Thanks in particular to Nia Forrester, Lily Java and Rae Lamar who are inspirations on and off the page. Y'all rock and I'm grateful to know you. And of course, to all of the readers who took the time to pick up this book, especially those of you who shared it with friends and/or left a review, THANK YOU. *Thank you. Thank you.* I don't take you for granted, like, at all. As always, thank The Lord Jesus for life, and life abundantly.

Sweet.

ABOUT THE AUTHOR

A longtime journalist and lifelong music lover, Jacinta Howard resides in the Atlanta area with her daughter and husband. She finds happiness in the pages of a great novel, on the beach, listening to good music and hanging with her family. She is the author of women's fiction and contemporary romance, a USA TODAY Must-Read Author and a two-time RONE Award nominee.

For more information:

www.jacintahoward.net

ALSO BY JACINTA HOWARD

THE PROTOTYPE SERIES

Happiness In Jersey

Finding Kennedy

THE LOVE ALWAYS SERIES

Better Than Okay

More Than Always

Less Than Forever

STANDALONE TITLES

Blind Expectations

COMING SOON:

Loving Cassie (Book 3 of The Prototype Series)

PLEASE CONSIDER LEAVING A REVIEW!

If you enjoyed *Keeping Willow* I'd be really grateful if you'd please consider leaving a review on Amazon and Goodreads!

Thank you!

CPSIA information can be obtained
at www.ICGtesting.com
Printed in the USA
BVHW080959260120
570519BV00001B/176

9 781974 289578